"JILL MARIE LANDIS
PROMISES TO BECOME A FAVORITE!"
—Affaire de C...

LAST ... of Last
Chan... Fighter
Lane ... past, it
was a...

AFT... ok to
be hou... ntana.
But h...

UNTI... o call
home-...

PAST ... t in
search ... ow-
boy po...

COME... ika
vowed ... as-
sion fla...

JADE: ... eauty captured the heart of a rugged rancher.
But could he forget the past—and love again?

ROSE: Across the golden frontier, her passionate heart dared to
dream of a love as boundless as the western sky...

WILDFLOWER: Amidst the untamed beauty of the Rocky
Mountains, two daring hearts forged a perilous passion...

SUNFLOWER: A spirited woman of the prairie. A handsome
half-breed who stole her heart. A love as wild as the wind...

Winner of the Romance Writers of America
Golden Heart and Golden Medallion Awards

JILL MARIE LANDIS
IS "ONE OF THE NEW STARS!"
—*Romantic Times*

JILL MARIE LANDIS

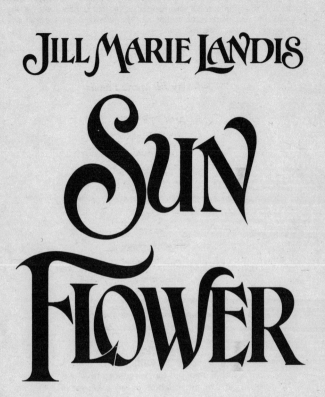

SUN FLOWER

JOVE BOOKS, NEW YORK

SUNFLOWER

A Jove Book / published by arrangement with
the author

PRINTING HISTORY
Berkley edition / June 1988
Jove edition / December 1990

ISBN: 0-515-10659-3

Jove Books are published by The Berkley Publishing Group,
200 Madison Avenue, New York, New York 10016.
The name "JOVE" and the "J" logo
are trademarks belonging to Jove Publications, Inc.

PRINTED IN THE UNITED STATES OF AMERICA

OPM   20   19   18   17   16   15   14   13   12   11

To my family and friends, for giving me the time to write
and for their enthusiastic encouragement;
to my Dutch friends, who helped with translations and recollections;
to the pathfinders, who are never afraid to seek change;
and to my dad,
who always believed I could do anything

Chapter One

Iowa, August 1870

August. Nothing moved in the oppressive humidity, not even the soft feather-light silk hanging from the cornstalks. The shimmering currents of heat, visible all day, had faded once the steel-gray clouds began to roll across the sky, obscuring the setting sun as they pushed and shoved against each other from horizon to horizon. As far as the eye could see, row upon row of tall, near-ripe cornstalks stood against the darkening sky, reaching up in supplication toward the rain trapped within the clouds. A narrow dirt road ran between the rows of corn like a long scar across the land. The passing of many wagons had packed the dirt hard into two long ribbons carved deep into the soil. In the spring, mud filled the ruts, but now, in late summer, the dirt road was cracked and dry, covered with a fine layer of dust that rose, when churned by hooves and wheels, to drift down upon weary travelers.

1

A clearing stood beside the road, an unplanted section that seemed to appear out of nowhere. Passersby on their way to the village knew that, once they reached the clearing and passed the tiny sod house set back from the road, the settlement was only four miles farther east.

Inside the soddie, Analisa Van Meeteren dried her hands and forearms on a cotton dish towel and hung it on a nail driven into the high wooden bench that served as a drainboard. Behind her in the one-room dwelling, all was in order. Her grandfather's bed claimed the corner next to the stove. Its warmth drove the chill from his bones when the winter raged. On the same wall, at the foot of Opa's bed, stood a pump organ, handcrafted in Europe and transported halfway around the world. It had been her mother's most prized possession, a link to their old life in Holland. Analisa kept it polished to a high gleam and covered with an embroidered linen cloth to protect the finish from the dust and bits of soil that continually sifted down from the sod ceiling.

A rocker sat near the organ, its high back draped with another hand-decorated linen cloth. A wooden crate served as a side table to the rocker, its rough, unfinished surface in stark contrast to the hand-turned finished oak of the chair. Across from the organ was Analisa's own high oak-framed bed, another object transported from the past. The bed was covered by a thick eiderdown comforter and a hand-pieced quilt with a bright red, yellow, and green tulip pattern of Analisa's own design. A small pallet was stored beneath the bed for Kase, Analisa's four-year-old son. The beds were near the front window where geraniums, growing in cans and chipped china dishes, lined the windowsill outside. During the summer months Analisa awoke to sunshine and flowers.

Blooms in similar containers outside the window above the kitchen bench caught her eye, and she reminded herself to water them tomorrow if the gathering clouds failed to produce rain. Wiping a forearm across her sweating brow, she gathered stray locks of hair off of the nape of her neck and tucked them into the loose knot atop her head. She secured the hairpins, which had slipped with the weight of her hair, and turned back to her work. She had soon washed the dishes and stacked them on the shelves on either side of the window frame. With strength born of necessity, she grasped the enameled dishpan handles and

hefted the pan off the makeshift counter. The sudsy water
sloshed close to the lip, but not a drop spilled as Analisa moved
with practiced ease to the open doorway. She stepped up and
over the sod threshold and out into the heat.

Analisa glanced skyward and watched the dark, heavy clouds
roll across the sky, driven by winds too high above the earth to
give the land ease from the heat. After tossing the murky water
out of the blue enamel pan, she watched it soak into the thirsty
ground. With the pan in one hand, she walked away from the
house of sod toward the wood and wire fence bordering the
yard. To Analisa it seemed that only the weather added variety
to her life on the prairie, and even that often remained
unchanged for weeks on end.

Four years had passed since Analisa had moved into the sod
house, four years that seemed like a lifetime. Most immigrant
families lived in the sod structures for a year or two, until they
could rebuild a permanent dwelling of wood. Not so, Analisa.
For four years she had battled the rigors of life in the soddie.
She refused to think about those years as she momentarily stood
idle, a rare occurrence in itself. Her long sleeves were rolled up
above her elbows, exposing fair skin baked to a golden tan from
working under the sun's glare. Long hair, bound as it was in a
loose knot atop her head, also showed signs of the sun's power;
the naturally honey-blonde hair framing her face had been
bleached nearly white. At first she had tried to remember to
wear a sunbonnet to shield her creamy skin from the sun, but
more often than not, it hung forgotten on the peg near the door
while she worked in the vegetable garden behind the sod house.

Analisa looked across the rutted road that ran parallel to the
rough fence. The corn was high and nearly ripe, thirsty for the
rain, which was sure to fall within the hour. Over the past few
years, she'd learned to smell the rain coming. Other signs were
in evidence, too; the thick, humid heat, the clouds backing up
on each other in the darkening sky.

Slowly her gaze left the cornfield and wandered to the road,
following it eastward toward the village, toward Pella. A deep
sigh escaped her, and Analisa shook her head, shaking off the
heavy sadness she sometimes felt but refused to let affect her for
very long. She knew very well that there was no going back, that
nothing could undo the past five years since she'd left Holland.
Before she turned to go back into the house, Analisa looked

down the road to the right, toward the west, and strained to see more clearly. The setting sun, low on the horizon, sent rays of light radiating from its center, casting the figure in the middle of the road into silhouette. Analisa could clearly see a lone rider slowly approaching. She watched for a moment, to be sure that the heat and the sun were not combining forces to fool her into seeing an apparition, but the figure grew larger as the horseman approached. Without another thought, she turned and ran toward the house.

The metal dishpan clattered noisily against the drainboard as she thrust it away and closed the door behind her. A hurried glance around the room told her that everything was in its place before she had a chance to wonder why that should matter. She had more to fear from a stranger than his opinion of the tidiness of her home.

"Anja? What is it?" Grandfather's voice startled her into action. Although his eyesight was poor, especially in the dim light of the thick-walled sod house, his sharp ears had picked up the sounds of her haste as she slammed down the dishpan and moved about the room. She forced a hollow calmness into her tone.

"There's a stranger coming down the road is all, Opa, but not to worry. He is likely to pass by. It is nearly dark, and he's on his way to Pella, I'm sure." She answered him in Dutch. "I will take up your gun and watch to be certain that he means no harm." It was hard to keep her voice light and easy with her heart lodged in her throat, yet she was reluctant to alarm the old man any more than she had to. With sure steps, Analisa crossed the dirt floor, stood on a smoothly carved wooden step stool, and drew the gun off of the pegs above the pump organ.

With the gun under one arm, she reached for a tin box labeled with gilt letters: Imperial Granum, the Unsweetened Wheat Food. Opening the lid, she dumped half a dozen shells into the pocket of her apron. Deftly she opened the breech-loading Sharps rifle and shoved a shell into the chamber. A quick glance over her shoulder at her grandfather prompted her to say, "Opa, please stay with Kase and don't let him come near the doorway." Her gaze rested for a fleeting moment on the small black-haired child playing with his carved wooden toys near his grandfather's feet. Then Analisa wiped her brow and, with sure, calm movements and a face devoid of emotion, walked to the window above the drainboard. Analisa would not hesitate to use the rifle if the need arose.

Cornstalk walls closed in on either side of the narrow dirt road, miles of green that stretched for as far as the eye could see. To Caleb Storm, who had been traveling the lonely stretch since before the sun was up, the rows of corn seemed to be pressing inward, meeting at a point along the road ahead of him, trapping him forever amid the thick, strong stalks. Somewhere in his muddled thoughts, Caleb knew it was only an illusion, a trick of his tired mind. His head throbbing from more than the heat, he suddenly became aware of the small clearing on the prairie between the rows of corn, the clearing with a small sod house set back off the road. As if sensing Caleb's need for rest, his jet-black stallion moved with a slow and careful gait until it came abreast of the opening in the rough wooden fence surrounding the open yard.

Pulling the reins to the right, Caleb nudged Scorpio into the dirt yard. A haze of gold surrounded the house like a halo, and in the waning sunlight Caleb discerned that the illusion was caused by a profusion of wild sunflowers that had rooted themselves in the flat sod roof of the dwelling. The blooms rose high above the house, some standing eight feet above the roof line and springing out of the ground along the base of the soddie as well. A picture flashed in his mind as he remembered a fairy tale his father often told him. The house might be the home of some elf or fairy creature. More than likely, though, the entire scene was just another mirage conjured by his feverish mind.

He dismounted slowly, surprised at his ability to do so without assistance. Caleb walked Scorpio nearer to the soddie, his eyes on the wooden door, which was closed against intrusion. As his gaze wandered the length of the dwelling, he thought he saw a flicker of movement behind the frame window to the left of the door, but knew that in his present state he could very well be mistaken. Caleb lifted his hat and mopped his forehead with a crumpled cotton bandanna pulled hastily from the back pocket of his closely fitted black trousers. He wiped the sweaty leather band inside the hat and replaced it. Scorpio followed his lead and walked to the long, rectangular water trough and drank deeply. Caleb could smell the rain coming, and somewhere behind him, lightning flashed. Within moments the distant sound of thunder rolled across the prairie. He plunged his sweat-soaked bandanna into the trough and squeezed the water out on the dry soil near his worn snakeskin boots. His mouth parched and dry, Caleb moved nearer the sod house, his destination the covered rain barrel near the door, which he hoped contained fresh water. With his next step, he froze instinctively as the door swung open far enough to reveal the dangerous end of a rifle aimed straight at the space between the brass buttons of his double-breasted shirt.

For a moment there was only silence, and in the stillness, lightning flashed closer, and soon after, thunder cracked. When no one spoke to him, Caleb tried to call out, only to find his voice too weak to utter more than a rasping croak. He pointed toward the water barrel and cleared his throat. "I need water for myself and my horse. If you could oblige, then I'll be on my way."

He took the lack of response to be permission and mustered his strength to walk the rest of the way to the rain barrel. The sod wall seemed to waver before his blurred vision, the sunflowers bobbing and weaving as they moved in a strange, enchanted dance. Rubbing a hand across his eyelids in an attempt to clear his sight, Caleb Storm felt helpless as the picture of the fairy house dimmed and he fell to the ground before the partly open door of the soddie.

As the sinister figure in black approached on horseback and turned into the yard, Analisa was filled with a cold terror that caused her heart to race while her hands held the rifle steady and her finger rested against the smooth metal of the trigger. She stood on tiptoe while she watched him through the window-pane. The rider was dust-coated and travel-weary. So much she discerned from his disheveled clothes and the tired slump of his shoulders. Ordinarily a lone traveler would have been welcome earlier in the day, but this rider, appearing out of the west at sunset, had a shining metal revolver strapped to his thigh.

When the stranger moved away from his horse as it drank from the trough and started walking toward the house, Analisa left the window and opened the door wide enough to stand back in the shadowed interior and stare down the sight of the long gun. She aimed to kill. No outward sign of fear exposed the raw terror clutching her heart.

When he spoke, the dark man's voice sounded strangely distant. At close range, she could see that his steps faltered and his face was flushed, but the brim of his dark hat hid the expression in his eyes. She decided he was drunk, a cowhand fired from a job and on his way to town. By the time his slurred speech registered in her mind and she translated his English into Dutch, the stranger had fallen face forward to the ground at her feet.

She stood stock still for a split second as she watched the motionless form stretched out before the doorway. Was it only a trick to lure her from the house, or had she pulled the trigger without realizing she had done so? When lightning split the sky above her and thunder shook the panes in the window frames, Analisa pushed the door open and stepped outside into the rapidly darkening yard. She knelt at the man's side and, tugging at his shoulder, rolled the stranger over on his back. She noted with relief that he had merely passed out. His hat had fallen off and lay in the dust near his head. She gingerly placed the rifle on the ground within reach and carefully brushed aside a shock of thick midnight hair and felt the man's forehead. It was burning with fever.

Large drops of rain began to fall, splattering the ground and filling the air with melodious sounds as they fell on wood, metal garden tools, the water in the trough, and the windowpanes. After another burst of thunder, Analisa grabbed the rifle and moved to collect the reins of the black horse. Oddly enough, the gelding remained quite still, only its eyes showing fear at each peal of thunder.

"Nice horse. Good, quiet horse," she whispered, her hand outstretched as she approached the tall dark shadow. Analisa wished the proud creature would not look down at her with such disdain. Despite his fierce demeanor, the horse was docile enough as she mustered her courage and grabbed the trailing reins. Analisa hurriedly led him around to a small shed built against the rear of the house where Tulip-the-Ox stood placidly staring at the wall. She tied the reins around a post and promised the animal she would return to remove its saddle and put out more feed. Then Analisa lifted her skirt and, still clutching the heavy gun in the other hand, ran back to the front of the house. The stranger had not moved, but Kase had ventured outside to sit on his haunches in the dust and eye the man with intense curiosity.

"*Wie is hij?* Who is he, Mama?"

"I don't know yet, Kase. Just a sick traveler. Don't get too close or you may get sick yourself," she warned.

"Like I was before?"

"*Ja.* Now go inside and take care of Opa."

The four-year-old hurried away, eager to be of help. She could hear him relating the conversation to his great-grandfather while she pondered the nature of the stranger's illness. Although she knew it would be dangerous to take him into the house without being certain of the cause of his fever, Analisa also realized that the falling rain was gathering intensity, and it boded ill for the stranger to lie in the dirt and become drenched. She carried the gun inside, unloaded it, and returned the shells to the tin, along with the ones she had put in her apron pocket. The task complete, she took a long match from the holder near the stove and lit the tall glass lamp that stood on top of the organ and then the one in the center of the table.

"Anja?" Her grandfather stood in the glow of the lamplight, squinting as he tried to study her expression. "Aren't you going to bring him in the house?"

"*Ja,* Opa. *Ja,* right now." She knew that her tone was impatient, but lately, between Kase and Opa and their demands on her, Analisa felt as if she were raising two children instead of only one.

Snuffing the match, she threw it into the cooling stove and brushed her sweating palms on her apron, pressing her skirts against her thighs. Without being aware that she did so, Analisa reached for the tiresome honey-gold strands of hair at the nape of her neck and pinned them up once again as she left the house.

Poor soul, she thought as she stood looking down at the stranger, deciding how best to maneuver him into the house. She picked up his wide-brimmed felt hat and dropped it on his chest, then walked around to his head and bent down to slip her hands beneath his shoulders and under his arms. She became aware of the solid feel of the man's corded muscles beneath the thin fabric of his shirt, his body so different from the soft ones of Opa and Kase. Grabbing him by his armpits she tugged and succeeded only in feeling a strain in her lower back. The rain pelted them fiercely, soaking through the back of her dress and forcing her hair down into her eyes. This time she braced her heavy *klompen* in the dirt and pulled with her legs as well as her arms. The man's deadweight began to slide through the dirt toward the doorway. Analisa pulled him the few feet to the threshold, then unceremoniously tugged him inside, letting his booted feet thud as they cleared the half-foot drop. She left the door open, welcoming the coolness of the falling rain inside the soddie.

"Please bring the lamp, Opa," she called over her shoulder.

The old man rose from his straight-back chair and shuffled around the table, his tall frame stooped with the burden of age, his once-bright eyes searching the dim light to see what manner of stranger his granddaughter had pulled into the house. The boy walked behind him, his dark hair and complexion so unlike the white hair and fair skin of his great-grandfather. Kase peered around Opa's legs, using them as a shield against the stranger's sickness. The man lay as still as death on the smooth dirt floor, surrounded by three figures staring silently down at him.

Ignoring Opa and Kase, Analisa raised her hand for the lamp her grandfather held, and he handed it to her without comment. She placed it on the floor near the stranger's head. Kneeling next to his shoulder, she reached across the prone figure for the dish towel hanging nearby and used it to mop away the rain from his face and push his hair back off of his forehead. For the first time she studied his strong features, noting the square jawline, the high, sharp cheekbones, and the straight, aristocratic nose. His brows were raven's wings arched above his eyes, and his hair, gloss-black and waving above his forehead, was neatly trimmed around his ears and gently curled around the nape of his neck. Analisa stared down at him and felt her hands trembling slightly. He could not be an Indian, she thought, not dressed so well and traveling alone toward Pella. Perhaps he was one of the Spanish from the south, from Mexico. Quickly she unfastened his gun belt and carefully untied the leather cord that held the holster tight against his hard thigh. Then she slowly slid the belt from beneath the stranger, expecting him to wake at any moment.

She glanced up quickly at Opa, who was beginning to ask questions, which she chose to ignore for the time being. Kase was staring down at the man who had dark hair so like his own. It was not often that the child saw anyone with such black hair, even when they went to the village.

Looking at her small son, with his straight, blue-black hair cut neatly into bangs across his forehead and bowl-shaped around his head, she had a sudden intuition as to the man's illness and began to pull the stranger's shirttail out of his trousers. Quickly, she unfastened the brass buttons and opened his double-breasted shirt. She noted with an expert's eye that it was tailored much like the shirts worn by the United States Army's soldiers. She wondered briefly at this choice of style, for although the shirt was similar to the uniforms, it was black instead of navy and devoid of any bar or buttons marked with the army's insignia.

Just as she suspected, Analisa saw that the man's stomach was aflame with a raised, mottled rash. She lifted his head and arms and wrestled with the shirt in order to pull it off of him. The insides of his arms were red as well. Analisa tried to ignore the otherwise cinnamon bronze tint of his upper body. She knew without looking that the rest of him would be of the same hue.

"What is wrong with the man, Analisa? Do you know?" Opa asked the question for the fourth time while Kase stood silent, hanging on to his great-grandfather's pantleg.

"*Ja.* I'm almost certain he has the measles, same as Kase had when he was so sick."

"A grown man fainting from the measles? You think so?"

"Please help me lift him, Opa," she spoke quickly, standing and moving the lamp to the table in the center of the room. "We'll put him on my bed." Analisa crossed the room and folded back the quilt and comforter, smoothing the clean sheet with her hand before she returned to her grandfather's side.

"Kase, put his hat on the chair and get back out of the way. There's no need to worry now, for you have already had the measles. You will not be sick again." With a quick, reassuring touch, she smoothed her son's silky hair and smiled into his china-blue eyes, a mirror image of her own and always startling in his brown face.

"What about his gun?" the boy asked.

Analisa carried the gun belt to the trunk beside her bed. She opened the lid of the chest and dropped the gun and holster inside, where they rested on her neatly folded clothes. She then returned to where Opa and Kase stood near the stranger.

"Come, Opa, take his feet," she instructed as she again lifted the man's shoulders to spare her grandfather the full weight. They carried the stranger a few feet before lowering him to the dirt floor again. Breathing heavily, Opa rested while Analisa waited, and in a few moments the pair lifted their burden once more. Walking with quick, short steps, they reached her bed and studied its height.

"I'll swing his shoulders up and you shove him onto the bed." Panting with exertion, Analisa swung the man's solid weight onto the bed. As momentum sent her sprawling across his broad chest, she struggled to pull her arms from beneath him while her head rested near his shoulder. Something froze inside her at the forced contact with the man's smooth, warm skin. Quickly, she twisted away from him and pulled her arms free. Her grandfather shoved the man's feet and legs up a second later, and Analisa, freed from the weight of the stranger's upper body, shoved his hips up and over the edge of the bed.

For a moment Analisa and her grandfather stood panting, trying to catch their breath while they watched the unconscious man. He did not stir.

"Thank you, Opa. Somehow we did it!" She smiled for the first time that evening, a glowing smile of accomplishment that lit her eyes and showed her even white teeth. A blush of color like that of a smooth, ripe peach warmed her cheeks, but Analisa gave no thought to her appearance as she turned to be sure the stranger was at ease. The knot atop her head forgotten, most of her thick hair had tumbled around her shoulders, the darker, honey-gold tresses hidden by the sun-bleached top layers, which fell from a natural center part. Droplets of sweat covered her brow and upper lip. She wiped them away with the back of her forearm. As Analisa walked toward the kitchen bench, she turned to her grandfather.

"Opa, I will pour you some clover tea, and then you should go to bed. It's getting late." She was anxious to tend to the man's needs without her grandfather's interference.

"Me, too?" Kase asked without taking his eyes off the strange dark man whose tall body lay stretched across his mother's bed.

"One cup, yes, with Opa, and then you will have to sleep.
I'll sleep in your bed with you tonight. Sit at the table and I will
get your tea."

Carefully, Analisa poured the tea into delicate porcelain cups
that seemed quite out of place in the house made of sod. The tea
had been brewed yesterday, for today they had managed with
cold meals in order to avoid heating the iron stove. While the
old man and the boy sat at the long table waiting for her to serve
them, she placed blue and white teacups, saucers, and bread
plates before them. Analisa worked with swift efficiency,
moving as if her life had not just been interrupted by a man
dropping on her doorstep. She served them slices of golden
cake, fresh two days ago, and taking nothing for herself, filled a
tall jar with water from the crockery pitcher on the bench and
returned to the half-naked man stretched out on her bed.

The man was beginning to stir. He was uncomfortable, she
knew. His head rolled from side to side as he mumbled
unintelligibly. She tried to capture his head in the crook of her
arm and force water between his lips, but her attempts failed.
The dish towel lay nearby, forgotten in their haste to move the
man to the bed. She moistened the end of the cloth with the
tepid water and smoothed it across his lips and brow. Analisa
repeated the movements until he quieted some and then
returned to her grandfather's side.

It was late into the night before Analisa was finally able to
slip her soft lawn nightgown over her head and roll the long
sleeves up to her elbows. She tied the ribbon below the prim
round neckline. The lace-edged collar and smocked bib front
broke the severity of the white gown.

After sending Opa and Kase to bed, she had wrestled with the
stranger's boots and finally succeeded in pulling them off.
When she unbuttoned the waistband of his trousers, Analisa had
discovered to her chagrin that the man was nude beneath the
dark material. After a moment's hesitation, she had covered
him with the lightweight tulip-patterned quilt and drawn his
pants down by tugging at them with her hands beneath the
cover. The task complete, Analisa had smiled at him, pleased at
her own ingenuity. Once the man was settled, with a cool
compress on his forehead, Analisa had seen to his horse.

Kase, she noticed, was sleeping soundly, his nightshirt

twisted up around his short legs, the white material a contrast against his brown skin even in the dark. The boy's pallet had been pulled out from beneath her bed, and since the stranger had usurped her place, Analisa would either have to share the pallet with Kase or sleep in the rocking chair. Not wishing to disturb the boy on such a hot night, Analisa chose the rocker.

The rain had stopped, and the house was still and dark. The familiar furnishings stood like mute ghosts around the room. Analisa wondered, as she had before, if her mother's spirit might linger among her belongings. She wondered, too, if that ghost would be whole and lucid, or like the confused soul who had lived in her mother's shell during the last year of her life.

An ivory-backed brush rested on the trunk near the head of Analisa's bed. She reached for it and drew the bristles through her tangled waist-length hair. With the appearance of the strange rider, Analisa had lost her opportunity to work during the early evening hours while Kase and Opa slept. It had been nearly two years since the luxury of a full night's sleep had been hers, but the results were more than worth her efforts. Before Kase was born, she had begun sewing for the women of Pella, at first taking in the mending and any decorative sewing they chose to let her complete. When it became apparent that Analisa had more than a little talent for sewing, the women grudgingly acknowledged it and began to trust more work to her. By experimenting on materials, which she bought with her earnings, Analisa discovered that she had a gift for copying styles from the ladies' magazines she was able to buy at Knapp's Dry Goods Store. Soon the women were bringing her less mending and more bolts of material, often accompanied by pictures of fashions from newspapers and magazines. Analisa was determined to turn none of them down, happy to take the money they offered for her work, and always finding a way to complete the tasks, despite the time it took for her to care for Opa, Kase, and the house and garden.

Yes, Analisa was aware that her name was well known in Pella. As she brushed out her hair she sighed, wishing with all her heart that it was not so.

Caleb tried to force his eyes open, but the burning, drumming pain behind his lids would not allow it. Someone would come along the road soon, he hoped. Someone would find him lying here baking in the relentless sun. When he had lost Scorpio he didn't know, but he hoped the horse had made its way to water.

A coolness touched his brow, easing the pain behind his eyes for a moment. His long lashes flickered and Caleb's eyes opened. He was surprised to discover that he was not lying out under the blistering sun, but surrounded by darkness illuminated only by moonlight filtering through a nearby window. He tried to speak and then attempted to moisten his lips with his tongue. A figure bent toward him, materializing out of the darkness. In the soft moonlight he studied the apparition, a face and shoulders leaning over him. Wisps of silver hair framed her face like a halo. Her eyes were wide and round, and Caleb realized he was disappointed at his inability to see the color of those eyes in the darkness. Dressed in white, the vision floated nearer and Caleb caught the sweet scent of her on the air. Suddenly he remembered the strange house covered with dancing flowers. Yes. Now he knew for certain. This was the fairy princess, the one his father had described in the old tale.

He was silent and let her gently raise his head and draw him near, to press the cool rim of a glass against his lips. With his eyes never wavering from hers, he drank deeply, the soothing liquid easing the fire in his throat. He licked his lips when she removed the glass and fought to keep his eyes locked on those of the fairy princess, but try as he would, Caleb failed in his attempt and drifted off as the vision continued to hold him in her arms.

Chapter Two

Caleb Storm was certain that he was dead. Eyes open, he lay staring at the sod ceiling above him and thought for a moment that he was staring up at the inside of his own grave. Tightly packed, twisted roots of thick buffalo grass held the sod together above him. Caleb rolled his head to the left and found that his face was just inches away from more thick, grass-filled sod. Too weak to panic and too numb to really care, he had all but resigned himself to his fate when he caught a glimpse of a window frame. He slowly glanced around and discovered he was in a small but comfortable sod house, similar to others he had seen on the open prairie. How he came to be so comfortably ensconced upon the high bed in one corner of the room, he had no recollection. A faint scent of lilacs lingered on the air, nudging his memory, but nothing came to mind except a fleeting picture of a fairy princess in a tale told by his father. He dismissed the image, for it gave him no clue as to how he had arrived in these surroundings.

Except for him, the room was deserted. Caleb sat up, propping the pillows against the headboard to serve as a backrest. His clothes seemed to be missing at the moment. He was more concerned as to the whereabouts of his gun belt and weapon, but he assumed that anyone who had obviously taken such pains to care for him would cause him no harm.

Caleb ran a hand through his tousled hair and felt the matted oiliness of it. He needed a bath and a shave in the worst way. He knew for certain that before he had reached this bed, whenever that was, that he had been traveling for three days. His skin was sticky from heat and sickness. Glancing around the room again in search of his clothes, he wondered how long it would be before he could move on. Caleb had a job to do, and no matter how unpleasant the task, he knew it had to be done. The question foremost in his mind was how in hell was he supposed to get up and moving without a pair of pants.

The sod house was so tidy that Caleb was reminded of his stepmother's home in the East. Everything seemed to be stored in its proper place or standing on display like an item in a curio shop. Blue and white dishes lined the shelves surrounding a window above a kitchen workbench. An enamel dishpan hung from a hook on the bench beside a dish towel, and on the work surface, large crocks stood in a row like soldiers against the sod wall. The table in the center of the room was uncluttered and draped with a runner. A small blue pitcher held flowers of red and yellow. Caleb stared at the flowers for a moment. They seemed to trigger something in his memory, but he knew not what.

An organ stood against one wall, the carved oak providing a stark contrast to the dark sod. Here and there around the room were small figurines or delicate hand-sewn pieces, making the small house an altogether appealing sight. He glanced out the window. The lower half of the view was blocked by a myriad of flowers and plants growing in various containers on the ledge, but above it all he could see an empty yard surrounded by a stake and wire fence with a cornfield beyond. Nothing looked familiar. The place appeared to be deserted.

Determined to find something to wear, Caleb threw aside the quilt and swung his legs over the side of the bed. When dizziness assailed him, he sat back down and braced his hands at his sides, trying to steady his shaking limbs. At the sound of movement outside and the opening of the door, Caleb turned to the intruder.

"Where are my clothes?" His voice was raspy, yet demanding, far more demanding than he had intended.

A young woman crossed the room wearing a getup the likes of which Caleb Storm had never seen. Long, baggy-legged pants reached to a point just above her ankles where the ragged hems showed signs of wear. Black suspenders were buttoned securely to the pants. A once-white linen collarless shirt was tucked into the brown slacks, its sleeves rolled up to the elbows. The suspenders held the shirt pressed against her breasts, and a faded calico sunbonnet hid her hair. Caleb stared at the heavy wooden clogs on her feet. Dutch? he wondered.

The ragbag figure approached him before she answered. Deftly she untied the bow beneath her chin and pushed the bonnet off of her head, retying the ribbons so that the hat would hang down her back. A halo of white-blond hair surrounded a suntanned face and wide, sapphire-blue eyes. All of this Caleb took in with a glance before his eyes came to rest on her pouting lower lip, which was smooth, pink, and inviting. He watched, fascinated, as the woman began to speak. She faced him, hands on her hips.

"This is the tanks I get?" she said.

"Thanks."

"You are welcome."

"No—I wasn't thanking you." He shook his head and explained, "The word is *thanks*. Th, th." Caleb pronounced the English digraph, emphasizing it for her, his tongue between his teeth. "The word's not *tanks;* it's *thanks*."

Her lush mouth hardened into a stubborn line as she stared back at him.

"This is all the *thanks* I get? I drag a stranger into my house, I save his life, I put aside my work to help him, and he is yelling, 'Where are my clothes?'!"

"I never yell." He was smiling broadly now.

As if she realized suddenly what he was asking for, the girl's complexion changed from sun-kissed pink to crimson. Without another word she spun away from him and ran toward the open door, which banged closed in her wake.

Caleb threw his head back and laughed heartily. Exhausted, he realized that he was still too weak to move. He guessed that the imp with the intriguing accent would reappear soon—with his clothes, he hoped—so he stretched out and pulled the quilt across his nakedness, intending to nap while he awaited her return.

Analisa stood immobile outside the door. She leaned against the house and put her hand on her breast where she could feel her heart beating so rapidly that she was sure it would burst.

What had she been thinking of? The man had been sitting on her bed stark naked, talking to her as if he were an English teacher in a schoolroom. The nerve of him to correct her speech! And him naked to boot! She looked around the yard. Kase and Opa were nowhere in sight, and she remembered that they were fishing at the creek. Good. She would have time to gather her wits. Analisa wasn't quite sure what to do next, but she knew one thing for certain: She would get the man's clothes back to him and shoo him on his way.

Somewhat calmer at last, Analisa brushed her hands on her pants and took a deep breath. The familiar smells surrounding her brought her back to reality and helped put her at ease. The herbs growing among the other plants on the windowsill next to her, the rich, warm earth, and even the farmyard scents helped calm her racing thoughts. He would soon be gone, the stranger, and Analisa could resume her normal routine.

She pushed herself away from the wall, forced by the *klompen* to walk slowly. Analisa had taken to wearing her brother Jan's clothes when she worked in the garden. They saved her own from soil and wear, and besides, Jan would never wear them again. For a fleeting moment the memory of her older brother lying so still, drenched in his own blood, appeared vividly in her mind. Analisa shook it away. Was there nothing she could think about safely this morning?

A strong clothesline hung between two slim cottonwoods behind the house. Analisa hurriedly took down the man's freshly laundered shirt and pants and smoothed them against her legs as she folded them. She knew she would never be able to walk back into the house with the clothes and face that man and his laughing eyes. Could she have imagined that his eyes were blue? His outward characteristics were those of a Spaniard or, at the worst, and Indian, but she would not let her mind dwell on such a thought. It was not possible that the stranger's eyes were as blue as the summer sky.

No matter, she thought. She might never have to see him again. Perhaps he would put on his clothes and ride away. She would have her grandfather take in the clothes and give them back to the man along with his gun. Opa would not understand a word the stranger said, and the old man's eyes were so poor that he would not wonder at the man's appearance. Yes. That was as good a plan as any she could devise so quickly. Analisa started across the yard to find Opa and Kase.

She could hear their voices before she actually saw them. They were standing beneath the cottonwoods along the creek that meandered across the prairie a short distance from the sod house. Part of the web of tributaries running into the Skunk River, the creek provided them with bullheads and catfish in the summer, quite a welcome change from cured pork and jerky. Analisa watched and listened to the two companions before she interrupted them. She heard Kase's high, piping child's voice clearly, but could not always hear the words Opa used to answer him.

Kase always spoke Dutch to his great-grandfather. Although the boy had not been exposed to much English, he knew that language as well and was able to converse with Analisa when she insisted they practice together.

"Opa, tell me what the old country was like." The boy looked up at his great-grandfather. He had asked the question many times, but Analisa knew he was always ready to listen to the stories Opa told about Holland.

"The old country was green and beautiful, Kase, not like this land." The old man waved his hand toward the flat, wide plain before him. "We lived on an island in the North Sea and spent our days fishing. There were great cities. Everyone was Dutch."

"Why did you leave there?" Kase looked up at the clouded blue eyes and wrinkled face of his great-grandfather and waited for a reply.

Edvard Van Meeteren sighed. Analisa watched his shoulders rise and fall with the weight of memories. She waited, like her son, for his answer, and blinked away her tears when it finally came.

"We came here because we needed work and room to grow.

The old country was beautiful, but it was hard to make a living from the land. Now the only ones who are left are your mama and myself, and we are not free.''

Analisa was deeply hurt by the sadness in his voice.

"Tell me about the others."

Analisa approached with rapid steps, calling out to them. "Kase! Opa!" She tried to sound lighthearted.

The boy always asked about the others, and the old man, forgetting how many times he'd told his great-grandchild about the family, would begin all over again. Analisa could not bear to hear their names, not today. Emmett, her father, Henrietta, her mama, and Jan, the older brother she had been so close to—all gone now. No, she did not want to hear it again. And what of Pieter and Meika? Would she ever see her younger brother and sister again? Analisa had wondered for four years. She would put it aside for now. There was the stranger to see to.

"Come to the house with me now. Oh, what fine fish, Kase! Opa, you must take the man his clothes so that he can leave. He is awake now."

Kase asked if the man could talk, eager no doubt to ply him with questions while Opa demanded to know who the stranger was and where he was going. They both spoke at once until Analisa laughed at their babble.

"Listen to us! Come home now. I'll wash up for dinner and you two will eat, but first you must clean these fish and see that the stranger leaves."

"Will he eat with us, Mama?"

"No."

"Why?" Kase questioned her in English, sensing from his mother's terse reply that she did not want the stranger around. He knew she might not want to share her reason with Opa.

"Because he has been here far too long already and needs to be on his way. Now, take Opa's hand and we will all go back to the house."

Analisa watched as Kase took the old man's hand in his own small one. Opa carried the thin pole and fishing line, and Analisa gathered up the bucket and the four shining bullheads that had been strung together through mouth and gill.

A strange foreboding crept along Analisa's spine as she stood alone beside the slow-moving creek, her grandfather and Kase having moved away from her across the grassy field. With a

sudden wariness brought on by the feeling, she turned her gaze
across the small stream and searched the low growth beneath
the cottonwoods. Unable to see anything threatening hidden
among the shining green leaves, Analisa shrugged at her
silliness and turned to follow the others.

Upon reaching the yard, Analisa called to Opa and gathered
the stranger's clothes from the fence rail where they hung,
neatly folded. She smoothed the dark material of the shirt one
last time, relishing its quality before she handed the pants and
shirt to her grandfather, instructing him to take them into the
house, give them to the traveler, and then fetch the man's
mount.

More than happy to be useful, Edvard nodded in agreement
and disappeared around the corner of the sod house. Kase
started to follow the bent figure, but his mother called him
back. She knew the boy could speak English well enough to
answer any questions the man might put to him and so sought to
keep from having to do so herself. The stranger could gain no
information from Opa and would, she hoped, be on his way
very soon.

Her stomach taut with nervousness, Analisa busied herself
filling the large bathtub behind the soddie. As soon as the man
was gone she planned to wash and change, then prepare the
midday meal. A tall windmill in the yard churned up the
precious water needed for life on the open prairie. A hand pump
served to force the water into whatever container was provided.
Analisa dreamed of having a pump inside the house someday so
that she could dispense with carrying the water indoors for
cooking and cleaning, but as poor as they were, she knew it was
a dream that would not be realized in the near future.

Analisa watched the water fill the large round oak tub,
laboriously working the pump handle until her grandfather's
shuffling gate disturbed her thoughts. She looked up from her
task to see him walking toward her, shaking his head in
confusion.

"Is he getting dressed, Opa?"

"*Nee*. The man is asleep again and I did not disturb him. He
seems to be feverish but not so bad as before. He will not be
able to leave yet, Analisa."

She turned away to hide her irritation. Was there no end to
the man's presence? Now she would be forced to face him

again, perhaps even tend to him if his illness worsened. If only he would recover enough to ride the few miles into town, he could rest there until completely well. Determined not to let the stranger disturb her life any more than he already had, Analisa straightened her shoulders and faced her grandfather once again.

"Thank you, Opa. Please see that Kase washes up and let him help you clean the fish. You can also light the stove, but quietly, so that the stranger is not disturbed. I'll wash up out here and then change. Dinner will soon be ready."

She issued the orders easily, not because she wanted to do so, but because the burden of running the household had fallen upon her shoulders since the attack on the family. Edvard Van Meeteren, nearly ninety and becoming more disoriented daily, accepted his granddaughter's role as head of the small household.

Stripping off her brother's shirt, Analisa stood in her camisole and rough homespun pants, quickly washing herself with a rag, which she dipped into the tub. The dampness felt refreshing against her skin as she lifted the hair sticking to the nape of her neck and wiped the cloth along the slender column, then down over the rise of her breasts. She had grown used to washing outdoors during the warm months of summer, and although she had not dared to bare herself completely and bathe in the tub behind the house, she felt secure and protected, having an unobstructed view of the open plains and cornfields surrounding the house. Her simple toilette complete, Analisa pulled on her shirt and went inside to gather up her clothes. While the stranger was in the house, she changed outside in the cow shed, preferring to dress alongside Tulip-the-Ox and the milk cow, Honey, or in their empty stalls. Analisa would indeed be grateful to see the back of him as he rode away.

A tempting aroma emanated from the cast-iron stove and drifted through Caleb's senses and into his mind. Soon the clatter of dishes and cooking utensils woke him. Motionless, with eyes hooded by lowered lids, he rested against the pillows in the high oak bed and watched a honey-blond figure move efficiently about her tasks across the room. He knew it was the same young woman he had seen earlier dressed in the ragged pants and oversize shirt, although she now wore a blue calico dress. Her back was turned to him as she stood before the stove, lifting the lids from simmering pots and stoking the oven with buffalo chips. She opened the oven door to peer inside, and Caleb admired the view of her firm, shapely backside. Now and again when she moved to work at the kitchen bench, he could just see her profile, a pert nose tilted slightly upward at the end, the thick wing of eyelashes, the soft, lush swell of her lower lip. He could see from where he lay that she worked without a smile, and for a moment he wondered what it would take to make her smile.

The room was empty save for the two of them, and Caleb began to wonder if the woman lived alone. He could not remember seeing anyone else earlier. After watching her silently for a few more moments, Caleb was about to speak when the door opened. For some unknown reason, he felt compelled to close his eyes once more, feigning sleep while he watched from beneath his lashes to see who had entered. It was a small boy whose dark head was barely visible above the end of the bed.

The boy ran toward his mother and threw his sturdy arms around her knees. Caleb did not understand any of the words the boy said except one, "Mama," and that one word was enough to add a vivid detail to the picture he was forming in his mind. He knew he had no right to feel disappointed upon learning the woman had a child. If anything, he should have been glad to learn that she did not live alone so far from a settlement, yet he knew that if she had a child she most assuredly also had a husband, and that knowledge strangely gave him a feeling of loss.

The woman laughed down into the boy's upturned face and stopped her work long enough to bend over and squeeze him tenderly. With a motherly gesture, she arranged his hair with her fingers, then turned back to her work. Dismissed, the boy crossed the room toward Caleb, who closed his eyes completely when he realized the child was standing next to the bed. The little boy was so close that Caleb could hear his soft, even breathing.

"Kase, come to the table. Where is Opa?" This time the woman spoke in English, her voice as softly accented as he remembered it earlier. Who was Opa? Caleb wondered. Could it be the boy's father?

Tired of his game, Caleb slowly opened his eyes and met a

pair of blue ones level with his own. As he studied the boy, Caleb felt as if he were gazing into a mirror, a mirror in which one could look backward through time. He was very sure of one fact: This child's father was either an Indian or a half-breed like himself.

Caleb and the boy exchanged silent stares, studying each other. The boy seemed to be weighing the man's worth. Caleb noted that the only feature which claimed him as the woman's son was his eyes, which were wide and blue, fringed by silky black lashes. The youngster's hair was neatly trimmed in a fashion the likes of which Caleb had never seen before. It looked as if the boy's mother had inverted a bowl on the child's head and trimmed around it. Though it was unusual, Caleb thought the haircut an appealing one, allowing the straight, dark hair to frame the boy's round face.

A wide smile appeared on the child's face when he realized Caleb was awake at last. Without moving, he turned and called out to his mother, speaking English this time.

"Mama! The stranger is awake! I may talk to him now?"

A pan clattered against the stove, drawing Caleb's eyes away from the child's to lock with the woman's. She stood frozen at the other end of the room, watching Caleb warily. What had he done to instill such fright in a woman he'd spoken to only briefly? Aware of her fear, Caleb smiled, trying to put her at ease. She did not move, nor did she return his smile as she wiped her hands nervously on her white apron. He wished she would walk toward him and lessen the distance between them.

"What's your name?" the child asked, stepping closer and leaning an elbow against the side of the bed.

"Caleb. What's yours?"

"Kase."

"That's a fine name. I've never heard it before."

"It's Dutch."

"I see." Caleb looked from the boy to the woman, who was watching their exchange. "So your mama is Dutch, too?"

"*Ja.* But I am not Dutch, only my name. I'm an American. I was born here, in this Iowa land."

"Kase." The woman called at last, her voice softly accented. "Leave the man alone. He is not feeling well."

Caleb welcomed the excuse to speak to her.

"He's no problem, ma'am." He wondered if she would refuse to speak directly to him much longer. He watched as she seemed to draw upon some inner strength, straightening her shoulders. Smoothing her apron, the woman walked toward the bed. She came to stand behind the child, keeping him between them, her slim fingers resting gently, protectively, on the boy's shoulders. She faced Caleb squarely, daring him to ask a question or make a comment about the boy.

"I am Analisa Van Meeteren. This is my son, Kase." As she spoke she held Caleb's eyes steady with her own.

"I'm Caleb Storm, ma'am. I'm sorry to have inconvenienced you. I don't know what happened. The last thing I remember is riding along the corn rows, needing a drink of water."

"It seems you have the measles, Mr. Storm. The illness has spread throughout the area this past spring and summer. It seems to affect some people more than others." Analisa's stare hardened as she explained. Caleb did not look away, but answered her unspoken question.

"I understand what you are hinting at, Mrs. Van Meeteren. I guess there's no need for me to tell you that I'm half Sioux. My looks give my heritage away. I know measles have wiped out a good part of the Indian population in this country. I didn't realize I'd been in contact with anyone who had them." He noticed that she did not volunteer any explanation regarding Kase and decided that perhaps she did not wish to speak in front of the child.

"How do you feel, Mr. Storm? Are you well enough to travel?"

Caleb smiled at her obvious impatience to be rid of him. He noted her discomfort. She avoided looking at his bare shoulders and midriff. Out of deference to her sensitivity he pulled the quilt up and held it securely beneath his arms. He knew that despite his light-headedness he would be able to travel if forced to do so, but for some inexplicable reason, Caleb couldn't bring himself to leave yet. He told himself the reason was his curiosity about the boy, but he knew, too, that the clear blue eyes and overripe lips of Analisa Van Meeteren had much to do with his sudden reluctance to move on.

"I still feel a little weak, ma'am." Caleb did his best to look helpless, but was unaccustomed to malingering and so doubted the success of his attempt. He was surprised when Analisa reached across the boy and placed her hand firmly on his brow.

She sighed resignedly before she spoke. "You do feel a bit feverish, Mr. Storm. Perhaps you should stay another night. Dinner will be ready soon, and I will fix you a plate."

"That would be fine, ma'am. I appreciate all you've done for me. It's not everyone who would take in a total stranger, especially one who's part Indian." He smiled up at her with genuine gratitude and was surprised when she turned away abruptly without so much as a nod.

"Where do you live?" The boy was still rooted next to the bed and curious.

"Kase!" The woman called out from where she stood near the stove. "Don't bother Mr. Storm."

"He's no bother, really, Mrs. Van Meeteren."

Kase smiled his thanks at Caleb and waited for an answer to his question.

"Well, I guess you could say I'm from the East, although I was born very near here."

"Are you going to Pella?"

"Just long enough to get supplies. I'm not planning to stay there very long."

"I've been to Pella once," Kase said proudly, his head bobbing as he spoke.

"Good for you!" Caleb smiled at the boy's enthusiasm and reached out to ruffle his hair.

"Kase," Analisa interrupted once again, "go out and find Opa, please. Tell him dinner is ready."

Kase was out of the door in a moment's time, anxious to find Opa and return to Caleb's side. Caleb watched with interest, wondering again if Opa could be the boy's father. Perhaps the boy was a foundling, an orphan the Dutch couple had adopted. Caleb doubted that, for he knew that Indians rarely gave their children away to anyone other than relatives.

He turned his attention to Analisa, who was sorting through a neatly stacked pile of clothing in a box she had pulled from beneath the cot near the stove. With a folded white cloth in her hands, she approached him again. Caleb noted the flush of embarrassment that burned her sun-darkened cheeks, the heightened color only adding to her soft loveliness.

"Mr. Storm, I have your clothes clean and ready for you to wear, but since you are not leaving yet, would you please wear this nightshirt?" She held the linen shirt out toward him by her fingertips, almost as if she was afraid to touch him. He found this strange after the casual way she had felt for his temperature moments before. Suddenly he remembered his demand for clothing as he had sat naked on the bed earlier, and her startled reaction when she realized he was nude.

"Mrs. Van Meeteren, I'm sorry about my . . . well, my rudeness earlier. It was uncalled for. I was disoriented when you first came in. I thought you were a boy." That was a bare-faced lie, and he chided himself for it, knowing there was no way he could have mistaken her round, lush buttocks and full breasts for a boy's, even in the ragged trousers and baggy shirt.

"A boy in a sunbonnet, Mr. Storm?"

"No stranger than a woman in trousers, Mrs. Van Meeteren."

"Please put on the nightshirt. I will get your plate ready for you." Without further comment, she turned away. Caleb smiled as he watched the decided swing of her hips.

As soon as she turned her back, Caleb slipped on the long, loose shirt. He was settled and covered again when the door opened and Kase led a tall, weathered old man into the house.

Analisa said something in Dutch to the old man, prompting him to swing his gaze toward Caleb, who nodded silently in turn. The young woman approached the bedside with a large plate laden with steaming food. She waited while Caleb adjusted himself against the pillows. When she started to place a napkin across his lap, color rushed to her cheeks once again. Caleb, aware of her discomfort, took the napkin and arranged it himself.

"This looks good enough to eat," he smiled up at her. "Thank you." Caleb's mouth watered as he stared at the plate heaped with pan-fried fish, boiled potatoes seasoned with a sprinkling of green chives, fresh-sliced tomatoes, and green beans. A thick slab of crusty bread slathered with creamy butter lay on the top of the food.

"I'll bring you some fresh water and a cup of coffee later." She bent to collect his empty water glass from the top of the trunk.

"This is a feast for a starving man."

For the first time, she turned to him with a smile, and Caleb was lost. Her soft, peach-hued skin and sky-blue eyes seemed to be lit from within and shining only for him. Her hair, spun gold and rich as honey shot through with strands of sunlight, fell softly about her shoulders where it had escaped the pins. He held her gaze captive with his own, willing her not to move. Kase's voice broke the spell.

"Mama?"

As she turned away, Caleb looked down at his plate. His appetite seemed to have diminished.

"Mr. Storm?"

It was as if the magic moment had never been when Caleb looked at Analisa. She stood near the old man who was seated at the long table. Caleb nodded again.

"This is my grandfather, Edvard Van Meeteren. We call him Opa in the Dutch way of saying Grandpapa." She then spoke to the old man, and Caleb heard her say his name, making the introduction in Dutch.

"Please thank him for me for the hospitality, Mrs. Van Meeteren."

She spoke quietly to the old man and then returned to Caleb's bedside. For a moment she looked down at her hands and then defiantly raised her eyes and chin, staring at Caleb, her discomfort apparent yet controlled.

"Mr. Storm," she began softly, her accent suddenly more pronounced, "I am not Mrs. Van Meeteren. I am not *Mrs.* anyone. I am just Analisa Van Meeteren."

Sensing that her defiance stemmed from humiliation and realizing that the boy, Kase, was indeed her son, Caleb knew the admission had cost Analisa dearly. Admiring her strength, he nodded in silent understanding.

"And I am just Caleb."

Consciously avoiding the eyes of the man across the room, Analisa turned her attention to the midday meal. She served Opa and Kase before she sat down to her own sparingly filled plate. The heat combined with the raw nervousness brought on by Caleb Storm's conversation had ruined her appetite. The three Van Meeterens bowed their heads in thanksgiving, and Analisa was aware of a cessation of sound from the corner as the man stopped eating in deference to their prayers. She lifted her fork at last and forced her eyes to remain fixed on her plate, but she could not still her mind as she thought about Caleb Storm.

He claimed to be a half-breed. Analisa would almost have believed him to be a full-blooded Indian, but his deep blue eyes gave testimony to the truth of his words. Memories and realities that she had forced out of her mind resurfaced as his words repeated themselves. "There's no need for me to tell you that I'm half Sioux," he'd said. He was right: There had been no need, for just as Kase's features and coloring could not be disguised, neither could Caleb Storm's. "It's not everyone who would take in a total stranger, especially one who's part Indian." His words exposed a cruel reality, only one of the many that her son would be forced to suffer during his lifetime. If only she had the power to change things, to guard and protect Kase always, to spare him the hurt that lay ahead. Analisa knew that was impossible, but often her mind dared to fancy a scheme that would spare him the humiliation of his inheritance. Oh, yes, she thought sadly, her mind could weave many plans, but there was no hope of seeing them fulfilled.

They ate in silence, Kase hurrying because he was so obviously eager to return to the man, Caleb Storm, to renew his questioning. Analisa could see that Opa had sensed her unease. Finally, she smiled at the old man and asked what he planned to do all afternoon.

"I am going to try to mend the section of fence that has a post missing."

Analisa knew how hard it was for her once-vigorous grandfather to sit idle. She never begrudged him the opportunity to remain useful, although more times than not she had been forced to repair whatever he decided to "fix." His projects did serve to keep him busy while she worked at her own tasks, however, and Opa usually allowed Kase to help him with his work. Lately, Analisa felt the little boy watched over the old man rather than the other way around. It mattered little, she thought with a smile, as long as they enjoyed each other's company.

The meal ended, Analisa rose and began to clear away the dishes. Her grandfather went outdoors to fetch a bucket of water. He left the front door open, and heat swept into the soddie. The walls were made of a double thickness of sod blocks nearly eighteen inches wide, making the finished walls a yard deep. Thus insulated, the house stayed cool in the summer and held its warmth in the winter. Analisa closed the door as she passed by to collect Caleb's plate and fork. She carried a cup of coffee to him, certain that he would relish a strong drink after so many days without it.

Without a word they exchanged dishes. Then Caleb spoke. "Thanks again, Analisa. That tasted as delicious as it smelled."

She stared at him in silence for a moment, stopped by the sound of her name on his lips. "Thank you, Mr. Storm, although I'm sure you were probably starving and would have eaten anything. You should regain your strength quickly now."

"I'm sure I will." He turned to stare out the window as she left the bedside. Through the forest of geraniums along the ledge he saw a stylish covered buggy turn into the yard and stop near the trough. A tall, stately matron stepped out and moved with the determined march of a general toward the soddie. He lost sight of her as she reached the door.

"It looks as if you have a caller."

Analisa was startled as Caleb's words and an insistent knocking rang out in the quiet room. Drying her hands on her apron, she hurried to the door. When she recognized Clara Heusinkveld, Analisa suppressed a groan. Of all the residents of Pella, Clara was undeniably the worst gossip, taking delight in spreading tales and embellishing them with her own details. Analisa knew that if Mevrou Heusinkveld saw Caleb Storm, she would spread the story over Pella faster than a prairie fire.

The woman was nearly through the doorway when Analisa stepped outside and closed the door. Mrs. Heusinkveld was startled by the abrupt rudeness, but Analisa feigned ignorance. *Let the old cow think I'm rude*, she thought. That would be better than allowing her inside.

"I wish to place an order for a very special gown," the visitor said. "I will need it before two weeks are over. I hope you will be able to complete the work on time. If you can, I will give you a bonus."

"I will certainly try, Mrs. Heusinkveld. Did you bring the material with you?"

"Of course, as well as the picture of *exactly* what I want." The woman stared at Analisa. "I'll get them and then explain what I would like you to do."

As the woman returned from her carriage with the package of fabric carefully wrapped in paper and tied with twine, Edvard appeared with the water bucket. He greeted the visitor in Dutch, but she offered no more than a polite nod. Analisa continued to block the door, forcing them to stand in the hot afternoon sun.

"Take Mevrou Heusinkveld inside, Anja," the old man said. "Where are your manners?"

Before she could protest, he had reached for the latch string and pulled it, swinging the door wide. Analisa closed her eyes in a brief moment of suppressed anger, then stepped over the threshold into the cool interior of the soddie.

Clara Heusinkveld's presence was a jarring intrusion in the small room. A high ruffled hat complete with a bobbing plume added to her already imposing height. Although Analisa was not short, the woman towered over her. A wide satin bow was tied beneath her chin, pushing the more than ample folds of skin forward. Her day dress of expensive watered silk was far grander than Analisa's simple calico. Her height, along with her light eyes and graying brown hair, proclaimed her Dutch heritage.

Standing aloof in the center of the room, Clara Heusinkveld let her eyes adjust to the dim light before she inspected the dwelling with a regal air. She watched while Edvard set the bucket of water near the stove and shuffled outside again. Her eyes took in the unwashed dishes stacked on the drainboard and the remnants of the finished meal on the stove. It was then that her attention was drawn to the hushed voices in the opposite corner of the room. Analisa's heart sank to her toes as Mevrou Heusinkveld's gaze came to rest on Caleb Storm and Kase.

The stranger was propped up against the pillows, Opa's white nightshirt open at the neck to reveal his smooth brown skin. Kase knelt on the trunk beside the bed, his wooden toys spread about the hills and valleys the man's long form created among the bedding. The two were moving the tiny figures about, ignoring the stares of the two women.

Mrs. Heusinkveld stood as if frozen to the spot for a few seconds before she spoke to Analisa.

"Well?" Her voice was icy as she demanded an explanation.

Analisa drew herself up to her full height and faced the woman squarely. If Clara Heusinkveld wanted information, Analisa was determined that she get all she needed directly from the source. Analisa knew she would be well within her rights to toss the nosy gossip out into the dust, but what Analisa refused to tell her could be construed as worse than the truth. Besides, the woman was one of Analisa's best customers.

Speaking in a whisper, unwilling to disturb the man and boy, Analisa explained Caleb Storm's presence in her home and, worse yet, in her bed.

"So you see," she concluded at last, "when he fainted right at our door there was nothing we could do but help him."

"Who is he?" the older woman asked, her brows knitted in question as she inspected Caleb.

"All I know is that his name is Mr. Storm and he is from the East."

"You haven't asked?"

"I did not feel I had the right to be rude, Mrs. Heusinkveld. Perhaps you would like to question him?"

The older woman missed the insult as she continued to stare. "He looks Spanish to me."

"Perhaps. I really don't know. May I see your material now?"

Distracted at last, the woman opened the parcel while Analisa studied the picture the woman had handed her. The dress was ornate with tucks and ruffles adorning the sleeves and skirt. The style was highly unsuitable for Mrs. Heusinkveld's overblown figure, but Analisa's services did not include suggestions about style. She was merely to copy the picture.

"I'll have to make the pattern first, Mevrou Heusinkveld. I have your measurements, but after I cut out the fabric and baste the pieces together you will need to have a fitting. I think perhaps in four days. Would that be all right?"

"Fine. I'll be back then. You're certain you will be finished in two weeks?"

"Yes. I'm quite sure." Analisa stood with her hand smoothing the heavy emerald satin the woman had purchased. The rich material slid through her fingers. It would be a joy to work with, and she could ill afford to tell the woman the task was too great. She would work day and night if need be to complete the gown in time. "Thank you, Mrs. Heusinkveld."

Analisa had opened the door before she noticed that Clara was once again gaping at Caleb and Kase. Glancing in the same direction, Analisa was startled by what she saw. Her son and Caleb had stopped their play momentarily to smile in innocent greeting to Mevrou Heusinkveld. With their heads close together, they were alike enough to be brothers, or father and son. A cold tremor shook Analisa, but she forced herself to dismiss the other woman in a firm voice. "Good day, Mrs. Heusinkveld."

Obviously anxious to be on her way to Pella, no doubt to spread the tale of the stranger in Analisa Van Meeteren's bed, Clara Heusinkveld hurriedly collected her reticule, straightened her hat, and rushed through the doorway without so much as a good day.

Chapter Three

"Why do I have the feeling that Mrs. Heusinkveld isn't going to waste time telling the town about the stranger you are harboring between your sheets?"

Analisa started visibly as Caleb spoke softly into her ear. As the door closed, hiding them from the older woman's view, he had left the bed and crossed the cool, hard-packed dirt floor to stand unnoticed beside Analisa. Deep in thought, she had stood staring at the door until his words disturbed her. She turned abruptly, unable to hide her dismay at finding him so close beside her.

Her lips were level with his collarbone. Caleb briefly imagined the feel of those lips and her warm breath against his skin before he forced his mind back to reality. He guessed her to be close to five feet eight, but Caleb, at six foot three, didn't feel intimidated by her height. Up close, he could see that her eyes were clear blue, the vivid blue of a cornflower, dusted with tiny slivers of silver. Thick honey-colored lashes hid her eyes when she blinked, almost as if they were trying to brush away his presence. She backed away from him quickly and tried to disguise her abrupt move by turning her back and attending to the stack of dishes.

"You should not be out of bed, Mr. Storm. Your fever may return." She ignored his earlier question about Clara Heusinkveld.

"I'm sure it already has," he quipped, referring to the heat stirring in his blood as he stood so near Analisa. "I do need to use the . . . convenience," he said. "I assume it's out back?"

"Yes."

She answered over her shoulder as she scraped the dishes clean, pushing the scraps into a bucket on the floor beneath the bench, and stacked the dishes in the enamel dishpan. To avoid facing Caleb, she reached for the teakettle and poured hot water over the dishes.

"I'll need my boots." He wished she'd turn around so that he could see her eyes once more, but she answered him without moving.

"They are at the end of the bed, near the door."

"About my gun . . ." While he was reclaiming his belongings, he decided it would be best to collect them all.

At last she turned around, a question in her eyes. "You need your gun to go to the outhouse?"

"No. I'd just like to know where it is."

"It is in a safe place. When you leave, I'll give it to you."

"I see. You'll toss it to me as I ride away?"

She turned her back on his teasing smile.

Caleb sat on the edge of the bed and put his boots on. The deep, soft mattress sank under his weight. Standing again, he walked to the door, feeling silly in the nightshirt, which hung down almost to the tops of his worn snakeskin boots. With a shrug he ran a hand through his tousled hair and across the stubble of beard. No wonder she wouldn't turn around. He guessed his appearance left a lot to be desired.

Kase ran to join Caleb, volunteering to show him the way to the outhouse. When Analisa started to protest, Caleb dismissed her objections with a smile.

"He's no bother."

The bright sunlight outside the soddie hurt his eyes. Caleb stood for a moment allowing his sight to adjust and then moved away from the house, rounding the corner behind his small guide. Kase chatted happily as he pointed out the important objects within his small world. As the little boy darted back and forth from Caleb to items of interest, things he was proud to show, the man assessed his surroundings.

A poorly mended fence made of thin stakes, cottonwood branches, and pieces of dismantled furniture was held together by assorted scraps of wire. The slipshod affair marked the perimeter of the yard. A sow and her brood of piglets roamed freely inside the boundary, as did a few scraggly hens and a rooster. A pile of wood collected from various sources was stacked near the house.

Once they had rounded the soddie and were facing the side opposite the door, Kase pointed out the small lean-to that served as a stable for a milk cow and an ox. The ox and cow had been set free to roam the yard, but Caleb found Scorpio still tethered in the shed. He untied the reins and removed the bridle and bit, slapping the horse on the rump and freeing it to roam at will and graze on the stubborn prairie grass growing in the yard. Caleb found his saddle and saddlebags on the floor of the shed, apparently too heavy for Analisa to move any farther. His rifle was hanging against the sod wall, well out of the boy's reach.

A large vegetable garden, meticulously weeded and neatly laid out in rows, occupied the southwest corner of the yard. He guessed that Analisa spent many hours, dressed in her strange ragged pants, suspenders, and faded bonnet, tending the garden. Good, he thought, smiling to himself. That meant he would have the pleasure of seeing her in those trousers again.

Caleb was somewhat surprised but also pleased to see that the Van Meeterens had the convenient luxury of a windmill in the yard. It would ensure them of a water supply when the dry season parched the land. Many settlers relied solely on rain barrels or nearby watering holes or creeks, which served only as long as there was rain. As he had traveled west, he'd been surprised at first to see windmills dotting the prairie landscape, but he had soon learned that the much needed devices could be purchased through farm journal advertisements and assembled at the site. Those farmers who could not afford to buy such luxuries sometimes built their own mills for a fraction of the cost by following instructions printed in the publications.

A splash of gold against the sky caught Caleb's attention. He lifted his gaze skyward and shielded his eyes against the sun's glare as he stared at the roof of the sod house. Sunflowers stood at various heights above the building, growing out of the roof. It was a sight the likes of which he had never seen, and as he took notice, Caleb saw that flowers surrounded the ground near the walls of the house as well. He had a sudden recollection of having seen the house covered with sunflowers before, and realized it must have been the night he arrived.

Kase called to him, impatient to resume his guided tour, and Caleb responded to his shout. After visiting the wooden water closet, Caleb stood near the fence at the south end of the yard while he waited for Kase. About a half-mile across the vast open grassland beyond the fence, he could see a stand of cottonwoods, and he assumed they were growing along a stream. At the thought of the clear, fresh running water, Caleb became aware of the uncomfortable itching of his skin and his scalp. He raked his fingers through the tangled mass of black hair, then rubbed the back of his neck with the palm of his hand.

"Kase?" He called the boy's name over his shoulder, and within seconds, Kase appeared eagerly at his side.

"What do you say we go for a swim in that creek over there?"

The boy looked up at him earnestly, his eyes wide. "I can't swim."

"Well, I need a bath in the worst way, so maybe you'd like to come along and make sure no one steals my boots." *They're welcome to the nightshirt*, he thought.

"Should I go and tell Mama?"

"No, you don't need to. We'll be back in a few minutes. Besides, I have a feeling she would object to my getting wet. Women have some strange ideas, Kase." Caleb opened the back gate and carefully looped the wire catch behind them. "Some of them are convinced that if you have any sort of sickness at all, a little water will put you right into your grave."

"We never bathe in the creek. We fish there, though."

"Where do you bathe?"

"I get into the big wooden tub behind the house, in the

summer. In the winter I wash by the stove. Mama and Opa, too.
But they never get in the big tub outside.''

While the boy chatted, Caleb glanced across the prairie,
surveying every direction for signs of riders. The area had been
settled for nearly twenty years, but away from the small prairie
towns, homesteads were miles apart. Roving bands of renegades
from the reservations were not unheard of. *And here you are,
Storm*, he thought, *ambling through the buffalo grass, hatless,
gunless, and dressed in a damned nightshirt*. He decided his bath
would be brief.

Large pieces of fabric, bits of knotted string, and odd-shaped
papers littered the top of the table. Mevrou Heusinkveld's dress
was beginning to take shape. Just as Analisa took precious time
away from her task to wonder why Kase and Caleb Storm had
failed to return, the boy ran into the house. She smiled at his
urgency as he tried to explain his mission. His English was
rapidly improving, now that he had a reason to use it, but he
stumbled over unfamiliar words.

''Mr. Storm need a . . . a *vatenwasbak*.'' He pointed to the
dishpan hanging near his head.

''Dishpan.''

''*Ja*. A dishpan. He wants to make a soapy water for taking
the hair off his face.''

''To shave.''

''*Ja*. He wants to shave, and so told me to get the pan,
please. You should see, Mama, he has everything he needs in
the bags in the shed, the ones that were strapped to his horse.
What are they called? Can I take the pan?''

''Yes, you *may* take the pan, and I don't know what to call
the bags. Ask Mr. Storm.''

''Mama, do you know that Mr. Storm goes into the creek
naked? I got to watch his boots for him while he washed
himself.''

The door closed on the image of her son struggling with the
dishpan nearly as large as he was. Intent once more, Analisa
carefully slid the scissors along the paper outline as she cut out
the emerald cloth. Suddenly, she slammed her scissors down on
the table and stared at the closed door. Just what had the boy
been talking about? Caleb Storm had a problem keeping his

clothes on, it seemed, and Analisa decided she need not put up with it any longer.

Furious, she charged out of the soddie and across the yard, dust flying up from beneath her pounding *klompen*. Chickens squawked and ran out of the way as her skirts swished around her ankles. She stopped short when she nearly collided with Caleb, who stood near the back wall of the house. He had balanced a small round mirror on the edge of an uneven sod block, and he was expertly plying a long, lethal straight-edge razor over the planes of his face, half of which was well lathered with soap.

"Analisa. Is something the matter?"

Her stormy expression told Caleb she was angry, but for the life of him, he couldn't figure out why she stood glaring at him, hands on hips, her eyes shooting sparks of blue fire.

"Don't call me that, Mr. Storm."

"What?"

"Analisa!" The order sounded ridiculous, even to her ears, and yet she could not seem to check her anger. The man had provoked her ever since he had fallen at her feet.

"Pardon me. I didn't realize it offended you, *Miss* Van Meeteren."

"It is bad enough that you sit naked and embarrass me this morning, but I want to know what gives you the right to expose yourself to my son and to take him to the creep without my permission."

"*Creek*." He tried to sort out her jumbled accusations. Had Analisa known Caleb Storm well, she would have noticed the tightening of his lips and the slight stiffening of his spine, but she did not know him at all and so provoked his rage.

"Listen here, Miss Van Meeteren, I'm sorry to have upset your tender sensibilities, but I don't like what you're hinting at. I needed to bathe. That's it. This kid's been my shadow since I woke up, so I let him tag after me. If you've got something against him seeing a man's body, then that boy is gonna have big problems later on." His eyes narrowed to slits as he leaned nearer to Analisa, his soft voice pressing the point home. She was reminded of a wild animal hunting down its prey. "Now I know why you've been avoiding me since I woke up. It must have set you off when *you* burst in on *me* this morning. Don't tell me you've never seen a man naked before, Miss Van Meeteren. This boy didn't just spring up out of the ground.'' He flung a hand toward Kase, who gawked at the pair as they faced each other down.

Analisa stood as if turned to stone while Caleb railed on, unaware that his words fell like a blacksmith's hammer against the fragile wall she'd erected around her emotions.

''You might be able to push an old man and a little boy around this place, lady, but don't try it on me.''

Run, Analisa's mind commanded, but her will won out over emotion. She faced him squarely, unaware of how ridiculous they appeared. Caleb, almost a head taller, wearing the baggy nightshirt and boots, half of his face caked with drying soap while the other was smooth-shaven, stared at Analisa. She in turn refused to back down. With that lock of loose hair brushing against her cheek, her hands clenched defiantly against her sides, she reminded Caleb of a ruffled mother hen.

''I want you out of here.'' She tried to match his tone, low and calm, not wild and angry as her own had been earlier. What was it he had said? ''I never yell.'' She realized he didn't have to. His words were like sharp, silent knives. They cut deep, without a sound. Analisa spared him not a glance but turned, head held high. With determination in her stride, she left Caleb staring after her.

As his anger ebbed, the pain behind his eyes returned and his head ached. He regretted his harsh words, but he regretted even more the look he saw in Kase's eyes before the boy cast his gaze toward the ground. Silently, Kase walked past Caleb, his small shoulders slumped, his head bowed, unwilling to meet the man's eyes as his feet scuffed the dirt.

''Listen, Kase—damn!'' The boy had disappeared around the corner of the house, and Caleb Storm, his anger spent, was left to finish his shave, no longer feeling quite as tall as he had moments before.

Inside, Analisa tried to ignore Kase, who sulked in the rocker. She took up her scissors and ruthlessly cut into Clara Heusinkveld's emerald cloth with a vengeance, wishing the fabric were Caleb Storm's hide or, better yet, his heart. She was convinced that would break the scissors, for his heart was surely made of stone. Analisa soon realized that in such an agitated state she might ruin the cloth beyond repair. Carefully, she put down her scissors and began to fold the pieces of cloth. She started with the larger sections of material, taking care not to dislodge the paper pattern pinned to the silk. It had taken the better part of the afternoon to sketch the pieces and then enlarge them in proportion to Clara Heusinkveld's size. Tomorrow would be a better time to cut out the rest of the material, she decided, after *he* was gone and she was in control of her anger.

First she folded the large panels that would be sewn together to form the skirt. Then she placed the smaller pattern pieces —the bodice, sleeves, collar, and cuffs—together and wrapped them inside the large uncut portion of material. She rewrapped the entire stack in butcher's paper to keep it clean and placed the bundle carefully on top of the organ. Behind her, the door opened and closed. Analisa stiffened, somehow knowing it was not Opa who entered, but him. Caleb Storm.

She kept her back to him and listened to the sound of his movements. He apparently chose to ignore her, and Kase as well. When the sound of his footsteps ceased, Analisa turned around slowly. Caleb stood beside her bed, his folded clothes in his hands as he stared out the window into the late afternoon light.

"I'm sorry about what I said out there." His words were clipped and awkward, as if the apology did not come easily. When she failed to answer him, he turned to face her. A darkness shadowed his eyes as they met Analisa's. He glanced at Kase. The boy was watching him silently from the rocker, his knees drawn protectively against his chest. His high-top laced boots, scuffed and covered with dust, rested on the oak seat of the chair, an offense Caleb knew Analisa would not tolerate in other circumstances.

"Go outside for a few minutes, Kase. I'd like to talk to your mama alone."

The child looked to his mother for permission. At her slight nod, Kase stood up. He slipped from the room while Caleb and Analisa faced each other silently.

"I meant what I said," Caleb began again, stepping toward Analisa, her look of discomfort checking his movement. "I'm sorry if I upset you. I had no reason to talk that way in front of the boy. It isn't the way I wanted to repay you for your kindness. You didn't have to save my life, but you did. Everything I own was on that horse when I rode in—my rifle, savings, clothes, everything. You could have robbed me, left me to die . . . but you didn't.''

She opened her mouth to protest, but Caleb ignored her. ''I'd like to stay for a while and help around here, to pay you back for your kindness. There's plenty of repair work to be done, chores that your grandfather can't handle. I'd like to leave knowing I've been able to help you in some way.''

''Mr. Storm, I really don't think—''

''I'll be on my best behavior, Miss Van Meeteren. I promise to keep my clothes on, too.'' A slow smile spread across his face, erasing the concern she had seen shadowing his eyes. Clean-shaven, with his thick hair still damp and swept back away from his face at forehead and temples, Caleb Storm's rugged handsomeness was suddenly all too apparent to Analisa. She realized as she stood gauging the depth of his sincerity, that she had not thought of him as handsome, at least not in the way she judged other men. Caleb Storm's dark hair and the cinnamon cast of his skin only enhanced his strong features. His deep blue eyes added mystery to the man. People would always wonder what manner of a man he was, where he was from. He was so very unlike the other handsome men Analisa had known—the blond, ruddy-skinned Dutchmen of her family, and the other immigrants who had traveled with them on the journey west. Although Caleb Storm was the opposite of those men, she was drawn to him, to this shadowy stranger who'd ridden into her life as storm clouds gathered.

Hypnotized by his steady blue stare, Analisa relaxed her guard slightly, shifting her weight as she placed one hand on the organ.

''I don't often apologize.'' He smiled again and waited for her response.

''I can tell that you don't, Mr. Storm. It seems a very hard thing for you to do.'' She took a deep breath and continued, ''So it seems to me that I must apologize also. I did not mean to accuse you unjustly about . . . about undressing in front of my son.'' She felt her face flame and fought the urge to cover her cheeks with her palms. ''But he is so innocent, so trusting. I'm afraid life will not be easy for Kase.''

''You can't protect him forever, Analisa. You may do him more harm than good.''

"I will try to protect him for as long as I can." When she looked away, lost in thought, Caleb moved toward the door.

"I'll change into my clothes in the cow shed. I assume you've accepted my apology and my offer to help out?"

"*Ja*—yes," she said, immediately correcting herself. "The next two weeks will be busy for me, with Mevrou Heusinkveld's dress to complete. Your help and your apology are accepted, Mr. Storm."

"I'd like it if you would call me Caleb."

She nodded, watching as Caleb Storm stepped out into the yard. As she went across the room to fill the stove with buffalo chips and scraps of wood, Analisa hoped she was not making a mistake.

Stars peppered the sky from horizon to horizon, some clustered together, others hanging alone, all sending their fiery light from distances Caleb knew he could never fathom. His mother's people told stories about the stars, stories as old as time, as old perhaps as the stars themselves. Someday he would write the stories down, translate them from the language of the Sioux into English so as to save them for the day when the Sioux were no more. If he had the time.

He shook his head, chiding himself as he lay on the ground, his head resting on the smooth, worn leather of his saddle. He was two weeks behind schedule already, and still he stayed at the Van Meeteren home, mending fences, rebuilding the hen-house, repairing the small wagon that was little more than a cart. With each task he completed, he told himself it was time to leave, but when he tried to say good-bye to Analisa, her cornflower-blue eyes stopped him. Instead of leaving, he would hear himself telling her what project he intended to take on next.

At first Caleb had told himself he was only biding his time until he recovered from the measles, but the illness was far behind him now. Caleb knew that if he didn't send word to Parker within a month or two, the man might become alarmed and send someone out in search of him. Soon, Caleb reminded himself for the hundredth time, he would have to move on.

The embers of the dying fire near his bedroll pulsed with what little life remained in them. Caleb watched the coals glowing red against the white ash and let his mind drift over the weeks he'd been helping Analisa. An awkward truce had existed between them during the first few days of his stay, but Caleb could sense Analisa's increasing gratitude as he worked with Opa and Kase. He had kept the old man and the boy occupied while Analisa worked from dawn until far into the night on the green satin gown. The dress had been ready when the pompous Clara Heusinkveld arrived to pick it up. Caleb had spent the day fishing at the creek with Kase and Edvard in order to avoid the woman's scrutiny and to spare Analisa embarrassment.

He watched a shooting star as it fell from the heavens. Behind him, the water in the creek splashed softly over the rocks and lulled him into a peaceful contentment. Caleb had been sleeping beside the stream under the cottonwoods since the day Analisa agreed he could stay to help out. He recalled their conversation after he had finally changed into his own clothes and returned to the house. When he handed the folded nightshirt to Analisa, Caleb had become aware of her scrutiny. She seemed surprised by his appearance, in a way almost wary of him. He sensed that it would be best to move out of the soddie and put her mind at ease. Now that he was up and dressed, their roles had changed. Analisa was no longer completely in control, and rather than unnerve her any further, Caleb felt it was best that he move out.

"I'll be sleeping outdoors now. I'm sure you need the space, anyway." He looked around for his hat and found it hanging on the wall near the window. "Where does the boy sleep?"

"He has a pallet under the bed; I pull it out at night for him."

"So you did give up your bed for me?"

He turned and caught her glance before she lowered her lashes and studied her hands, hiding the thoughts he tried to read in her eyes.

"You needed it. I slept in the rocker."

"One more reason for me to repay you."

"I told you that is not necessary."

He could see by the sudden protest that she did not wish to be beholden to him.

"It's something I'd like to do, Analisa, not something I have to do."

There was an awkward silence in the room while he pulled up the comforter in an attempt to straighten the bedclothes.

"I will tend to the bed. You are welcome to take your meals

with us, Mr. Storm. I'm sure that you should rest for a few days until you feel stronger.''

"Thanks. I'd appreciate the meals. If you don't mind, I'd like my gun and holster back.'' At her questioning look he hurried on, "I'll keep it with my gear out back, but I would feel better knowing where I can get my hands on it.''

She walked to the trunk that served as her bedside table. After carefully setting the medicine bottles and water on the floor, she opened the lid and lifted out Caleb's gun and the dark leather holster. As if she were carrying a live snake, Analisa crossed the room and held the gun and holster out to him at arm's length.

"Are you afraid of guns, Analisa?''

"No, just respectful.''

"I see.''

"I'm not afraid of much anymore, Mr. Storm.'' She tilted her head and raised an arched brow as she stared at him. "Do you remember anything about the night you arrived?''

"No.'' He hid his puzzlement.

"I was the one who aimed a shotgun at your heart. I thought perhaps you would remember.''

"No, I can't honestly say I do . . . but I'll keep it in mind, if that's a warning.''

She smiled, and Caleb laughed with her. He admired her spirit, and although there was much she kept locked inside herself, he found the quiet mystery surrounding her only made her more appealing to him.

The smooth leather creaked as he shifted his head on the hard surface of the saddle. The fire had died to a low mound of glowing embers. Dawn would come early and with it another chance to talk with Analisa, to watch that quick smile light her eyes, to hear her soft laughter as she watched Kase at play.

You'd better get riding, Storm, he mentally warned himself, knowing he would have to leave soon or he might not leave at all.

The kerosene lamp flared and sputtered, smoke trailing up the glass chimney. Analisa folded the material she'd been stitching and extinguished the lamp. She moved through the darkened room to the window and glanced out at the quiet yard. Nothing moved in the darkness beyond the glass panes. In one corner of the room, Opa snored softly. Analisa rolled her head from side to side, kneading the tight muscles at the base of her neck.

Since Caleb had begun helping with the outdoor work, she was able to devote more time to the sewing orders she received, happy to relegate the farming tasks to his capable hands. It would be difficult to adjust when he left and she was forced to resume the chores. Analisa was surprised at how much the man had accomplished in so little time. He'd set Kase and Opa working at jobs Analisa had always done herself for fear that the boy and the old man would find them too taxing. She quickly learned that Kase was more than capable of gathering eggs and weeding the garden. Kase's attention often drifted from the task at hand, but Caleb praised him for the work he accomplished and taught him how to do a fairly good job. Although Edvard could not understand much of what Caleb said, the two men were able to work side by side, making their wishes known to each other.

Analisa moved closer to her bed and reached across Kase, who was sound asleep on his pallet on the floor. She changed into her nightgown, then stepped carefully over the sleeping boy and climbed into bed.

Stars burned in the heavens outside her window. Analisa lay awake, watching them hanging against the midnight sky. She felt too exhausted to sleep. It was strange, she thought, how quickly she fell asleep after working outside, while sewing all day only led to cramped shoulders and restlessness. Closing her weary eyes, she shut out the sight of the star-spattered sky and tried to relax, but sleep did not come. Instead, somewhere between sleep and full consciousness, the nightmares began to appear in her mind, scenes from the past that Analisa could not forget. Her memory would not let go of them. She often managed to live for weeks at peace, but then suddenly the memories would return to tear apart all of her well-constructed defenses.

Suddenly she saw them all again: Jan, his body twisted in death, his blood soaking the ground; Papa, staring with unseeing eyes into the blue prairie sky; Meika, screaming for Analisa's help before dark hands reached into the wagon bed to carry the girl away; and little Pieter, only eight years old, eyes wide with fear as he sat on a racing pony, held in the grip of his captor.

Her heart began to pound as the scenes flashed rapidly behind her shuttered eyes. The sight of the dark man standing over her in the wagon bed, the feel of his rough hands as they tore at her clothes, the sound of her own cries, harsh and shrill, reverberated through her mind until finally she could almost feel the white-hot searing pain of the knife that slid into her flesh when he was through with her body. Her struggling had saved her life, but the blade had grazed her ribs, leaving the crescent-shaped slash that curled down from her right breast almost to her waist.

Analisa forced her eyes open. She was breathing heavily, as if she'd been running for her life; her mouth was dry. She sat up, listening for a sound from Kase or Opa, afraid she might have cried out. They were still sleeping soundly. When the tremors started, Analisa tried to still her body's reaction to the nightmarish scenes. She had to move, to get out of the room before her tears began. With a quick movement, taking care not to disturb Kase, she scrambled out of bed. Swift, soundless steps carried her to the door.

Drinking in the cool night air, Analisa stopped just outside, pressing her back against the sod wall. Silent tears coursed down her cheeks as she stared unseeing into the darkness of the yard, her arms wrapped around herself below her breasts, her lungs heaving with the need for air.

Caleb found her thus as he rounded the corner of the sod house. Wary of frightening her, he called her name softly in the darkness, but his words went unheeded. He moved to her side and, without hesitation, pulled her into his arms. She did not resist his touch, nor did she pull away as he half expected, but stood stiffly within his embrace, much like one of the porcelain figures in his stepmother's parlor. He could feel the tremors moving through her in waves and so stood as silent as she, waiting for her fear to subside before he spoke to her.

Deep inside herself, Analisa was aware that she was enfolded in Caleb Storm's arms. She knew it was wrong and that she should pull away; yet it felt so good to be wrapped securely against harm. How long had it been since she'd been taken care of, held close by another human being? After the attack on the wagon and the loss of so many loved ones, Analisa had been forced to be the strong one, the giver of comfort. Now it was her turn to receive and, although her mind told her to pull away, her heart surrendered to Caleb's silent strength.

As she felt his hand move slowly up and down her spine, gentling her as he would a frightened child, Analisa's silent tears gave way to choking sobs. She pressed her face against the warmth of his neck, letting her arms encircle Caleb as she clung to him for support.

As he felt her relax against him and listened to her anguished sobs, Caleb knew that the reason for her tears was buried deep inside her. He knew, too, that the cause of her sorrow held the answer to the riddle of her son, Kase. The longer she forced the past to stay buried deep inside herself, the more the pain would grow and fester like an untreated wound. Caleb hoped that soon she would feel free to unburden herself. But, for now, he could only offer whatever comfort she would accept.

Her fear subsiding, Analisa stood with eyes closed, pressed against Caleb's hard frame, blessing him for his silence, but wondering how to extricate herself from his embrace. She wished the pleasant, comforting sensation she was experiencing in his arms would never have to end. A quiet strength emanated from him. His dark clothing was scented with wood smoke and leather. Slowly, regretfully, Analisa pulled away from him, wiping her eyes on the sleeve of her nightgown, trying to avoid his gaze. She could almost feel his eyes reaching her through the darkness, questioning silently.

"Feeling better?" he finally asked, forcing lightness into his tone.

She nodded.

"How about a walk?" Caleb hated to let her go inside alone, wrapped once more in her cold, protective shell.

"No shoes." She spoke in a whisper as she curled her toes up out of the dirt.

They stood in silence, Analisa's back brushing the outer wall of the soddie as Caleb stood before her, a breath away. He reached out and touched her hair, which was plaited into a long, thick braid that hung forward over her left shoulder. He rubbed the end of the braid between his thumb and forefinger, then untied the ribbon and combed the strands of honey gold with his fingers. Analisa's hair slipped through his hands like fine silk. Caleb arranged it around her shoulders in a golden cape that fell nearly to the small of her back. He stared down into her eyes and even in the darkness could see confusion mingled with fear reflected in them. He lowered his hands and looped his thumbs in the pockets of his pants, but he did not move away. He glanced up at the roofline, a black silhouette against the sky.

"Do you know what I thought of the first time I saw all these damned flowers sprouting up out of the roof?"

She shook her head, afraid to speak, afraid to break the spell.

"I thought of how much they reminded me of you, beautiful and golden, but stubborn. You and these sunflowers are determined to grow here in the middle of nowhere."

She looked away from him, her gaze moving along the wall to where she could see the tall shadows of the sunflower stalks growing near the corner of the house. With a smile, she sighed and faced Caleb again.

"They have no choice. The seeds are scattered by the winds and the birds, and they grow where they happen to take root."

"Like you, perhaps?"

"Perhaps."

"And how did you get here, Analisa?"

She knew what he was asking, knew that he would listen if she chose to tell him her story, but she knew, too, that she wasn't ready. To voice all that had happened, to put it into words, would bring the past to life. The nightmares might never end. Nor could she face the look of scorn and contempt that would fill his eyes once she had told him. He would hear it all soon enough, as soon as he rode into Pella. The townspeople would be eager to tell him, once they learned he had stayed at the Van Meeteren place.

"The story is long and complicated, Caleb, and better told another time."

"Just remember that I'm willing to listen."

Analisa was quiet with embarrassment. She straightened to leave, looking toward the door, but stopped to face Caleb again.

"I'm . . . I'm sorry about this. I hope I didn't make you uncomfortable. What were you doing out here anyway?"

He answered her question with his usual directness. "Before I bed down, I always take a walk around the place to be sure everything is all right. I'm glad I was able to help."

"Thank you." Her eyes studied his shadowed features and were drawn irresistibly to his lips. What was it about this mysterious stranger that warmed her so? She knew nothing at all about him and was almost afraid to ask. He surrounded his identity with silence. She only knew that he was a half-breed

like her son. How was it that he claimed his home was in the
East? Why was he in Iowa? Why did she wish he would lean
closer and press his warm lips against her own?

As Analisa watched him in the darkness, Caleb tried to sense
her feelings. He was close enough to lean forward and touch her
lips with his own, but he feared that taking such a liberty would
frighten her into distrusting him again. He shifted his weight
and, unwilling to stand in awkward silence while Analisa waited
for him to leave, Caleb bid her good night and walked in to the
shadows.

She waited until the sound of his footsteps receded, then
stealthily entered the soddie and climbed back into bed.
Emotionally exhausted, but at the same time refreshed by the
cleansing effect of her tears, Analisa closed her eyes at last and
slept.

"Another cup of coffee, Mr. Storm?"

Caleb had long ago given up trying to persuade Analisa to call
him by his given name. With a broad smile he looked up into
her eyes and shook his head.

"No thanks, Miss Van Meeteren." He addressed her formally in the presence of Kase and Opa. Her composure, he noticed,
had been restored since the nightmares of last night. "That
breakfast was more than enough for two men. I'm going to have
to labor mighty hard to work up an appetite for dinner."

She returned his smile, knowing full well that he would do
justice to the dinner at noon. For breakfast Analisa had
prepared one of Opa's favorites, sausage and fried bread. She
suspected Caleb was becoming fond of the rich golden-brown
slabs of bread fried in bacon grease, then dusted with sugar and
topped with warm maple syrup.

"What are we fixing today, Caleb?" Kase asked.

Analisa was more than aware of the growing camaraderie
Caleb shared with her son. As she turned back to the stove, she
frowned, deep in thought, hoping that Kase would quickly
recover from the disappointment he would surely feel when
Storm left. *And what of you?* she asked herself, remembering
the feel of his strong arms about her.

"Miss Van Meeteren?"

"Yes?" Analisa's attention was drawn back to Caleb.

"I was asking your leave to take Edvard and the boy into

town. I've got the wagon mended, and I figure Scorpio won't balk too badly if I put him in the harness. I thought I'd pick up some nails and any supplies you might be needing.''

Caleb watched Analisa sweep her hand up the back of her neck to the thick coil of hair on top of her head, tucking in the stray wisps that continually escaped the pins. He had noticed it was a habit she unthinkingly fell into when confronted with a problem, as she was now, trying to decide whether or not to allow her son to accompany him into town.

"You're welcome to come along, too," he added with a smile. "We could all take the morning off."

Her first instinct was to fold her apron and join him and Opa and Kase on their ride into Pella, to walk freely through the streets and shops, smiling and nodding to the inhabitants as they passed by. But what then? To face the humiliation as the righteous townsfolk turned away from her to speak together in hushed tones? Would she let them stare and point at Kase, her beautiful, smiling son? Opa would surely suffer; he would understand the slurs spoken against her in his own tongue. Worst of all, she would be shamed before Caleb, her one friend in the new land, the one person who knew her only as Analisa, who spoke to her with respect and friendship, offering her his quiet strength. Soon enough he would learn the truth. It was best he go into town alone. Perhaps he would choose to ride on and never return to the soddie.

"Mr. Storm, I think perhaps—"

"Daar komt iemand," Kase interrupted. "Someone is coming." In his excitement, he spoke Dutch.

Opa stood and moved away from the table, eager to greet the passengers in the buggy pulling up before the soddie.

Caleb watched as Analisa registered his presence with a fleeting look of dismay. He felt a swift sense of hurt at her reaction until he realized his being there as a single man was as condemning in the eyes of the visitors as the fact that he was a half-breed.

"I'll get out of here as soon as I can." He rose and began to move away from the table. He watched her eyes move away from his as she realized he had seen her reaction.

"I'm sorry," she said softly. "There's no need for you to leave." Analisa squared her shoulders and followed her grandfather to the door.

Kase looked up at Caleb, rolled his eyes with a shrug, and followed his mother and Opa outside.

Caleb realized it was far too late to leave unnoticed, unless he climbed out a window. He had never run from a fight; his only regret was that Analisa might suffer further embarrassment because of his presence. Deciding there was not much he could do, he began stacking the breakfast dishes on the kitchen bench.

Outside the house, Analisa watched warily as Dominie Wierstra, the young assistant pastor of the Reform Church of Pella, descended from the buggy with Clara Heusinkveld. She felt her face flame with color. Although she had never been introduced to the man, she identified him by his clerical garb, the black woolen suit and stiff-collared white shirt. His pale yellow hair gave almost no contrast to the sallow color of his skin; his eyes were limpid pools of blue-green above his high cheekbones. Mevrou Heusinkveld was beside him now, standing aloof, trying to ignore the flurry of squawking hens surrounding them in the yard.

The clothing of both visitors was impeccably styled and only slightly dusty from the four-mile drive from the village. Analisa knew her own plain blue cotton gown was far from adequate for greeting visitors. She was all too aware of the dust coating her clogs and the hem of her worn gown. Suddenly the yard seemed small and dirty, the house smaller and shabbier. Dominie Wierstra, the new assistant minister, was used to visiting the houses in the village of Pella, wooden houses furnished with fine European treasures and surrounded by carefully tended lawns. In the spring, tulips bloomed in profusion before such homes, but here only dust and the wild sunflowers greeted the young minister. Trying to hide her embarrassment, holding her head high, her shoulders rigid, Analisa welcomed the visitors, inviting them into the house.

Kase bounded inside before the others, informing Caleb in hushed whispers that the guests were none other than the "holy man" from the *dorp* and Mevrou Heusinkveld. Caleb was eager to see what Kase's idea of a holy man was and had no notion at all as to what *dorp* meant, but he knew who Mevrou Heusinkveld was and so was anxious to leave as soon as he could get past the group coming in the door. Their language was an odd mixture of Dutch and English, Clara Heusinkveld valiantly refusing to speak Dutch in Analisa's presence; the holy man, who Caleb could plainly see was a minister, was speaking in Dutch for Edvard's benefit; and Analisa used one language or the other, depending on the person she addressed.

Everything in the house was in its place, and for that Analisa was thankful. She noted that Caleb had helped her by clearing away the dishes, and her eyes caught him standing near the door, hat in hand, ready to slip away. She flashed him a grateful smile, which drew Clara Heusinkveld's attention.

"Ah, Dominie Wierstra, this is the man I was telling you about. Mr. Storm, isn't it?" Her inquisitive gaze bored into Caleb. "From the East?" She turned away from Caleb without waiting for him to answer and continued talking to the young minister. "As I was telling you, it seems Mr. Storm fell ill, and so Analisa took him in. A perfect stranger, though, isn't that correct, Analisa?"

Analisa was beginning to understand the reason for Clara Heusinkveld's surprise visit with the minister in tow. It was obvious the man had little enthusiasm for his task. He appeared to grow more uncomfortable the longer the older woman spoke.

"Please," Analisa interrupted, "sit down, everyone. I have some coffee ready, and some cookies if you'd like."

"If you'll excuse me, I have work to do outside." Seeing his chance to escape, Caleb stepped toward the open doorway, nodding to the group as a whole.

"Just a moment, Mr. Storm." Mevrou Heusinkveld's voice sounded shrill and authoritative in the small room. "Actually, you're the reason Dominie Wierstra and I have come to speak to Analisa. Perhaps it would be best for you to stay." She sent an encouraging look in young Dominie Wierstra's direction, forcing him to speak.

"Yes. Please stay, Mr. Storm. I hope that this will only take a few moments of your time." His words were almost an appeal for Caleb's understanding.

Mrs. Heusinkveld sat beside the young minister on one side of the table while Edvard took a seat on the bench across from them, speaking to the man in rapid Dutch, eager to glean what news he could of Pella. Caleb chose to remain standing, his hips leaning against the tall wooden workbench, his legs crossed at the ankles.

"Kase, please leave us," Analisa commanded the boy as he began to climb onto the bench beside Edvard.

Starting to protest, Kase looked to Caleb for support.

"Run outside and check Scorpio." Caleb spoke softly to the boy. "Be sure he has feed and water. Can you do that for me? We'll save you some cookies."

As Kase scampered away, happy to do Caleb's bidding, Analisa noticed the smug look Mevrou Heusinkveld exchanged with the minister.

While Dominie Wierstra and Edvard continued their conversation, Analisa set out cups and saucers and a plate of cookies. Caleb watched in silence, noting Analisa's high color and the rigid set of her shoulders as she avoided the eyes of the young minister. She eased herself quietly onto the bench beside her grandfather as if she hoped to remain unnoticed.

Apparently unable to stand Analisa's silence, Clara Heusinkveld drew herself nearer the table, straightening her spine and raising her ample breasts, looking ready to do battle.

"Analisa, I think we should come right to the point of our visit." Clara's blue eyes flashed a challenge as they bored into Analisa's. "I informed Dominie Wierstra of the fact that you had a man living here with you, and . . . well, he felt it was his duty to investigate the situation. Naturally, the church community is concerned that you may be in need of guidance, if not protection." She risked a quick glance at Caleb, who was standing in ominous silence behind her, his arms now crossed over his chest. "As an unmarried woman, Analisa, you must be fully conscious of the circumstances you place yourself in, even though you do not live within the confines of the *dorp.*"

As Mrs. Heusinkveld continued speaking, she seemed unaware of the angry set to Analisa's tense posture and the ice-blue glint in her eyes. The minister sat in silence beside Mevrou Heusinkveld, allowing her full rein, his pale face flushed to the hairline with embarrassment as the woman carried on.

"Katrine Oldorph came directly to me last week after she had driven out here to order a new gown from you, and I can tell you very honestly that she was in quite a state. She told me that the stranger you had taken in was still here. That was quite a surprise to me, Analisa, since you had told me he'd be leaving as soon as he was able, and quite a startling surprise to her as well. Katrine, like myself, noticed the striking likeness between your . . . your friend, Mr. Storm, and your son. Naturally, the conclusion one *might* draw is that perhaps he is someone you knew in the East, someone you met on the journey to Iowa. We feel it is possible that your son might not be, as you claimed, the product of the attack on your family, but of your previous *knowledge* of this man.''

''Mevrou Heusink—'' Analisa began to protest but the older woman raised her hand dramatically in a signal for silence.

''Please allow me to finish, Analisa. Your grandfather is too old and feeble to protest your shocking behavior. He is probably not even aware of what is going on around him anymore. It is a sorry state of affairs here, I can see that, what with you refusing to give up the boy and then taking in this—''

''Excuse me, Mevrou Heusinkveld, if I may.'' Dominie Wierstra turned politely to the now sweating matron. He spoke in soft unaccented English, returning his gaze to Analisa, who continued to sit in stunned silence.

''Miss Van Meeteren,'' the young man began, ''I realize that I have not met you until now, and so whatever facts I've gained have come to me secondhand, but since there has been quite a bit of talk in town lately, I felt it best to accompany Mevrou Heusinkveld here and speak with you personally. Our only concern is to stop the gossip already circulating among the townspeople.''

He paused. Analisa nodded in understanding, and the young man continued.

''I am sure you have a perfectly good explanation for Mr. Storm's continuing presence in your home?''

The question hung in the air as Analisa stared into the minister's pale blue-green eyes, trying to collect her scattered thoughts. She could feel Caleb's anger from across the room, but she spared him not even a glance as she laced her trembling fingers together beneath the table. Facing the young minister squarely, she met his gaze and spoke in a strong, even voice that belied the turmoil seething below her cool surface.

''Yes, Dominie, it is true you never came to visit my grandfather properly as head of this household. I'm glad he cannot follow our conversation, for he would have asked you to leave before now. As you say, you know little of the circumstances surrounding my family, at least as I would explain them to you, but I realize you have been given a thorough accounting by Mevrou Heusinkveld and the other ladies of the congregation. You have been told that I am unmarried and have a four-year-old son. I'm certain you were informed of the circumstances surrounding his birth?''

Forced to answer her question the minister only nodded.

''Yes. I can see by your embarrassment that you have learned my son is half Indian, a half-breed as such children are called. I was attacked and left for dead in a raid that took the lives of my father and older brother, left my mother unbalanced, and saw my younger sister and brother taken captive.''

''Miss Van Meeteren, you need not—''

''Oh, yes, Dominie,'' she interrupted, shooting a cold glance in Clara Heusinkveld's direction, ''I need to explain, obviously, once more. Following the attack, the people of Pella gave us this abandoned soddie to live in and offered us ways to earn a meager living.

''My sin was that I lived after the attack, although no one had expected me to recover. I found I was carrying a child. At first I wished I had died at the hands of the murderers, but I lived and took care of Opa and my mother. She lived for two years, a helpless, mindless soul.

''When Kase was born, the people of Pella urged me to send him away to be raised on a reservation. They wanted him elsewhere so that they would not have to be faced with a child of mixed blood, a child born not of love but of rape and murder. My second sin is that I refused.

''We live apart from the community, and we ask for nothing, except to be left alone. For that reason I will not explain Mr. Storm's presence in my home, nor will I defend my action in taking him in. Let the good people of Pella think what they will.'' Analisa rose and stared down at Clara Heusinkveld and the minister.

''Miss Van Meeteren, please.'' The minister stood as well, tugging on the rumpled sleeves of his black coat and then running a finger around his stiff white collar. ''I agree that the circumstances were not of your making, but the Lord has afforded you a chance to make up for the past. You must remember that you are, and always will be, subject to public criticism. Such is the nature of humanity. I'm sure that Mr. Storm''—he nodded in Caleb's direction—''understands that his presence here is but another smear against your name. Surely now he will be more than willing to—''

"That is beside the point, Dominie Wierstra. I am free to choose whom I will shelter under my roof. Mr. Storm is here at my invitation and welcome to stay for as long as he cares to."

"You see?" Clara Heusinkveld exploded, her cheeks flaring with color, her jowls shaking above the wattles of her neck. A purple satin bow tied beneath her chin held a bobbing ruffle-edged hat on her head. An amethyst brooch glittered against the stiff bodice of her gown.

Unable to stand any more of the scene unfolding before him, Caleb pushed his dark-clad form away from the workbench and stepped forward. He moved to stand behind Analisa's rigid form and placed a hand on her shoulder. Analisa was too angry to protest the familiarity of the action.

Caleb looked steadily at the younger man, ignoring the matron. "I would ask the privilege of speaking for myself. Your accusations against Miss Van Meeteren are quite unfounded. They are as offensive to me as they are to her. If this were my home, I would have shown you the door long ago."

The two townspeople sat listening to the tall man who spoke to them with such aristocratic grace. The contrast between his rough appearance and his polished eloquence served to confound the listeners. He was dressed like a cowhand, and yet he spoke like an educated leader of men. His blue-black hair accented the brilliant sky blue of his eyes, eyes that now sparked with stubborn pride and anger, and his lips were set in a firm line.

Caleb could feel Analisa trembling beneath his fingertips as he gripped her shoulder. He'd listened in stunned silence as she spoke of the outrage committed against her. In his mind he saw her as she must have been before the attack, an innocent young woman, a stranger in a strange land. Anger shook him as he heard the exchange between Analisa and the two self-righteous hypocrites who proclaimed themselves God-fearing Christians. He wanted to lash out against them, to watch them suffer pain as deep as that they so callously inflicted upon Analisa. The unfairness of her situation had troubled him all along, and now that he knew the details of Analisa's past, Caleb was moved by an emotion more intense than any he had ever experienced.

Staring at the stunned listeners, he spoke in quiet, menacing tones. His gut-churning anger drew him out of himself, and it seemed to Caleb he was watching the scene act itself out, watching himself, unaware of what his words would be until they were spoken.

"This woman has more forgiveness in her than your entire congregation. She has more faith in God and herself, more love for her fellowman than all of you rolled into one. Analisa could have cast her son away as you asked her to, left her grandfather here alone, and moved on to begin again, but she didn't. She chose to stay and give of herself. I, too, was a recipient of her kindness. She took me in." He paused in order to emphasize his next words. "I was a total stranger, and yet she saw me through my illness. I believe the lady has defended herself to you for the last time. You are welcome to leave now, and if you feel a need to report to the congregation, tell them that Analisa Van Meeteren has no further need of your meddling 'protection,' as you like to call it. She does not need it," he added curtly, "because she has agreed to become my wife, and I take care of my own."

Attempting to rise and protest, Analisa found her progress hampered by the force of Caleb's hand pressing down on her shoulder. His fingers were nearly embedded beneath her collarbone, his terse announcement echoing in her mind. Wife? *His* wife? What was the man thinking of? Surely he had spoken in anger and haste. He had only wished to defend her before Mrs. Heusinkveld and the minister. He could not possibly have meant those words.

Clara needed only to glance at Analisa's shocked expression to guess correctly that the man, Storm, had spoken in haste. She would force his hand to get to the truth of the matter.

"Then it is quite lucky we arrived, is it not, Dominie Wierstra, to set matters aright? Analisa would not be permitted a church ceremony under the circumstances, so you can marry them this morning, right here in her home." The older woman glanced slyly at Analisa and was rewarded in her efforts to uncover the deception when the girl began to protest.

"I—that is, we—" Analisa met Caleb's eyes with a haunted expression that all but begged him to save her from the awkward situation.

"We'd be delighted. If we could have a moment alone . . ." Caleb's voice expressed many emotions, the least of which was delight.

Relieved, the minister grasped Clara Heusinkveld's plump elbow and began to walk her toward the door. "We'll wait outdoors for a few moments while you gather your thoughts before the ceremony." Before the older woman could speak, adding any further to the strained atmosphere in the room, he had propelled her through the doorway.

Chapter Four

For a moment, Analisa was tempted to cradle her head in her arms and sob, but she collected herself and stood on trembling legs when Caleb released her shoulder. Without sparing a glance in his direction, yet painfully aware of his rigid presence behind her, she moved to speak softly to her grandfather, explaining to him that she wished to speak to Caleb alone. Analisa then ushered Edvard outside, fully aware of the damage the others might do when they told him what had been discussed. There was nothing she could do to prevent it. For now, she needed to face Caleb.

"What have you done?" Her china-blue eyes questioned his, afraid of whatever answer he might give.

"I don't know."

It was a reply she'd never expected. She watched him turn away, his thumbs looped in his belt. He stared out into the yard.

"At least you are honest."

Neither of them moved. Analisa watched dust motes fall in the stream of light filtering in through the front window. The room itself was quite still, the sounds from the visitors outside muffled by the thick sod walls. The minutes passed as Caleb stared into the sunlit yard. Finally, he turned and walked back across the room to stand before Analisa once again. He met her gaze unflinchingly before his eyes roved over her face.

"I couldn't let them hurt you any more. I wanted to stop them, to stop the hurt." He smiled crookedly at her, his eyes taking on a faraway look. "When I was a boy, growing up with my mother's people, I came upon some children torturing a rabbit. When I discovered what they were doing, I killed it swiftly, ending its pain. I did not stop to consider the consequences; I merely reacted."

"Just as you did today."

"Yes."

"Then we must go outside and tell them to go away." She turned toward the door. A gentle touch on her upper arm stopped her.

"Wait, Analisa." Caleb turned her by her shoulders, and she stood facing him, forced to tip her head back to look up into his deep blue eyes. "I've had time to think since I spoke out."

"Only minutes."

"Why should we not be married?" He went on as if she had not spoken. "I'll admit we hardly know each other, but you do need the protection of a man's name, not only for your sake, but for the boy's. I'm willing to marry you to salvage your name and to silence these people once and for all. If you wish, my protection is all you will ever have to take from this marriage."

"No."

"I care about your boy. He deserves better than what he'll have to face if you continue to fight them all alone. Hell, let them think he is mine for all I care."

"No!" Her refusal was stronger this time.

Caleb stared at her for a moment, trying to read the expression in her eyes. "I see. You don't want to marry a 'breed, is that it?"

"Not at all, Mr. Storm. If you believe that, you haven't learned much about me, have you? I refuse because I don't *need* your noble sacrifice, nor does my son. We have managed up to now—''

"How?" His voice was a cold demand. "By hiding yourself out here on this godforsaken farm, afraid to go into town, afraid to let that child out of your sight? You have shut yourself into a shell, Analisa, a small, fragile shell. Like that of an egg, it could break at any moment. Then where would you be? Where would the boy be?" He pointed toward the door. "I wouldn't put it past those people to ride out here one day and demand that you give Kase up, hand him over to them. They'll bundle him off to some mission school, and you'll never see him again." Caleb watched the sudden fear in her eyes and hated what he was doing, but the longer he spoke, the more determined he became to bend her to his will, to make sure her future was assured. "I don't know why or how, but you've had a hold over me ever since I met you, Analisa. I've never been in love before, and I sure as hell can't say that I am now, but something has been holding me here. When I ride away, I want to know that you'll be better off than you were before I came, and the only thing I can leave you with right now is my name."

Shaken by the force of his words, her mind reeling with the thought of losing Kase, Analisa was silent. She stood frozen, lost in thought as Caleb reached out and gently, carefully pulled her to him, holding her much as he had the night before in an embrace that made no demands upon her, offering only comfort and support. She allowed herself a moment of warmth before she pulled back to look up once again into his eyes. She wanted so to believe him, needing to trust in someone. Could he make life sane again?

Slowly, in a silent response, she nodded her assent.

Less than an hour later, Analisa found herself wondering how it had come to pass that she was standing in the small sod house on the Iowa prairie, dressed in an everyday homespun gown and apron, her hair hastily recombed and wound into a loose knot on the crown of her head. She clutched an array of wilting wildflowers, an offering from Kase, who stood in front of her and Caleb, not sure what the strange ceremony meant, but happy and excited nonetheless. Edvard stood quietly near his granddaughter's shoulder.

Dominie Wierstra held a small, worn Bible, its once shining leather cover worn thin at the corners and showing signs of long years of use. It had been Analisa's mother's Bible, and it had passed through the many hands and many lives of her forebears. Analisa had quietly but firmly insisted the minister use it during the ceremony.

Caleb stood strong and silent by her side, responding to the minister's questions in a firm, even voice that lessened Analisa's trepidation. She forced her mind not to stray to the hours and days that would follow this moment. Even in her dreams, when she had allowed herself to dream, Analisa had never envisioned her own wedding. She had convinced herself she was unworthy of marriage. What man would want a woman who'd been soiled in such a foul manner? Yet here she stood beside Caleb Storm, a man she knew virtually nothing about, repeating the vows read by Dominie Wierstra. For all she knew of him, Caleb could be a hired killer or an outlaw on the run, the kind of gunman she had read about in newspaper serials.

The longer she was forced to stand beside him in the close air of the tiny room, the more fearful Analisa became about the outcome of her hasty decision. She studiously avoided Clara Heusinkveld's stare and concentrated instead on the dying beauty of the wildflowers clutched too tightly in her hand.

The ceremony ended as abruptly as it had begun. Prompted by the minister to kiss the bride, Caleb firmly grasped Analisa's shoulders and drew her toward him. His lips brushed her temple before he pressed them warmly against her mouth. Analisa stood wide-eyed, her lips closed against the kiss, unsure of the feelings he had aroused in her. Caleb released her before she had time to respond to his touch. Her face flamed with color. An awkward silence ensued while all eyes stared at the newly wedded couple.

Finally Dominie Wierstra cleared his throat and extended his hand, returning Analisa's Bible. "You'll want to enter the marriage." The minister's attempt at light conversation failed as Analisa offered no response to his comment. "I will fill out the proper certificates when I get to town. For now, I'll just sign in the book and you can do so as well."

While the adults tended to the business aspects of the marriage—Analisa searching for paper, pen, and ink, Mevrou

Heusinkveld staring thoughtfully while Edvard chatted with the minister—Kase's voice piped up above the babble. "What happens now?"

It was Caleb's turn to darken with embarrassment in response to the boy's innocent statement. He turned away from the group to collect his hat from a peg near the door.

"What happens now," he began, his composure tightly controlled once again, "is that we get back to work. Let's go Kase, Edvard." As he swung the door open, Caleb turned to nod a curt dismissal to Dominie Wierstra and Mrs. Heusinkveld. "Reverend, ma'am." Edvard shook the minister's hand heartily and said good-bye. The door closed behind the visitors as he and Kase moved off into the yard behind Caleb.

"Well, Analisa, I'm sure you'll be needing some time to yourselves, now that you and Mr. Storm have married. Newlyweds and all that." The overblown woman took delight in embarrassing Analisa.

Dominie Wierstra, pushed to anger by the woman's tone, stepped closer to Analisa, diverting the older woman's attention. "Miss . . . Mrs. Storm, I wish you every happiness in your new marriage. If you ever need anything, please feel free to come and see me." Analisa noted that the man looked doubtful, as if regretting his actions.

Outwardly she was cool and aloof, showing no response to what had passed in the small room. Her mind was so filled with questions that she paid little attention to what was being said to her. She managed to nod in the minister's direction. If the two townspeople thought it strange that the groom had resumed his daily chores, they said nothing to Analisa. Exchanging a look with Clara Heusinkveld to let her know he was more than ready to depart, Dominie Wierstra moved toward the door.

Rousing herself from her contemplation, Analisa followed them as far as the threshold and stood watching as they mounted the carriage and drove through the open gateway before turning toward Pella. She looked down at her hands. The Bible and the wildflowers were still clutched in her grasp. Releasing a long, slow sigh, Analisa walked to the table and lowered herself onto the end of the bench, her movements those of one walking in a dream. She stared at the flowers and the Bible for a moment before she set them gently on the table beside her. She rested her elbow alongside them and let her fingertips slide back and forth across the embroidered stitches of the linen table runner.

A chicken squawked somewhere outside, and the distant sound of hammering drifted on the air. Caleb, Kase, and Edvard had indeed resumed their duties. Should she begin the noon meal preparations as if nothing at all had occurred? Numbly, Analisa shook her head, hoping to clear her vision. She didn't get up.

There was a quick knock on the door, but before she could open it, the wooden portal swung inward and Caleb entered. Analisa watched as he crossed the short distance between them and dropped down on one knee to look up at her. He'd left his hat outside, near the pump, she surmised from the fresh-washed appearance of his face and the slick look of his neatly combed jet-black hair. The collar of his shirt was stained with water spots. He reached for her hand. Analisa stared at the strong, dark fingers holding her own and then lifted her eyes to meet Caleb's.

"I imagine you're feeling as confused as I am right now." His voice was low and steady while his fingers played idly with Analisa's.

She smiled, thankful for his understanding, aware that his confusion was as real as her own.

"I'm not quite sure what I'm to do just now," she began, the smile fading as she watched his blue eyes, then studied his high forehead and his nose and lips. "Am I to make dinner as usual or begin sewing or merely sit and wonder at what I've done this day? I don't ever remember being so uncertain. There's always been so much to do."

"We can't hide from this, Analisa. We are married, that's a fact."

Analisa stiffened involuntarily and immediately regretted it, for Caleb let go of her hand, as if sensing her panic.

"Hey." He smiled again, rising from his crouched position to join her on the bench. "I meant what I said. This marriage will be whatever you want it to be."

Analisa was silent, her eyes fixed on a point across the room. What *did* she want? she asked herself.

"I think the least we could do under the circumstances is take the afternoon off," Caleb said. "I've set Kase and Opa to fence-mending. Why don't you pack us a cold picnic and leave something here for them? We'll walk down by the stream and talk things out. I told you earlier that I'll be leaving here soon, and I need to explain some things to you. How about it?''

A day without work. A day to walk with Caleb, to talk and to enjoy a few moments of leisure. He had promised to demand nothing of her. Analisa returned her gaze to Caleb and nodded.

"I promise not to swim in front of you."

She tried to hold back the smile, but she was unsuccessful and felt herself smiling openly while she spoke to him. "I will give you the hardest task. You shall explain to Kase that he may not join us. The picmick will be ready in a few minutes."

Caleb threw his head back in laughter, startling Analisa. *"Picnic,"* he said.

Pointedly ignoring his laughter, Analisa brushed at the full skirt of her dress as she stood and began opening tins and bags of food. Caleb's laughter filled the room and followed him outside.

The cottonwoods along the stream offered a shaded retreat from the September sunshine. With the remains of their picnic spread out on a piece of calico between them, Analisa and Caleb rested in silence, awkward with their new status as man and wife. A jackrabbit hopped tentatively near the silent figures and froze as Caleb slowly raised his hand to draw Analisa's attention to the curious creature crouched amid the scrub. She watched it with a smile until the animal darted away into the brush.

"Thank you for the meal." Caleb's voice mingled with the sound of the stream sliding over the rocks along the bank. "And for the company."

Analisa nodded in acknowledgment and continued to relax in silence. She fought to keep her eyes from straying too often toward the handsome figure beside her. Caleb had changed into a crisp white cotton shirt and had left the collar open. Although creased from being folded in his saddlebag for so long, the shirt was clean and made of quality material. The white of the cloth enhanced his dark skin and magnified the deep blue of his eyes. She wondered for a moment how he would look in a shirt the color of the sky.

"I've never seen that dress before," he said. "I like it. Did you make it?"

Analisa blushed. She thought he hadn't noticed her change of clothes. The dress was one she'd designed herself, a deep rose-colored cotton with simple lines, suitable for everyday wear, but ornamented with ruffles around the neckline and cuffs. The high collar that graced her long neck also gave Analisa a regal appearance and enhanced the smooth bodice, which outlined her firm, full breasts. A wide sash encircled her waist. Although it was made of inexpensive yard goods, the dress was Analisa's best, and she was secretly warmed to hear that Caleb liked it.

"Yes, I made it. Thank you. There's not much cause for me to own the fancy gowns the ladies of Pella order. I have never worn this dress before today."

Caleb was at once reminded of women he knew in the East, women with wardrobes full of gowns from France, worn once and then discarded. Analisa lived a life altogether unsuited for such possessions, a life not all that different from that of his Sioux mother's people. Indeed, like Caleb himself, Analisa lived somewhere between two cultures.

"You said you are leaving soon?" She brushed some dust from the toe of her wooden shoe and then, on impulse, slipped the clogs off and set them beside her.

Caleb pushed the brim of his hat back and unfolded his long legs, then lay back in the grass, propping himself up on one elbow.

"Tomorrow." He lifted a sugar cookie from a round, shallow tin. Taking a bite, he let his eyes roam over Analisa's trim form. She was leaning against the trunk of a cottonwood, her knees bent, legs pulled up against her. She reminded him of a child, the way she held the hem of her skirt tight against her ankles. The tips of her socks peeked from beneath her dress. She said nothing.

"I've been here too long already. I can't put off leaving another day."

"Someone's expecting you?" *A woman?* She left the second question unasked.

"Yes." He looked away.

Analisa felt her stomach knot. Caleb turned to face her again, and she raised her head off of her arms to look directly into his eyes.

"Analisa, I can't tell you anything yet about what I'm doing out here. I hope I'll be able to explain when I get back.''

''Are you out of the law?''

He stared for a moment trying to make sense out of her question. ''You mean an outlaw?''

She nodded.

He could see by the fear creeping into her eyes that she was afraid he would admit that he was. ''No, Analisa. I'm not an outlaw. I'd tell you all about myself if I could. As it is, though, you'll just have to trust me. If you were worried, why didn't you ask me anything before now?''

''It's for you to tell me. You never asked about Kase. I've tried not to ask about you.''

''Today I found out about Kase.''

It was her turn to look away.

''Analisa, listen to me. It doesn't matter to me what happened to you in the past . . . Do you believe that?''

She nodded but refused to look at him.

''I'm surprised you don't hate all Indians, after what happened to you. I wouldn't blame you if you never wanted . . .'' Caleb found himself backed into a very tight corner. He picked up a blade of grass, twirled it between his fingers, and then tossed it away. ''Let's just say I'll give you all the time you need. We can talk about it when I get back.''

She looked at him again and, seeing the questions in his eyes, tried to explain. ''I can't blame all for the acts of a few. My son is Indian. I know how deep the white hatred runs.'' She was thinking of Kase and they both knew it. ''Each man must be judged on his own, if one dares to judge. I can't even remember what the man looked like. I was spared the memory when I was knocked unconscious. When I woke up, all I saw was his knife. He meant to kill me, but I struggled so hard he only cut me.''

Caleb rose and with two easy strides stood next to her. She lowered her eyes and studied the silver-gray snakeskin of his boots. When he remained silent, standing so near, Analisa looked up along the columns of his long legs, past the broad wall of his chest, to his eyes, burning with crystal intensity. He held out his hand, and placing her fingers in his warm palm, Analisa allowed him to pull her up beside him. They stood toe to toe.

A bird called out its sweet song from somewhere overhead.

She was drawn toward Caleb, moving without moving, leaning into him as he leaned toward her, his head lowered to accommodate her height, drawn to her lips as a man who thirsts for water is drawn to a stream.

It was gentle, that first kiss, as gentle as the sound of the water in the creek sliding over the smooth stones. Caleb's lips touched Analisa's for a moment and then drew away, only to return a heartbeat later and linger this time. She let his lips capture hers without returning the kiss as yet, merely savoring such close contact with another being. He still held her hand. She could feel his fingers tighten as they laced between hers. As this last sweet kiss ended, his fingers lessened their hold until Caleb released her hand, only to wrap his arms around her, pressing his palms into her shoulderblades, enfolding her against the hard wall of his chest.

This time his lips met hers with little of their former gentleness. Hot, demanding, Caleb's kiss forced Analisa to realize this was not a dream. As his mouth moved over hers, his tongue seeking entrance, Analisa began to feel an overwhelming need rising within her. A slow heat spread throughout her body, its origin the very core of her womanhood.

He buried his hands in the thickness of her hair and urged her head back, arching her neck as his mouth worked its magic against hers. Analisa's lips parted, wanting more from Caleb's kiss, needing to ease the ache that was pulsating through her with the ferocity of a summer storm. She clung to Caleb's strong form, caught up in the fury of his passion. Feelings she had locked deep inside herself for so many years were bursting through her now, pushing out and overwhelming her from every nerve ending and every pore. The intensity of the wanting overshadowed her fear. She felt a warm moisture between her thighs.

Caleb took a step with Analisa in his arms, and she leaned against the rough bark of the cottonwood for support. His hands stroked her hair, sending the pins flying and letting the golden, sun-streaked mass tumble in disarray around her shoulders. His lips left hers, and he began to nuzzle the sensitive flesh around her ear.

Desperate to taste his lips on hers, Analisa grasped his face between her hands and urged him with her touch to capture her mouth again with his own. Caleb welcomed the invitation, pressing her hard against the rough trunk of the tree. His hands stopped their search while he pressed his length against her. Analisa felt her breasts crushed against his chest and welcomed the sensation, which heightened her pleasure.

Thigh touched thigh. Seeking to ease the thrumming, bursting need that drove her on, Analisa dared to move against Caleb, pressing her hips and groin against his, imitating his movements. She was startled by his response, for he reacted first by meeting her thrusts and then holding himself away. A second later his lips left hers and their eyes met.

She wondered if his fevered look was reflected in her own eyes and watched as emotions moved across Caleb's face like clouds across the summer sky.

"I want you, Analisa."

The heat from his eyes scorched her. She turned her face away. "You've lost your hat." Her voice sounded distant to her own ears.

His finger resting lightly beneath her chin pulled her gaze back to his. "I want you."

"We should clean up the . . . the picnic." Her eyes could not leave his lips.

"You want me, too."

"Yes."

The word had barely passed her lips before Analisa realized that she did want what Caleb wanted. She wanted him to make love to her. She longed to experience all that life had cheated her of. She wanted him to let loose in her the emotions she'd kept locked deep inside herself for so long. If he never returned to her, if she could keep only his name for the rest of her life, Analisa knew without a doubt that the coming moments would change her forever, healing the old wounds inflicted by the act of brutality. Besides, she reasoned, he'd unselfishly given her his protection today. She could in turn give him what he craved, and what she, too, craved—the pleasure of her body. Afterward, she would let him go. They would owe each other nothing.

Caleb took her hand and led her closer to the stream. Soft, tall grass grew abundantly near the water's edge.

"Stay here," he said unnecessarily. Analisa knew she could not leave now even if she desired to do so.

He tossed the food hastily into the deep basket and shook out the calico cloth. Analisa watched him walk toward her with smooth, sure steps. She opened her arms, and he entered them as if it were an old habit.

"I don't want you to ruin your best dress," he explained, spreading the cloth on the soft grass.

"Is it the custom to wear clothes?" A smile pulled at the corners of her mouth. Caleb covered it with his lips. His hands slid to the back of her neck and began working open the long row of buttons that ran along her spine.

"Did you pack a button hook in that basket?"

"You promised only a picnic."

"I didn't know my new wife was so eager to have me."

"I didn't either."

They spoke over each other's shoulders as his fingers fought with the buttons, the light banter taking the edge off of their embarrassment. Caleb hoped his delay with the buttons would not give Analisa time to build up a wall of fear. Had he known her true thoughts, he wouldn't have been so worried. She was as eager to receive pleasure as she was to pleasure him.

Feeling her dress give way at last, Analisa drew the high collar away from her neck and pulled her arms out of the sleeves. The top half of the gown hung around her waist. Caleb let his thirsty eyes drink in the picture of her full breasts beneath the cotton camisole. She wore no stays. Her hardened nipples were outlined vividly through the soft, worn cotton. He lowered his head and covered the peak of one breast with his lips. As she felt the warm wetness of Caleb's mouth draw upon her, Analisa moaned low in her throat. She could not hold back the explosion inside herself, and the ripples of ecstasy that burst through her caught her unaware. She could only cling to Caleb, her fingernails digging into his shoulders as she pressed herself against him.

He waited until she was still, her ragged breathing slowed, and then drew her down to the cloth. He left her arms while he tugged at the snakeskin boots, tossing them left and right into the grass.

Staring wide-eyed at the canopy of leaves high overhead, Analisa lay still, relishing the feel of the final pulsations that had rocked her at Caleb's touch. They slowly ebbed away. She had thought to give him pleasure, to repay him for his sacrifice to herself and Kase, but instead, she was discovering there was as much to receive from the act of love as to give. If he left her now, at this very moment, she would have memories to last a lifetime.

A touch on her shoulder brought her eyes back to the man beside her. Naked, he stretched his long, lean form out beside her. Analisa felt as if she were a part of the earth with this tall, handsome man so close to her. She could feel the heat of his body where his skin touched hers, feel it even through the thickness of her skirt and the bodice of her dress still bunched at her waist. Raising her hand to his lips, she traced their outline and then ran her thumb back and forth across his full lower lip. She sighed at the wonder of him and watched, breathless, as Caleb lowered his lips to hers.

Lost for a time in his kiss, Analisa felt the fire within her rekindle. His hands were moving slowly, languidly about her body, over her shoulders, through her long hair, along the length of her hip and down her thigh. He pushed the hem of her skirt up to her thigh and moved his hand slowly and sensuously beneath it. His fingers toyed with the waistband of her pantalets. After fumbling with the ties for a moment, he was soon rewarded as the material separated. Caleb pushed the undergarment down toward her knees. Analisa released his lips reluctantly as he bent to push the offending garment down her legs and over one foot. She could feel it still looped around her left ankle.

As he pressed himself against her once more, Analisa closed her eyes, daring to touch him, to run her hands over the smooth skin of his shoulders, down the small of his back, and over his hips. Caleb possessed not an ounce of spare flesh, and yet the muscles bunched tight beneath the bronzed skin kept him from appearing thin. Those muscles were relaxed now, allowing Analisa's trembling fingertips to explore questioningly. Caleb's hands were anything but still as they caressed Analisa's body.

When his hand stole between her thighs and he pressed his palm against the soft, warm mound hidden there, Analisa reeled with sensation. She raised herself against his hand, moving gently, aware now of the pleasure his touch could evoke. Would he receive such pleasure if she touched him in the same way? Moving her hand slowly over his hipbone and then along the top of his thigh, she slid it toward his loins and touched the silken length of him.

His movement stilled as Caleb fought to control his response to her feather-light touch. His lips moved down along her throat to the sensitive hollow at its base. With her hand cupped around him gently, she drew him near, urging him to lie across her thighs.

Straddling her, Caleb roused himself long enough to pull away and slip both hands beneath her and untie her sash. Analisa stared up into his eyes, trusting, giving him full command over her. He gathered the rose material in his hands and pushed the gown and camisole up over her breasts, over her head, then flung it free. Kneeling over her, his legs astride her hips, Caleb ran the palms of his hands down the length of her and up again to her breasts. With a slow, determined movement, he traced the crescent scar that ran along her rib cage on the right side. His hands returned to her breasts, gently stroking them before he kissed them, drawing deeply on her erect nipples. Analisa thrashed her head from side to side, lost in this new world of sensations he was arousing in her.

Lowering himself over her, Caleb gently nudged her thighs apart with one knee. Her breath caught in her throat as Analisa felt him move between her legs. The silken tip of his manhood was seeking admittance. Gently, tentatively, he moved against the moist entrance to her body, as if awaiting her permission.

Analisa slid her hands down his rib cage to his hips and pulled him close in silent invitation. His lips covered hers as he began to enter her, sliding into her inch by inch, filling her slowly until he was encased inside. She felt him hold himself rigidly above her, as if he, too, was fighting to capture the moment and savor it for a lifetime. When he began to pull away, as slowly as he had entered her, Analisa tore her lips from his and whispered, "No!"

Caleb moaned low in his throat. She felt his warm breath as his lips moved near her ear.

"I'm not going anywhere. We're just getting started."

He let his lips play along her shoulder, toying with her with his teeth, and began his assault inside her once again, moving slowly, filling her to the limit and then drawing away again. Her breath was ragged, every fiber of her beating with the intensity of a savage drum. Analisa began to respond to Caleb's movements, meeting his forward motion until they lunged and thrust together, blending their souls in a harmony of pulsing movement, sending each other skyward until finally mingled cries of passion were torn from them to blend with the sounds of the surrounding landscape.

His thirst for her slaked for the time being, Caleb lifted himself onto his elbows to spare Analisa his weight. He gathered handfuls of her golden hair and pressed his face against it. Analisa lay watching him closely.

"Thank you," she whispered.

"The pleasure was all mine."

"Not entirely all."

He smiled into her eyes, let go of her hair and pressed a quick, loud kiss on her lips. "Now we swim."

"But, Mr. Storm," she began, a teasing smile on her lips, "you promised you would not swim nude."

"That was hours ago. Besides, how was I to know then that you would make me take off my clothes . . . not to mention yours?"

Analisa blushed crimson.

"Up."

When he stood and offered her his hand, Analisa was surprised at her calm acceptance of his nudity. It seemed the most natural thing in the world to see Caleb standing unclothed, surrounded by the sun-dappled leaves and trees. It was her own nakedness that made her uneasy, but as she looked down at her body, so rarely uncovered, she was secretly pleased that her muscles were firm and her skin smooth.

She started to laugh when she saw her pantalets looped about one ankle and noticed that she was still wearing her thick socks. She owned no silken hose or ruffled garters.

Caleb turned from where he walked a few paces ahead of her and smiled at the sound of her laughter.

"*Sokken,*" she explained and waved him on toward the water. She quickly stripped off the socks and wrapped the calico cloth around her, securing it across her breasts. At the edge of the shallow stream she called out to Caleb. "I cannot swim."

"Well, you can't drown in here! Wade on over here." He was sitting submerged up to his chest in a shallow pool in the center of the stream. Watching Analisa as she dropped the cloth and carefully picked her way across the slippery rocks to his side, he smiled at the change in her. Her eyes were shining for him, her cheeks tinted with a warm blush. His plan had been to leave her and return to Washington until they had time to decide what feelings they had for each other. What if he were to take her with him? An idea began to formulate in his thoughts until he remembered Kase and Edvard. There was no way he could ready the three of them and arrive in the East in time to report to Parker.

"Caleb?" She was next to him now, seated precariously on a submerged rock.

"I'm sorry, I was thinking." He dropped his thoughts of leaving for a time. "How do you like it?"

"I thought it was wonderful," she answered honestly and felt her cheeks flush.

Caleb put an arm about her shoulders and drew her to him before he whispered in her ear, "I meant the swim."

An embarrassed "Oh" formed on her lips. She splashed at a water bug as it floated lazily past.

They sat for a time, soothed by the cool water. Caleb made a great show of ducking and splashing water over his head and face before Analisa interrupted his sport.

"We must go back. I would hate for Opa to come looking for us. What if he decides to bring Kase fishing?"

"Come here."

"Please, Caleb."

"Come here. Please."

With an exaggerated sigh, Analisa crossed the small distance between them and was again enfolded in his embrace. Her reward was a wet and highly enthusiastic kiss. She dropped her eyes to the smooth, gloss-wet surface of his bronze chest as she struggled to keep her breasts submerged beneath the shimmering water. Bracing the palms of her hands against his shoulders, Analisa held herself away from him, as far as his strong arms would allow, to drink in his features—his dark brows, winged and fine above the azure of his eyes, his straight firm lips curved into a beguiling smile. She let her eyes feast upon his sensual, primitive handsomeness, tracing his lips with her fingers, searching them with her touch as a blind man might, lightly, carefully, getting to know him through her newly awakened sense of touch.

Her life had been turned upside down with the arrival of the pastor and Clara Heusinkveld. Never could she have imagined the overwhelming metamorphosis Caleb's lovemaking would work on her. Stubborn, independent Analisa Van Meeteren, capable of carving out a life on the vast prairie, suddenly smiled in wonder. Surely what had passed between them was meant to be. How could such a force strike with mere randomness? She had forgotten where they were, who they were, even what the future might bring, while he held her in his arms.

"You're smiling." He spoke between kisses as his lips moved over hers.

"Hmmm."

"The first time I saw you, I was lying in your bed, watching you work at the stove, and I wondered what it would take to make you smile."

"And?"

"Had I known then, I would have been about it much sooner."

"Caleb." She pulled away, all too aware now of where they were and afraid of being discovered by Edvard or Kase. "We have to go back."

He seemed suddenly grave, his eyes full of concern, his smile fading. Analisa's deep instincts sent a cold warning along her spine.

"It's going to be hard for me to leave you tomorrow."

She began instinctively to draw back into place the sheath that protected her emotions, all the while fighting against her urge to cling to him, to beg him to stay or, at the very least, to take her with him. But he still intended to leave her, despite all that had passed between them in the last hour. Slowly, having developed expert control during long years of practice, Analisa steeled herself against her emotions. Caleb was going away. She had no idea of his destination, nor did she understand the commitment that compelled him to return East. Perhaps another woman waited to welcome his kiss, to awaken to his touch.

Determined to let him go without clinging, she sought to free him from any obligation he might feel toward her because of his hasty offer of marriage. "I want you to know, Caleb, that if you should decide never to come back here again, I will understand."

He was still for a moment, staring into her eyes as if trying to plumb the depths of her soul. "What do you mean by that?"

The words were quiet, calm, but she was forced to look away from the intensity of his stare.

"You have done so much for us already. I know this marriage was impulsive and that you never really thought of marrying me before the minister called. I want you to know how grateful I am for what you did for Kase, and for me and Opa, and I want you to know, too, that I will understand perfectly if you decide that this has all been a mistake."

"Just like that? What do you propose I do, then, in the event that I do 'decide this has all been a mistake,' as you put it?" His words drew her eyes back to lock with his.

She was confused by the dark, quiet anger changing his features, confused by his reaction. Analisa forced a light tone into her voice as she tried to explain. "You could get a divorce. I have no family to object, and your family need never know. I would still be Mrs. Storm to the people of Pella. All they ever wanted was for me to become respectable."

"How about what just passed between us? How do you explain that away?"

Did his sullen anger mask the hurt she had inflicted on him with her easy release? If he cared so deeply, how was it that he could not postpone his departure? Confused, Analisa tried to explain in a way that would leave him free and her pride intact. "I . . . you've done so much for me, for all of us. I wanted to give you something in return, that's all. Caleb, I have nothing else to give."

"So to show me the depths of your gratitude, you offer to sacrifice yourself once again for the sake of Kase and Edvard?" His words were cutting, cold.

"No. That's not what I meant. I mean . . . if you are in the East and decide that this was all a mistake, I will understand."

"Are you telling me that if I decide not to bother coming back, that is just fine and dandy with you?"

"Yes." She hid her pain behind a false smile. "This has all been very sudden. You may regret what you've done."

"Just as you might now be regretting what you've done? After all, what you did today was just a way of saying thank you."

"Yes." She nodded, not sure why he seemed so angry.

"Next time, why don't you just say *tanks?*" He was very angry now, but she found he had spoken the truth when he'd said, "I never yell." She almost wished he would. His cold, contemplative stare would be her undoing.

"Caleb . . ."

He pulled himself out of the water and moved across the shallows to the shore, Analisa trailing slowly behind him, her arms extended in order to balance herself on the slippery rocks below the water.

While he brushed the water off of himself with his hands, Analisa dried her body with the calico and then offered it to Caleb. He turned his back to her and began to ram his legs into his britches. Suddenly awkward, embarrassed by their nudity, Analisa dressed hurriedly. By the time she was ready, he was moving through the cottonwoods in the direction of the soddie. She grabbed the basket and hurried after him.

If he thought she would chase him all the way to the house, he was mistaken, she decided, but she proceeded to do just that. He slowed his steps until she caught up with him, but as they crossed the open prairie side by side, he remained ominously silent.

"Caleb, I don't understand your anger." Panting from the effort of matching his long strides, Analisa tugged at his arm to slow him down. Caleb stopped walking long enough to turn seething blue eyes in her direction and grab her arm above the elbow.

"Let me see if I have this straight. I ask you to marry me in order to give Kase a name. To pay me back for such a sacrifice, you make love to me today, and now, debt free, you release me until such time as I decide to return. If I choose not to return, I'm to obtain a divorce, and my decision doesn't matter to you in the least. Is that correct?"

"I think so, but when I form the words in my mind, they don't sound as bad as you make them seem. Perhaps I have not said it correctly?"

"No, lady, for once I think you've said it pretty damn straight. I was just fool enough to think for a while back there that this might work out."

"Are you angry because you don't think I enjoyed what happened between us today?"

"Ha!" He started to walk away again, his words drifting over his shoulder. "No, you don't have to ask that. I may be a fool, but I do know that you enjoyed our little romp as much as or more than I did.''

''Romp?'' The word was strange to her. ''More than you did?'' She was hurt to think he had not shared the passion she felt.

''Oh, that stings, does it? Good.'' But he felt far from good about his harsh words.

Caleb had not known he'd possessed such deep feelings before she had shaken him to the core with her cool dismissal. Had he taken the time to think instead of react, he would have seen her as the actress she had become, able to hide her most intense emotion from the world behind a stolid, collected exterior. What had he expected, after all? Did he want her to beg him not to go? All he knew for certain was that he had to get far away from the bewitching picture she now made, flushed and satiated in the soft rose gown, and sort out his feelings. Love? He thought not. At least he never thought of love as this gut-wrenching, overwhelming uneasiness. Lust was more like it. Perhaps she was right. It was time he left to report to Parker and clear the slate. Then he could decide exactly what his feelings were for this strange girl.

They were marching now, Caleb's boot heels digging into the ragged buffalo grass beside Analisa's own pounding steps. She wasn't sure exactly why they were so angry with each other. She hadn't expected Caleb to be hurt by her attempt to release him from his obligation to her. If she told him now that she would die a little each day until he returned, would it make a difference to him? She doubted it, and decided not to further humiliate herself by doing so.

When they reached the back gate, he held it open until she passed through and then slammed it shut behind them. He moved beside her as far as the shed, then stepped inside to saddle Scorpio and retrieve his rifle. She stopped walking and stood still, holding the basket in front of her with both hands. When she realized his intentions, she let the basket drop to the ground beside her and moved toward him.

''Where are you going?''

''There's plenty of daylight left. I can get to Pella tonight. If there's no train, I can head up to Des Moines and catch one tomorrow. Seeing as how I'm leaving, it doesn't matter where I sleep tonight, does it? I can be on the east-bound train by tomorrow noon if I get going.'' He slapped Scorpio's reins against his thigh with impatience and watched while Analisa straightened her shoulders as he'd seen her do in so many tight situations. Too bad her hair was unpinned, he thought; ordinarily she'd be trying to smooth it up into place.

Finally she spoke. ''Good-bye, Caleb Storm. I will not say thank you, as it seems to make you angry.''

''I'll write you.''

She nodded, unbelieving.

He reached deep into the pocket of his pants and pulled out a handful of gold coins. ''Here. See that you have everything you need for the winter.'' He dropped five twenty-dollar gold pieces into her hand.

Shaking her head, the golden mass of hair shimmering in the late afternoon sunlight, she was about to protest when Kase ran up to join them. Caleb's words tore at her insides. She was to get what she needed for the winter. He would not be coming back.

''Where are you going, Caleb?'' Kase looked up at him with curiosity, his blue eyes bright. ''Can I go with you?''

Caleb hunkered down and ran his hand over Kase's blue-black hair. Seeing Caleb's solemn expression, Kase put his hand on the man's shoulder. Analisa looked away, her heart constricting at the sight of them.

''I have to go back east, to the city I came from, but I'll send you a big surprise for Christmas.''

''Do you have to go?''

Caleb looked up over the boy's head at his mother. ''Yes.''

''Be careful.''

''I will.''

Pulling the boy to him, Caleb gave Kase a ferocious growling bear-hug that helped to ease his own sadness. The hug made Caleb think of his father and the many times Clinton Storm had comforted him. Without touching Analisa again, he swung himself up onto Scorpio's back and tipped the brim of his dark hat to Analisa. Then, without further ceremony, he rode toward the back gate and his camp near the stream.

''When will Caleb be back, Mama?''

''I'm not sure, Kase.'' Analisa choked back the sob that threatened to burst from the aching lump in her throat.

"I would rather have Caleb here every day than a Christmas present. Wouldn't you, Mama? . . . Mama?"

When Kase finally turned to demand an answer from her, he saw that his mother had left his side and was running toward the soddie. With a last look in the direction of the man riding away from the homestead, the boy picked up the forgotten picnic basket and walked slowly toward the house.

Chapter Five

Silent snowflakes fell from gray skies, slowly molding themselves into drifts around the soddie. Inside, secure behind the thick walls and warmed by the low, ever present fire in the stove, Kase and Opa occupied themselves on the far side of the room while Analisa concentrated on fitting the pieces of a velvet gown together. It was the first time she'd attempted to make one of the newly designed gowns with a bustle. The dress was a special order placed well ahead of the approaching holiday season. As Analisa carefully gathered a long ruffle onto her needle and pushed the material along the thread, spreading the folds evenly along its length, her thoughts drifted like the soft snow outside.

It was the tenth day of November, two months since Caleb had left for the East. During that time not a day passed that Analisa did not spend time thinking of him. Shut inside by the cold weather, she watched the long days stretch on as she lost herself in the thousands of stitches she plied. Her business seemed to have doubled since September, the month Caleb left, the month they were wed.

Mevrou Heusinkveld had wasted little time, it seemed, spreading the news about Analisa Van Meeteren's new husband and the details of their impromptu wedding. At least twice a week one or more of the fair ladies of Pella would arrive at the soddie, material in hand, to place an order. Analisa would politely invite them in and offer refreshment, which they would politely refuse. The women waited curiously for Caleb to appear. It galled Analisa that they never inquired after him, just watched the door expectantly. They called her Mrs. Storm in deference to her new status, but refrained from asking her husband's whereabouts. Stubbornly, she never offered them an explanation.

Edvard moved away from the corner where he had been teaching Kase to make hats from folded newspaper. Analisa glanced up from her work long enough to smile and nod at her grandfather when he donned his woolen jacket and stepped outside into the softly falling snow.

"Kase," she called out, demanding her son's attention, "do you need to go with Opa?" With the snowdrifts deepening, Analisa preferred Kase did not go out to the privy alone. When he shook his head, she turned once again to her work. The long silk ruffle finally gathered, she began to baste it near the hem of the rich brown velvet with long, smooth stitches.

Her concern regarding her grandfather had mounted as the fall passed and winter set in. Edvard, ninety years old in October, seemed to be slipping into a world of his own. Often, like Kase, he would ask about Caleb, but unlike her son, he thought his granddaughter's husband was just outside working on some task and due back any moment. Other times he would speak of his own son, Emmett, Analisa's father. When she reminded him that Emmett and Henrietta were no longer alive, he would reply, *"Ik begijp het niet.* I don't understand," shaking his head in sad confusion, his blue eyes dim and watery.

She turned the thick material as she worked, resting the heavy folds against the tabletop until, at last, the long ruffle of contrasting gold silk lay in place against the warm, deep velvet.

Placing both palms against the small of her back, Analisa straightened her spine and stretched her tired muscles. A cup of tea was just what she needed to break the monotony of her work.

"Kase, would you like tea and cookies?"

The boy had built himself a playhouse from a sheet draped over the rocking chair, anchored at each corner by a book.

"Mama, come and see my house." His eyes sparkled with mischief as he thrust his head from between the overlapping edges forming the door to his tent house. Analisa walked across the room to inspect her son's handiwork and, as she did, realized that Edvard had not yet returned. Had she been so intent on her work that she missed his entrance? Had he come inside and then gone out again without her knowledge?

"Kase, did Opa come back in yet?"

No answer.

"Kase!"

"What?"

"Did Opa come back inside?"

Silence. Finally, the boy stuck his head out again and smiled up at his mother. "Not yet. Maybe he is feeding Tulip-the-Ox."

Analisa fought her immediate reaction of fear. There was nothing to worry about, she told herself. Opa was just outside seeing to the animals, perhaps checking the latch on the chicken coop; it had blown open two days ago. Everything was all right.

Quickly, she went to the window and tried to see outside. Condensation fogged the panes, obscuring her view. She wiped the pane with a swift, circular motion and, still unable to see outside, quickly went to the door and opened it far enough to look out into the stark whiteness beyond. The gently drifting flakes of an hour ago had gathered in intensity until now they were falling in thick, clotted sheets. The cloud carrying them had sunk to earth as well, enshrouding the silent, white flakes in a dense fog. Analisa could not see more than an arm's length.

"Opa!"

The sound of her voice seemed muffled by the thick snow. Analisa listened intently for even a hint of a sound from her grandfather. Snow sifted in the open door, chilling her. She closed the door and pulled her long, gray woolen coat from the peg beside the door, trying to still the wild beating of her heart as she prepared to go outside in search of her grandfather.

"Kase?" Wrapping a fringed shawl about her neck, she pulled a pair of woolen gloves from her coat pocket and began to put them on. When Kase failed to respond, she called him again impatiently. "Kase! Please come here."

Aware of the command in his mother's tone, the boy wriggled out from beneath his cloth structure and crossed the room to stand before Analisa, his bent paper hat cocked to one side on his shining black hair. "Yes, Mama?"

"I am going out after Opa. The snow is falling heavily now, and I don't want you going out at all. Do you understand me?"

Never had his mother spoken so harshly to him. Kase nodded in silent response.

Aware of the fear creeping into the child's innocent eyes, Analisa knelt before him and pulled him into her embrace. "Kase, I'm sorry. I am just worried about Opa. I will be right back. You be a big boy and stay in the house. Promise me."

"Yes, Mama," Kase whispered against her shoulder, his mother's fear having communicated itself to him.

Pulling the shawl up over her hair and tight against her mouth, Analisa knotted the ends behind her neck. She opened the door and stepped into the snow, her leather shoes crunching in the deep powder. Analisa knew the risks of straying too far from the soddie. Settlers caught in blizzards had been frozen to death a few feet from their homes.

One hand against the rough, frozen sod wall, Analisa felt her way slowly along the house. The snow was deep and unpacked. With each step, she sank up to her knees. At the corner of the building, Analisa turned toward the back of the soddie. Her movements were slow and exhausting, the wet, clinging snow soaking her through to the skin. She kept on until she rounded the final turn along the wall and entered the cow shed.

Snow had piled up outside the open doorway, and Analisa could not find purchase. One foot and then the other went out from under her, and she landed heavily on the straw-covered floor. Righting herself, she brushed the snow from her wool clothing. She was soaked through, yet warm from the exertion of winding her way through the snow. The muffler was sodden and clinging to her mouth and nose, dampened by the warmth of her breath. It itched unbearably, and so Analisa unwound the shawl and draped it across her shoulders.

A quick glance in their direction told her that Tulip-the-Ox and Honey were comfortable and oblivious of the storm outside, their heavy bodies filling the small room with a close warmth. They turned their gaze on Analisa as if expecting her to rub their noses and whisper nonsense words to them as she usually did. But not today.

Standing just inside the snow-filled doorway, Analisa tried in vain to see across the fog-shrouded yard.

"Opa!"

She called his name in a loud, clear voice, first in the direction of the outhouse, and then to the left and right, in case Opa had become disoriented. Her attempts brought no results, and silence met her on every side. Frustrated, Analisa was aware that if she stepped a few feet from the soddie she, too, would become lost. She struggled against tears. "Think!" she admonished herself.

The idea came on her in a sudden flash of inspiration. Analisa whirled around and lifted a coil of rope from a hook on the wall. The rope was stiff from the cold and barely manageable. She peeled her gloves off and stuffed them into her coat pocket. Willing the rope to cooperate, Analisa tied one end around an iron ring embedded in the shed wall. She pulled on the rope to test the knots. After tying the other end of the rope around her waist, she examined the coil to be sure it was free of tangles. She then began to climb up the bank of snow in the doorway.

Carefully gauging the position of the outhouse in relation to where she stood, Analisa began moving forward, calling for Edvard every few steps. Realizing he could have collapsed inches from her and might now be covered with a fine layer of snow, Analisa beat the powder with her hands. No sign of Edvard appeared to relieve her fears. Struggling forward, Analisa felt the rope pull taut all too soon; she had not yet reached the outhouse. Turning, she looked back in the direction of the soddie. It had disappeared from view and was now enshrouded in snow and fog. The rope trailed off to disappear in the snow as well. It was impossible to see where the sky stopped and the earth began. The silent white world had an eerie, almost magical quality. For a moment Analisa was distracted from her search as she stared around her, heavy flakes falling on her cheeks and lashes.

After one last frantic shout, Analisa sighed, admitting defeat, and turned back, pulling herself along, letting the rope guide her to the shed. The deep footprints she had left behind her were already nearly obliterated by the snow. Struggling on, she was determined to return to the house as quickly as possible; she was worried that Kase might become frightened enough to step out in search of her.

"Please, God, keep him safe indoors."

By the time she entered the soddie and felt the warmth of the small room surround her, Analisa was trembling violently from exhaustion and fear. She dropped the heavy weight of the rope to the floor. Kase ran to her side, his usually bright, eager expression clouded with worry.

"Did you find Opa?" His eyes told her he knew the truth although he asked anyway, hoping that perhaps his great-grandpapa would come in on Analisa's heels.

Still standing inside the door, her sodden clothing clinging to her, the snow melting to form a puddle on the earthen floor, Analisa met her son's gaze intently. There was no story she could tell, no lie that would shield him from Edvard's fate. An angel from heaven had not swooped down to carry the old man away. It would be cruel to lie to the boy when she never had before.

Slowly she unwound the shawl from around her shoulders and hung it over the bench near the fire. She pulled the balled woolen gloves from her coat pockets, straightened the fingers, and put them beside the shawl. The smell of wet wool filled the air.

"Mama?" Kase followed her to the bench, where she sat down heavily and unbuttoned her coat. She wanted to hold him when she explained. Thankful that the bodice and sleeves of her dress were still relatively dry, she shrugged her coat aside and held out her arm to him. The little boy scrambled up onto the bench, and Analisa drew him close.

"I couldn't find Opa, Kase. I went to the shed and used the rope as a guide so I wouldn't lose my way. I called and called, but he did not answer."

"Were you scared?"

"A little."

"Will Opa ever come back?"

"I don't know, Kase. Perhaps he has found shelter and is waiting for the storm to lift." She smoothed his forehead with her fingertips.

"Do you think he's buried in the snow?"

"I hope not, but I'm so afraid he might be."

The boy was silent. Analisa knew he was conjuring up scenes of Opa trapped beneath the snow, cold, frightened, dying.

"Kase." She drew him closer and looked at him steadily, hoping to make her thoughts clear without frightening him. "Everyone—you, me, Opa, Caleb, all the other people you've ever known—everyone has to die someday. We learn this when we come into the world. We will die, but at our own special time. We never know when that time will come. Opa is a very old man and he's had a very long, good life. Perhaps his time to die was today."

"Did it hurt Opa to die?"

"If he is dead, I'm sure he simply drifted off to sleep in the snow."

They sat quietly for a time, Analisa's arms about her son, her cheek resting against his glossy black hair. Absently, she rocked him back and forth as she'd done so many times when he was a baby.

"Mama?"

"Yes?"

"Don't die."

His words were a soft whisper in the room. She squeezed him tight and gave him the only answer that would suffice and, in doing so, prayed that nothing would befall her before he was old enough to care for himself, for there was no one else left.

"I won't."

In the middle of the long night Analisa, lying awake in her bed, heard Kase moving restlessly on his pallet beside her. A thick comforter kept him warm, and she had seen to it that his bed was dry and free from the bone-chilling cold. She listened for a few moments before she whispered to him in the darkness, "Are you awake, Kase?"

He answered immediately. "Mama, may I get into bed with you?"

"Ja."

Kase scrambled into Analisa's bed, snuggling against her protective warmth. Their minds were intent on the man lost somewhere beyond the safety of the sod walls.

"I wish Caleb was here." It was the hundredth time in the past two months the boy had wished for Caleb. How the man had created such a bond between himself and her son she could not fathom, but then, hadn't Caleb carved himself a place in her own heart as well? She, too, wished Caleb were here, for even if he could have done nothing to save Opa from his fate, his presence would have offered them consolation.

"I know," she whispered to Kase, covering them with her comforter, "but he's not here, and he may never come back. We can take care of ourselves."

By morning the storm had lifted. Dazzling snow reflected the sun's brilliance as it shone in an unclouded aquamarine sky. The air was crisp with cold, and as far as the eye could see, the ground lay shrouded in white. Mile upon mile of gently rolling, sparkling landscape surrounded the soddie. Analisa and Kase arose early, thoughts of their missing grandfather having plagued their rest. Snow reached halfway up the cabin door, and the better part of the morning passed as Analisa shoveled and tossed the thick mass up and over the banks she created as she carved out a path. Exhausted by midafternoon, she realized the futility of searching for Edvard now. She would have to wait until some of the snow had melted.

She set Kase to work sweeping an already clean floor and then resorted to having him help her make an apple pie. As she worked, adding spices to apples dried earlier in the fall, Kase rolled and rerolled his portion of pie dough on the floured surface of the table. Once he tired of rolling and reshaping the dough, he cut it into various shapes with tin cookie cutters and sprinkled them with cinnamon and sugar. The treats made of excess dough were always a favorite.

Occasionally he would glance toward Opa's bed in the corner near the stove and cease his chatter, his eyes meeting Analisa's own, his brows knit in worry. She wondered, as she watched the movements of his sturdy, capable brown hands, if he at all resembled the man who had fathered him. Perhaps only his coloring came from the Sioux? His features could belong to a distant relative of hers. And yet, she argued with herself, he looked so like Caleb, who was of Indian blood himself, that Kase must have inherited his features from the man who fathered him. It mattered little, she told herself, because no matter who the boy favored, he was her flesh and blood and she loved him beyond a doubt.

The first day after the storm passed into the second and then the third. Finally the earth began to warm gradually and the crust that had formed atop the settling snow began to soften. Analisa wrapped herself once again in her heaviest clothes, this time donning Jan's long-legged underwear and trousers before she tramped about in the snow in the yard. Kase was bundled to the ears, unwilling to stay indoors and needing his time outside in the fresh air and sunlight. She allowed him to roam the short path she had made outside the door and to roll and play in the well-packed snow near the soddie. Analisa supplied Tulip-the-Ox and Honey with feed for the next week and piled more hay near the shed. She sank the edge of the shovel into the snow behind the soddie, methodically testing the ground inch by inch in her search for Opa. In her heart she dreaded finding him, but also knew that she must continue the search until she did.

It was thus Dominie Julius Wierstra found her as he made his way into the yard driving a sleigh pulled by a heavy-sided draft horse. She heard the merry sound of the sleighbells before he was near the front of the property, and so stopped her search to stand with Kase at the gate to meet him. They followed the sleigh into the yard and watched as the young assistant pastor jumped down from the high seat.

"Welcome, Dominie Wierstra."

"Analisa." He nodded politely to her and then looked to the boy. "And this is Kase, isn't it? I was out traveling the road to see how the folks on the outlying homesteads weathered the storm. The roads have been quite impassable for the last three days, so I had to wait until the snow became packed a bit before I set out. You came through the storm without mishap?"

Analisa noted that he had not inquired about Caleb and wondered if word of her husband's absence had been reported in the village.

"My grandfather is missing."

There was no subtle way to tell the man, but Analisa saw by his reaction to her words that he must think her unmoved.

"What? Surely not, Mrs. Storm."

"He went out the day of the blizzard and didn't return. I searched for him until I feared that I, too, would be lost. This is the first day I have been able to get across the snow to continue searching."

"Where is your husband? Shouldn't he be helping you?" The man's gaze registered her appearance. Her face was flushed with the effects of the sharp air and the sun reflecting off of the snow, her eyes a brilliant blue above the ruddy cheeks. Tendrils of yellow-gold hair escaped her tightly wound scarf, framing her face and creating an innocent, appealing air.

"Caleb is away on a business trip to the East. I'm not sure when he will return."

Or if he will return, the man thought to himself. He'd long ago regretted letting Clara Heusinkveld push him into marrying Analisa and Storm. Mrs. Heusinkveld and her gaggle of biddies were overly concerned with the morals of other people, but the pastor would not let him ignore one of the *dorp*'s most generous contributors to the church.

"Do you have any idea where Edvard might be?" he asked.

"If I did, Dominie Wierstra, I would have found him by now."

"Yes. Well . . ." How was it this young woman could make him feel so inept? Her ice-blue eyes did not waver as she continued.

"He is lost somewhere within the yard. I think he must have become disoriented by the storm on his way in from the outhouse."

The minister blushed red to the roots of his hair, and Analisa looked away to avoid his embarrassment. Caleb, no doubt, would have laughed aloud at the man's discomfort over the mere mention of the outhouse.

"Miss Van Meeteren—that is, Mrs. Storm—I can't let you go on searching for your grandfather alone. He is entitled to a Christian burial, and I will brook no interference from the townspeople on this score. I'm returning to Pella at once to organize the men to accompany me out here to search for Edvard. We have ignored your plight for far too long."

"Dominie Wierstra—" She started to object, then stopped as she thought of her grandfather's body lying somewhere beneath the snow. This was no time to let stubborn pride stand in the way. "That would be most welcome help. My father, mother, and older brother are buried in the cemetery in Pella. I know that Opa would be content to lie beside them."

"Then I'll be on my way and will return as soon as I can gather the men."

"Would you like some hot coffee first, perhaps some breakfast?"

"No. I needn't waste the time. Perhaps you will have food ready for the men when they arrive?"

Analisa nodded in agreement and stood aside as he mounted the sled again and turned the heavy horse back toward the gate. She watched as the snow packed itself under the runners.

It was two hours before the sleighbells could again be heard singing across the frozen landscape as the minister's sleigh, filled with four well-bundled men, moved into the yard. Behind it was a smaller sleigh driven by a tall blond man. The five men of the village seemed to need no direction as they hopped from the rigs and began to work their way around the yard. Each carried a long pole or the handle of a rake or hoe. Moving in a determined line, the men carefully searched through the snow-drifts for some sign of Edvard Van Meeteren.

Unable to watch, Analisa went inside and stood near the stove, arms folded against her breasts, trying to still the tremors that began as she waited in dread of a word or shout from one of the men. She kept Kase indoors on the pretext of helping her with the food she would serve. Dominie Wierstra divided his time between the kitchen and the yard, often bringing one or two of the men indoors with him for hot coffee and thick slabs of warm bread. Analisa served them with distracted politeness. She had met few of the townspeople during the time she'd lived in Iowa, and she did not know any of these men, but one or two names were familiar to her, their wives having placed orders for gowns. All treated her with a quiet reserve, attempting to study her when her attention was drawn away from them. More than once Analisa found them staring at her and wondered what questions their minds held. Uncomfortable under the scrutiny, she turned away from their prying eyes, all the while hating herself for her cowardice.

For his part, Kase kept out of the way, sensing his mother's unease and the way the men stared at both of them. Caleb had been different from these men. The boy discovered that fact when the men in the room failed to pay him any attention beyond curious stares in his direction. Unlike his mother, Kase met their questioning looks with luminous blue eyes that were disarming in their honesty. When he found that the men turned away from any open attempt at friendship, he stayed near his mother.

After what seemed like an eternity, Analisa heard a shout from the yard. The heavy sound of the men pushing away from the table and their boots tramping across the floor filled the room. Talk turned to speculation as they shrugged into heavy coats and mufflers, shoving their hands into woolen mittens and gloves as they filed outdoors.

Dominie Wierstra turned to Analisa and met her wide, frightened eyes across the room. He thought of the disservice the small, narrow-minded congregation had done this young woman, casting her out to fend for herself and the old man simply because she was forced to bear a child conceived during a brutal attack. If he had been the pastor of Pella four years ago, he asked himself, would he have had the strength and courage to stand up to the openly hostile church members in defense of Analisa? How different would her life have been if he had? As he looked across the room and met her deep blue eyes, eyes filled with fear of what the shout in the yard would bring, he felt an overwhelming compassion for the young beauty and knew that beneath his compassion dwelt some stronger feeling. He pushed the acknowledgment of that feeling aside and became the comforting minister he'd been trained to be.

"Mrs. Storm, would you like me to go out alone?"

"No. I will go with you."

Somehow he had known that would be her answer. He stepped aside as she crossed the room, drew her heavy coat off of the peg, and pulled it on. The dark gray wool did little to dull her appearance. Instead it called attention to her corn-silk hair and bright eyes, her cheeks flushed from nervousness. He watched her take a deep breath and then turn toward him as she drew on her gloves.

"Will you walk with me, Dominie?"

"Of course." Julius was sorry that she had felt the need to ask.

She instructed Kase to wait inside, fearing he would balk at her request. Her son's eyes were bright with tears, but he held them back bravely and sat at the table to await her return.

The men were speculating in hushed tones, a mixture of Dutch and English words floating on the air around them. They stood in a circle around a spot not far from the outhouse but beyond it. As Analisa and Dominie Wierstra approached the men, the circle broke and widened to admit them. Standing tall and proud, slowly drawing the cold air into her lungs, the shock of its iciness helping to calm her, Analisa looked down at the figure of her grandfather. Edvard Van Meeteren looked as peaceful as if he had just fallen into a deep sleep. Her fear slid away. Analisa knelt in the snow and looked carefully into Opa's face. His eyes were closed as if in sleep, snow still clinging to his hair and clothing where the men had not brushed it away. He looked almost young, the creases of his skin less noticeable. Leaning close to him, Analisa whispered, "Be happy now, Opa. You are with the others." She knelt near him a few moments longer, the men respecting her grief and standing silently; shifting their feet and blowing on their mittened hands to ward off the cold.

Analisa rose and, looking slowly around the circle of men, drew their attention with her silence. "My grandfather was a good man, a simple man," she said at last. "He was a fisherman in the old country, working the seas around the north islands. He came here because of my father's dream of a new life, no doubt the same dream you or perhaps your fathers came to find. Now he is at peace. My son and I thank you for your help."

She spoke clearly in English, her Dutch accent apparent but not obscuring her words. When she had finished, Analisa turned away from the men without waiting for them to respond. Julius Wierstra followed her, gently holding her elbow to guide her across the snow. He saved Analisa the embarrassment of inquiring into the procedure for her grandfather's burial by taking the initiative in directing events.

"Close up your home and get your son ready to leave. We will take your grandfather's body back into Pella and make arrangements for him to be buried in the church cemetery as soon as possible. You will stay the night in the village." Seeing that she was prepared to object, he forestalled the interruption with a shake of his head. "The pastor is away for two months, spending the holidays in the East. If need be, you will stay in the parsonage with your son, and I will find other lodgings. I will accept no excuses, Mrs. Storm. Surely you will do this for your grandfather?"

She watched the man's open features as he stood next to her, a figure wrapped in dark, heavy clothing, a stark contrast against the bright blue winter sky. The land all around them was vast and white with snow. Analisa suddenly felt small and insignificant, lost against the wide horizon, blue meeting white where the sky dipped to the earth, surrounding them in every direction. She had to get away from this house, away from the terrible, stark aloneness of the open prairie, if only for a day or two.

"We will be ready." She turned toward the soddie and then remembered to thank the quiet young man who stood watching her with such a forlorn expression. Turning back toward the minister, she reached out tentatively to shake his hand. As he closed the space between them to take her hand, she fought the tears that had welled up in her eyes and whispered, "Thank you."

As the sleigh traveled through the snow-packed streets of Pella, Analisa and Kase huddled beneath a lap robe, surveying the town from the high seat. The late afternoon cold had driven the townsfolk indoors as the sunlight began to wane. Pella stretched out in neat straight lines on the flat, unbroken landscape, halfway between the Skunk and Des Moines rivers. Settled in 1847 by Dominie Hendrike Pieter Scholte and his congregation of eight hundred men, women, and children, the town had taken root and flourished on the plains much like the precious tulip bulbs the immigrants carried with them.

Analisa watched as the sleigh slipped past houses and stores. A grand white structure, the Reverend Mr. Scholte's two-story home, stood in quiet splendor on Washington Street, many of its windows shuttered against the cold. At the corner of First and Washington, the minister's sleigh turned north and stopped before his own small white frame house.

The sound of their footsteps against the polished floor disturbed the serenity of Dominie Wierstra's home. Analisa was tempted to tiptoe as she crossed the glossy oak floor in the small entryway. Hat in hand, Kase released his mother's fingers but stayed near her side, his eyes taking in every detail of the wooden structure. The house was warmed by glowing fires in the drawing room and in the kitchen. The delicious aroma of cinnamon and nutmeg wafted through the house.

Although the house was small by town standards, built to house visiting clergymen and the assistant pastor, Analisa knew it must seem like a palace to Kase, who had never set foot inside a home other than his own. She smiled down at him reassuringly and followed Julius Wierstra into the drawing room.

"Let me take your coats, and if you'll just have a seat, I'll tell Mrs. Eide, my housekeeper, to serve us some coffee as soon as she can have it ready. Excuse me." He bowed slightly, awkward and formal even in his own home.

Analisa arranged her heavy wheat-colored shawl around her shoulders and straightened the skirt of her plaid wool dress before she sat down carefully on the brocade settee opposite the fireplace. The dress had been her mother's and was the fashion of a decade ago, with its wide full skirt and long sleeves gathered at the cuff. It was her warmest presentable winter gown. Settling Kase beside her, Analisa took in the peaceful room.

A small but ornate Belgian rug lay before the fireplace, the settee and two tall wing chairs drawn up in a comfortable grouping around it. Against the wall behind them, a tall standing clock chimed the quarter-hour and ticked away the minutes, breaking the silence in the room. Exhausted, Analisa could do little more than let her eyes wander about the room. She realized how little she'd slept since Opa's disappearance. She was certain she would sleep soundly tonight no matter where she was.

Glancing down at Kase, she felt a tug at her heart. The little boy was sitting straight and still, his spine pressed against the firm back of the settee, his short legs straight out before him, feet dangling in space. The high tops of his boots were exposed where his pantlegs had hiked up. His sturdy garments were clean and well tailored, made by Analisa herself. Short trousers of wool, a thick flannel shirt, and a woolen jacket completed his outfit. His thick socks kept his feet warm and dry and extended to above his knees. His hair, she noticed, was sorely in need of a trim.

Kase looked quite foreign in the polished atmosphere and traditional surroundings of the minister's house. The stiff formal furniture, fabric-covered walls, and gilt-edged books lining the bookcase served as an unlikely backdrop for her half-breed son. It was hard for Analisa to imagine him in such surroundings for long. Yet, where did he belong? Surely not in a mission on some reservation, among barely civilized nomads. Would he ever live in a world that accepted him? Analisa wished she'd been able to talk to Caleb about his own life, to ask him how he had come to terms with his heritage. For her son's sake she should have put aside her pride and asked.

Her thoughts were interrupted by the minister's entrance. His housekeeper and cook, Mrs. Eide, followed, carrying a large silver tray laden with fine china cups and saucers, a silver coffee service, and an assortment of turnovers. The minister drew a low table up in front of the fire, and the woman set the tray before them.

Mrs. Eide was a short, elderly woman whose figure gave testimony to her skill as a cook. Her round-collared long-sleeved dress with its row of tiny buttons down the bodice was typical of the old-country style. A full, starched white apron covered the dress front and back, allowing only the collar, sleeves, and six inches of the skirt hem to show. A tiny white cap was perched atop the woman's thick gray curls. Her blue eyes snapped above ruddy pink cheeks as she sullenly met Analisa's gaze. At Julius's introduction, the woman nodded, gave Analisa a cursory "Pleased," and, ignoring Kase entirely, swept from the room.

"Would you like to serve the coffee, Mrs. Storm?"

Julius Wierstra drew her attention away from Mrs. Eide's rude exit, attempting to set her at ease. He smiled at Kase and extended the plate of turnovers.

"I seem to have upset your cook," Analisa said softly, handing him a cup and saucer.

"I fail to understand the depth of the hostility these people carry." He shook his head in puzzlement.

"I like to believe it isn't really me they hate, Dominie; it's what I remind them of. Nearly everyone has been hurt by an uprising, or their friends, cousins, and neighbors have. It isn't easy for me, but I try to understand."

"But none of it was your fault," he argued.

"No. But I am here. I'm someone to vent their anger on."

"You've quite resigned yourself to your fate, is that it?"

"What else can I do?" She shrugged.

"I don't know if I could be so strong. What will you do now that Edvard is gone?"

Analisa was quiet, contemplating the question she had not yet asked herself.

"You could take the boy and move East, begin a new life," he suggested. "If you need funds, I can see that you have them. Perhaps the congregation would not object to a new project for charitable work. I feel they owe it to you."

Analisa shook her head, returning his smile, noting his slim hands as they held the porcelain cup. "Where would I go? At least here I have my sewing orders and the land around the soddie. I would not like to begin again." She watched her son as he walked carefully on silent feet around the room, leaning close to study the books on the shelves, touch a brass paper-weight in the shape of a bumblebee, and examine a small, faded daguerreotype displayed on a side table.

"And what of Kase?" she asked. "Do you think he would be any better received in the East?" She was not sure that moving would change their lives.

"I think he might, Mrs. Storm."

Analisa was silent. She set her cup on the tray and watched the fire glow. The heat brought a flush to her cheeks.

"Is your husband due to return soon?"

Should she lie to a man of the church or tell him the truth? She didn't know whether Caleb would return to Iowa or not. They had avoided speaking of him at all until now.

"I'm not sure when Caleb will return, Dominie. He has business in the East. He left us well provided for, in any case." She took a sip of coffee. "I meant to tell you I will insist on paying for my grandfather's burial."

"We'll speak of that later."

The sound of the door knocker echoing in the entry hall interrupted his words. The minister excused himself and left Analisa and Kase in the drawing room while he answered the summons. Hushed whispers filled the hallway. Minutes later, Dominie Wierstra reentered the room and stood aside to admit a young woman near Analisa's own age. The woman was a few inches shorter than Analisa and appeared to be very thin despite the thick layers of warm clothing she wore. Her gray wool coat was closely fitted to her figure and edged with fur at collar and cuffs. A pert fur hat sat at a jaunty tilt atop her thick chestnut curls. Her features were small and finely drawn—round sable eyes, a button nose, and full, pouting lips. Analisa did not recall ever having seen the young woman before.

"Analisa Van Meeteren Storm, I would like to introduce you to Sophie Allen. Sophie's husband, Jon, was one of the men who joined in the search for your grandfather. They are new to Pella."

"Mrs. Allen." Analisa acknowledged the young woman, unsure of how she should react to the bright, pleasant smile lighting the young woman's face.

"Mrs. Storm," the woman said, "I will come right to the point. When he returned home today, my husband told me all about you and your son, as well as about your grandfather's death. I must insist that you stay with us while you are in town. We have a large home and more than enough room."

Overwhelmed by the girl's invitation, Analisa's first reaction was one of suspicion. Her feelings must have been apparent, but failed to daunt Sophie Allen. She waved away Analisa's unspoken protest and continued.

"Oh, I know all about your past. As a matter of fact, I grew quite tired of hearing the local biddies discuss your shortcomings when I first arrived here in Pella. I've been dying to meet you so that I could decide for myself just what kind of a woman you are."

"Sophie and Jon were married last summer and moved to Pella from Minnesota," the minister interjected. "He plans to open a lumber business."

"Yes, and I've yet to find a friend my own age. Please say you will stay with us, at least for the night?"

"Well . . . I have my son with me." Analisa's gaze drifted to her son, who was now leaning over the tray of turnovers, trying to decide which one to eat. She watched for Sophie to display the usual reaction at the sight of him. Instead, the young woman sidestepped Analisa and crossed the room to kneel beside Kase.

"Hello." Her voice was bright, beguiling. "I'm Sophie. Who are you?"

The child smiled at her, his eyes alight at having someone to talk to. The adults had been too concerned with Opa's death to pay him much attention this day.

"I'm Kase Van Meeteren. Would you like to eat a turnover? They have some apples inside."

"They do look good." Sophie watched the boy as he took a bite of his second treat.

"Do you live here?" His usual curiosity forged a link between them as he talked with Sophie.

"In this house?"

Kase nodded.

"No. I live down the road. Would you like to see my home?"

"Yes."

"You and your mother are certainly invited." Sophie stood and moved back to where Analisa quietly watched the exchange. "Please believe me, Mrs. Storm; I am sincere. Jon and I would like to have you and your son stay with us for as long as you like. I would appreciate your company."

Wanting to believe in the warmth she saw in the girl's dark eyes, Analisa looked to Julius Wierstra for his advice.

"Would you like to, Analisa?" She noticed the minister used her first name.

Daring to hope that she and this enchanting girl could become friends, Analisa nodded to Sophie and was rewarded with a cry of delight.

Chapter Six

Washington, D.C., December 1870
A whistle shrilled, and as the train began to pull away from the station, Caleb took a last look out of the window at the nation's capital. A dense sleet was falling, but the frozen mass melted when it hit the ground, and was churned to a thick brown slush by the grinding wheels of the street traffic. He was glad to be out of the foul weather and more than glad to be out of the muck and mire of Washington politics. Choosing to sit in a section of vacant seats, Caleb stretched his long legs beneath the seat opposite him. The brim of his hat pulled down over his eyes, he slouched low and rested the back of his head against the padded seat, pretending to sleep. Now that his report had been delivered and his plans laid for a return trip to the West, Caleb planned to spend the last few weeks of his leave visiting his home in Boston.

The months he'd spent in Washington had been filled with

long, tedious meetings and endless social obligations. He recalled the way his freedom had come to an end as soon as he had arrived in the capital, and headed directly to Parker's office to file his report. At least Ely Parker's welcome had been genuine.

"Caleb! I'm relieved to see you've finally returned." Reaching out to pump Caleb's hand, the tall full-blooded Seneca rounded his massive cherrywood desk, which was strewn with files and ink-covered pages. Parker's dark copper-colored skin was deeply creased about the eyes from many years of exposure to the sun. Although only ten years Caleb's senior, he seemed to have aged rapidly in the few months while Caleb was on assignment in the Indian territory.

Ely Parker was the first of his race to be appointed commissioner of the Bureau of Indian Affairs, but except for the fact that he was Indian, he was no different from the many other friends and army companions who had been appointed to office by the newly elected President, Ulysses S. Grant. Determined to achieve the reforms called for by numerous committee findings filed over the previous decades, Grant had placed Ely Parker at the head of the bureau in the hope that he would act swiftly and fairly to end injustices committed against the Indians who were being forced to live on reservations under the unsympathetic control of the military.

"Your father would come back to haunt me if anything had happened to you while you were working for me, Caleb." With an easy motion, Parker directed Caleb toward a pair of deep leather armchairs near the windows. "I was ready to send out a search party."

Caleb smiled. "And just who would you have them search for?" he asked, crooking a skeptical eyebrow at his superior. "A renegade Sioux or a Spanish grandee studying the flora and fauna of the West?"

"You're right there, Caleb. I wasn't sure which identity you had assumed," Parker admitted. "I wasn't even sure where to look for you."

"I cut a pretty wide trail, General. I ended up in Iowa, where I inconveniently caught the measles." Caleb was still for a moment as he pushed the memory of Analisa from his thoughts. "That held me up for a good month."

Caleb shifted in his chair before he continued. "Things are as bad as the commission reports indicated, perhaps even worse. I'm ready to give you the full details, but I'm afraid it will take quite a bit of time."

"Time seems to be a commodity there's no end of here in Washington." Parker tapped the arm of his chair with a long forefinger. "The President wants his peace policy implemented as soon as possible, so that should help things move a little more swiftly. While you were gone, Congress passed a bill forbidding military personnel to hold civil office."

"That means any military men doubling as Indian agents will be ousted." Caleb sat forward in his chair.

"Right. And Grant wants the changes accomplished as soon as possible. He's decided the Indian agency appointments should go to men who've been recommended by religious leaders, and he has the support of the newly appointed Board of Indian Commissioners."

Leaning forward, his forearms on his knees, Caleb stared intently at Parker as he spoke. "General, it may take months or even years to replace all the Indian agents in the territories. Meanwhile, the crooked ones will still be duping the government by misappropriating funds and holding back supplies promised to the Indians on reservations. They're starving already. The ones who are no longer willing to be treated like animals become renegades."

Ely Parker stood and walked to the window, pulling aside the curtain to stare out at the bright sunlight of a late summer day. Always the military man, he kept his spine ramrod straight, his shoulders squared. The September heat was close and still. Noise from the traffic on the street below drifted up into the second-story windows.

"You're the last to return, Caleb. All of the reports have been grim, I'm afraid." Slowly, hands in his pockets, Parker turned toward him, his face lined with worry. "If you've no objections, I'd like to send you back out there after we've met with Grant and you've filed your report. You aren't under any obligations to accept the assignment, of course, and you know I hate to ask you to put your law practice on hold any longer, but very few men have your qualifications and your ability to infiltrate both sides—white and Indian. If you accept, you'll be in a dangerous position, so I won't blame you if you refuse. Things are going to heat up fast, especially when military men are forced to give up their agency appointments. I have a feeling they aren't going to accept the changes very readily and will be looking for ways to circumvent the orders.''

"Meaning they might find civilians they can control and try to put them into the positions the army is in charge of now?"

"Exactly."

Caleb stirred as the northbound train gathered speed. He had listened intently that day, giving needed firsthand information to Parker, noting the sincere worry and frustration of the man as he faced the monumental task of restructuring an unwieldy government agency. Caleb had known, too, when Ely Parker suggested that he return to the West, that he would accept the assignment. He wanted to help end the suffering of his mother's people, and he valued the commissioner's high opinion of him. Parker, an aide to General Grant, had worked his way up to brigadier general by the end of the war. It was his hand that had copied the terms of surrender signed by Lee at Appomattox, after Grant first scratched out the dictates on the pages of his order book.

When the Civil War broke out, Caleb's father had insisted that his son complete his education before he enlisted. Caleb was twenty-one the year Clinton Storm died, and he would wait no longer. The year was 1863. As a soldier in the Army of the United States, Caleb had served under General Parker, admiring the older man's determination to rise above the prejudice he faced because of his Indian blood.

It was Ely Parker who had encouraged Caleb to enter Boston College after the war and earn a law degree, something Parker himself had been denied. When the conflict was over, Caleb resigned from the army and did as Parker suggested. He was admitted to the Massachusetts bar in 1869. When his former general asked him to serve as a secret agent in the Indian territories, working for the cause of his mother's people and, indeed, all Indian peoples, Caleb could do no less than accept the challenge.

The train slowed and pulled to a stop, drawing Caleb's thoughts back to the present. A glance at the frosted window told him the sleet was still falling. Thoughts crowded his mind, and at the forefront of those thoughts was Analisa. She had haunted his waking hours and walked in his dreams. Parker was sending him west again. He could return to Analisa if he chose to.

If he chose to? How could he not? he thought. What man in his right mind could walk away from a woman like her? He crossed his arms over his chest and tucked his hands in his armpits to warm his fingers. The car was cold and drafty, the seat next to him still empty. Slowly the train began to roll forward once again. Within a few moments, Caleb had fallen into a peaceful sleep. He rode out the rest of the journey toward Boston dreaming of Analisa's cornflower-blue eyes.

The back door of the imposing town house swung open noiselessly as Caleb, surefooted and silent, his saddlebag slung over one shoulder, entered the warmth of the kitchen. With a quick look around, he took in the pots and cooking utensils lined up against the brick walls and hanging on hooks from the low ceiling beams. Across the room, near a sturdy chopping block, a plump woman in a white muslin cap and thick wool dressing gown stood with her back to him. A long silver plait hung down her back and swung slightly as she worked. He could not see what she was doing, but was certain she was preparing a midnight snack. She worked with speed and in silence. With gliding steps, he moved up behind her. He slid one arm around her ample waist, drew her against him, and leaned down to whisper in her ear.

"If you aren't careful, I won't be able to get my arms around you, and I know you will miss my amorous attentions." With that he nuzzled the smooth, warm skin near her ear, enjoying the kitchen smells that mingled with the scent of her talcum.

The pipe clenched between her teeth forced her to speak out of the side of her mouth. "Unhand me this minute, you sneaking red-blooded scoundrel!" She raised a long-handled wooden spoon and rapped it sharply against his head and shoulders, hard enough to make him notice without doing any real harm.

Caleb threw back his head and laughed, enjoying the old woman's curses of disgust. "My, but it's good to be home again." He continued to ignore her struggles. "Do you know how much I've missed your cooking, Abbie Oats?"

His question stilled her movements and with a twinkle in her eye she squirmed around to face him and looked at him flirtatiously.

"No. Just how much have you missed my cooking?"

"Enough to travel all the way from Washington in this weather just to have a taste of your—" he stopped long enough to see what it was she was working on, then added—"fresh-baked apple pie."

"Here," she said, handing him the wedge she had already cut. "You can sit for a spell and start on this while I get you a mug of milk. Or would you prefer coffee?"

"Milk would be fine. You always did know how to please a man." He gave her a smacking kiss on the cheek, then he took the plate to the table near the fire. "Is Ruth here?"

"Of course. She'll be surprised and happy to see you, Caleb. You know she worries about you as if you were her own son."

"I know, and I should have written more often, but sometimes it's hard to get a letter off when you are out in the middle of nowhere."

"I'm sure she understands. I'll go call her. She went up to bed not two minutes ago, so I'll probably catch her even before she has time to change."

"Maybe you should wait. I can see her in the morning." His mouth full of pie, Caleb's words were a mere mumble.

"Lose your manners out there? Don't talk with your mouth full."

"Some things never change."

"I'm going up to get Ruth. She'll be mad if I don't let her know you're home. You just finish up and meet her in the hallway."

"Thanks, Abbie," Caleb called out as the stout figure disappeared through the doorway. He looked around the room and thought of the many hours he'd spent here in the warm kitchen with Abigail Oats. She'd been the cook at the Storm house for a good thirty years and was more in charge of the place than its true owners were. Having befriended Caleb when his father brought him to Boston after his mother's death, she was, for a time, his only companion other than his headstrong father. Clinton Storm had been determined, after the death of his Sioux wife, Gentle Rain, that his son would learn to live in the white world, and so he had returned east with Caleb to claim his inheritance, one of Boston's most prosperous shipping companies.

"You're home!"

Ruth Decateur Storm moved quickly down the steep wooden staircase, appearing exactly the way Caleb remembered her. Her violet wool gown was partly hidden by a paisley shawl that blazed in a riot of yellow, gold, black, and green. It had been knotted over one shoulder, carelessly draped across the other, and then forgotten. Thick eyeglasses rode precariously atop her head, the stems thrust into her mass of wildly curling hair, which was only slightly laced with gray and had been tucked and pinned on top of her head with no thought to fashion or sophistication. She was a short woman—the top of her head came to a point just below his collarbone—and yet Caleb felt that she could fill a room with her presence. Exuberant, determined, positive—all of these things Caleb thought of when he thought of Ruth. Blinking her warm hazel eyes, she scanned her stepson quickly from head to toe and back again before she reached up to embrace Caleb in welcome.

Clinton Storm had remarried when Caleb was nineteen. Ruth Decateur, half Clinton Storm's age, had been a wealthy, eccentric spinster of thirty-eight when she had met and fallen in love with the handsome widower. She soon became more than a stepmother to Caleb; she was his friend and as close a confidante as he had ever let anyone become. After Clinton's death, Ruth had remained in the Boston house, always happy to greet Caleb and determined to make him feel the place was still his home. She even saw to it that the maids left the dusting and care of his "savage museum pieces" to her, for his room was a storehouse of Sioux artifacts. Its walls were lined with an assortment of beaded and feathered reminders of his Indian heritage. Powder horns, spoons, and ladles fashioned from buffalo horns, a hide painted with images that told the story of Caleb's ancestry, a quill-decorated breastplate and horse mask, a quiver of painted arrows, and a bow fashioned by Caleb himself—these were but a few of the pieces stored in the room that had been his refuge during the lonely years when he'd walked a thin line between the white world and that of the Indian.

"You look wonderful, Caleb. Your mysterious mission must have agreed with you!" She took in his tall figure, his neatly trimmed hair, and the fine arched eyebrows. Dressed in a well-tailored suit of wool tweed, he looked quite polished and sophisticated, from his starched white shirt collar to the somewhat muddied but obviously new shoes. "Come in now, and tell me all about it."

He looped his saddlebag around the newel post, tucked her arm into the crook of his elbow, and walked her down the long, narrow hallway. They separated to enter the small informal parlor at the end of the hallway. A deep armchair and ottoman stood near the fireplace. Caleb, like his father before him, always chose to sit there, so Ruth moved to sit on the floral-print straight-backed settee.

"I hope you're here to stay for a while, Caleb. It seems so long since you've been home. Are you planning to spend Christmas with me?"

Caleb eased himself into the chair before he answered. "I'm not sure yet, Ruth. I do intend to stay at least a week, but General Parker wants me to go back out west as soon as I can."

"You have an important decision to make in the next few days."

Ruth's comment was a statement of fact, not a question. Caleb wondered again at her uncanny knack for knowing what was in his mind. He didn't want to give her the satisfaction of learning she was right just yet. It was disturbing enough to think she knew what preoccupied him.

"I'm not reading your mind, Caleb, so don't look so concerned." She ignored his startled expression as she made herself comfortable. "Your chart shows you have some strange energy around you. I wouldn't be at all surprised if you didn't have some sort of major decision to make. Why, with Mars in conjunction with your moon, as it was in late August, anything could have happened." She watched him closely as she added, "It might have been a good time for romance. Did you meet anyone interesting last August?"

Caleb wondered how Ruth would react to the news of his sudden marriage to Analisa? And how could he explain the reason for the marriage? If he knew Ruth, and he felt he knew her well, she had already spread his astrological charts over the library floor. He pictured her trying to determine by the position of the stars exactly which day would be right for him to meet the woman who would fulfill his destiny. But Caleb sensed there was more to Ruth's insight than her ability to read the charts. It was as if her hazel eyes could see through him.

He knew that he would eventually seek his stepmother's advice. Not that he'd follow it, he told himself, but he valued her opinion. One thing he knew for certain: He would return to the sunflower house. What would happen after that, even Ruth's stars might not foretell.

"We'll get to all that in due time, Ruth!" Caleb laughed, feeling at ease with himself for the first time in months. It was good to see that his stepmother hadn't changed at all. He still couldn't fathom half of what she rambled on about. Mars in his moon? "How does a thirsty man get something to drink around here?"

"Oh, Caleb! I'm so sorry. I don't know where my manners are. I was so excited to see you that I totally forgot to ask if you've had any supper. I'm sure Mrs. Oats can put together a meal for you if you'd like."

"No, thanks, Ruth. She's already stuffed me with a piece of apple pie, but I would like a brandy and a chance to relax before I tell you all about the last few months."

Ruth moved to a gleaming cherrywood sideboard opposite the fireplace. A crystal decanter of amber brandy surrounded by a collection of mismatched stemmed goblets and snifters rested on a silver tray. She poured a liberal portion into a tulip-shaped snifter and carried it to her stepson.

They sat in silence for a time, content in their reunion and comfortable in the warm atmosphere of the room. Caleb stared into the fire, his thoughts far away.

"You look tired, Caleb."

His attention was drawn to his stepmother. She was amazing. Ruth was close to forty-eight now, but she looked ten years younger. Ruth hadn't aged a day since she'd married his father. He knew it was her zest for life that kept her young.

"You're right, I am tired. Rattling up here on the train was exhausting. I haven't had any real exercise since I returned to the East, and that usually makes me sluggish."

Ruth stood as the clock on the mantelpiece chimed half past one. "It's long past my bedtime, too. We'll have plenty of time to talk tomorrow." She gave Caleb a long, hard stare before she added, "Then you can tell me what's really on your mind." She leaned down to plant a kiss on his shining hair. "I'm so glad you're home for a while, Caleb!" She smiled down at him warmly before she turned away to leave him alone in the quiet room.

"Good night, Ruth," he called after her, and as his gaze returned to the fire he shook his head and smiled to himself. It was comforting to know that some things never changed.

As the wind howled, driving a freezing winter storm down upon the eastern seaboard, Ruth and Caleb sat closeted in Clinton Storm's library. Caleb's law books filled nearly two-thirds of the shelves along one wall; beside the worn classics his father had collected stood Ruth's favorites. The usually tidy desk was littered with sheets of paper covered with circles, each of which had been divided into wedges, like a pie. Jotted on these wheels were Ruth's astrological forecasts for her friends and relations—many of whom were convinced she was quietly going insane. Astrology was a passion she had inherited from her mother, who had learned the skill from a great-grandmother. Ruth loved to tell Caleb her version of her ancestors' life story; she was thrilled to have a Gypsy on her family tree.

Caleb slouched deep in an armchair before the fire, a book of poetry open on his lap but forgotten as he sat lost in thought, watching the flames play around the glowing embers. Had it really been three months since he stared into the dying fire on the open prairie behind Analisa's house?

"Caleb?" Ruth called to him softly from the far side of the room, drawing him back through time. "Where have you gone?" she asked as she watched him shrug off his thoughtful mood.

"I was in Iowa." He smiled at her. Something in his eyes told her he was concerned with matters of the heart.

"Did you finally meet a woman you couldn't manage to escape?"

Closing the book carefully and unfolding his tall form, Caleb stood and stretched his long arms above his head before he turned to answer Ruth. Moving with calm, sure strides, he crossed the room and joined her where she sat on the thick Oriental carpet, her full plaid skirt settled about her in deep folds, her kid-slippered feet tucked beneath her. Caleb sat cross-legged before her.

"Do you think I'm going daft, believing in all of this?"

He smiled. "Not really. The Sioux have always believed that visions and dreams can forecast the future. Why not the stars? You do realize that two hundred years ago you might have been burned on the commons, don't you?"

"Of course, but times haven't changed all that much, Caleb. I try to keep my work a secret, except that all my family and friends know about it, so I guess you could say it's not much of a secret after all. This could get me into a lot of trouble if the wrong people found out about it." She toyed with the cover of the book for a moment before she spoke. "Caleb, I hope you're ready to talk about what's bothering you."

"Are you so sure I really do have something nagging at me?"

"Yes, so don't try to hide it from me. I know you, Caleb, and I know you aren't one to sit and brood unless something is eating at you. You've always been a man of action."

"It's quite a long story."

She looked toward the frosted windows and the gray skies outside. "I'm not going anywhere."

Omitting no detail, Caleb related the story of how he'd come upon the soddie and literally fallen at Analisa's feet. She laughed as he described their first real meeting when he had sat nude on her bed and demanded she bring him his clothes. Kase, Opa, and the Iowa countryside all came alive for Ruth. Clara Heusinkveld and even the minister, Mr. Wierstra, were vividly portrayed as Caleb's Indian inheritance, a natural gift for storytelling, took over.

As Ruth watched Caleb and listened to the tale, she knew without a doubt that his feelings for this young woman ran deep. That was apparent in the words he chose to describe Analisa, as if by creating a vivid image for Ruth, he could bring her memory back to life for himself as well. Frustration and anger clouded his handsome features as he told her of the scene before the minister on the day when he had finally learned the details of Analisa's past. By the time he fell silent and looked to her for advice, and perhaps even approval, Ruth was more than convinced that he was deeply in love with Analisa, even though he had married under such unusual circumstances.

"Does she return your feelings, Caleb?"

His brows knit in thought, casting his clear blue eyes in shadow. He replied honestly, shaking his head. "I don't know. I didn't leave her under the best of circumstances. I've gone over our last few hours together countless times, and I realize I'm seeing this whole affair only from my point of view. I took offense at her letting me go so easily."

Ruth waited in silence for him to explain his last remark.

"She seemed so . . . well, blasé after what to me was such an overwhelming act of love." Caleb's deep color darkened with embarrassment, but he continued talking in the hope that another woman could perhaps explain Analisa's actions. "Analisa said that if I wanted to return to her, that would be fine, and if I decided never to return, that would be just fine, too."

"Would you rather she had begged you not to leave at all?"

"No, of course not."

"You're sure?"

"Yes . . . No . . . Hell, Ruth, I don't know." Frustrated, he glanced away and watched the heavy snow falling outside the window. "Yes. I guess my male pride wanted to hear her say she wouldn't be able to live without me. I think in a way I wanted her to beg me to stay, but at the same time I knew I had to leave. I guess I expected too much."

Ruth gathered her thoughts before she answered his unspoken question. "From all you've told me, I get a picture of a woman who has learned to stand up and face all kinds of hurt and humiliation. I would guess that she expects very little in the way of lasting joy or pleasure. Am I right?"

He shrugged, unable or unwilling to answer until he'd heard more.

"Think, Caleb," Ruth admonished him. "If Analisa had begged you to stay, she would have been letting down her last defense, turning herself into the helpless, dependent creature she's fought so long and hard not to let herself become. She must feel that she and her boy would be a burden to you, or to any man. I'm sure that by letting you go she only meant to release you from that burden, no matter how much pain she must have suffered in doing so."

"Do you think so?" The unguarded, hopeful look in Caleb's eyes pulled Ruth's heart into her throat. She hoped she wasn't wrong about what his Analisa was feeling.

"From all that you've told me, yes, I do think so." She took his hands in her own. "Caleb, a woman who has faced all that she has, and who has fought so hard to keep what she has, isn't going to lower her standards and give herself to the first man who comes along—unless she does love him." Ruth gave his hands a squeeze before reaching up to place one palm on his shoulder. "I'm sure she loves you."

As Caleb sat weighing all she'd just said, Ruth began to stack the books scattered around her on the floor. Then she stood, shaking out her skirt, and extended a hand to Caleb.

"Now," she began, once he stood facing her, "let's get moving." A woman with a mission, Ruth glanced up at Caleb as she moved toward the desk. "When is her birthday?"

"I don't know."

"Never mind, then, but as soon as you get back there, be sure to write and let me know when and where she was born, so that I can get to work on her astrological chart." She turned when he failed to follow her to the door. "Don't just stand there, Caleb. If you hurry, we'll be able to get some decent gifts for that new family of yours, and you will be back in Iowa in time for Christmas!"

Chapter Seven

"I'm going to burst my buttons if I have one more bite!"

Jon Allen flashed a knowing smile first at Analisa and then to Sophie, who chose to ignore his exaggeration. As Analisa watched them exchange smiles, she envied Sophie her happiness with Jon. Although the man was not exceedingly handsome, he was confident and always smiling, and very obviously in love with his charming wife. Analisa wondered if Caleb would ever look at her that way, then pushed the thought to the back of her mind. Caleb was not here and might never return. There was no sense in thinking about things that might not be.

Her attention was drawn to Jon's face again as she watched him tease Kase. The man was tall and slender, almost gangly, with light brown hair that was already thinning in places. His eyes, like those of most of the Dutch, were blue—not as vivid a blue as hers, or even Caleb's, but a lighter blue, as if the coloring was not as strong.

"What of you, Kase?" the man asked. "Are you near to burstin', too?"

Kase shook his head and smiled at his friend. "Not yet. I still have room left inside."

"Would you like some more of that fine goose, then?" Sophie asked, pretending to rise to serve the boy more of the leftover bird.

"No! I mean, no, thank you, ma'am. I am saving room for the *appelflappen*. Can we have it now, Mama?"

The adults all knew that Kase could hardly wait to taste the deep-fried batter-coated apple rings. He'd waited for them all afternoon as the scent of cinnamon permeated the air inside the soddie, tempting them all. Analisa laughed and ruffled his hair before she stood up and collected the dishes.

Sophie joined Analisa, and as the two women began working, Analisa said, "First, Kase, you and Jon must wait until we have cleared the table and made some coffee. Maybe he'll play a tune for us?"

She looked at Jon, knowing he would enjoy entertaining the boy while she and Sophie scraped the plates and cleared the table. Jon nodded his assent before he and Kase moved across the room. The man lifted a case from the bed and, with quiet ceremony, carefully took out a fiddle and a bow. Kase eagerly hopped up on the bed while Jon tuned his instrument.

Analisa watched them for a moment before turning back to join Sophie as she removed the remains of the goose dinner from the table. The young couple had arrived at the soddie early in the day with a fat Christmas goose and all the trimmings, surprising Analisa and her son, infecting them both with their high spirits.

"Sophie, I really don't mind cleaning up. Why don't you join Jon and Kase?" Analisa said.

"Nonsense." Sophie tossed her chestnut curls and continued scraping food into the bucket under the kitchen cabinet. "Two pairs of hands make the work go faster."

Analisa laughed. Her friend seemed to have a proverb handy for every occasion, and as usual, she was right, for the work did go quickly.

"Sophie?" Analisa stopped the other woman as she turned away from the stove. "I want to thank you again for everything. You have done so much for Kase, and for me, too—especially by helping me learn to read English so much better. Your friendship is the greatest gift I could have received this Christmas."

The slight figure in wine-red watered silk did not try to brush aside her words. Instead, Sophie took Analisa's hands in her own and looked up at her friend. "You needn't worry about repaying me, Analisa. I am so happy to have finally found a friend that anything I can do for you in return is little in comparison."

Sophie's gaze traveled across the room to where her husband was entertaining the small dark-haired boy. "Just look at them." She nodded toward the man and boy. "Jon loves children. He's had such fun with Kase." Sophie's eyes took on a wistful look that Analisa knew stemmed from her longing to give Jon the child he desired. So far she had been unable to conceive. Sophie reached out and hugged her friend. "Oh, Analisa, I hope that the coming year brings you the happiness you deserve."

"Thank you, Sophie. And you, too." Hearing the wish and seeing her friend's secret smile, Analisa knew she was referring to Caleb. A few weeks before, feeling the need to explain her hasty marriage, Analisa had told Sophie why she'd entered into a union with a man she barely knew.

"I'm a hopeless romantic," Sophie had told her then, "so I'll wish the best for you. I can't wait to see this dark, mysterious stranger you've married."

Analisa remembered how she'd flamed in embarrassment at Sophie's words, knowing inside that her wish for herself was the same.

"The coffee is nearly ready. Shall we join our men?" Sophie lightened the mood as she nodded toward the two across the room.

"*Ja.*" Analisa smiled and linked arms with her friend as they moved across the hard-packed floor.

Hat pulled low to meet the collar of his coat and shield his neck from the drifting snowflakes, Caleb made his way across the flat, open plain toward the golden squares of light that singled out the soddie in the darkness ahead of him. The light shining from the windows was a beacon drawing him home. Drawing him to Analisa. The last few yards seemed the longest as he rode surrounded by the silence, the only sounds in the chill of the evening the creaking of his leather saddle and the muffled footsteps of his horse. How would Analisa react to his return? He'd written her only one terse note since September, a note that was cold and impersonal. He wouldn't blame her if she turned him away at the door.

Caleb shrugged off the cold and pulled on the reins, guiding Scorpio through the packed powder along the road. What if Analisa didn't love him? What if Ruth was wrong? He remembered his stepmother's enthusiasm as she'd accompanied him on a shopping trip in Boston, choosing items of clothing for Analisa and Kase, caught up in the spirit of Christmas giving and the thought of his new family somewhere in the West. She'd seen him off at the station a week later, boxes and parcels wrapped and tagged for Analisa, Kase, and Edvard, together with his own luggage and instructions from Parker.

He rode Scorpio from Pella, intending to return to the train depot to collect the remainder of his goods once he was certain of his wife's welcome. He was determined to arrive at the soddie while it was still Christmas Eve, and so he had strapped only the lightest of the parcels to the back of his horse.

Caleb took a deep breath of cold air to calm himself as he approached the soddie and nudged Scorpio forward. He couldn't recall ever having felt as nervous as he did just now, watching the distance close between himself and the bleak sod house. He told himself there was no need for the tension building inside him. If he was not welcome, he would simply leave. For a man who'd fought his way out of more than one impossible situation he was acting quite the fool, and knew it.

Caleb turned into the yard and quickly took note of the black carriage standing near the house. All thought of his nervousness fled as he listened to the soft strains of music drifting on the air outside the soddie and remembered the organ standing against the far wall of the room. The strained, slow music was soon joined by the sound of a fiddle, and Caleb found himself wondering with a sharp sense of unease who could be with the

Van Meeterens. He had never imagined a rival for Analisa's affections and now he felt his stomach knot with anxiety as he imagined who might be inside.

With an easy motion that was second nature to him, Caleb dismounted, letting the reins trail to the ground, a signal to the well-trained horse to stand and wait. While the music continued, Caleb untied the parcels from his horse and balanced them precariously on one arm while he piled them one upon the other.

Analisa pumped the organ pedals and played "Sinterklaas Kapoentje," a Dutch Christmas favorite, the only tune she could play with some confidence. Jon tried his best to accompany her on his fiddle. The result was unique, if not memorable, Sophie and Kase exchanging pained looks while the musicians' backs were turned. Kase glanced toward the door when he heard a soft knock, and before Sophie could join him, the boy had crossed the floor and opened the door wide.

"Caleb!"

Before the man took a step into the room, the child wrapped his arms around Caleb's knees, rendering him helpless. His arms filled with gifts, Caleb teetered precariously on the threshold.

"Take it easy, Kase. I'm about to drop your presents!" Caleb was reassured of the boy's affection at once. The problem now was extricating himself from Kase's hold so that he could determine Analisa's response to his arrival.

Aware of Caleb's uncertain foothold in the doorway, Sophie moved to take the packages from his arms. The confusion in the doorway drew the attention of Analisa and Jon, who stopped playing. Jon put his fiddle down and walked to the doorway to greet the visitor, who was obviously no stranger to Kase. Analisa sat in stunned silence, unable to move and join her friends as they ushered her husband into the tiny room.

Sophie stepped aside and set the packages on the table as her husband greeted Caleb and welcomed him into the house. His hands free of the bulky parcels, Caleb bent and scooped Kase up into his embrace. After a quick, intense hug, Caleb held him at arm's length, studied his healthy complexion, and hugged him again before setting him down. His eyes skimmed the room, ignoring Jon and Sophie for a moment as he sought out and soon found Analisa. She was lovelier than he remembered, her hair a halo of golden braids wrapped about her head, her eyes shining a silent welcome across the room. In a heartbeat he noted the plaid wool dress she wore as well as the bright flush of her cheeks against the pale ivory of her skin. She seemed unwilling or unable to cross the room to meet him, and he wanted nothing more at that moment than to take her into his arms, but he was all too aware of the couple in the doorway and the boy tugging at his coat sleeve.

"Caleb! Caleb!" The child's voice brought his attention back to the trio surrounding him. "Caleb, we have some friends now. This is Jon and Sophie . . . and Jon made me some ice skaters and I learned how to do it. He's gonna make me a fiddle, too, when I grow bigger."

Caleb studied the other man, a tall slender blond, taller than he, who pumped his hand with a vigorous shake of welcome. The man looked well dressed and prosperous, the cut of his suit and quality of the materials attesting to his wealth, as did the expensive rig outside. His thin brown hair had been carefully parted and slicked down for the occasion. Caleb tried to smile, but failed in the attempt. He longed to grab the man by his collar and shake him.

"Happy Christmas, and welcome, Mr. Storm. Allow me to introduce myself properly. I'm Sophie Allen, and this"—she grabbed Jon's elbow and drew him near—"is my husband, Jon Allen. We've just finished quite a wonderful Christmas dinner, but there is plenty left over. We'll be happy to fix something for you. I'm sure you want to come in and rest after your journey."

A genuine smile lit Caleb's eyes as he listened to Sophie Allen's introduction. He could tell by the relieved look on her face that she had read his feelings perfectly, and he felt himself blush at the thought of his loss of control where Analisa was concerned. He took a liking to this petite Sophie at once and knew, too, that he would have to guard his thoughts around her, as her intuition about his feelings seemed to be as sharp as Ruth's. Caleb noted that, like her husband, Sophie was dressed in the latest style. He'd become all too knowledgeable about fashion during his week of shopping with Ruth. The simple but elegant pearls the young woman wore bespoke wealth. He was

anxious to hear just how the couple had become acquainted
with Analisa, but it seemed that in the hubbub created by his
entrance, he would be forced to wait a while to find out.

As they moved into the room, Caleb shrugged out of his long
wool coat and hat and handed them to Jon, who hung them on
the pegs near the door. Sophie crossed the room to join Analisa,
who had finally managed to rise on shaking limbs. Analisa
stood with one hand against the organ for support as she
watched Caleb cross the room with Kase in tow. She knew she
had to move, to speak, to say something in greeting, lest he
think she was not happy to see him, and yet she had no strength;
her will to act seemed to have vanished at the sight of him
standing in the doorway. The space between them narrowed to a
few feet and then to inches before Analisa could make any
response to him at all. She felt Sophie touch her shoulder, but
was unable to take her eyes off of Caleb.

"Analisa, Jon and I will fix a plate for Caleb while you say
hello," Sophie prompted.

Analisa was afraid she would be forced to stand dumb-
founded forever. She knew her friends were fast becoming
aware that she'd kept the intensity of her feelings for Caleb
deeply hidden . . . but what good did her attempts at secrecy
amount to now as she stood openly gaping at him?

"We have to think about leaving, too, as it is getting quite
late."

Sophie's words suddenly registered in Analisa's mind.
Would they truly leave her alone with this dark, silent man who
was once again a stranger to her?

"No!" Analisa turned to Sophie, her eyes pleading as she
tried to soften her reaction to her friend's announcement. "No,
please, Sophie. It's still early, and we've not yet served the
dessert." Analisa looked back at Caleb once more, shaken out
of her state of shock. She smiled in greeting. A slow, warm
smile. She was unsure of herself and of his reaction to her as
well. What was he doing here? Did he intend to stay this time?
Analisa knew it was best her friends stay until she felt able to
deal with his sudden appearance. Suddenly she did feel like
celebrating. For the first time she spoke directly to Caleb,
avoiding any greeting at all, but slipping into her own safe,
familiar role.

"We have a special Christmas treat, Caleb, *appelflappen*,

which I'm sure you'll like, and you must get acquainted with Jon and Sophie, our new friends.''

The stiff formality of her words frightened him for a moment. He could see the tension in her determined stance and fought the urge to reach out and pull her to him. Caleb knew that for a while he would have to be content to go along with her need to become familiar with him once again, and hoped that she had not surrounded her heart with the barriers he'd broken through once before. In that moment he knew that he had been right to come back to her, whether she loved him or not. Seeing her standing there, so alone and yet willing to face being alone for his sake, Caleb knew that his heart belonged to this tall, striking woman, and had since he'd first laid eyes on her. It had taken time and Ruth's perception to make him aware of his love.

Analisa tried to read the emotion she saw in Caleb's eyes as she stared into them across the space that still separated her from him. He could hardly pull her into his arms in front of the others, and yet that was what she secretly wished he would do. All around them, confusion reigned. Sophie stood near the stove, lifting pan lids and banging them down again in her haste and excitement as she prepared a plate for Caleb. Kase had joined Jon and Sophie near the table where he eyed the packages and scanned the snow-dampened paper tags in search of the one word he had learned to read—his own name.

"K-a-s-e. Kase! This one is for me, *ja*, Caleb?"

The boy's enthusiastic shout drew Caleb and Analisa back to reality. Caleb turned away from her with a smile that promised much, and walked to the table where the little boy waited anxiously for permission to open his present. Analisa watched him go, admiring his slow, confident grace as he crossed the room. His movements were all so familiar to her, and yet it was only now, seeing him walk, that she realized just how much she had missed him. Afraid that she would wake to find this just another one of her dreams, Analisa joined the boisterous couple near the stove. She poured coffee for the adults and mixed a cup of milk with the warm, dark brew for Kase. The *appelflappen* he'd waited for was finally placed on the table amid the confusion of Caleb's dinner, the coffee cups, and all of the packages as well.

Caleb lifted the gift with the boy's name spelled out in carefully printed letters. "This one does have your name on it,

Kase. How about that? I didn't realize I had a package this big for you.'' Caleb handed the gift to the boy, then sat down at his place near the end of the table.

Kase smiled and would not allow himself to be teased. ''Don't you remember that when you left you said you would bring me a present?''

The talk around the table became hushed as Caleb met Analisa's eyes for a brief second, each remembering the circumstances of his leaving. Caleb covered the awkward moment easily as he continued talking to Kase. ''That's right. And I knew a tough *hombre* like you would hold me to my promise.''

''Kase,'' Analisa interrupted, ''you should have good manners and wait until Caleb is finished eating before you open the gift.''

''On Christmas Eve?'' Caleb crooked an eyebrow at her. ''That's what the evening's for, isn't it? I would say we could dispense with manners for one night.'' He cut into the tender slice of goose on his plate, his appetite growing with every bite, now that his initial nervousness had fled. He was back, Analisa was beside him, and Caleb felt he had all the time in the world to relish the complete feeling that washed over him each time he looked at her.

''We don't celebrate Christmas Eve with gifts, Caleb; it's a holy night,'' Jon explained. ''Gifts are exchanged on Sinterklaasdag, December fifth. That's when Sinterklaas flies over the houses on his white horse and brings gifts for the children, who leave hay in their *klompen* for his animal.''

''*Ja*,'' Kase added with enthusiasm, his eyes shining bright with the memory of the treats he'd received. ''I left my shoes outside the door, and Sinterklaas left me some candies inside. Jon made me some skates, too, for Sinterklaasdag, but they were from him, not from Sinterklaas.''

''Well, these are from me, and a good friend of mine whom I will tell you about later. Why don't you open yours now while I finish this delicious meal?'' Caleb nodded his appreciation to Sophie, who beamed at his recognition.

''Analisa cooked most of the meal, Caleb. Jon and I just brought out the goose early in the day and sort of invited ourselves to dinner.'' As Caleb continued to eat, Sophie explained further how she and Jon had moved to Pella and were without family in the area. "So, you see, even though Jon's family is Dutch, they all live in Minnesota. I am a Canadian, and a Catholic, so you might say I haven't too many friends here yet."

Analisa turned to her friend. Before she spoke she realized her shyness in front of Caleb was ebbing slowly. Still, she could think of nothing to say to him directly. "You'll have plenty of friends, Sophie, as soon as Jon's business is opened and everyone gets a chance to meet you."

Kase had soon unwrapped his parcel and tossed the brown paper and string to the floor. Impatiently, he lifted the lid off the box and gazed at the small newspaper-wrapped bundles inside. Removing one, he unrolled the paper covering and soon held a tin soldier in his hands. The figure was perfect, painted carefully to represent a United States Army officer. He stood the toy soldier on the table and continued to unwrap each figure in turn, exclaiming over the uniforms as he stood them one by one on the table. Jon was nearly as excited as the boy and examined each figure as it appeared. Caleb explained the rank and duties of the soldiers as Kase lined them up. Analisa listened in amazement and realized that Caleb must have served in the army at one time. She wondered if he'd been in Indian campaigns like the ones that plagued the army now. Had he fought against his own mother's people, then?

Caleb soon cleaned his plate as he alternately watched the boy unwrap the soldiers and took bites of food. In no time at all, the goose, creamed potatoes, beans, and honeyed bread disappeared. Analisa moved his plate to the sideboard and replaced it with a dessert dish. As she refilled his coffee cup, Caleb suddenly looked around the room as if seeking a missing detail. His eyes met Analisa's as she sat back down on the bench across from him.

"Where is Edvard?"

He asked the question quietly, his voice nearly a whisper, but Sophie caught his words. She drew Kase's attention from Caleb and his mother, giving Analisa a chance to explain.

Caleb knew immediately by the sadness that filled Analisa's eyes that Edvard was dead. He wished he had waited to ask.

Leaning forward, her arms folded against her rib cage, her voice soft yet steady, she told him of her grandfather's disappearance during the snowstorm. Quickly, with as little detail as possible, Analisa explained how the minister had brought the volunteers, Jon among them, to search for Opa, and how Sophie and Jon had taken Kase and her in as guests until the burial was over. She didn't tell him that the four of them had been the only ones to attend the old man's funeral, nor did she tell him of the way the townsfolk chose to ignore her loss.

"Caleb?"

He had failed to hear Kase call his name the first time, but now turned to the boy.

"May I open another gift?"

"Only if your name is on it. I want your mother to open the one I brought for her, too."

"I found another one with my name," Kase explained, then added, "a big one!"

"Then go right ahead." Caleb turned to Jon, who was seated next to Analisa. "Jon, why don't you pass Analisa that big box?"

Suddenly, unbidden color stained Analisa's cheeks as Sophie, Jon, and Caleb watched her take the large gift. Slowly, trying to calm her shaking fingers, she untied the twine and began to pull off the thick brown wrapping.

Kase was exclaiming over his gift, a suit cut to his size with long wool trousers, a finely tailored jacket of matching tweed, and a round-collared white shirt. A pair of black suspenders was tucked into the box as well. In his eagerness to try on the new clothes, he jumped up from the bench and carried the box to his mother's bed and began to unbutton his cotton flannel shirt and tug it off.

"Don't look until I am ready," he called over his shoulder, giving the adults the opportunity to study Analisa's package once again.

She lifted the lid and then the thin paper inside to reveal the gift. As Caleb took a sip of warm coffee, Analisa stared at the contents of the box while Sophie leaned over the table to get a closer look.

"Oh, Anja!" Her friend spoke with a swift intake of breath. "It's beautiful."

Analisa slowly pulled the delicate rose-color dress from the box, relishing the feel of the soft, expensive wool. The dress was cut in the latest style, much like the ones she'd made for the women of Pella. Her eyes deftly took in the tucks and stitches and knew that this dress had cost no little amount. It was cut for a bustle in the back and fell into a sweeping ruffle across the front near the knees. Tucked inside the box was a pair of the finest kid gloves, dyed a matching shade of rose. Analisa recalled with a sharp twinge of feeling that the dress she'd worn on the day Caleb left was the simple cotton of the same shade, the plain dress she called her best.

"Analisa, stand up and hold it up to you. Let us see," Sophie pleaded. "That color will be lovely on you. Caleb, it is perfect. You have to teach Jon how to shop . . . and soon!"

Caleb laughed, his eyes glowing appreciatively as Analisa stood up and held the dress before her. He could see that she was embarrassed by all the attention, and so smiled encouragement to her. She sat down quickly, carefully folding the dress back into the box. He pointed to another package, which Sophie was quick to push toward him. "This," he said in a tone that would brook no argument, "is to open later. But this one is to open now." He pulled the last box toward Analisa.

"Caleb, I don't know what to say." She shook her head.

"Say, 'Merry Christmas,' and open the gift."

Analisa made swift work of opening the present. Inside a deep nest of straw was a fat china teapot hand painted with a bouquet of violets in shades that varied from the deepest purple to the palest lavender. She found the small lid wrapped in paper and tucked into the package beside the teapot.

Smiling up at Caleb, she let her fingertips play over the painted surface of the porcelain teapot. "It's too beautiful to use."

"I had a feeling you would say something like that. I want to drink tea made in it tomorrow." He laughed, knowing how thrifty she was and how she used only serviceable goods for herself.

Tomorrow. The word rang in Analisa's mind. *Tomorrow.* He planned to be here tomorrow . . . but what of tonight? Suddenly, the room seemed to close in on her, and she sat in silence, a smile frozen on her lips, her mind racing miles away from the activity around her. Kase was parading in his new clothes. He looked quite the gentleman, a smaller version of Caleb, who also wore a fine wool suit.

"Play us a tune, Jon," Analisa heard Sophie say, and watched while Jon and Caleb stood to admire her son in his new outfit. Caleb knelt down on one knee and adjusted the boy's suspenders, as if he'd been taking care of children for years. Both men made quite a fuss over Kase and his new finery until Sophie asked the little boy for a dance.

All at once the noise and movement in the small, warm room were too much for Analisa. Caleb, standing with her new friends, was a sight she'd thought never to see, no matter what her heart might have wished. Happiness was an illusion she was afraid to indulge in. Why had he come back? Could she possibly hope that time had healed the rift between them? Would he be able to stay with them now and leave the mystery of his life behind? The questions crowded in on her like the suffocating air in the room. Analisa knew she had to slip away and be alone. After so many years of facing her problems on her own and living in the quiet soddie with only Kase and Edvard, she found the merriment of the evening, coupled with Caleb's return, unnerving. Quickly reaching for the coal bucket she used for carrying in dried cow chips for the fire, Analisa stood up and slipped from the room unnoticed, welcoming the solitude of the darkness outside.

Chapter Eight

The cold night air was a shock against her skin, yet it brought Analisa welcome relief from both the warmth of the soddie and the suffocating intensity of her own thoughts. She left the house without a wrap of any kind, knowing the trip outdoors would have to be short, but she welcomed the few moments to herself. She needed time to think about Caleb's sudden appearance and what it meant.

She noticed Caleb still rode the huge black horse, but she spared Scorpio only a glance as she turned to make her way around the house. She would share the warmth of the animals in the cow shed and extend her time alone a while longer. Analisa stopped just outside the lean-to in order to fill the bucket with cow chips for the fire, hoping to use the task to cover her sudden departure. She heard the muffled sound of the fiddle music through the thick sod wall and knew that Jon still entertained the others. With a glance around the darkened yard, Analisa stepped inside the shed where Honey and Tulip-the-Ox stood, ever patient as they awaited the morning, when they would be turned loose outside to wander the hard-packed yard. In the far corner, Jon Allen's well-bred carriage horse nickered softly.

Absentmindedly petting the cow's smooth nose, she stared out through the open doorway at the scattering of stars in the dark sky. Slowly drifting clouds passed by, reminding her of wisps of smoke on a silent journey across the otherwise clear sky. The slow sprinkling of snow had stopped, leaving the air crisp and clear. Analisa sighed as she looked out on the peaceful scene, trying to regain control of her pent-up emotions.

She knew she needed to sort out her own feelings rather than question Caleb's return. Analisa would never forget the intense pounding of her heart that had begun the moment she saw him standing in the doorway. He had not changed since September; if anything, he had grown more handsome. His raven hair was neatly trimmed, the uncontrollable waves above his forehead and at the nape of his neck still refusing to be tamed. His skin had retained its warm hue even though his dark tan, like Kase's, had faded during the winter months. His clear blue eyes seemed to look through her to the very core of her soul. Caleb's clothes were a silent complement to his strong, well-muscled body and did little to hide his easy movements and natural grace.

Analisa wondered about his clothes and the expensive gifts he'd brought them. When she saw the quality of the dress and the care he had obviously taken to choose it for her, she was assailed by questions, realizing again how little she knew of him. Where did his money come from? Her mind still held a picture of the man who had ridden into the yard last summer, a man carrying few possessions, unwilling to tell her where he was from or where he was going. He had assured her he was not doing anything against the law, and she had chosen to believe him, listening with her heart rather than her common sense. Would she care, even now, if she found out that he had lied back then? She tried to convince herself she would have to turn him out if she learned he was an outlaw, but even as she thought those words, Analisa felt her heart trip as she remembered the touch of his hands and the feel of his kiss on her lips.

Reason fought with her emotions, and as she began to feel the chill of the evening, Analisa knew that she must face Caleb with her doubts and questions before she could resume their tenuous relationship. She was determined to do so before the evening was over, but whether or not she could send him away was another matter.

The frosty air began to seep beneath her skin, chilling her to the bone. Analisa rubbed her hands together and blew on them for warmth, then picked up the bucket of chips and returned to the house.

When Caleb straightened from where he'd knelt on the earthen floor after adjusting Kase's suspenders and rolling up the new trousers, he noticed that Analisa's place at the table was empty. His first inclination was to go to her, but instead he decided to give her a few moments alone. Kase was trying to guide Sophie around the room by making up the steps to a dance while Jon set the pace on his fiddle. The three of them seemed content to amuse themselves, and so Caleb paced to the window above the kitchen sideboard and tried to look out into the blackness beyond. Condensation on the windowpane prevented him from seeing outdoors. He glanced once more at Sophie, Jon, and Kase, then quietly opened the door and slipped outside. He knew the time had come for them to face each other alone.

Lifting Scorpio's reins, he led the horse around the Allens' rig toward the shed behind the house. There was no sense in leaving the animal out in the cold any longer, now that Caleb knew he intended to stay the night. He hoped that he would not have a problem convincing Analisa, for he had no inkling as to her feelings. She had looked shocked and disbelieving rather than pleased when he'd arrived, but he knew he could not really blame her for her startled reaction to his sudden appearance. Caleb took a deep breath as he rounded the corner to the shed, determined to let her know that he could be as stubborn as she if he chose.

Analisa nearly collided with him in the shadowy darkness as Caleb led Scorpio into the shelter. She stepped back inside, unsure of what to say, shivering with cold and anticipation while she watched him unbuckle the saddle and slide it off the big mount. Caleb seemed to ignore her as he set the saddle against the far wall and slipped off the bit and bridle. With a slap on the horse's rump, Caleb turned to face Analisa while Scorpio ambled past the other animals toward the feed bin.

"You're getting a little low on feed. I'll get some when I go into town to pick up my baggage." He stepped closer in order to see her expression in the soft glow from the window.

"You are staying?" She spoke through chattering teeth as she tried to still her shivering.

Caleb stood silent for a moment, debating his next move. She had not protested his comment, but simply asked if he was staying. Would she leave the choice up to him?

"Come here. You must be freezing to death without your coat." Caleb stepped up next to her when she refused to move toward him, opened the front of his wool jacket and enfolded her inside.

Drawn by the warmth he offered, she slipped her arms around him underneath the heavy jacket and felt the heat of his back through the fabric of his shirt. She longed to rest her cheek against the strong, even beat of his heart, but resisted, determined to put emotion aside and ask him the questions that were tugging at the corners of her mind. Analisa tilted her head back and loosened her hold on him, trying to see his eyes in the dim light.

"Why did you come back?" She was afraid she would miss his answer as she listened to her own heart thundering in her ears.

"I had to." He bent and kissed the tip of her nose, her forehead, her temple, with just a teasingly light touch of his lips.

"You had to?"

"Yes. I would find myself thinking of you at the oddest times. Once I was in a roomful of people." He looked over her head as if he recalled every detail as he spoke. "It was a ball, as a matter of fact. I was surrounded by ladies and gentlemen in fine gowns and suits—silks, satins, jewels—and suddenly, there you were. I saw you as I'd seen you so many times. You know, the way your hair falls out of the pins and slides down your neck." He touched her throat with his lips before he continued the hushed words. "You had on your apron and the faded blue dress you always wear when you're working. You seemed so real, I nearly spoke to you, until I realized you weren't there at all." He stopped kissing her and held her close, his cheek pressed against hers as he rocked her gently from side to side. "You might say I came back because I was haunted by you. Do you know what that means?"

She nodded. "You were at a ball . . . a dance?"

"Yes. Many. But no one I met compared to you."

Analisa pulled away again, intending to look into his eyes, but her gaze was drawn to his full lips. She cleared her throat, suddenly finding the words lodged there. "Where did you get the money for all of those gifts?"

"The bank."

"You robbed a bank?"

Caleb laughed as he rubbed her shoulderblades with his open palms. He pressed his hands against the small of her back, forcing her against his length. "No, I didn't rob a bank. Must you always make me out to be an outlaw, Analisa? You seem to doubt my ability to earn a living."

"You have told me nothing of yourself, Caleb. You left me with one hundred dollars in gold, with no explanation and no word all these months . . ."

"Didn't you get my letter?"

"Oh, yes . . . I have it committed to memory: 'Analisa. Hope that you, Kase, and Edvard are well. If you need anything, you can reach me through Ruth Storm in Boston, Massachusetts. Caleb.'"

Thankful for the darkness, Caleb felt himself color as she recited the terse words of his note. It had been cooler than he remembered, and the only communication she'd received from him in three months. She had every right to toss him out.

"I have many more questions, Caleb." Analisa no longer felt the cold, pressed as tight as she was to his body and warmed by the anger she aimed at herself as she let him take over her senses so easily.

"Ask away." He moved with her, gently pushing her farther back into the shed until she was pinned between his warm body and the sod wall of the house. His lips were playing with her ear, and he felt a tremor run through her as his teeth gently pulled against its soft lobe.

"Who is Ruth Storm?" Analisa's words were fading into a whisper as he toyed with her ear.

"My stepmother."

"How do you work, to put this money in the bank?" She was

beginning not to care what his answers were as his hands drew her nearer and played along her waist.

"Sometimes," he said between kisses as he teased her lips with his own, "I am a lawyer . . . and I live off an inheritance . . . and I also work for the government of the United States . . ." Caleb tried to continue but drew back for a moment to look into her eyes. "Do you really have to know all of this right now?"

Pressed against the sod wall, Analisa could feel the rough earth and buffalo grass scratching through the material of her dress. Enfolded inside Caleb's coat and his tight embrace, she could think of little except the man who held her and the way her body responded to his touch. She had dreamed of him for so long, remembered their lovemaking so often, that now she was almost afraid to believe he'd become a reality, and yet she needed to experience the fullness and satisfaction she knew he could give her. She stared up into his eyes and asked the only question she truly wanted answered.

"Why did you come back?"

"I had to have you again."

Caleb's words were lost in a whisper against her lips as he pressed his mouth to hers in a searing, demanding kiss. Unable to restrain her need for him, Analisa let her arms move to encircle Caleb's neck and pulled him closer. Her hands played in the waves of his hair at the nape of his neck, her fingertips delighted by the satin thickness of the soft curls. She felt his hands at her waist, on her breasts, and finally caressing her lower back and hips as he drew her against him. She became aware of the rigidity of his arousal pressing against her. Analisa was driven to seek the feel of his smooth skin against her own. She pulled at his shirt and heard Caleb's low throaty laugh of delight as she worked the shirttail free of his waistband. Ignoring the sound, she slipped the palms of her hands under the shirt and pressed them flat against his smooth skin, skin that was hot to her touch.

The fiddle music slowed to a waltz, the notes drifting on the night air around them. Vaguely, Analisa could hear her mind telling her that it was rude to leave her guests, rude to let them wonder what she was doing alone with Caleb, but she could not seem to control her driving need for him. She felt his hands reach for the crown of braids wrapped around her head, and as his fingers began searching for the pins that bound the plaits, she pulled her lips away from his.

"Caleb, no . . . They will know, then, if you take down my hair."

"They probably know now." Aware that Analisa would be embarrassed to face her friends with her golden hair spilling past her shoulders in disarray, he lowered his hands and began to draw her skirt up along her thighs. When his palm came in contact with her cotton pantalets, Caleb tugged at the waistband and sought the drawstring tie.

"Don't wear these while I'm home," he mumbled against her lips.

"No. I won't."

Finally, Caleb felt the offending undergarment fall free and bent to draw it off of Analisa's legs. He ignored the rending tear he heard as he impatiently tugged the garment over her shoe and stuffed it into his coat pocket. While he worked to remove her drawers, Analisa's fingers had nimbly unbuttoned the front of Caleb's woolen trousers and pushed them low on his hips. She was rewarded with the feel of him as he thrust against her.

"I can't wait to have you, lady. I'm sorry."

With the words barely spoken, Caleb lifted Analisa against the wall and pressed upward, lowering her suddenly, sheathing himself within the warm depths of her body. He covered her mouth with his own as she began to moan and cry out, clutching him nearer, drawing him even farther into herself. He had been afraid of hurting her in his haste, and so was greatly pleased to find her as ready as he. Holding himself still within her, Caleb stood rigid, pressing Analisa against the rough wall, knowing full well that any slight movement on her part would bring him to fulfillment.

Time stopped for Analisa when Caleb drew her onto himself. Forgotten were the freezing cold of the night and the restless animals moving next to them. She was only slightly aware that Jon's fiddle continued to play, the music adding a strange, haunting quality to the scene. It seemed that in this one suspended moment, she could feel the earth turning beneath her as it moved through the heavens. As her body pulsed with the rhythm of life, she sought to draw Caleb into herself, to lose herself in him and him in her. Unable to hold back the desperate need within, Analisa wrapped her legs around Caleb's hips and surrendered to the throbbing force.

Through a haze of sensation, she heard him call her name as he thrust deep into her once, twice, three times, and then held her wrapped in his embrace as he poured his love into her. His breath was searing hot against her ear, their ragged gasps for air echoing in the stillness of the tiny shed. Slowly, as their breathing returned to normal and the pulsing sensations died away, Caleb hugged Analisa to him once more and gently slid away from her. She wanted to cry out at the feeling of loss she experienced as he left her body, but instead opened her eyes and was satisfied to know he was really there.

Caleb ran a shaking hand through his hair and pulled Analisa's undergarment out of his pocket. She could tell he was smiling by the tone of his voice and could see a hint of his wide smile reflected in the glow from the window. He leaned forward and planted a swift kiss on her lips.

"Your drawers, my lady." With a formal bow he presented her with the pantalets. "Would you like me to wait for you, or do you think we should go back inside separately?"

Analisa stared up at him wide-eyed, unsure of how to answer. What she craved most was to wash, put on a clean nightgown and crawl between the sheets . . . with Caleb. Reality told her that her dream was impossible, that she had to return to face her new friends, her son, and a pile of dirty dishes. For an instant she wanted to wish them all away, but only for an instant. Hesitantly, she returned Caleb's quick kiss and turned him away from her. He seemed to understand her need for privacy and walked out of the shed to stand just beyond her vision, fastening his own trousers as he went.

While Analisa readjusted her clothing, Caleb leaned back against the outer wall of the shed and looked up at the winter sky. A wide, satisfied smile lit his face as he stood with his hands deep in his pockets. Of all the homecomings he could have imagined, none could have been as much of a surprise or delight as the one he'd just received. "Thanks for the advice, Ruth," he whispered as he looked up at the stars and, still smiling, turned as he sensed Analisa's presence near him. He reached out to take her elbow and escort his lady back into the soddie.

During the brief walk, Caleb and Analisa decided not to offer any excuse for their absence, and upon entering, they were met by Sophie and Jon, who had obviously decided not to ask. Kase was lost in concentration as he lined the tin soldiers up on the table. Sophie bustled from the dishpan to the stove while Jon, his fiddle stowed in its case, sat at the table and lit his pipe.

"Caleb," Jon called out, a smile lighting his face. "Come and join me for a Christmas toast while the women finish up the dishes." He pulled a flat silver flask from his hip pocket and poured a hearty draft of whiskey into his coffee cup.

Caleb looked to Analisa, who was tying an apron over her plaid wool dress and, at her slight nod of encouragement, seated himself on the bench beside Jon. The two men began to talk of business ventures while Sophie and Analisa made quick work of the dishes and pans.

"Anja, listen," Sophie said softly while the men talked amiably. "Jon and I want to take Kase home with us tonight, if you would agree. We haven't mentioned it to him yet, because I wanted to see if you had any objections."

Analisa began to protest, but Sophie hurried on. "We would love to have him stay with us. Besides, it would give you and Caleb time to work things out. What do you think?"

"Oh, Sophie . . . I don't know . . ." Analisa shook her head, a worried expression darkening her radiant glow. "Kase has never been away from me, not even for a night, since the day he was born."

"You know we will care for him as if he were our own. It's only for a night or two. Whatever you decide."

Glancing over her shoulder at Kase playing quietly by himself and then toward Caleb, who sent her a secret smile that warmed her to her toes, Analisa turned back to Sophie with her answer.

"You can ask Kase. If he wants to go, he has my permission. I think you are right, Sophie. This first night with Caleb back will be quite awkward with the three of us here, but Kase may want to be with Caleb, too."

Sophie called the boy to her side. "Kase, would you like to come back to town with Jon and me and stay with us for Christmas Day and night?"

Looking at his mother with excitement shining in his eyes, Kase nodded enthusiastically. *"Ja,* Mama? I can go with Sophie?"

"If you'd like to, Kase. You will have to get your nightshirt and change into your other clothes. Find a brush for your hair, too."

"Can I take my soldiers?"

"Yes." Analisa nodded, watching Caleb's reaction to the news of the boy's sudden departure. Lifting his coffee, he met her eyes over the rim of the cup and sent her another secret smile.

"Bring your skates, too, Kase, and we will try the pond near the edge of town," Jon added as he went outside to hitch his horse to the rig.

Finally, they were ready to go, Jon and Sophie standing just inside the doorway, wrapped in their heavy coats, Kase bundled between them. Analisa bent to kiss her son good-bye.

The boy noticed her worried look and suddenly turned to Caleb. "Caleb, are you going to be here while I'm gone?"

His gaze steady, the man answered, "Yes. And when you get back, too."

"Good, because I couldn't leave Mama here all by herself if you were not going to stay with her."

The adults laughed to cover their embarrassment, and Caleb knelt to say his own farewell to Kase. They spoke quietly, heads together as they talked while Caleb pulled the collar of Kase's thick coat up around his neck.

"You have a good time with the Allens and don't worry about your mother, all right?"

"All right, Caleb. Don't feel bad. We will play with the new soldiers when I get back."

"Good. I'll ride into town to pick you up day after tomorrow, so you be ready, you hear?" Standing once more, Caleb slipped an arm around Analisa's shoulders and watched the boy walk out of the house with Sophie and climb into the rig. Wrapped in lap robes and bundled to their noses, Sophie and Kase huddled near Jon as he turned the horse and buggy and headed out the gate. Sleighbells added a magical sound to the special night. Caleb and Analisa watched them until the carriage was swallowed up by the darkness.

Closing the door, Caleb drew the latch into place, then turned and noticed the tears shimmering in Analisa's eyes. He drew her into his arms and heard her sigh.

"What is it?" He kissed her brow.

"He's never been away from me before . . ."

Caleb heard her breath catch in her throat, lifted her chin with his forefinger, and watched as the tears brimmed over and slid down her cheeks.

"I'll try to take your mind off of him," Caleb told her as he lowered his lips to hers and began to replace her thoughts of Kase with new sensations.

Sunlight streaked through the windowpanes, melting the tiny frost crystals that had formed on them during the hours of darkness. The beams of light spread across the high bed beside the window, jumped its shadow, and streaked across the floor, dispersing the chill that had crept into the room the night before.

Lying still beneath the warm down coverlet, Analisa watched dust motes play in the sunbeams. She'd grown used to the constant settling and shifting of dust from the earthen ceiling of the sod house. Quiet moments passed before she turned her thoughts away from the dancing specks to the man sleeping beside her, his long form stretched out full length on her bed.

The thick comforter hid all of him except his nose, eyes, and blue-black hair as he slept, unaware of her scrutiny. He was nude beneath the covers. Analisa was tempted to run her hand along his side, to feel the firm muscles bunched beneath the smooth skin of his hips and powerful thighs, but she chose to let him sleep on.

The day and two nights since Caleb's return had passed all too quickly as they had used the precious moments to grow acquainted with their new love in the quiet solitude. Analisa smiled to herself as she remembered the way they had hurried through the daily chores, feeding the animals, stoking the stove, barely taking time to eat. Like children, they had created a private world of their own, free from intrusion and filled with laughter. Analisa sought to etch the precious memories on her mind as she lay quietly watching Caleb sleep.

She recalled the way he'd asked about her family, wanting to gain some knowledge of her people. She had climbed from the bed and rummaged through her trunk to retrieve a photograph of the Van Meeterens. Without looking at it herself, she'd handed it to Caleb.

He held it quietly for a time, seemingly aware of her inner

struggle as she steeled herself to look at the photograph. When Analisa felt his arm slip around her shoulders and draw her near, she took her strength from his and reached for the pictures. Memories came flooding back.

The picture had been taken in New York. Photographers had waited at the docks to entice the boatloads of immigrants to purchase mementos of their arrival in the New World. Her father, Emmett Van Meeteren, so proud of his decision to move to a new land of wealth and promise, had chosen to part with a portion of their stake in the future and so lined his family up for the portrait.

Analisa had tried to view the picture as Caleb might. The Van Meeterens stood proud and ramrod straight, adults and older children arranged behind the two youngsters. Jan, Analisa's nineteen-year-old brother, stood on the far left next to Mama, then Edvard, standing between Mama and Papa, and then Analisa herself. *How young I look,* she'd thought, staring at herself at sixteen. Two long braids hung over her shoulders and across her breasts. Her blue eyes appeared nearly transparent in the photograph, the subjects all portrayed in black, white, and shades of gray. *So very young* and *so very innocent,* she'd added. Her eyes were as wondering as Pieter's and Meika's. While she stared at the picture, she had wondered if the children's expressions still held that look of innocence, the look she'd lost long ago. What was life among the Indians doing to them?

It was then Analisa had told Caleb about her hope of one day being reunited with Meika and Pieter. She prayed they would escape their captors and make their way to a white settlement. Caleb's silence, his refusal to reassure her, had hurt Analisa, darkening the moment. She'd returned the photograph to the safety of the trunk and vowed to hold on to her hope.

As if he sensed her distress, Caleb had tried to lighten the mood. She remembered answering his questions about the name Anja.

"It's just a childhood name. A way to say, Little Anna," she explained. "Do you have any such name, Caleb?"

"That's what we would call a nickname. There is none for Caleb, that I know of. It's good to know what a name means. The Sioux choose names that describe a person or tell of an important event in one's life. Some Indians even change their names after a significant experience."

Before he could continue, she interrupted.

"What is your . . . Sioux name?" She wanted to understand the one facet of Caleb's past that frightened her the most.

"The name my mother gave me was Raven's Shadow, because my hair was so black and glossy. That was only my infant name, though. My father wanted me to have a white name as well, and so he chose Caleb. It's a Hebrew name that means 'bold one.' It can also mean 'dog.' "

"They all seem to suit you very well," she laughed. "You are lucky to have so many names."

"Oh, I have more." His smile had been mischievous as he continued his explanation. "My Sioux grandfather later named me, One-Who-Walks-in-Two-Worlds, for obvious reasons. And when I'm working for General Parker, I often have to assume other names."

"So it seems I have married many men?"

She watched the laughter in his eyes as he lowered his lips to hers.

"And I have just my Anja."

The memories faded as Analisa's thoughts returned to the present. Today Caleb was to ride into town and return with Kase as well as his own belongings. She looked forward to welcoming her son home again, but at the same time wondered how the boy would react to Caleb's sleeping in her bed. Analisa refused to consider the complications that were sure to arise with the three of them living together in one small room. When she voiced her worries to Caleb, he'd merely laughed at her embarrassment and said he wouldn't mind a few more sessions in the cow shed. She had taken a swipe at him with her dish towel, but ended up laughing as she did so often now. Perhaps, after the spring rains let up and it was dry enough to cut more sod, they could add another room to the house. Analisa decided to suggest the idea to Caleb. For now she was content to watch him sleep as she continued to sort out the thoughts that had awakened her long before dawn.

When she asked about his family, Caleb had told her the story of his father's return to Boston after years of living out west, and his own reluctant introduction to his white heritage. A description of his years at school, his time in the army, and his friendship with Ruth followed. Analisa listened intently, trying to understand, asking questions whenever they came to mind.

As he told her about the work he did for Ely Parker and the Bureau of Indian Affairs, she'd sensed hesitation on his part and realized Caleb was leaving many details untold. He'd avoided any mention of how he would carry out his assignments from Pella, and now his obvious omission of facts hung heavy on her mind.

Feeling like a child, eager to be up and out of bed, Analisa forced herself to lie still a little longer. It was only an hour past dawn, but she'd been awake long before the sun gathered enough strength to force its way into the room. Analisa closed her eyes against the light, intending to give Caleb a few more minutes before she roused him . . .

"I thought you wanted to be up and about early to send me off after Kase, yet here you are sleeping away the morning."

Drifting back to consciousness, Analisa listened to Caleb's soft words spoken very near her ear. She smiled, eyes closed, and threw her arm across her eyes to avoid the daylight.

"*I* was awake before dawn, but you, Caleb, slept on and on until I just gave up." A smile peeked out from beneath the downy white sleeve of her nightgown.

"Why didn't you wake me up?" He leaned over her and lifted her wrist slowly to uncover her eyes. Caleb then planted a kiss on her closed lips. "Is this how you *really* are? Too lazy to fix breakfast for your starving husband? I can't recall the last time I sat down to a decent meal in this house. Christmas Eve, I think. I'll have to ask Sophie to make me something while I'm in town."

"You must do that," she teased. "I am getting very used to being so lazy, but if you light the stove, I will cook."

"That sounds fair enough."

"Then you must collect Kase and your things. Sophie always says she rots him. He will be very rotted by now."

"Rots?" Caleb stopped where he was, half out of bed, and turned to face her. "Rots him?" He repeated.

She looked thoughtful, her brow furrowed as she tried to remember the expression Sophie used so frequently. "Ruins?" she tried again.

Caleb thought for a moment. "Spoils?" he countered.

"Yes! That's what she said she does. Spoils him rots."

Caleb rolled his eyes toward the ceiling, stepped from the bed, and reached for the pile of clothing draped across the rocker.

"Repeat after me." He looked at her while standing on one leg, thrusting the other into the pantleg. "Sophie spoils Kase rotten."

"No."

"Why not?"

"You are laughing at me." Analisa folded her arms across her breasts and stared up at the ceiling.

"I'm not laughing at you," he began, engaged in the process of buttoning his shirt. "I admire your creative ability to change the language, that's all." When a glance in her direction warned him that she was not enjoying his joke, he moved to the edge of the bed. "Really, Analisa, I'm not teasing you. I think it's remarkable that you taught yourself English at all. It's just that the way you turn words around sometimes is very . . . entertaining." He gave her a slow smile and extended a hand to help her out of bed. "I'm sorry if I hurt your feelings."

Unable to resist the warmth of his smile and his apparent sincerity, Analisa slipped out from beneath the covers and put her arms about his neck. She could feel the rough wool of his tweed pants through the soft cotton of her long-sleeved nightgown.

Caleb kissed her thoroughly before relinquishing possession of her lips.

"You do want me to go get Kase, don't you?"

She nodded.

"Then you'd better get dressed and let me go." His clear blue eyes sought the depths of hers. He was still for a moment before he added, "I have something important to tell you, so get dressed while I light the stove and start the coffee."

"Caleb . . ." Analisa was worried by his words. Was he going to leave again soon? This time if she threw aside her stubborn pride and asked him to stay, would he go anyway?

She felt cold and alone as she watched him move toward the stove, then turned away to dress hurriedly while trying to still the anxious beat of her heart.

*   *   *

"Fort Sully . . ."

Analisa repeated the name and tried it on her tongue while she sought to create a picture in her mind. Nothing materialized.

"Where is this Fort Sully?" She met his straightforward gaze across the table, her plate of fried ham and eggs forgotten. Caleb's "something important" was not what she expected. She had been sure that he would tell her he was leaving soon, but Caleb had surprised Analisa with the news that he wanted her to leave Iowa and move with him to Fort Sully.

"Actually," he said, "it's on the Missouri River in what the army calls the Department of the Dakotas. Right now, the most flagrant misuse of Indian funds stems from that area."

Analisa sat in silence, not quite able to understand all Caleb said.

Aware of her confusion, he tried to explain as briefly as he could. "At first, when General Parker gave me the assignment, I decided to go out there alone. I didn't think it was feasible to take you and Kase along, but the more I've thought it through, the more it seems like a good idea. You two could provide a cover for me as well as constant contact with the fort."

He reached across the table and took her right hand in his. "Besides, now that I have you, I'm not so willing to give you up. For anything."

Analisa felt herself blush at his words. "Nor I you." She dropped her eyes to avoid the intensity of his gaze. "But, Caleb"—she looked up again—"I never dreamed I'd leave here." Her gaze took in the interior of the soddie. "What about my things?"

He squeezed her hand, relieved at the lack of resistance she'd shown, and smiled reassuringly. "We'll move everything you cannot replace and sell the rest. You'll have to sell the livestock, too, and the homestead."

"Sell Tulip and Honey?"

He nodded. "It would be too expensive to ship them, and we won't have any place to keep them at the fort."

"Maybe Sophie and Jon will take them." She looked thoughtful before she added, "The house and the land belong to the church. They let us come here after the attack. I suppose we should just give it back."

"That will be easy enough. I hate to think you owe them

anything.'' Caleb glanced around the room. The congregation had felt quite righteous, no doubt, allowing the Van Meeterens to live in the run-down sod house. He'd be glad to see Analisa well away from Pella at last. "Then it's settled. I'll leave next week and return as soon as I can get things set up for you and Kase, probably early March. You should be packed and ready to leave by then.''

Caleb let go of her hand with another squeeze and stood, pushing away from the table. He was on his way to Pella to collect Kase and his own belongings. He looked back to see her sitting lost in thought.

"Anja? Are you sure you want to move?''

She nodded with confidence. "Yes. I am sure. It will be good to begin again . . . but I am thinking, if you are to be gone for three months''—she met his gaze with a tempting smile—"are you sure you want to rush off after Kase right now?''

Caleb rounded the table and stood by her side. She tilted her head back and stared up at him, feeling the need for his touch surge through her once again.

"Aren't you afraid he's been thoroughly 'rotted' by Sophie?'' His hand slipped into the knot upon her head, and he watched the heavy golden locks cascade around her shoulders. Caleb lowered himself beside Analisa on the wooden bench.

"No,'' she began, as his lips descended toward hers, "only a little ruined.''

Chapter Nine

An insistent wind tugged at the wet shirt as Analisa fought to hang it on the clothesline. When she refused to loosen her hold on the garment, the shirt was buffeted backward, slapping her across the face. Frustrated, she balled the freezing fabric in her wind-chapped hands and flung it back into the laundry tub. She thrust her numbed fingers inside the pockets of her worn wool coat and watched as Kase ran into the shed to find a hammer. He was building something, he said.

"Don't look, Mama. It's a surprise."

"Kase," she called to him above the moan of the wind, "I'm going to hang the clothes inside."

She heard his response, a muffled *Ja,* and lifted the copper boiling tub. Hauling the heavy, wet load to waist height, she rested it on her hip and started around the house toward the door.

This was no day to hang clothes outside, she admitted to herself in defeat. The sky was leaden, a sheet of gray tin that pressed down upon the land like the underside of an upturned tub. The relentless prairie wind howled across the bare, frozen ground. The land appeared desolate, now that the snow had melted. The buds of new life lay dormant, sleeping just below the surface of the hard earth, content to remain huddled and hidden the last few weeks before spring arrived. Analisa felt no such compulsion.

It was March 7, 1871, and she was ready for the spring, ready to watch the buds open and see the tulips push above the ground. Lovingly transported from Holland, the tulips reminded Analisa of her mother, and she remembered her own tears as she had placed the bulbs in the ground that first year. Heavily burdened with her unborn child, a constant reminder of her shame, Analisa had fought the hard sod, burying the tulip bulbs deep in the new land. She'd willed them to grow and they had obeyed. Like her, they had lived, if not exactly thriving, after the shock. Now she longed to see them bloom again, but more than anything she longed to see Caleb.

She went inside and hung the clothes on a cord stretched across the room, then decided to refill the tub and indulge in a sponge bath. Sophie had given her a jar of skin cream guaranteed to "soften and luxuriate," and now Analisa was determined to pamper herself. She couldn't remember a winter as long and miserable as this one. It must have been the waiting that had made the days stretch on endlessly.

Now that Caleb had entered her life, Analisa knew she would no longer be content to live without him. She was sure the decision to move to Fort Sully had been the right one, and she was anxious to see the move accomplished. If only Caleb would arrive and take them to their new home. Everything had been in readiness for weeks.

Analisa hung the last piece of clothing, her mended pantaloons, and smiled as an idea crossed her mind. After her bath, she would don the silk undergarments Caleb had given her for Christmas. She'd found them tucked into a box he'd hidden beneath the table on Christmas Eve after the Allens left with Kase. She thrilled at the touch of the heavenly ivory silk drawers and camisole, but she had put them safely back inside the tissue along with the silk stockings. Today, she was determined to slip into them and feel the raw silk against her skin.

As she refilled the tub at the pump, carried it back inside, and heated the water on the old stove, Analisa mentally checked her preparations for the move. Jon and Sophie had agreed to take Tulip and Honey; they would keep them in the small barn behind their house in Pella. The Allens had also informed the Reverend Mr. Wierstra of Analisa's impending move. The sod house would revert back to the church.

All of her household goods, except the most necessary items, were already packed in crates and awaited the departure. The room was bare of the few decorative Delft pieces, the lace and embroidery work that had lessened the severity of the soddie and made it a home.

Stripping off her threadbare blue homespun dress, Analisa debated throwing it away. She could no longer afford to look unpresentable, for they'd be living in close contact with others at Fort Sully. Still, her good clothes were few in number, and she hated to wear them while doing household chores. Choosing to decide the fate of the blue dress later, she tossed it over the bench. Perhaps she would cut it apart and use the soft blue material for scraps.

She stoked the stove to heat the room and dipped a linen washcloth into the steaming water, lathering it with a scrap of lemon-scented soap. Dropping the shoulder straps of her cotton chemise, Analisa soaped and then rinsed her body absentmindedly as her thoughts dwelt on Caleb's letters and the move north. Once again she was thankful to Sophie for her reading and writing lessons.

Caleb had written her six precious letters, which were now carefully stored in her trunk. Analisa had carried each one in the pocket of her apron until she knew the lines by heart and had shared the news with Kase, Jon, and Sophie. The words of love she kept for herself alone, and locked them in her heart.

In the last letter, Caleb informed her that housing was finally available at the fort. In the meantime, he was living with the newly appointed commander, Major Frank Williamson, but would be returning before mid-March "to collect his family." A warmth spread through her at his use of the word. Family. She realized he was trying to put her mind at ease. Analisa would never again let herself doubt Caleb's sincerity and feelings for her—for that doubt had nearly destroyed their love in the very beginning.

The house they were assigned was partially furnished already. The former occupants had been transferred to the Southeast and decided not to take their heavy belongings with them. They accepted Caleb's offer to buy the pieces from them. He wrote that Analisa now owned a table with six chairs along with a sideboard in the dining room. Analisa asked Jon to explain what a sideboard was and he translated it into Dutch for her: *buffet*. She would feel like a queen with a dining table and chairs, let alone a *buffet*, too. She tried to remember to call it by the English name.

Her own bed would be moved for Kase. No longer would he need to sleep on Edvard's cot. A complete bedroom set awaited her at the fort. The rocker, organ, her trunk, and Kase's belongings as well as Caleb's were all packed, along with the bedding, dishes, and kitchen utensils. The stove, table, and benches would remain for the soddie's next occupants.

The wind blew steadily against the windows as she hurried to put on the silk garments. Almost stealthily, Analisa slid the ivory camisole over her head, relishing the cool feel of the silk as it slipped along her skin. She never wore a corset, but was determined to have one to wear under the new rose dress Caleb had given her. For now, she merely stepped into the matching silk drawers, which were cut wide-legged and edged with lace that brushed against her upper thighs. To replace the old blue homespun, she dug through her trunk and shook out a serviceable yellow calico she had not worn since last spring. She had made the dress years ago, and repaired and altered it many times since she arrived in Iowa. Free of adornment, the calico had long full sleeves that ended in plain cuffs buttoned tight around her wrists. She found an old lace collar, yellowed with age, one of the few items she possessed that had been her grandmother Van Meeteren's.

Analisa tied the collar around her neck and straightened the squared edges of lace about her shoulders. She would not wear the silk stockings and fancy garters Caleb had given her, afraid she might ruin them before the departure for Fort Sully. Instead, she drew on thick wool socks and then slipped into her heavy *klompen*. They kept the hem of her skirt above the dirt floor.

Dressed to suit herself at last, Analisa took up her hairbrush and let down her hair, working the bristles through the long, thick strands. She brushed her scalp until it tingled and then set the brush down on the trunk lid and took up the jar of cream. Opening the lid, she held the fragrant stuff beneath her nose and inhaled the sweet scent of roses. Analisa dipped a finger into the thick, rich substance and worked it into the thirsty skin of her hands. She applied a second helping to the backs of her hands and between her fingers.

Refreshed, her spirit revived, Analisa wrung out her wash-cloth and towel and hung them across the laundry cord. A slight metallic sound carried on the wind caused her heart to stand still as her breath caught in her throat. She closed her eyes, daring to hope, at the same time warning herself it was probably just a trick of the wind. Analisa turned to look through the window. She stood on tiptoe, stretched herself over the kitchen bench, and leaned near the windowpanes.

Silhouetted against the gray sky was the lone figure of a man on horseback. She recognized him. It was Caleb. Then, after watching a split second longer, Analisa was sure it was not he. The man was of the same height and build, yet sat his mount awkwardly, as if unaccustomed to the saddle. The hat was all wrong, too. As he turned into the yard and approached the house, she could see that he wore a bowler and round-lensed spectacles. His legs were thrust stiffly into the stirrups and stood away from the horse's sides at right angles. She recognized the horse, Scorpio, and now that he was close enough to see clearly, she knew the man was Caleb—but was not Caleb.

Puzzled, Analisa continued to watch as he struggled to dismount, drew an umbrella from the back of his saddle . . . an umbrella? . . . and stood looking at her from just outside the window.

Analisa thrust her arms into a heavy wool sweater and, holding it closed with her hands, rushed outdoors. She stopped short a few feet from the man.

"Caleb?" She didn't know how she could be so sure and unsure at the same time.

"*Perdón, señora.*" He touched the brim of his hat with the hand still holding the reins of the horse. His right arm he held away from his body, elbow bent, wrist cocked, holding the umbrella above the ground. Small round glasses were perched on the end of his nose. He peered over them in her direction.

"Perdón, señora," he repeated. His next words were so heavily laced with a Spanish accent that she barely understood them. "Allow me to introduce myself."

He bowed deeply from the waist, nearly losing the bowler and making a grab at it with the hand that clutched the umbrella. Shoving the hat down securely around his ears, he seemed unaware of the dent formed in the top by the carved umbrella handle.

"I am Don Ricardo Corona de la Vega, at your service. If you would be so kind as to show me how to tie this beast so that he will not escape," he lifted the reins in her direction, "I will be most grateful."

Analisa watched in amazement as he bowed again. She could see that his hair was tied at the nape of his neck with a black stain bow, reminiscent of the style of a century ago.

"Caleb?"

"Señora," he began again, his voice rising in exasperation, "if you insist upon calling me by another's name, the least you could do is to greet me as you might this"—he waved his hand limply in an expression of disgust—"this Caleb."

With that his eyes twinkled at her over the rims of his glasses and he dropped the reins to step toward her. It *was* Caleb. Analisa was certain as she watched his lips curve into a wide grin. She reached up and carefully drew the fragile glasses off of his nose, folded the thin wire stems, and slipped them into his coat pocket. She then removed the ridiculous hat and handed it to him. Finally, she reached behind his head to loosen the ribbon and free his curls. Not until she was finished did Analisa speak.

"Welcome home," she whispered before she pressed her hungry lips to his.

He drew her into his embrace and his arms locked about her. His lips crushed hers. Heady with the warmth and smell of him, Analisa let herself forget the world as she reveled in the sensation of being in Caleb's arms once again. The rough wool of his coat scratched her smooth cheek. His lips were hot against hers, a sharp contrast to the chilly wind that tossed and tangled her unbound hair. Eyes closed, she savored his presence and tasted his tongue against hers. The kiss seemed endless as they rejoiced in each other and their reunion.

"Hey, Caleb! Say hello to me, too!"

Reluctantly, Caleb ended the kiss, forced to acknowledge the small boy tugging at his pantleg. He continued to hold Analisa in his arms while he glanced down at Kase who stood staring up at him solemnly.

"Hello, Kase." Caleb nudged Analisa, directing her attention to her son. "How can I resist that look?"

She peered down at Kase over the circle of Caleb's strong arms and sighed, "You can't, and neither can I."

Analisa stepped back, allowing Caleb the freedom to scoop Kase up in one arm. The boy looped an arm around Caleb's neck and one around his mother's.

"Now we are all together again," Kase proclaimed. *"Komop, wij gaan nu*—Come on. Let's go now!'"

The only sound in the soddie was the slow, rhythmic squeal of the ancient oak rocker. The soft hush of evening had descended with the darkness, and weak, flickering light from the oil lamps filled the room. Caleb occupied the rocking chair, Kase asleep in his arms. The man kissed the top of the boy's head and stood up slowly. Caleb carried him across the room and, after tucking the child into the cot beside the stove, returned to join Analisa.

He watched her for a moment as she sat lost in her work, repairing a tear in Kase's play clothes. She was sitting on the near side of her bed, leaning against the oak headboard, her head and hands straining toward the lamp on the trunk beside the bed. The yellow calico skirt was spread wide across the coverlet, the colorful print muted by the bright tulip quilt. Her hair was still hanging free, at his request, and he marveled at the life it possessed as it rippled around her shoulders. Silently, Caleb reached out and lifted a strand of her hair between his thumb and forefinger, savoring the silken texture of the golden locks.

Analisa set her sewing aside and raised her arms to him in greeting and invitation. He lowered himself onto the edge of the bed beside her and leaned over her.

"Kase is asleep," he announced unnecessarily.

"Now will you tell me why you have become Don Ricardo

Corona de la Vega?'' The question had played on her mind all evening. Caleb had refused to explain earlier, afraid that Kase would overhear.

"I hoped perhaps you wished something more of me, beautiful *señora*.'' His eyes flashed in the lamplight.

"I can't understand you when you talk that way.'' Her tone held a note of mild complaint. Her nerves taut from waiting for his explanation, she pushed him away.

Ever persistent, Caleb leaned forward again, slipping his hands behind her as he sought the ties of her lace collar.

"You failed to mention how you knew I was arriving today.'' He toyed with the buttons at the back of her gown, ignoring her impatience.

"What do you mean?''

"You are all dressed up.'' His eyes slowly appraised her. "Perfume and lace. I hope it was in honor of my homecoming?'' His right hand pushed up her skirt and began to trail along her thigh. As he touched the silken drawers, Caleb's lips formed a sly half-smile. "My, my. Silk undies, too.''

"I didn't know you were returning today.''

"So who were you expecting?'' He pulled back to look into her eyes.

"I was expecting spring, but since it is so slow in coming, I decided to treat myself to the pleasure of a bath, clean clothes, and the feel of silk. I am spoiled by you already. I think I will only wear silk underclothes from now on.''

"I would prefer you wear nothing.'' His hand slid easily beneath the loose-fitting drawers.

Caleb awoke well before dawn and drew Analisa into his arms. She barely stirred, burrowing into him as she sought his warmth. He teased her awake by nibbling on her ear and letting his hands rove over her velvet skin.

"Anja?''

"Mmmm?''

"Wake up. We need to talk before Kase is up.''

She stretched and rolled over, fitting herself against the protective shell of his body, her back pressed against him. Caleb felt his passion mount at the touch of her rounded backside pressed so intimately against him.

"Anja.''

His whisper insistent against her ear, Analisa could no longer hide in the world of dreams. She opened her eyes in the weak light before dawn and whispered back, "I'm awake."

"I need to tell you about Fort Sully and Don Ricardo."

When she failed to respond, he, too, remained silent, thinking her asleep again.

"What about them?"

"No one there knows who I really am. Even Major Williamson believes I am Don Ricardo Corona de la Vega. Until I know for certain where his sympathies lie, I must keep him in the dark about my true identity and activities." He shifted his position slightly, drawing her nearer.

The sensations he aroused in her excited Analisa as she fought to concentrate on his words.

"My identity papers state that I am a Spanish professor traveling the United States to study the West. As an inept, foppish sort, I won't be suspected of spying for the Bureau of Indian Affairs. Only President Grant and General Parker know my true identity and assignment."

"You are in danger."

It was not a question. Analisa realized for the first time the extent of Caleb's involvement.

Caleb remained silent as he gathered his thoughts in order to deal with her honestly. He knew she would be forced to spend many days and nights alone at the fort, and he sought to keep her from worrying about him.

"Not necessarily. I will pose as Don Ricardo when I am living at the fort." He paused before adding, "The Sioux will know me only as a half-breed, Raven's Shadow, who scorns the whites and has given up his half-white heritage."

Analisa lay tense beside him, her arousal ebbing as she tried to sort through the new information. It was slowly becoming apparent that his true identity was a dangerous secret that must be guarded at all costs. What of Kase? How could they trust the four-year-old not to innocently betray him? Analisa envisioned endless days of tension and worry, on guard against her son's every word and deed.

"How will we keep Kase from calling you Caleb? And how will you explain the fact that I am not Spanish? Kase is enough like you to be your son, but he speaks no Spanish. What if he should speak Dutch in front of someone? What will we do if . . ."

He ran his hand over her arm and sought to quiet her. He lowered his voice to a hushed whisper, speaking in the slow, confident tone she was so familiar with.

"If it's all right with you, I'd like him to call me Papa. If he starts now, it'll become natural to him by the time we reach the fort." He took the time to tease the back of her neck with his lips.

"I have a story all worked out, and I think it's quite plausible. I told Williamson that I met you in Europe. We were married there, and Kase was born in Holland before we came to the States. I have been teaching in the East for three years, so naturally, you both speak English quite well. I haven't had time to teach either of you much Spanish."

She marveled at the intricacy of his explanation and became caught up in the cover story. "So you went ahead to Fort Sully to make arrangements for us to move there, and now you are supposedly in the East, collecting your wife and son?"

"Exactly. What do you think?"

"What does this Major Williamson think?"

"He believes me. He has no reason not to; my introductory papers are very official and in order. He is to make sure I have all the assistance I require, and the freedom to come and go from the fort to study the surroundings. Naturally, he thinks I'm a bit crazy to ride out into hostile territory alone. After meeting Don Ricardo, how can you blame him?"

"Yes. The professor I saw ride up to my door this morning was lucky to know which end of the horse to lead." She felt him laughing silently. "What will you really do among the Indians?"

"They are renegades—runaways from the reservation. I'll infiltrate their camp and work to persuade them to return to the reservation before they are hunted down and killed." He avoided explaining the rest of his mission, hoping to ensure her safety by keeping her unaware of the details.

"Part of the time you'll be living with . . . them?"

"Yes, and while I am you will have to cover for me at the fort. I wanted to spare you that, but there is no other way this will work."

Analisa was so silent for a time that Caleb finally nudged her gently.

"Anja?"

"I was just thinking."

"And . . ."

"You have entrusted me with much responsibility, Caleb."

"I trust you with my life."

Analisa closed her eyes and prayed silently, hoping she would prove worthy of that trust.

"Mama? Can I get in bed with you, too?" Her eyes flew open immediately and saw the round-eyed face of her child standing beside the bed staring at the two of them. She wondered how Kase had crossed the room so silently. He was becoming as graceful and stealthy as Caleb. Wanting to hide and draw the covers over her head in embarrassment, she was unable to answer Kase and so kicked Caleb in the shin.

He took over immediately. "Run along and dress, Kase. We'll be up in a minute."

Not the least bit offended by the abrupt dismissal, for he was always willing to please Caleb, the youngster moved off to his side of the room.

"How long has he been standing there?" Analisa whispered from behind the hands she pressed against her burning face.

"I'm not sure. I was concentrating on your neck." He placed a gentle kiss on the soft skin at the edge of her hairline.

After Christmas they'd played a waiting game with Kase, making certain he was asleep before they went to bed and that they were up and dressed before the boy awoke. Analisa had hoped he would not find out they shared a bed, but Caleb was certain that sooner or later he would know. Now that the truth was out, the boy seemed not to care in the least.

"Kase?" Caleb called out, noting that youngster was nearly dressed. The call drew Kase to the bedside once more.

"Go outside and lead Scorpio into the yard for me. He needs to stretch his legs. Can you do it?"

Happy to be given such a great responsibility, Kase shrugged into his coat and was out the door in seconds. At the sound of the wooden portal closing securely behind him, Analisa bounded from the bed and grabbed her clothes.

"Need these?"

Caleb had retrieved her new satin underclothes from between

the sheets and tossed them to her. Within moments they were both dressed and nervously awaiting Kase's return.

"I'll go out and get him." Caleb strode to the door and grabbed his own coat. Analisa, too embarrassed to face either of them, kept her back to him while she added cow chips to the fire with improvised wooden tongs.

Kase ran up to greet Caleb as the man rounded the corner of the house. The wind drove the mill above him, setting a frantic pace as the blades spun around and around. The sky remained lackluster gray, although dark clouds streaked it with charcoal. Rain was imminent.

"I let him out, Caleb," Kase announced proudly, pointing to Scorpio as the big horse moved about the yard.

"You're not afraid of him at all, are you?" Caleb asked the boy, the pride apparent in his voice.

"*Nee*. I like horses."

"It's about time you had one of your own."

Kase stopped kicking the toe of his worn leather boot against a dirt clod and looked up at Caleb in disbelief. "My own horse?" His child's voice rose an octave in excitement.

Caleb merely nodded. He'd see that the boy had a mount and riding lessons, too, as soon as they reached Fort Sully.

"Let's go in. Breakfast should be about ready." Caleb shoved his hands deep in his pockets and headed toward the front of the house.

"Caleb?"

"Yep." The man knew from the tone of the boy's voice what was coming next. He held his breath.

"How come you were in bed with my mama?"

Caleb hunkered down on his haunches and met Kase's honest, questioning eyes.

"Do you remember when the minister came here last summer and your mama and I got married?"

Kase nodded.

"Well, that's what married people do: They sleep in the same bed together and keep each other company."

"Do Jon and Sophie?"

"Yep."

"Why?"

"That's just the way it is, son. Married folks sleep in the same bed."

Kase was silent again, thoughtfully sorting this new information.

"Any more questions?" Caleb asked, silently imploring all of the gods that there were not.

"What kind of a horse will I have?"

Caleb released a pent-up sigh of relief. He stood and took the boy's hand as they moved toward the door. "Just the right kind, Kase. I'll pick out a special one just for you."

Analisa stared at the reflection in the long oval mirror in Sophie's guest room. Surely this could not possibly be her, even though the image matched her every move. The round, luminous eyes fringed with golden lashes and the sun-kissed hair swept into a high-perched chignon were definitely hers, and yet the elegantly attired figure in soft rose-colored wool looked far too sophisticated to be Analisa Van Meeteren.

She appraised herself with a critical eye and then remembered: She did not look like herself because she was no longer Analisa Van Meeteren. Mrs. Caleb Storm would definitely be a woman of quality, one who cut a fine figure indeed, for didn't Caleb know the President of the United States personally? The thought did little to bolster her courage, but unwilling to be intimidated by her new status, Analisa straightened her shoulders, worked her kid gloves onto her hands, brushed a piece of lint from her jacket, and turned to inspect the bustle under her wool skirt. Gleaming leather boots hugged her feet and ankles, their buttons and loops fastened securely. At Sophie's insistence she'd chosen a light gray pair, highly impractical and yet a fitting complement to the expensive dress Caleb had given her. She had purchased the bustle and a whalebone corset at Knapp's Dry Goods in Pella. The two items were necessary to achieve the required fashionable figure beneath the stylish dress.

The hat was sheer folly, but Sophie had insisted she buy it and had finally won out by using devious tactics. She'd told Caleb about the hat and about Analisa's stubborn refusal to spend any more of his money on herself. Sophie had described the jaunty gray hat in such detail that a blind man could have found it at the millinery store. Caleb had purchased it almost immediately and had threatened to leave Analisa at the depot if she appeared without it.

Analisa lifted the little gray confection carefully out of its box, brushed the peacock-blue feather with her gloved fingers, and carefully perched the hat on the coil of gleaming hair. The feather tilted and waved rakishly to one side, and she frowned back at the image in the mirror. The hat was just not right, she decided, and only served to make the regal figure in the mirror more frightening. She felt as if she were masquerading as someone else and was afraid of being found out. With trembling fingers she thrust a long, deadly-looking hat pin through the soft gray felt and secured it to her hair. Caleb wanted her to wear it and so she would. Perhaps she would eventually forget it was up there.

With a last look in the mirror and a bemused shrug, Analisa accepted her fate and quickly surveyed the room. None of her possessions remained; they had been taken downstairs with Caleb's things. Jon and Sophie had insisted that the Storms stay with them for a few days before their departure. Gratefully, Analisa had accepted. A strong storm front had boiled across the plains, dumping inches of rain and hail on the prairie and turning the ground into a sea of mud.

Analisa was thankful that she would no longer be forced to endure the spring rains in the soddie. Each year the rains came, soaking the yard, seeping through the sod-lined ceiling and into the dirt floor. Muddy water spattered and dripped unceasingly into the room. Pots and pans caught the biggest drips while oilcloths and rags, old canvas and newspaper protected the furniture. Life during the rainy season went on in a sea of mud, and Analisa was glad to be going far away from it.

Sophie and Jon's two-story house was made of wood. Set away from the center of town, on Liberty Street, the house represented a far different way of life than the one Analisa had known. Shops were located nearby, as were the neighbors Analisa had lived without. It reminded her of life in the old country—housewives walking to market in the morning, horses and buggies passing by, busy people leading active lives and keeping in touch with one another. Would Fort Sully be like this? she wondered. No one would know her there. Perhaps she would be able to join in the stream of life around her instead of existing far removed from everything.

Analisa took one last look around the room, admiring the way the sunlight played upon the high polish of the floor and wondered if her new home at Fort Sully would be half as elegant. She doubted that she could adjust to living in such luxury, and then laughed at herself for worrying over something she could not foresee. With a shake of her head at the vision in the mirror, Analisa set the peacock feather bobbing. She groaned in exasperation, then turned and left the room without a backward glance.

The sun, flooding in through lace-draped windows, warmed the cheery front parlor of the Allens' wood frame house. Caleb felt that the room welcomed visitors as he looked around for the last time. A large stone fireplace stood in the center of the far wall. Sophie's eye for elegant but unpretentious detail was evident in the appointments she had chosen for the room. The walls were papered with a soft floral pattern of spring colors accented by a white wooden chair rail. Blue and white Delft pieces adorned the plate rack and the thick mantelpiece. Touches of lace and crocheted doilies softened the spider-legged tables, and a yellow-striped settee and matching wing chair near the tall windows beckoned visitors to sit in the sunlight.

When Kase asked Jon to play him a song on the fiddle, Caleb noticed the sadness in the tall man's eyes and realized how sorely the Allens would miss Kase. As Jon quietly explained that there wasn't time for him to play a tune, Caleb drew on the long chain of his watch, slipped the timepiece out of his vest pocket, and pressed the catch to release the lid. The gold watch had once belonged to his father and so held special memories for Caleb. One glance at the slender hands told him it was time to leave for the depot. Deftly he pressed the lid closed and returned the watch to his pocket, then went to the foot of the stairs to call to Analisa.

The sound of her footsteps ringing on the wooden floor above him stopped his words. He waited silently for her appearance, then watched as she paused, tentative and unsure, on the landing. She was lovely, a vision of quiet sophistication and elegance, the deep rose of the gown reflected in the color that suffused her cheeks. She descended the stairs slowly, the toes of her gray kid shoes peeping from beneath the swaying wool hem. Her hands were encased in the soft smoke-colored gloves, and the jaunty feathered hat rode atop her flaxen hair. As she noticed him, her wide blue eyes sought his approval, but Caleb remained speechless until she reached the bottom step and stood facing him, her eyes level with his own.

Finally he spoke, words whispered in Sioux, his first tongue, the language of his soul. The words faded away upon the air, and silence fell between them. He translated for her. "You are beautiful. You do me great honor."

He felt her eyes on his lips, his face. Leaning forward, Caleb warmly pressed his mouth against hers. It was a slow, unhurried kiss, a sharing of warmth, passion held on a tight rein because of their surroundings. The time had come to leave, to embark upon a new life, and both were aware of the need to pull apart. They did so, slowly, simultaneously, and with regret.

Conscious once again of her appearance, Analisa reached up to see if the hat was secure.

Caleb watched. A wide smile appeared on his face. "Sophie was right," he agreed. "The hat's perfect."

"With luck I will forget I am wearing it." She rolled her eyes and blew at the feather.

He extended his arm to her, elbow crooked, and she allowed him to lead her into the parlor where her friends waited to say farewell.

Sophie called out, her voice high with nervous excitement, "You look wonderful, Anja! You'll be the most glamorous woman at Fort Sully."

"I can already assure you of that," Caleb broke in, "for I've met all the others, and not one of them compares with my Anja." He bent to whisper against her ear, "At Fort Sully or anywhere else, for that matter."

Embarrassed by so much praise and attention, Analisa sought to convince them she remained unchanged by the fashionable trappings. "When they see the hands beneath these gloves, people will know for certain I am no lady of quality. I have calluses that will last a lifetime."

"There's nothing wrong with that," Jon said. "You've worked hard because you've had to."

Unsure how to respond, Analisa looked away and noticed Kase sitting alone and uncertain on the raised hearth. She realized she must look like a stranger to him. Gently withdrawing her hand from Caleb's arm, she went to her son. His blue eyes stared up at her from beneath the straight fringe of blue-black hair, his face unsmiling and thoughtful. She reached for his hand, and when Kase stood, she drew him into a warm embrace.

"You look very special in your new suit. You are the most handsome man I've ever seen."

"More than . . . more handsome than Papa?"

She nodded. A tender feeling warmed her whenever she heard the child call Caleb Papa. Analisa whispered her reply. "Yes, but don't tell him that I said so." She smiled a secret smile, and Kase bobbed his head, agreeing to keep the secret.

"What are you two up to now?"

Analisa turned to face Caleb, her son's hand tightly enclosed by her gloved fingers.

"Oh, just sharing a little secret is all. Is it time to go?"

"I'm afraid so." Caleb turned to Jon. "Why don't we see to the carriage while Analisa and Sophie say good-bye?"

"Go with Papa, Kase." Analisa urged him forward.

Analisa fought the tears threatening to spill from her eyes as Sophie held out two gifts. "These are for you."

Analisa took the gifts, one a small soft object wrapped in brown paper, the other a heavy muslin bag filled with shifting, heavy lumps. Analisa knew at a touch what the bag contained. "Bulbs?"

"Yes." Sophie nodded, her long curls bobbing about her shoulders. "Tulips for your new home. I know how much you love flowers, and I'm sure you'll find something to plant there, but knowing how you Dutch love to take your tulips with you, I got these for you. Some of each color."

Analisa smiled and wiped her eyes with the tip of her finger. "My mother brought tulip bulbs all the way from Holland. I didn't dig any of them up to take with me. It seemed fitting that they stay here, with the spirits of my family. Your gift is very special to me, Sophie."

"Open the other."

Carefully, Analisa removed the wrapping to reveal a black satin reticule, delicately beaded with jet and adorned with fringe. Satin drawstrings held the pouch closed.

"It's lovely!" Analisa exclaimed and slipped the strings over her wrist, allowing the purse to dangle at her side. "I will think of you each time I carry it."

Realizing the time had come to depart, Sophie smiled at Analisa and shook off her sadness. "I wish you every happiness, Anja."

"And I you."

Their attention was drawn to the front porch where Caleb called out for them to hurry. With one last quick hug, the two women went outside.

Caleb handed Sophie and Analisa into the carriage where Jon waited, reins in hand, to drive them to the depot. Lifting Kase onto Scorpio's back, Caleb then swung himself up behind the boy and followed the carriage as it made its way down muddy Liberty Street toward Main. After three days of constant driving rain the thoroughfares were churned to mud beneath the wheels of the carriages and horses' hooves.

Her senses alive as she looked over the town for the last time, Analisa was aware of the steam rising from the shaked rooftops along Main Street as the sun baked the rain-soaked wood. The smell of fresh-baked bread rode upon the clean, crisp March air as they passed the bakery. Above the muddy streets townfolk strolled along the high planked walkways that were washed down every morning by the shop owners. She saw many of them take notice of the Allens' carriage, some stopping to stare openly when they recognized her. Analisa thought they must make quite a procession—she and Sophie dressed in their finery; Jon, handsome and strong, driving them through town; Caleb following close behind, with Kase before him on the saddle. Still, she could not force down the feeling of humiliation and tension that swept over her when she met the curious stares of the onlookers. Analisa sat rigid beside Sophie, her friend holding tight to her hand, offering encouragement as well as reassurance.

As if sensing Analisa's nervousness, Sophie whispered to her as the carriage pulled up before the wooden platform of the depot. "It's good you are leaving, Anja. You have a chance to begin again."

"It's not that I am afraid of their stares." Her eyes mirrored her feelings as Analisa tried to explain. "It's just that when they look at me that way, as if I am unclean, I am forced to remember it all again. No one here will let me forget."

At that moment Analisa indeed felt grateful for the chance to make a new life for herself and Kase. *I have Caleb to thank for this second chance,* she thought, as she watched him approach the carriage.

Caleb dismounted and reached up to help her down from the carriage. Rather than set her on the muddy ground, he carried her the few short steps to where Kase waited on the platform. As Analisa turned to straighten the boy's high shirt collar, she noticed a familiar carriage passing by. She immediately recognized the stout figure of Clara Heusinkveld holding the reins. The older woman, failing to hold her amazement in check, openly gaped at Analisa. The buggy slowed. With a slight smile, Analisa bobbed her head in Mevrou Heusinkveld's direction, acknowledging the woman's obvious amazement. Caught gawking, the gray-haired matron slapped the reins against the chestnut horse's rump, and the carriage rolled past with a sudden lurch.

The Union Pacific train pulled into the station in a whirlwind of steam, clanging bells, and screaming wheels, demanding the attention of the small group waiting on the rough wooden platform. Scorpio whinnied in protest as a station employee led him to the stock car. The noise and last-minute activity infused everyone with an overwhelming sense of urgency. Sophie gave Analisa one more hug before she turned to tell Caleb good-bye. The two men shook hands over Kase's head, and then it was the boy's turn to be the center of attention as Jon and Sophie knelt to bid him farewell with promises of a visit very soon.

Analisa felt Caleb's hand at her waist urging her toward the steps. The final moment was here, she realized: She was leaving Pella. Analisa turned, one foot on the lowest step that hung above the platform, one hand clutching the bag of tulip bulbs. With a final, hurried wave over her shoulder, she moved upward into the dark interior of the car.

Chapter Ten

Dakota, April 1871

"I see you are the best dressed again today, Private Jensen."

Analisa could not help smiling as she spoke to the young man who stood at rigid attention on her wooden porch. Behind him on the parade ground, the rhythmic pounding of horses' hooves blended with the creak of leather and the rattle of sabers as shouted commands rose above the steady, monotonous cadence of moving men and animals. Shoulder to shoulder, the men of the Twenty-second Regiment moved past the row of small wood-frame houses with a precision born of long hours of drill.

Each morning before guard mount the men best "turned-out" were excused from guard and fatigue duties to act as orderlies. The coveted positions allowed a chosen few to serve the commanding officers. Major Williamson, the acting commander, saw to it that Caleb and Analisa were assigned an orderly at least three days a week. Tor Jensen, a fresh faced and eager Swede of barely eighteen, managed to win the detail two out of three days.

Analisa noticed that whenever Tor blushed, as he was doing just now, the red hue spread from his throat up to his hairline. The high collar of his shirt pushed tight against his massive neck, and his shoulders strained at the seams of the navy wool uniform. Like many other Swedes, Tor had thick, straight white-blond hair, which was carefully slicked into place. He was shy and polite, and Analisa had appreciated his help and companionship as she became accustomed to her new surroundings.

Still at attention, the young soldier spoke, his English singing with a heavy accent. "Should I bring around the wagon, Mrs. de la Vega?"

"Yes, Private. I need to go to the trader's store to pick up a few things."

"Yes, ma'am. I'll be right back."

She suppressed a giggle when he started to salute her and caught herself, afraid of hurting the serious young man's feelings. Tor was off the porch in a moment and heading for the stables.

Analisa leaned against the door frame of the small wooden house assigned to Caleb and watched the soldiers drill. The monotonous routine of army life was becoming all too familiar. The enlisted men's lives revolved around the bugle calls that summoned them to various duties and daily drills. She found the bugle calls a way to mark the slowly passing hours while Caleb was away on an assignment and Kase was off on his daily round of riding lessons and adventures with his new friends.

Tor would return soon, she reminded herself, and so closed the door behind her and crossed the parlor. Pen and ink sat beside a neatly lettered sheet of paper on the dining table. Analisa sat down once again on the high ladder-back chair and searched for the correct words to finish a letter to Sophie. Although writing in English was still a struggle, Analisa held to her promise and wrote her friend at least once a week. In the month since the Storms had arrived at the fort, no news had arrived from Pella, but she was confident that the next shipment of mail would contain word from the Allens.

Her fingers toyed with the pen as she tried to find a way to onclude the letter. She wrote, "Caleb has been gone for over a week now, and I look forward to his return." She could not add that she feared for his safety, nor would she let her friends know that the reason behind Caleb's frequent comings and goings was till a secret he kept from her.

Analisa put the pen back into the ink pot and cradled her chin in her hands, elbows braced upon the table. She was determined not to become angry with Caleb because he would not confide in her, but she found it increasingly difficult to hold her temper as the days turned into weeks.

"It's for your own protection, Anja," he had said when she asked him why he could not at least tell her where he was going the last time he left. "The less you know right now, the better. If anything should happen to me . . ." He paused a moment before he continued, "Nothing will happen to me, Anja. Nothing. Believe me."

As she sat staring across the room, Analisa fought against the fear that caused her anger. What if Caleb never returned? She and Kase would be all alone. She shuddered at the thought. *You're not afraid of being alone,* her conscience scolded, *for being alone is nothing new to you.* Then Analisa forced herself to face the basis of her fear: *I'm scared to death of losing Caleb.*

When had it happened? she asked herself, leaning back in the chair and rubbing her upper arms, suddenly chilled. When had Caleb taken over her every waking thought, her very soul? He worked such magic on her that she remembered only the hours he was beside her, what he said, what they did. Nothing else seemed important anymore. Only Kase was allowed into their glowing circle of love; only Kase and Caleb mattered.

Her thoughts were far too scattered to allow her to complete Sophie's letter, and so Analisa carefully folded the paper and stood, pushing the chair away from the table. She unconsciously smoothed the thick *tafelkleed,* a tightly woven patterned table-cloth of blood-red tones edged with fringe. Too precious to use in the soddie, it now covered the round dining table. Collecting the writing utensils, she carried them to the buffet, where she reserved one of the small, upper drawers for her stationery. Unconsciously, she ran her fingertips across the fine mahogany finish of the sideboard and then turned to survey the room.

Analisa was happy with her accomplishments here. Now that

she had mixed her few precious possessions with the variou pieces left behind by the previous tenants, the place wa beginning to feel like home.

As she crossed the parlor intent upon readying herself fo Tor's return, she glanced down at the carpet that covered almos the entire floor. It was her most prized possession. Caleb had helped to spread fresh straw beneath it, not only to provide additional padding but also to insulate the room from the bone-chilling cold that spread beneath the floorboards. Conten with the appearance of the room, Analisa went into the bedroom she shared with Caleb. Although small, the room afforded them the privacy the soddie had lacked.

On tiptoe, she retrieved a soft, lightweight shawl she had folded away among her other clothing on the shelf. As she wrapped the pale yellow material about her shoulders, Analisa stopped before the oval mirror above the dresser and repinned her hair. The black beaded reticule, her precious gift from Sophie, lay on the dresser amid pin boxes and tins of buttons and sewing notions. She slipped the drawstrings over her wrist and felt the purse dangle heavily from her arm. Caleb always insisted on leaving more money than she needed while he was away. She weighed the bag in the palm of her hand, certain that she could live for a year on the sum he'd left behind. Opening the purse, she placed half of the coins in the top drawer of the dresser and then left the room. She passed through the parlor and stepped out onto the porch to await Private Jensen.

The air outdoors was fresh and unusually warm: only a hint of coolness touched her as she stood in the shade of the overhang. The house itself—or the guests' quarters, as it was referred to—was made of rough-hewn cottonwood logs. Although it was a far cry from the soddie, the structure was nearly as crude in many respects. Clay mud had been used to chink the cracks and openings between the logs, and the place was often cold and drafty. Still, she no longer fought a constant battle with sifting dust and dirt as she had done in the sod house.

Analisa moved forward into the patch of sunlight that crept across the front edge of the plank porch, laced her fingers together, and held her locked hands against the folds of her gray skirt. How often had she stood in the doorway of the soddie, gazing out upon the empty, rolling miles of prairie, wondering if she would ever see what lay beyond the horizon? These days

Analisa often marveled at the way her life had changed. A year ago her acquaintances had been limited to a handful of people. Now, at Fort Sully, she moved among the residents of the outpost, who accepted her as the wife of Don Ricardo de la Vega. As yet, Analisa had met no one among the officers' and enlisted men's wives who might become as dear to her as Sophie. She felt more comfortable with the wives of the enlisted men, but Caleb had warned her against befriending any of them.

"For appearances' sake," he'd told her. She was to play the role of a woman of a certain standing, the wife of a foreign professor. As such, he had explained, she would be used to having servants and should not choose to become familiar with the enlisted men's wives. Analisa thought it a ridiculous stricture. Now that the world was open to her and none of her new acquaintances were aware of her past, she was forced to live a lie.

Straightening the shawl, which slipped off of her shoulder, she wondered what was keeping Private Jensen. A small sigh escaped her. Analisa scraped the toe of her black leather shoe against a splinter between the planks and then squinted into the sunlight. The increasing sense of boredom and lethargy was beginning to weary her and she was determined to find something to occupy her idle hours. She refused to tell Caleb that she was unhappy here only a few weeks after their arrival, but her thoughts weighed heavily on her mind as she surveyed her surroundings. In Iowa there had been more than enough work to fill the hours of the day. Caring for Kase, gardening, keeping house, tending to the animals, and sewing had demanded all of Analisa's attention. Now her life had changed abruptly; the fading yellow calluses on her hands attested silently to her transformation.

Perhaps today she would find some new materials that would inspire her to sew. Now that the curtains were hung and she had two new day dresses, Analisa felt there was nothing to do but wait for Caleb's return. She loathed the feeling of dependence that the waiting forced upon her. Even Kase always seemed to be occupied elsewhere. He had gone off early that morning, eager for his morning riding lesson. Later that day, he would chatter endlessly about his riding and about "Soldier Zach," the scout who lived behind the store.

This morning she watched with eager anticipation as the open buckboard wagon driven by Tor Jensen rounded the corner of the barracks and traveled the length of the row of houses, finally pulling up before the porch. As Analisa moved off the low step, the private climbed down from the high seat and walked around the rear of the wagon to lend her a hand up. The young, smooth-faced man flushed red to his hairline as he assisted Analisa onto the high wagon seat.

Aware of his embarrassment she tried putting him at ease and ignored his nervousness. He was only a few years younger than she, but she felt they were a lifetime apart in experience. Tor had left his parents' homestead, hoping to ease their burden of eleven other children. He earned his own pay, thirteen dollars a month, had a place to sleep, regular meals, and a chance to learn English. When he signed up, he had never seen an Indian or ridden more than a few miles on horseback. He'd wanted to become a soldier in the U.S. Army and so he had. Analisa gleaned the information bit by bit from the quiet man whenever he served as the de la Vegas' orderly.

Content to ride in silence, Analisa enjoyed the morning air and the deep, azure canopy of the sky, and filled her lungs with the heady smell of early spring. Although the Missouri River was too far west to be visible, Analisa marked its location by the thick growth of trees lining the banks. The land immediately around the fort was a virtually treeless plain that afforded a clear view in every direction. There was plenty of well water and enough grazing land for the cavalry horses.

"You wish to go to the store first, Mrs. de la Vega?"

"I think we should go to the stables. I'd like to watch Kase. He's been begging me to see his progress."

"He is doing well," Tor volunteered. "The old man told me Kase has a natural way with horses."

"Ca . . . His father, Don Ricardo, wants him to have his own horse," Analisa continued after correcting her near mistake. "I'm worried that he is too young."

"He's a good rider, Mrs. de la Vega. You shouldn't worry." He tried to reassure her. "He's already a much better horseman than some of the recruits!" Tor laughed aloud, and Analisa was glad the young man was becoming more at ease in her presence.

Tor stopped the wagon a short distance from the corral where Kase sat astride a prancing chestnut mare. Analisa held her breath as she watched her son. He looked so vulnerable perched atop the horse, his sturdy legs gripping its sides, far too short to reach the stirrups.

The man Kase called ''soldier Zach'' was leading the horse in a wide circle while Kase practiced holding the reins and clinging to the wide body of the animal with his knees. A triumphant glow lit the boy's face as he successfully completed the exercise, and Zach slowed the mare to a walk.

Analisa realized she'd twisted the strings of the reticule unconsciously as she watched her son perform on the horse. She released her pent-up breath and tried to smile. The lessons were important to Kase, and Caleb had insisted the boy learn to ride; if it had been up to Analisa alone, Kase would have waited until he was older.

''Mama!''

Kase called out to her over the distance that separated them, and Tor slapped the reins, signaling the horse to move forward.

Moments later, Kase was standing beside his mother, tugging on her hand.

''Did you see, Mama? Did you see me ride? Soldier Zach says I'm the best rider here! Come watch me.'' Unable to wait, he let go of her hand and ran ahead. ''Tell her, Soldier Zach. Tell her how good I am.''

Stepping carefully over the uneven ground pockmarked by hundreds of hoofprints, Analisa, followed closely by Private Jensen, approached the corral. The old soldier sauntered forward with a rolling gait, Kase on his left and the mare trailing behind.

''Howdy, Miz de la Vega.'' The man's voice was gravelly and stern, but Analisa knew his gruffness was a facade that hid a kind heart. Kase idolized the man, and the child was not easily fooled by strangers.

''Hello again, Mr. Elliot. Kase insisted I come to watch, so here I am.'' She reached out to shake the man's rough hand and noticed the beginning of a smile forming at one corner of his mouth. Before he took her hand, he brushed his own against his pantleg. Stiffening at the contact, he shook hands and nodded in greeting. She was certain he felt uncomfortable around women and wore his gruff demeanor as a form of protection.

His appearance was startling to say the least, but failed to frighten Analisa. She'd heard some of the officers' wives make cruel comments about Zach on more than one occasion, but their snobbery only served to spur Analisa's determination to show the old man every kindness.

Zach Elliot stood at medium height, his skin baked dark by the sun and creased with lines. His beard seemed to be in a perpetual state of stubble, never long, never clean-shaven. A thick white mustache hid his upper lip and trailed down along the corners of his mouth, outlining his lips with a perpetual frown. One deep-set brown eye glistened intently as he watched Analisa. His left eye had been replaced with thick scar tissue, the result of his years as an Indian fighter, so the stories claimed; a jagged scar trailed from the empty socket down the side of his face to his lower jaw. A wide, floppy-brimmed hat, the crown battered out of shape, rode just above his unruly white eyebrows, hiding his hair. Everything about him was long and bent. He looked as used and worn as his hat, his nose twisted slightly to one side, his legs long and bowed from years of riding. A combination of army issue and buckskin, his clothing hung on his spare frame, the entire ensemble coated with dust. Analisa guessed that Zach was far younger than anyone suspected, but he held his peace, never correcting their assumptions. Word was that he was the best Indian tracker at the fort, better even than the Crow scouts on the army payroll. He seemed to see more with his one eye than most people saw with two.

"Your boy there's got the makin's of a fine horseman, Miz de la Vega. Takes to it like an Injun." A stream of tobacco juice shot from the side of his mouth and landed a few feet away.

His words set her heart beating in alarmed warning. She forced herself to meet his sharp one-eyed stare. Did he suspect the truth about Kase's heritage? Analisa wondered, then berated herself for her suspicions. How could Zach possibly know what Kase didn't even know himself? Analisa knew her features must have registered surprise, for Zach immediately sought to apologize.

"No offense intended, ma'am. Nothin' I admire more than a good rider."

She felt him watching her, waiting for further reaction. For a moment she feared he saw through the facade and into her past, but calmed herself. He had no way of knowing. She was Mrs.

Ricardo Corona de la Vega now. She met his stare. "I'm sure his father will be pleased."

Zach merely nodded.

She heard Kase calling to her from the corral gate.

"I came to watch Kase ride, if you don't mind my taking a few more minutes of your time."

"Not at all, ma'am."

At that the man ejected another stream of tobacco juice and turned on the worn heel of his boot to lead the big mare back into the enclosure. Analisa followed Kase, who clung to her hand as he hurried her along. She stood outside the corral and watched as Zach tossed Kase into the saddle and led him around the wide ring, slowly at first and then faster until Kase clung to the saddle horn with both hands. Surprisingly enough, considering his size, he sat the horse well, riding smoothly and accommodating his own movements to the horse's gait.

"Watch, Mama! Look at me!"

"I am!" she called back, laughing. Tor stepped up beside her, smiling and calling out encouragement to the boy. In a few short weeks Kase had become quite a favorite among the troops, especially Tor. She fought the questions that came to mind whenever she saw him talking to the soldiers. Would the more seasoned Indian fighters treat him so kindly if they knew he was not Spanish but half Indian? She discovered early on that living a lie was as complicated as living with the truth.

Dampness crept up between the floorboards of the building that housed the trader's store. Originally built with a dirt floor, the room had never lost the musty smell of wet earth. Wilber Gentry, agent for Durfee and Peck, the franchised traders, stocked every sort of merchandise and crowded it all into one room.

When Analisa arrived, the store was empty except for Gentry, who was trying to create space for newly arrived merchandise. After purchasing a few kitchen supplies, a small garden trowel, and some flower seeds, Analisa bade the trader good day. The door opened before she could turn the handle and Millicent Boynton, followed by her husband, Captain Danfield Boynton, stepped inside. The woman stopped for a moment, allowing her vision to adjust to the dim light, and recognized Analisa. Weeks ago, at their first meeting, Analisa had hoped they might become friends, but later on, she had found the other woman so vastly different from herself in attitude and spirit that she had chosen not to pursue a closer friendship.

The delicate blonde reminded Analisa of a hothouse plant far from its natural environment. Millicent preferred to stay indoors most of the time, reclining on the settee in her own house a few doors from Analisa's.

"Good morning, Mrs. Boynton, Captain." Analisa could feel Millicent inspecting her from head to toe, and so she stood tall, stretching to her full height in order to give the woman a better view. She was not ashamed of the simple lines of the gray batiste gown she'd made for herself shortly after her arrival at the fort.

The dress Millicent wore would have suited someone much younger than thirty-six. Adorned with ribbon and covered with sprigs of embroidered flowers, the style was far too girlish for a woman of Millicent's age. The gown had none of the crisp tailored lines Analisa admired.

Captain Boynton merely nodded in Analisa's direction. Although he was nearly forty, his slight stature and youthful build combined to give the impression of a much younger man. He wore thick-lensed wire-rimmed glasses and continually pushed them upward along his pointed nose. His face, usually shaded by his wide-brimmed cavalry hat, remained pale despite his years spent outdoors. She wondered how he managed to keep his skin so white, in sharp contrast to his faded brown mustache. The man's reed-thin neck stuck out of his braid-trimmed collar.

"I hear your husband is out on another of his flower-gathering missions, ma'am." As Boynton turned his stare in her direction, he slid his spectacles along his nose with his forefinger.

She chose to ignore the sarcasm in his tone. It was obvious that Danfield Boynton thought Caleb less a man because of his supposed profession.

"That's right, Captain, but I expect him to return soon."

"I assume he's been warned that those red bastards out there wouldn't think twice about lifting his scalp."

Analisa swallowed hard, taken aback by the menace in the

man's stare. "Well, he . . ." When she failed to respond quickly enough, Boynton ignored her struggle and continued to rail against the renegade Sioux.

"If I had my way," he said as he jabbed a cocked thumb toward his chest and glanced around to see who might be listening, "I'd round up every last one of them—man, woman, and child—and put 'em out of their misery."

"Now, Danfield"—his wife beamed as she proudly squeezed his arm—"don't you go off on your high horse again." She shrugged and smiled at Analisa. "Sometimes he gets himself so worked up."

"I would," he reiterated. "I'd clean 'em all out. 'Nits make lice,' remember." His chest swelled with pride as he quoted his hero, Colonel Chiviagton. He paused long enough to pull a gold watch out of his pocket and check the time before he spoke again. "I'll see you later, m'dear." Always the gentleman, Boynton bowed slightly to his wife and nodded in Analisa's direction before he left the store. As the door closed behind him, Millicent moved farther into the room.

"Mrs. de la Vega . . ." Millicent stopped beside a pickle barrel and glanced around the room, leaning close to Analisa before she continued. "I'm glad I ran into you. My sister-in-law is arriving within the month from Chicago, and I am planning to hold a soiree in her honor. Nothing too extravagant, mind you . . ." The woman patted her perfectly formed corkscrew curls into place.

"Just punch and some desserts. I'm sure I can talk the major into letting the company band perform, and perhaps we can use the Officers' Club, but if not, the hall will have to do, I suppose."

Unable to comment on Millicent's notion of a "small soiree," Analisa merely nodded.

"Anyway, I hope you'll be willing to help me when the time comes. There's no way we can hope to decorate well enough to hide the *dismal reality* of this place." She fanned her hand languidly, her wrist limp. "But if the others are as *deathly bored* out here as I am, they will certainly welcome any sort of diversion." There was a slight pause while she caught her breath and then added, "Don't you agree?" Her pinched brown eyes bored into Analisa's.

"I'll be happy to help in any way I can."

"I'll let you know about the date as soon as I know myself. I'll need to ask Major Williamson for his permission of course. It's a shame he isn't married. It's up to the commanding officer's wife to provide us with social entertainment, you know." She stopped and glanced outside through the glass-paneled door, hastily smoothing her skirt and then straightening the bodice with a gloved hand. "Then again, I'm glad he isn't married. He's certainly an attractive man, don't you think?"

Before she could answer, Analisa heard booted feet scrape across the walkway outside and turned to look through the doors herself. Millicent had seen the major approaching from outside.

The man paused just inside the entry, hat in hand, to speak to the two women. Frank Williamson reminded Analisa of Caleb, although physically, the acting commander of Fort Sully was nothing like her husband. The similarity was in the way the two men moved. They could not be ignored when they entered a room, especially by women, even though Major Williamson was twenty years older than Caleb. Both were at ease with themselves, confidence showing in every step. Where Caleb's features were dark and arresting, however, Frank Williamson's more open, smiling appeal was highlighted by snapping green eyes and thick, unruly auburn hair. The major sported a neatly trimmed mustache of the same rich color, which drew attention to the broad smile always in place beneath it. Analisa had never heard a disparaging remark from the major and admired the way he extended a kind greeting to everyone. His calm assurance put her at ease, and she appreciated his concern. He stopped by frequently to see how she and Kase were getting along and to offer his help. Analisa looked forward to his calls and enjoyed the easy openness of the man—but not, she realized, in the same way Millicent Boynton enjoyed his company.

"Major Williamson, what a surprise!" Millicent's voice rose as she greeted the striking figure. Analisa stood by silently while Millicent touched his coat sleeve as she emphasized her greeting. "What a relief! I'd just mentioned you to Mrs. de la Vega. We're both *so* hoping that you'll agree to let the company band play for a party in a few weeks. You see, I have company coming to visit and—"

"Hello, Mrs. de la Vega. Mrs. Boynton." The major nodded

to each in turn, seemingly unaware that he'd cut the woman off in midsentence. His eyes lingered a moment longer on Analisa before he turned to Millicent. "I'm sure something can be arranged, Mrs. Boynton. You need to speak to Sergeant Terry in my office. He'll make all the arrangements." Easily dismissing the issue, he again studied Analisa. "Are you getting settled, Mrs. de la Vega?"

"Yes, Major. Thank you."

"Fort Sully's such a change for you. I hope you aren't too bored."

"Actually, I'm quite used to being alone, and I have Kase."

"You must miss the excitement and bustle of Boston."

For a moment she was taken aback, then hesitantly answered, "No, actually, I prefer to be alone."

Millicent included herself in the conversation. "Well, I *loathe* it here. Believe me, I'd rather have Danfield stationed anywhere else. The weather out here is dreadful—it's either too hot or freezing cold—and not a night passes but what I don't fear for my scalp."

"I'm afraid you don't give the regiment much credit, Mrs. Boynton. Besides, there are far worse forts than Sully. The only problems we have here right now are a few renegade Indians who refuse to turn themselves in."

"Those renegades continually attack the work details," Millicent complained. "There's not even a stockade around this place. It doesn't seem much like a fort to me."

"I'm sure the troops are more diligent because of that fact, ma'am. They've no walls to hide behind." Dismissing her, he let his quick glance inspect Analisa's packages. "I hope you found all you need?"

"Yes." She nodded. "I am going to plant a few seeds, if that's all right? I'd like to have some flowers near the porch."

"That sounds like a fine idea." His eyes softened as he looked away, staring through the glass door for the briefest moment. "My mother always kept flower boxes along the edge of the porch."

Millicent's razor-edged voice cut in, drawing the conversation back to herself. "I've never found the time to fiddle with flowers. Besides it's such nasty work, all that *dirt* and all." She visibly shuddered at the thought.

"Mrs. de la Vega," the major began again, ignoring Millicent's comment, "would you like me to have a man build a couple of flower boxes for your porch?"

"Oh, Major, I don't mean to make any trouble. I just want to plant a few seeds."

"It's no problem. I insist. Right now we've got more men than I know what to do with. The only important detail out working today is the one escorting the paymaster the last few miles back to the fort." He brushed his hat against his pantleg and shifted his weight. "I'll send someone over after the noon meal."

Analisa paused, embarrassed by his suggestion, but grateful nonetheless. Gardening would help her pass the time. "My thanks, Major Williamson." Anxious to return home before Kase finished his lesson, Analisa bade them both good day.

"Mrs. de la Vega." With a curt nod, Millicent dismissed Analisa and began to lead Major Williamson toward the center of the store. "Now, Major, I'd like to discuss a few more details with you . . ." The sound of Millicent's voice drifted away as the door closed behind Analisa.

"How long will it be before the flowers bloom?"

The major's deep voice, so close to her ear, startled Analisa. He'd come upon her without warning and was standing next to the porch, watching her as she bent over one of the newly made flower boxes.

"I see the boxes were completed quickly," he went on. "Do they meet your approval?" As he smiled she noted the slight space between his two front teeth. The red highlights in his hair were set aflame by the bright afternoon sunlight.

Resuming her work, Analisa broke up the heavy dirt clods in the box with her new trowel. "Yes, Major. I must say the man you sent over knew exactly what to do. The boxes were finished in no time. I can't wait until they are full of flowers."

"And how long will that be?" he asked.

"At least six to eight weeks before they sprout. I plan to put a few sunflowers around the porch, too. They'll bloom late in the summer."

Removing his hat, the major sat down on the edge of the porch and leaned against the post that supported the roof. He sat quietly for a time, toying with the braid that circled the crown of his hat while Analisa continued to press the dirt over the seeds. When she finished, she sat back on her heels, kneeling on the rough wooden planks, and brushed the dirt from her hands. With her wrist, Analisa pushed at the wisps of hair escaping the knot on top of her head, then stood and moved closer to the door. The major remained relaxed, leaning against the post, watching the comings and goings of the men across the square.

"Can I get you some tea, Major? I was just about to have some myself. I'm sure the water is still hot."

"Thanks, Mrs. de la Vega. That would be just fine."

When the tea was ready, Analisa used a bread board as a tray and carried out two cups and saucers, her violet teapot, and a plate of *koekjes* for the major. He gingerly set his cup of tea beside him on the porch and took the cookie plate.

"You certainly know how to spoil a man, Mrs. de la Vega. I'm not surprised that your husband was so anxious to bring you out here." He watched while she settled onto the straight-back chair against the wall of the house.

After taking an ample bite, the major glanced at Analisa. "How did you meet your husband? If you don't mind my asking, that is."

"Not at all." Analisa kept her voice steady while her mind raced ahead. "We met in Europe. Ricardo studied for a few months in Holland, where he became acquainted with my father through the university. Ricardo is a very famous botanist."

"His credentials are quite impressive. I understand you've lived all over the world?"

She tried to speculate as to the tack his questioning was taking, worried that she might become trapped in the web she spun.

"Not the whole world, Major." She remembered to smile and suddenly hated having to force her emotions. "We lived in Holland for a time, then moved to Boston. Of course, we stopped in Spain to visit with my husband's people. We've lived in the States nearly four years, so Kase knows little else. That is why his English is so good." She looked away, unable to meet his steady gaze.

"You speak Spanish?" He spoke between bites. Was he watching her too intently?

"Actually, no . . . well, very little." Her nerves taut, her stomach twisted into a knot, Analisa changed the course of the conversation. "Tell me about the reservation, Major. Why is it so hard to keep the Indians there?"

"If I knew that, Mrs. de la Vega, I would be a man without a problem." He set his empty plate down and picked up his cup. The china looked too small for his large hands, but he held the saucer gently and raised the cup to his lips before he answered.

"The Indians are used to life without boundaries. Before whites settled here, they lived a nomadic life, following the buffalo and other game. They lived to hunt and hunted to live. Now we expect them to live in one place, to stay put while we build homes and plant crops on the land they once roamed freely. They can't or won't adjust."

"Can you blame them?"

"No. No, I can't say I do. But the army is in a rough position. We are supposed to corral the Indians and keep the peace. If they won't stay civilized—that is, live in one place and abide by our rules—we're supposed to ride them down and put them back on the reservation. The problem is, there are men in command who see our job as a license to kill the Indians off. Some officers think that's the only way we'll ever end the conflict. Just get rid of them."

"But aren't the Indians cared for on the reservations? Isn't the government supposed to provide for them and teach them to provide for themselves?"

"That sounds real good in theory, on paper in Washington. But by the time the money filters out here, most of what's due the Indians has been skimmed off the top. They get the worst of the bargain, moldy meat and mealy flour. I haven't met an Indian agent yet who isn't a crook. Buff Hardy at the agency nearby is one of the worst."

"Why don't you get rid of him?"

"The system won't let me do that. He's been there for years, and the BIA recently took away what little power the army had over the agents."

"BIA?" Analisa asked.

"Bureau of Indian Affairs."

Caleb had already explained all of this to Analisa, but she pretended to be ignorant of it. If Caleb were actually a botany professor, she would have little knowledge of the Indian situation.

"Perhaps you'd like to visit the reservation, Mrs. de la Vega? You might find it interesting."

"I never—"

"You might be moved to do something for the Indians out there. None of the other women around here seem to care, but I have the feeling you would think differently."

To imagine herself moving among the Sioux frightened her to death. But did she owe it to Caleb and Kase to try? Perhaps she could understand a part of them that was unknown to her. Besides, working at the reservation would help fill her idle hours. As the idea began to take shape in her mind, Analisa questioned the major. "Are there many children on the reservation?"

"Yes, kids and old folks mainly. The strong young ones take to the hills and try to stay one step ahead of us. They live off of raids or an occasional hunt. Of course, with the railroads expanding so quickly now that the war has ended, it's getting tougher on them every day. If something isn't done soon, I'm afraid there'll be all-out bloodshed. Neither side wants that."

"No." She noticed his empty cup. "Can I get you more tea, Major?"

"Thank you, no. It's time I got back to work." Unfolding his tall form, Frank Williamson set the cup and saucer on the plate and offered them to Analisa, who walked across the porch to stand above him.

"I'm glad you stopped by, Major." Her smile was genuine, for she appreciated his company as well as his suggestion, which had set her mind on a plan to relieve her boredom. "And thank you once again for the flower boxes."

"I'm always happy to oblige, ma'am."

Too late she noticed the soft warmth in his voice as he lifted her free hand to his lips. She felt the heat of his breath on her skin before his lips touched the back of her hand. The whole experience was over before she could pull her hand away. Major Williamson stood tall and smiled casually as if the kiss had been nothing but a polite formality—and yet a vague uneasiness nagged at Analisa. Had he meant it to be something more?

He pushed his hat down over his wavy hair. "Let me know if you decide to ride over to the reservation. I'd be happy to show you around."

Both the major and Analisa were startled by the sound of a heavily accented voice.

"I'm sure you would be, Major, but I am also quite sure that an Indian reservation is no place for my wife."

The major turned to lock eyes with the man behind him while Analisa, her face surprised and then welcoming, recognized Caleb.

"Don Ricardo," the other man began smoothly, extending a hand in greeting, "welcome home."

Chapter Eleven

Caleb shook the major's hand briefly and waited for Williamson to move away from Analisa. Obviously ignoring Caleb's biting words, Williamson tipped his hat in Analisa's direction and walked away from the house.

One glance at Caleb revealed his anger. Analisa tried to see past the ridiculous round glasses to look deep into his eyes and gauge his feelings. Fatigue shadowed the depressions under his eyes and weighed heavily on his eyelids. Beneath the bowler hat, his hair looked dull and unwashed, its usual sheen dimmed by dust and grime. She could tell he was uncomfortable in the stiff, high-collared shirt, for he stood at attention, holding to the foppish pose he assumed with the role of Don Ricardo Corona de la Vega. He clutched a variety of plant cuttings in his hand. More plants filled a wooden box at his feet. She longed to

encircle him in her embrace and welcome him home properly,
but was all too aware of the constant activity across the square.
Instead, she stepped aside, her hands filled with cups and
saucers, as he lifted the box and strode past her without a word.
Retrieving the bread board, she stacked the service and followed
him into the house.

Caleb was not in the parlor. Analisa passed through to the
kitchen and found him drinking a glass of water. Finished in
seconds, he poured another glass full and drank it, then set the
glass on the drainboard and turned to face her. With his hat off
and the spectacles in his breast pocket, he looked more like
himself, but the anger on his face was clearly visible to her.
Afraid of the coldness she saw in his eyes, Analisa stood rooted
to the spot. Suddenly unsure how to react to his mood, she did
nothing, although she longed to go to him and melt the
expression that tightened his lips.

"I need a bath." His icy words matched the cold blue steel in
his eyes.

"I'll heat the water for you."

"Fine." His voice a gruff whisper, he brushed past her on his
way to the bedroom. Confused, Analisa reached beneath the
sink for a bucket and then added wood to the stove. She lifted
the kettle and crossed the room again to fill it with water from
the crock. Something had gone wrong; that much was certain.
She wondered if he held her to blame? Determined to clear the
air, Analisa waited impatiently for the water to heat before she
went to face him.

Stripped to the waist, Caleb folded back the fragile screen
that surrounded the tub. He walked to the dresser and glanced at
his reflection in the mirror while he ran a hand across the light
stubble of beard on his usually clean-shaven face. He untied the
twisted queue at the nape of his neck. He knew the men at the
fort thought him strange indeed, but what did he care? he asked
himself. It was all part of the ruse. His problem was that he did
care—he cared too much what Analisa thought. He cared about
her and the boy, and he was becoming more convinced as the
days dragged on that he should never have brought them to Fort
Sully.

Nothing was going right. He pulled his near-shoulder-length
hair out of the knot and let it hang loose. He'd greased it down

in the Sioux custom to keep it from flying into his face, and now it felt as heavy as his spirit. He sat on the bed and began to pull off his boots, wishing they were the familiar, worn snakeskins. Unbidden, the disturbing picture of Frank Williamson and Analisa engaged in idle conversation on the front porch sliced through his thoughts. He felt his gut churn and was hit by an urge to toss his boot against the wall. Instead, slowly, intently, he pulled off the other one, picked both boots up, and walked in stocking feet across the room to set them down silently beside the door. Discipline. Silence. He wasn't a wild man, he told himself, and refused to give in to the raging anger inside him. He owed her the chance to explain.

Everything in the room was in order, just as he had known it would be. He'd looked forward to coming home, even though he could stay only one night. But to return to the cozy sight of Frank Williamson kissing his wife's hand—it was not what he'd bargained for, and he certainly didn't have time to deal with it right now.

Living a dual life was not easy, especially since life in the renegade camp was so hard. The Sioux who refused to live on the reservation scraped out an existence on the run. It was a far cry from the Indian way of life he'd known in his youth. Two weeks ago he'd located the renegade camp, hidden in a quiet meadow between the bluffs along one of the many offshoots of the river. The leader of the band was a man named Red Dog, a warrior from a northern clan. Openly suspicious of the half-breed who claimed to side with them, Red Dog had spoken out against Caleb and wanted him gone until some of the older men, men who'd known of Caleb's grandfather, agreed that he be allowed to stay and prove himself. So far Caleb had not been forced to participate in any raids against the white settlements nearby, but he feared the time would come when he would no longer be able to avoid a confrontation. He would have to prove his loyalty.

With thoughts of the past two weeks heavy on his mind, Caleb poured water from the pitcher on the dresser into the washbowl and wet the soap cake in his shaving mug. Lathering his face with a boar-bristle brush, he tried to concentrate on shaving.

At the sound of quiet tapping, Caleb bade Analisa enter.

"The water is heating."

"Thank you."

She carried the first bucket full of steaming water to the tub and dumped it in. Caleb turned to watch her, wiping away the little islands of lather that remained on his face and neck as he did so.

"I'm sorry," he began slowly. "I didn't realize you were already carrying a bucketful. I'll bring in the rest."

Silent, Analisa stared at him from across the room. Bare to the waist, his body was lean and hard, his bronze skin glistening over tautly molded muscle. It was the color of dark golden honey fresh from the comb. She knew his trousers hid thighs and legs as lean and strong as the rest of him. Disappointment swept over her when he turned away, until the sight of his slim hips and tight buttocks beneath the wool tweed pants sent an aching throb through her. She longed to touch him.

"Would you like me to trim your hair?"

"No."

He tossed his head, shaking the hair away from his eyes. "I have to leave it long. Besides, it's too dirty."

She closed the distance between them, reaching out to touch his shoulder, and saw him stiffen as she approached. His silence frightened her.

Her words were hurried. "I'll go see about the rest of the water."

Analisa closed the bedroom door behind her and fled into the kitchen. While she waited for another kettle of water to boil, she busied herself with dinner, hoping to release the tension she felt. What in the world was wrong with Caleb? She'd never seen him so visibly angry, not even the day they were married, the day he rode out of her life for three months. Venting her own anger while she began to prepare supper, Analisa realized her mistake as soon as her eyes began to flow with tears. She looked down at the onion, which she had minced to a pulp. Sniffing and wiping at her eyes with the backs of her hands, she stepped away from the overpowering scent and backed into Caleb.

"Oh!" She pressed her hands to her eyes to stop the stinging as well as the flow of tears. Fingertips heavily scented with onion only made matters worse.

"Are you crying?" She heard doubt in his voice.

"No. I'm chopping onions. I never cry." She waved her hands beneath his nose and he winced.

"Oh."

Silence again.

Didn't he realize she was teasing him, reminding him of his own words, "I never yell"?

Caleb opened his mouth to speak and, thinking better of it, closed it again. Desire pulsed through him at the sight of her flushed cheeks and the haunted expression in her eyes. All he wanted at that moment was to take her in his arms then and there, to taste the nectar of her lips and hold her to him. He studied her, wanting to read desire in her eyes. He saw only tears. Could they be real? Doubt assailed him, blotting out reason. Analisa'd never met another eligible man before he'd ridden up to her door. No one from Pella would have married her, of that he was certain, but what if she'd had a chance to leave the Dutch community and meet a man elsewhere, someone more like herself, someone of her own choice? Someone like the major?

Doubting himself, Caleb was sure in an instant that she would never have chosen him. If that was true, was it fair of him to keep her, to press her into holding on to a marriage that had no real reason for being? Did it matter at all that he'd come to love her? Wiping his open palms against his thighs, Caleb turned away.

Analisa dried her tears with the corner of her apron and pretended not to notice as he hefted a kettle off of the stove and carried it into the bedroom without another word. His footsteps beat a soft tattoo against the floorboards as he walked back and forth, cooling the boiling water in the tub with a bucket of cold water from the barrel on the back stoop. The footsteps stopped soon after she heard the bedroom door close.

She would give him ten minutes, she decided. Ten minutes, and then she'd go right in there and ask him face to face what he was so mad about. Having finally decided on a course of action, Analisa scooped the onion and some butter into a frying pan and set it on the sideboard. Then she washed and dried her hands, smoothed her hair, and paced the room for nine minutes.

The door swung open soundlessly. Analisa moved into the bedroom on tiptoe, her heart racing. Caleb sat low in the tub, unmoving, his head against the high rounded backrest, his eyes closed. Intending to offer to wash his back, she walked toward him silently. Caleb's chest rose and fell heavily; he was asleep. She knew he was thoroughly exhausted, for the slightest sound usually woke him.

His hands were folded across his chest, his fingers intertwined. The thick, corded muscles of his upper arms contrasted with the serenity etched on his face as he slept. His dark lashes were half moons against the high-cheekboned planes of his face. His knees were drawn up to accommodate his length, extending well above the surface of the water while one leg lay against the side of the tub. Clouded with soap, the milky water hid his lower body from view, but the knowledge of what lurked just below the surface was enough to send a rush of heat to her cheeks.

Unwilling to disturb him, Analisa began to walk away. The soft rustle of her skirt and the brush of the fabric against the side of his face roused him. With a warrior's instinct, Caleb sat up, instantly alert, yet for a split second unsure of where he was.

Damn. He chided himself for his laxness. Had she been an enemy, he'd be dead now, he thought, and knew he was more tired than he had realized.

He watched Analisa over his shoulder as she placed folded linen towels on the bed. As if aware of his eyes on her, she turned to face him. Selfish pride and possessiveness overwhelmed him. God, he loved her. No one else would have her, he'd be damned sure of that, for he couldn't let her go. Not to the major, not to anyone, even if the other man was more suited to her than he was.

"Caleb, we have to talk."

It took all of her courage to utter the words. Something was wrong; she saw it in his eyes and felt it in the very air around him. She unfolded a wide linen towel and carried it to him. Awkward with his nudity, she draped it over the screen and busied herself, tidying up his shaving items. The mirror over the dresser afforded her a view without forcing her to face him directly. He stood in the tub and briskly toweled his hair, shaking the loose strands and rubbing it until it no longer dripped profusely. He swiped at the beaded water on his skin and dried his body before stepping out. She watched the muscles in his arms bunch and relax with his movements. He kept his back to her until he had draped the towel around his hips and tucked in the ends. She turned to face him just as he turned to face her.

He felt everything inside him flop upside down at her words. She wanted to talk. Well, he would listen, he told himself, even if she told him what he feared most. He'd listen, but refuse to let her go.

"What do you want to talk about?"

His steps took him within inches of her. He didn't realize he'd pinned her against the dresser.

"I . . . I just want to know what's bothering you, Caleb. I have never seen you like this." Her eyes moved over his face. It was grim and determined. "That is, not since last year. Before you went to Boston."

They both knew she was avoiding mention of that day by the stream.

"Should something be bothering me?"

"What?"

"What is there for me to worry about, Analisa?"

"How should I know?" Her mind raced. Why hadn't he called her Anja as was his habit now? Why hadn't he spoken her name with the loving caress in his voice she'd grown used to?

"Where's Kase?" he demanded.

The abrupt change of subject confused her for a moment.

"Kase?" Her brow furrowed in thought. "Kase is with Private Jensen. They went out rabbit hunting."

His expression changed to one of concern.

"Where?"

"Not far. Toward the river, I think. I'm sure Tor will be careful with him."

"That kid can barely take care of himself, let alone Kase."

"They should be back soon. Besides, I think Tor misses his family deeply. Kase reminds him of his own brothers and sisters; that's why the major assigns him to us as orderly whenever he can."

As soon as the words were spoken, Analisa knew she'd said something wrong. She knew now how the prey of a hawk must feel in its final moments.

"The major." A muscle tensed in his jaw and failed to relax.

"Yes, the major. He's very perceptive."

"Perceptive?"

"Yes."

"Where did you learn the word *perceptive?*"

"Reading. I've had plenty of time for reading. You have been gone two weeks."

"You don't have to tell me how long I've been gone. I can count. I'm sure the major was very solicitous while I was away, inquiring as to your needs and wishes. Have you learned what *solicitous* means?"

She shook her head. She could feel the edge of the dresser pressing against her hips. Caleb towered over her; for some reason he was trying to intimidate her. That was more than enough to raise her ire. Analisa straightened, ready to do battle, ready to clear the air.

"He was very polite, yes."

"Coming up with all sorts of suggestions and ways to keep you amused? Outings to the reservation to visit the poor and the downtrodden? That sort of thing?"

"Among others. There's to be a party. A dance in honor of Captain Boynton's sister."

"And Williamson asked to escort you? I'm sure he hoped your husband would still be away."

The searing hatred that suddenly flashed in his eyes warned her not to push him further.

"Of course not." She tried to temper her tone, but failed, as her own anger mounted. What kind of woman did he think she was?

Suddenly, as if he'd slapped her, her heart constricted inside her breast. Caleb sounded no different from the people of Pella. Because she'd been raped and had borne a child of that rape, they assumed she would not care about her reputation because she had none to care about.

She let out a heavy sigh. Stubborn pride strengthened by long years of facing such prejudice helped her maintain her proud stance, but she could not meet his eyes and so simply looked away.

Caleb reached out and grabbed her shoulders, his fingers biting into the tender skin beneath the gray batiste. He wanted to shake her, force her to deny that there was anything between her and Frank Williamson. Instead, he studied her profile. Her mouth was set in a stubborn pout, the lush bottom lip all but begging him to kiss it. Standing so close, he could smell the subtle fragrance of her flowery talcum. It was his undoing.

Slowly, he released his iron grip on her shoulders and lifted his right hand to her chin, gently turning her face until their eyes met. Caleb dipped his head until his lips touched hers, tentatively at first, unsure of her acceptance. When he felt her arms slide beneath his and her hands press against his spine, Caleb deepened his kiss, pulling her closer, molding her to him, thigh against thigh, their hearts beating wildly against each other in welcome, saying all that their words left unsaid.

His tongue explored the depths of her mouth, his skin felt warm from the bathwater, and Analisa reveled in his clean scent as his damp hair brushed her cheek. The days of separation had heightened her need for him, and she sensed that same pulsing need in Caleb. He held her so tightly, bending her over the dresser, that she felt as if she would break in two. Sliding her hands to his sides, she pushed against the solid wall of him, trying to break free.

Caleb's lips released hers. He raised his head but did not relinquish his hold. "You're mine, Anja." He ground the words out, his voice low, threatening. "I won't let anyone else have you."

"No one else wants me." She fully believed her own words.

He straightened, his arms still around her waist, as he held her possessively. "Either you're playing me for a fool or you're more naive than I thought."

"Caleb, why are you treating me like this?"

"Like what? I have every right to be jealous. You are a beautiful woman."

"I am your wife. Not some . . . *hoer*." She waved her hand in frustration. "I don't know the English. I am not some woman who goes from man to man. Caleb, you are my husband."

"What choice did you have, even in that?"

"You gave me a choice. I chose to marry you."

"Yes, but you were forced into it by that spineless minister who catered to the whims of those controlling the collection plate. If you'd had a real choice, you'd never have chosen me. I was the only one around and the first to ask. We're from two different worlds."

He released her and took a step backward, but his eyes never left her face. The bodice of her dress outlined the ripe swell of her breasts, drawing his attention away from her thoughtful stare. Her figure had filled out since their arrival at the fort, the little weight she'd gained adding a lushness to her form that had been lacking before. She was rounded now, softer, while retaining her strong Junoesque stature. A sense of wonder overwhelmed him at times when he realized she was his. Perhaps there was something behind Ruth's belief in a destiny charted by the stars; maybe his marriage to Analisa proved it. Never could he have foreseen marriage to a woman like her. Perhaps their meeting had been part of a plan set in motion long before he passed out at her door.

His own mother, Gentle Rain, had been a typical Sioux woman. Small of stature, her body had been soft and lush, much like those of the other women he'd known in his youthful summers while he lived among her people. He'd surmised early on that if he ever took a wife, she would most likely be Sioux. The women he'd met in his father's social circle in Boston had not been much to his liking, and he'd sensed that he was nothing more to them than an exotic curiosity, someone to experiment with, but not a man they would seriously consider marrying. Even his wealth had not been enough to disguise the fact that he was a half-breed.

Now, as he studied his Dutch wife, with her shining sun-kissed hair, her pert nose, her lips tender from his kiss, he felt his heart swell with pride and determination. She was his, but he would have to guard her well, for Analisa was quite unaware of her own beauty and powerful sensuality.

"Forced into it?" She repeated his words. "No one forces me into anything, Caleb. Not anymore. I take care of myself and Kase. I listened to you that day, and believed I was doing what was right for my son, but I was not forced."

"But now you are out of that life. Here no one knows you, Analisa. You can start over if you want to, without being haunted by the past."

She shook her head, unsure of what he was hinting at.

"I have started over, Caleb . . . with you."

She couldn't fathom the reason behind his words. Hadn't her kiss told him all he needed to know? She longed for him to stop talking and take her into his arms again. Should she reach out to him, tell him with her body that he was the man she desired, the only one she needed? Uncertain, afraid of being condemned by her forwardness, she stood immobile, waiting for Caleb to move. Perhaps she was becoming too free in her desire for him. Was it wrong to lust after one's own husband? She hoped not, for if it was, she was surely lost.

Reaching out, she touched his shoulder, her fingertips thrilling to the satin smooth feel of his skin. "Caleb . . ."

The words she was about to speak were cut off as the back door slammed shut. They heard Kase running through the kitchen.

"Mama? Mama, I'm back. We shot a rabbit!"

Without another word, Analisa dropped her hand and turned away from Caleb to go to her son. She stepped out of the room and closed the door behind her, allowing Caleb to dress in privacy before Kase charged in, eager to see him.

"Papa's home, Kase. He'll be out in a moment."

"I have to tell him all about the rabbit. Tor shot it, and then we rode over and picked it up. It's all ready for you to cook. He let me watch him skin it, and he's going to give me the fur. Do you think we could make something out of it?" Kase chattered to her over his shoulder, leading Analisa back into the kitchen where Tor Jensen waited with the skinned rabbit.

"Will you stay to dinner, Tor, and help us eat your catch? My husband returned this afternoon. I'm sure he'd enjoy your company."

The young private blushed and shook his head. "No, tanks, Mrs. de la Vega. I have to report back." In his accented English, he explained, "Riders just came in with news the paymaster's wagon been attacked by Sioux before the guard detail reached them. The driver been killed and the pay chest stolen."

Analisa blanched as she fought to keep her tone light. "It looks as if your pay will be late again this month."

"Someting always keeping me from getting paid, but nutting this bad happened before." He laid the rabbit on the drainboard and turned to leave. "Well, I suppose we all be out on detail tomorrow, chasin' after the Indians and findin' nutting. Tanks for the offer of dinner, Mrs. de la Vega. Good night, ma'am."

"*Wel te ruste,* Private."

Absently, she bade him good night in her own language and

attempted to hush Kase. The boy wanted to relate every detail of his day while she tried to collect her scattered thoughts. Had Caleb been with the party that attacked and killed the paymaster or had he been on his way back to the fort by that time? Perhaps knowledge of the ambush was the reason behind his ill temper. She began to prepare the evening meal, quartering the rabbit and browning it with the onions in the skillet. Kase gave up trying to capture her attention and went to pester Caleb while his mother cooked. The pungent smell of onion browning in butter filled the air, but she was oblivious to the scent, her hands working at the task while her mind churned.

Analisa shook her head, wondering how a day that had begun as usual could suddenly be turned upside down by Caleb's return. Their argument remained unsettled, and she now faced the additional worry about the attack and Caleb's possible involvement in it. First things first, she decided. They would eat a quiet supper for Kase's sake. Then after the boy was tucked in, things would be settled. She'd make certain of that.

The small house chilled with the increasing hours of darkness. The scent of onion and boiled cabbage lingered in the rooms as Analisa made a last tour of the house in the darkness, checking on the fire in the stove, securing the latch on the front door. Kase was safely tucked in bed. He fell asleep nearly as soon as his head hit the pillow. She guessed he dreamed of riding and rabbits, and she felt content knowing that the boy had been happier since their move to the fort.

Supper had ended quickly. Caleb had eaten as if he had not seen food for the past two weeks. Perhaps he had not. Kase's early enthusiasm had waned as exhaustion overtook him, and he'd asked to be excused as soon as he finished eating. The boy had sat on the settee, where Caleb read him a story while Analisa cleared the table and washed the dishes. When she returned to the parlor, both Kase and Caleb had been gone; she'd found Kase asleep in his bed. Now it was time to lock up and join Caleb.

The lamp was out in the bedroom. The moonless night swathed the room in inky blackness. Her arms extended before her, she felt her way to the far wall and began to unfasten her dress. Dropping it to the floor, she stepped out of the voluminous folds of material and then shook it out softly and hung it on a hook. Her long cotton petticoat went next, and she was left standing in her silk chemise and pantalets. She bent to remove her shoes, struggling with the hooks in the darkness, unwilling to light the lamp and disturb Caleb. She could hear him breathing softly from across the room. She reached for her nightgown, letting her hands search for it in the darkness. When her fingers recognized the texture of the cotton and the shape of the gown, she took the nightie from the hook.

Never had she gone to Caleb nude. It seemed far too daring a step. A considerate lover, he knew how inexperienced she was, and Analisa sensed that much of Caleb's light humor and gentleness when they were together was meant to put her at ease. She would have to let him know somehow that he'd banished her nightmares. She never feared the act of love, because of his tenderness, and never would she fear Caleb. Maybe he didn't realize how much she cared for him. She had doubted if that was possible, but now she wondered if his harsh words earlier had stemmed from jealousy. Could he believe she would look twice at another man after having known his love?

She hung the nightgown back on its hook. The evening chill in the room began to seep into her skin. She shivered, briskly rubbing her arms to ward off the cold. Her skin was dimpled with goose bumps. Hastily she slid down her garters and stockings. The silk pantalets whispered as they slipped off of her body. She drew the camisole over her head and laid it aside. Hurrying now because of the cold, she pulled the pins from her hair and shook it free. She would not brush it out tonight, for if she had her way, it would be mussed very soon anyway. She felt above the hooks for the shelf and dropped the hairpins somewhere near the edge. She was ready.

The bed dipped as she entered it, and the sheets felt cold against her skin. Caleb's warmth radiated near his body but did little to heat her side of the bed. He was so still she could not tell if he was asleep or merely lying in silence. When he made no move to touch her, she debated with herself over her next move. Should she reach out to him? Would he think her brazen? Before she could decide how to approach him, Caleb's voice reached out across the darkness.

"I'm sorry about the way I acted today, Anja."

He made no move to touch her. They lay as still as statues, close but without making contact. Analisa felt her skin tingle all down the side closest to him.

"I think I understand now," she whispered. "I have been thinking about everything you said. Are you jealous of the major?" Her voice sounded incredulous as she spoke to the ceiling.

"I've never been jealous before, and when it hit me I couldn't really believe it. I have such strong feelings where you are concerned." He sighed into the darkness but did not move toward her. "I made a fool of myself, I guess."

"No, Caleb. Never that. I must admit, your temper frightens me, but not so much as your silence. I didn't know how to deal with it."

"Yes, you do. You take on that stubborn Dutch pride and look me square in the eye. Don't ever stop standing up to me when I need it, Anja."

"You know I care nothing for Major Williamson, don't you, Caleb? He's a friend and is concerned about us."

"You might think of him as a friend, but I'd wager to guess that he would not think twice about cutting me out. He knows me only as Don Ricardo, Analisa." She felt him prop himself up on his elbow and look down at her, his outline barely discernible. "He probably can't figure out what a woman like you sees in a greenhorn like the professor."

Her laughter floated on the air. "Yes, but I know you are nothing like the man you pretend to be, and that is more than enough for me. Please don't be jealous anymore, Caleb. You have no need."

"No? Somehow I've been lucky enough to marry one of the most beautiful women in the world."

"*One* of the most beautiful?"

He leaned over her and unerringly found her lips in the darkness. "Definitely *the* most beautiful."

His arms encircled her and he pulled her close. His hands explored her nude form, tracing the outline of her shoulders, her waist, and the swell of her hip.

"What's this?"

Shy in the face of his question, suddenly embarrassed by her own boldness, Analisa shrugged in his arms, thankful for the darkness.

"You've been lying here like this all the time and you let me rattle on, apologizing?" His lips teased hers.

"Yes. I . . . I really missed you, Caleb. I was so worried that something would happen to you. All I wanted earlier was for you to hold me, to . . . well, you know. And all you did was rant and rave and act like a beast."

"Ha. I guess I did that."

"Yes, you did. I decided I should take things into my own hands, but once I got into bed, my courage died."

"Perhaps you should take things into your own hands now?"

Slowly, silently, she slipped her hands between them until she found that part of him which always drove her to such heights. She cupped him with her hands, gently massaging him until he groaned low in his throat.

"Anja, sweet Anja."

He pressed her onto the pillow, his mouth assaulting hers, his tongue dipping and tasting her sweet nectar. He moved his lips to her breast and heard her gasping for release. He drew gently on one ripe peak and then the other, teasing her with his teeth. She whispered his name over and over in a joyous litany of welcome.

She beckoned him to enter as she opened her legs and moved sensuously against him, rousing him to a throbbing urgency. No longer able to withstand her whispered encouragement, Caleb thrust between her thighs and found the moist warmth that would guide him to her very core. He drove his length into her, sheathed at last in the honeyed depths, and followed her lead as she began to move against him, faster, faster, until he could no longer hold back the force driving to burst free.

As he reached the summit of ecstasy, Analisa called his name and clasped him to her, tipping her hips higher in order to fully receive his precious gift of love.

Analisa savored the pulsing sensations deep inside until they slowly began to fade. She peppered his neck and shoulder with kisses before he lifted his head and kissed her thoroughly. Feather-light strokes of his hair teased her face as the raven tresses hung free. He whispered against her lips.

"Now I'm really too tired to move."

"Perhaps the Dutch are stronger than the Sioux."

"No doubt about it. Besides, I'm only half Indian. My blood is thin."

"But your body is not. You're too heavy." She pushed against him, shifting his weight off of her ribs.

"You weren't complaining a minute ago."

"A minute ago you were not lying here like a deadweight."

He rolled off her to his own side of the bed and pulled her close to rest her head in the crook of his shoulder. She pressed her hand above his heart and measured its steady beat until she drifted off to sleep.

Chapter Twelve

"Fine. If you won't take me, I'll find someone who will."

"Can you ride?" Zach peered up at Analisa, a skeptical look in his one eye. He didn't bother to stand when she approached, just sat where he was, perched on the edge of the stoop that led to the back door of the trader's store. The twisted cutting of wood in his hand was as thin as the gnarled fingers that clutched it. He continued to scrutinize her as he reached into the deerskin sheath hanging from his belt to pull out a razor-sharp ivory-handled knife.

Refusing to let his unwavering stare unnerve her, Analisa waited, hands on hips, harnessing her temper before she answered him. She pulled aside a lock of hair driven across her lips by the incessant wind. "Of course I can ride."

It was nearly the truth, she assured herself. It had been true five years ago, for Analisa had learned to ride on the journey west. Why should she tell him she hadn't ridden since?

"I ain't takin' no buckboard, and there ain't no fancy sidesaddles." He spat as if to emphasize his distaste.

She wondered what a sidesaddle was. "I don't mind."

Analisa pulled her sweater tight against the wind and watched him squint at the sky from beneath the brim of the battered hat that looked as if it single-handedly won the war.

"Don't look like the weather's done actin' up yet."

Exasperated, but aware that Zach was her only hope of visiting the reservation, Analisa held her tongue. He seemed content to let her stand awkwardly awaiting his answer. She decided to quit begging and try a new tack.

"The wind has blown the storm out. Even now it seems calmer than when I walked over here. I'll be ready about noon, Mr. Elliot. I'll fix you dinner before we go."

Zach settled back against the wall of the building, tossed aside the wood he had been holding, and used the knife point to flick a chunk of dried mud off the side of his boot. Unexpected fear gripped Analisa the moment she noticed a long rawhide thong ornamented with colored trade beads dangling from the carved handle. Her eyes traveled from Zach's knife to his face. Analisa thought she saw him staring at her curiously.

"You wouldn't be tryin' to bribe me, would you now, Miz de la Vega?"

"If I have to, I will." She raised her chin a notch and saw his stern lower lip twitch with a smile. His mustache hid his expressions well, but she sensed a crack in his reserve.

"Then I guess I'll have to get to your house a little before noon so's I can collect my bribe."

"Fine." Thinking the exchange over, she started to turn away. His next words stopped her.

"What does Señor de la Vega think about your wantin' to trek out and stare at the curiosities?"

"He does not dictate to me, Mr. Elliot."

"Nope. I imagine not."

"What do you mean . . . curiosities?"

"Oh, jest wonderin' why a nice, clean city lady such as yourself wants to ride into a Sioux agency. I didn't take you as the type who'd get a thrill out of lookin' at the poor caged-up

critters that live out there. Just sight-seein', ma'am? It ain't a
pretty picture.''

"The major suggested that I might find the visit interesting.
There may be something I could do to help."

"Most of those folks don't need any more 'help.' ''

His expression challenged her, but she ignored his comment.
"I'll see you at noon, then."

Without waiting for his reply, Analisa turned and crossed the
muddy stable yard. She watched every step, carefully avoiding
the deep horseshoe depressions filled with trapped rainwater
and mud. She'd donned her thick wooden clogs and welcomed
the familiar feel of the smooth wood against the thick woolen
socks that protected her feet from blisters.

During the night, a weak storm front had blown across the
plains, washing down the dust and unlocking the heady scent of
the surrounding countryside. Early spring wildflowers in bloom
on the prairie filled the air with their fragrance. Analisa inhaled
deeply, her senses awakening with the change of weather and
signs of spring.

Once clear of the uneven ground near the stables, she walked
along the narrow, hard-packed road that wound its way past the
buildings of the fort. The plains spread out in every direction,
gently rolling swells of land reminiscent of the Atlantic.
Enjoying the view, Analisa let her gaze wander as she length-
ened her stride and inhaled deeply of the myriad scents clinging
to the clean air. She wondered where Caleb might be now. He'd
left again that morning, having stayed at home longer than he'd
planned to. As soon as he had ridden out of sight, Analisa had
come to ask Zach to accompany her to the Sioux agency. She'd
lied to Zach, for before Caleb left he had expressly forbidden
her to visit the reservation with anyone.

Recognizing Tor Jensen among a group of enlisted men
across the parade ground, Analisa waved, then remembered he
was on duty. Even so he nodded slightly in her direction,
sharing a secret smile of greeting.

She continued along the road that edged the parade ground
and curved to front the row of private housing. As she walked,
Analisa's thoughts drifted to her confrontation with Caleb last
night when he'd issued his ultimatum concerning her visit to the
agency. They'd been seated at the dinner table, Kase watching

them intently as he spooned thick barley beef stew into his mouth, Caleb crumbling biscuits on top of his own portion.

"Fine." Analisa agreed on one point only. "I won't ride out to the reservation with the major, but I see no reason why I cannot go with someone else."

"For instance?" His eyes met hers as he continued to eat, his head lowered over his plate.

"For instance, Tor or Zach Elliot." She knew immediately by his darkening expression that he felt them unworthy escorts.

"Anja, I can't discuss this with you now." He nodded toward Kase. "But I do have my reasons. I don't want you anywhere near there."

"That's not fair, Caleb."

"Fair?"

"Yes. It's not fair that I am left to wait with nothing to do but worry while you are off God knows where."

"It seems to me there's more than enough to keep you busy."

"Such as?"

She picked up the serving bowl and moved to stand at his right shoulder, the dish of stew balanced in one hand as she plopped another hearty spoonful, none too graciously, onto his plate. He shot her a warning glance out of the corner of his eye, which only tempted her to dump the entire contents of the bowl over his head. Analisa listened to him expound on ways to keep busy as she walked into the kitchen to bring back the remaining biscuits.

"Sew, read." He glanced around the room. "Play the organ, go visiting." Caleb looked up again as she reentered the room. "Tea parties."

With a slam that rattled his plate against the table she set the tin of biscuits beside his spoon.

"You've ruled out tea parties already."

Caleb's eyes flashed in her direction.

"Besides," she went on, unwilling to give up the argument, "the only other woman I am supposed to associate with is Millicent Boynton, and we are not . . . not . . . She's not like me, Caleb."

"Compatible." He supplied the word for her.

"Yes."

They were silent for a time while the business of eating provided the only sounds in the stillness.

"I've made two new dresses. The house is in order. You've hired a woman to do the laundry, and because I'm supposed to be a lady of *quality,* I'm not *allowed* to put in a garden. And I can't play the organ well enough to enjoy it."

"So, practice." He crumbled another biscuit onto his stew.

Minutes ticked by silently, neither of them willing to continue the argument. Analisa felt a wad of tension growing in the pit of her stomach. She hated to argue with Caleb. His abrupt homecoming and the jealous scene over the major's attention had caused enough friction, but she felt determined to fight for her own independence. If she lost ground now, what would the ensuing years hold for her? Her struggle to survive alone on the prairie had been hard fought, and Analisa was determined not to give up being her own person simply because she'd married Caleb.

"May I be excused?"

As if aware of the tension between the two adults, Kase moved quickly at Caleb's nod of assent, slipping to the edge of the chair and stretching his toes down to reach the floor. He walked into his room without a backward glance.

Analisa stood and began to clear the plates immediately, not bothering to ask Caleb if he cared for anything more. After two noisy trips back and forth to the kitchen, she noticed that Caleb continued to ignore the clanking and slamming of pots and pans, and chided herself for her own childish behavior. Forcing herself to calm down, she picked up the wooden bucket and went outside to the water barrel that was refilled daily by the water wagon detail. She returned and placed the bucket on the drainboard. A kettle of water simmered on the stove. She poured the dishpan half full of hot water, then added tepid water from the bucket until it was cool enough to use.

As she slipped the first dish into the pan, she heard Caleb enter the room. He placed his empty plate with the others and slipped his hands around her waist. He drew her against his length as he nuzzled her neck with his lips. "Pouting?"

The warm breath and sound of his husky voice playing about her ear nearly caused her legs to buckle as something deep within her ran liquid, like warm butter. She forced her hands to continue their task.

"Decided never to speak to me again?"

His tongue traced the shape of her ear before his teeth pulled on the lobe. Chills ran down her spine, and her hands gripped the lip of the dishpan. She tried to speak, but was forced to clear away the constricting lump in her throat.

"Caleb, please don't try to kiss this away."

She turned in his arms to stand facing him, locked within the circle of muscular flesh. Analisa stretched to the right to draw a dish towel off of the rope that was stretched across the corner of the room above the drainboard. Still within the boundary of his arms, she dried her hands and then raised them to his shoulders. The fingers of one hand toyed with the dark waving hair at the nape of his neck while the other dangled the dish towel behind him.

Her eyes searched his and saw his love reflected there. She knew without a doubt that Caleb loved her; it was apparent in his every action. Even his jealousy and anger over the major had sprung from his love for her. Analisa realized in that moment that more anger on her part would not persuade Caleb to share the secret of his mission. She would call upon her love for him to gain his trust and help unlock the reason behind his frequent absence.

Tipping her head back, she welcomed his kiss. His tongue teased, as smooth as velvet against her own parted lips before it delved deeper. Her hand tightened around the satin hair that spilled almost to his shoulders while the dish towel fluttered forgotten to the floor. As the exchange slowly ended and Caleb raised his head, Analisa drew a deep breath. Her eyes returned his heated stare measure for measure, and she felt him teasingly rub against her in invitation.

"You can do the dishes tomorrow after I've gone."

Although he'd told her earlier that he would leave the next morning, she'd pushed the thought away. She took a deep breath, hating to dispel the warmth surrounding her, and hoped Caleb would understand.

"Caleb, when you asked me to marry you, for my sake, and for Kase's—I did. When you went away to Boston, I waited. I moved here when you asked . . . but I cannot go through any more waiting without knowing where you are or what you are doing or why." She tried to appeal to his heart. Would it hear her when his mind would not? "Fear is making me crazy, Caleb. I love you, but I refuse to be afraid anymore."

He pulled her close and held her gently, passion replaced by something more, something true and lasting. Analisa sensed it in his stillness, his thoughtfulness. She heard him sigh before he released her.

"Come," he said. "It's time we talked."

The sight of Millicent Boynton standing on Analisa's front porch interrupted her reminiscence. Although the clear April air was brisk, the wind blowing gently, the woman was bundled up in a full-length fitted coat, the collar sporting a jaunty fur trim. Analisa wondered what Millicent wore during the dead of winter. Straightening her sweater, Analisa waved as she approached. Millicent stepped off of the porch and waited for Analisa to join her. As was her usual habit, Millicent inspected her from head to toe, her gaze lingering on the wooden clogs and thick woolen stockings. She made no comment on the footgear, but greeted Analisa with unusual warmth.

"Hello! I just came over to give you the news." Millicent smiled up radiantly at Analisa, her usually dour expression missing, her pale cheeks pink with excitement. "I've received word from my sister-in-law that she'll be arriving today. That means we will have to make plans for the soiree. Can you come over this afternoon?"

"I have plans." Analisa knew the woman would not be content without further explanation. "Zach wants to take Kase out riding and I want to go along. Perhaps we should wait and include your sister-in-law in the planning?"

Millicent frowned, the lines formed about her eyes and lips aging her instantly. Then, as suddenly as her features had darkened, they cleared. "Why, you might be right! That will give me time to get everything else ready before she gets here. Doesn't the steamboat arrive in the late afternoon?"

"Ours did," Analisa assured her, recalling the steamboats that plied the Missouri carrying every type of cargo—human, animal, and otherwise. A nearby landing at the bend in the river served both Fort Sully and the Indian agency. At the sound of the steamboat whistle, a detail was sent to the dock to transport passengers and supplies to the fort. Analisa had gotten her first glimpse of the outpost from the swaying seat of a wagon loaded high with their household goods.

"Well, I'll just have to wait until I hear the whistle. Hasn't it been nearly two weeks since the last one arrived?"

"I'm not sure."

Rattling on as if Analisa had never answered, Millicent fluffed her corkscrew curls while her eyes darted about the parade ground. More than once she glanced at the rambling administration building across the square.

"Perhaps I should give Major Williamson my thanks for sending an orderly over with the telegram?"

Analisa realized Millicent asked questions without expecting answers. Before she could respond, the woman was off with a wave of her hand, moving across the open area on short, flitting footsteps. Her bouncing yellow curls soon disappeared inside Major Williamson's office.

"Kase?" Analisa called out as she entered the house, then nearly tripped over her son as she walked across the parlor.

"I was looking for you." She smiled down at him and watched as he continued to line the tin soldiers up on the carpet and behind the legs of the settee. "I'm going to start dinner now, and after you eat we are going for a ride with Zach. I'll call you when it's time to set the table."

"*Ja*, Mama."

When they were alone she always spoke to him in Dutch, hoping that Kase would not forget his first language. He was growing so fast, she realized, as she watched him play quietly by himself. Soon he would be ready for a new pair of pants.

She bustled about the kitchen, pulling potatoes out of the sack leaning against the wall and taking onions from a drawer that served as a bin. She then began to prepare a dish of fried bacon, onions, and potatoes for Zach. It would be luxury to have fresh tomatoes and string beans again. She had seen a work detail of men turning the earth in the fort's garden plot this morning and knew that in a few weeks' time the results of their labors would be for sale.

At the thought of the impending visit to the Sioux agency, her stomach knotted in anticipation. She fought down the nervous feeling caused by going against Caleb's wishes, but since their intimate conversation last night, she was more determined than ever to acquaint herself with conditions on the reservation and to meet the agent, Buff Hardy.

She added half a cup of water to the simmering mixture in the cast-iron fry pan and covered it with a lid. Within minutes she mixed and rolled out biscuit dough on the floured surface of the square cutting board. Her hands worked without pause preparing the meal while her mind recalled the details Caleb had revealed to her concerning his work for the Bureau of Indian Affairs.

"It's time we talked." She remembered the words he'd uttered last evening as she stood in his embrace, her hips pressed against the kitchen bench, the warm, delicious food smells in the room tinged with the sharp scent of the lye soap in the dishpan.

His eyes had held a promise of more than lust or passion. She knew he weighed his trust in her and found her worthy. Suddenly apprehensive over the prospect of sharing his secret, Analisa had rubbed her cheek against the starched linen of his shirt and then squeezed him tightly before she pulled back to look up at him again.

"I'll finish the dishes while you get Kase to bed. Then we'll talk," she had said.

"Fair enough."

He gave her a quick buss on the lips and released her. As he strode toward the doorway, Caleb turned and sent her a look she assumed he intended to melt her to the core. It did.

"I don't plan to waste my entire last night at home talking, though." His heated gaze had held her riveted to the spot long after he disappeared through the doorway. She could hear the two of them chatting together as the boy prepared for bed.

Caleb moved the oil lamp from the dining table to a small side table near the settee, then used a long-handled snuffer to extinguish the lamp that hung on a chain from the ceiling.

Realizing that she would concentrate more fully if she stayed out of his reach, Analisa sat in the rocker near the settee. She smoothed out the skirt of her gray dress, the one she usually wore when her husband was home.

Caleb went to the buffet and poured himself half a tumbler of brandy. Without asking, he poured Analisa the same amount and crossed the room. After she took the glass from him, he sat at the end of the settee, stretched his long legs out before him, and crossed his booted feet at the ankles. Analisa smiled at the pose that had become so familiar to her.

The pungent aroma of the brandy warned her of the heady taste even before the liquid touched her tongue. Cautiously she took a sip and let the brandy coat her tongue. It scorched a trail down her throat, but she found its searing effect somewhat pleasant.

They sat in the stillness, surrounded by shadows lurking in the corners of the room. A ring of light made a halo on the wooden ceiling above the lamp, the flames creating dancing, leaping circles.

Analisa cradled the brandy glass in her hands, resting them on her lap. With her feet pressed together at the ankles, she slowly pushed against the carpet with the toes of her gray kid shoes to rock the chair gently back and forth.

Finally, the deep resonant sound of Caleb's voice broke the stillness, his words spoken so that she barely heard them. "I told you I work for the government."

She nodded and pronounced each word distinctly. "The Bureau of Indian Affairs."

He stared at the lamp as if the flame held an unknown secret.

"For years the army, on behalf of different Presidents, has made useless treaties with various Indian leaders. Most of them are invalid. The problem stems mainly from the fact that the government doesn't understand that each one of the Indian clans and nations is a separate entity." He paused to glance in her direction. She nodded again to let him know that she understood so far.

"No one man can speak for other clans of the same nation. So any treaty made by, let's say, a Sioux war chief is not binding for others—only for his band."

"I see." Analisa sipped the brandy again as she rocked.

"When the other Sioux clans continue to raid the white settlements, all are blamed for breaking a treaty that never included them in the first place. The army is sent to punish the criminals and ordered to bring them onto agency land."

"But they don't want to live there."

"No. Why should they? Most reservations are no better than prisons."

She watched the side of his jaw tense with suppressed anger. He tossed down the last of his brandy.

"The Indian is being cut off from his land. Railroads are dividing the plains into smaller and smaller sections and bringing in more settlers." Sadness replaced the anger in his voice. "The old way of life is dying, and the Indian people will die with it if they can't adjust to living in the white world."

"But you're only one man. What can you do?"

"Very little, I'm afraid." He sighed.

"Still, you are here for some purpose."

Caleb went to refill his glass, then sat on the floor near her feet and leaned back against the settee.

"Sometimes I wonder what I am doing here. Other times, I realize I couldn't be anywhere else. I cannot turn my back on my past even though I've chosen to live another life."

"How can you help them, Caleb?"

"I hope I can at least save a few lives, perhaps put an end to the slaughter for a time. That's why I'm here."

"You still haven't told me anything." She took a deep breath. "Where do you go when you leave here?"

"To a renegade stronghold along the river. It's not far, just very well hidden."

Her heart began to pound with fear. "They accept you there?"

"Not as Caleb Storm. Nor as de la Vega. They know me by my Sioux name, Raven's Shadow. I claimed to have renounced my father's name and told them I had come back to fight with them."

"These are your mother's people?"

"No. But some of the older men knew of my grandfather. The men believe me, but their leader is not so sure. He's been suspicious of me, thinks I may be scouting for the army. He's had me trailed, but so far I've managed to keep my life here a secret."

"If . . . if you *were* followed, found out . . ." Her words hung on the air.

He shrugged. Without words he told her his life would be forfeit.

"But how can you leave there and return here to the fort? Aren't they becoming . . . suspect?"

"Suspicious. Not yet. I've set myself up as something of a loner. When I say I'm going off to hunt, I usually return with a rifle or a rustled steer, something to share with them to prove my loyalty. They don't know that I purchase the 'stolen' goods with white man's money."

"Were you part of the raid on the paymaster's wagon?" She tried to control the quiver in her voice but failed. He reached up and took one of her hands in his own and held it against her lap, the brandy in the other hand forgotten.

"No."

His eyes said all. She believed him.

"I left the renegade camp that morning. I suspect the raid was already planned, but Red Dog kept the knowledge of it from me."

"Red Dog?"

"He's their leader. Not quite twenty-two, I'd guess, but he's as sharp as a finely honed knife and twice as dangerous. And he's running scared. After all, he's responsible for the lives of all the renegades, women and children included."

"How many live in the camp?"

"It's a good-size band, so it would be hard to keep them on the run. Nearly a hundred and fifty."

"Oh."

He squeezed her hand while she took another drink. The strong, pungent liquor numbed her tongue and made swallowing the stuff easier as the level in the glass began to sink.

"Where will all of this lead? Are you spying on them, Caleb? Is it your job to turn them in?"

"No, it's not as simple as that. I'm to convince them that they'll be safer at the agency."

"But how can you succeed? If you even mention the BIA or a return to the agency, won't they lose trust in you?"

"Yes. But I don't intend to do any such thing until I can remove the one barrier that keeps them from coming to the reservation voluntarily."

Her thoughts raced ahead. What barrier could he possibly mean? The army?

"*Ik begryp het niet.*" She knew he was now familiar with the Dutch phrase that meant "I don't understand."

"The agent—Buff Hardy. He's the reason they won't surrender. He's also the reason so many have become renegades."

Caleb set his empty glass beside him on the carpet. "And he's also the reason I don't want you anywhere near the reservation, Anja. Not until he's gone."

"But . . . how do you plan to get rid of him?"

"I have to come up with enough evidence to present a strong case against him, but Hardy's covered his tracks so well that he looks good on paper in Washington. That makes my job harder, but I'll get evidence sooner or later to prove that Hardy is corrupt and cruel. The men in Red Dog's camp have already told me that Hardy gives very little food to the Sioux on the reservation, and what he does provide is of low quality. I also know that the government sends an abundance of goods to the Indians and that Hardy sells most of it to the white settlers or keeps it for himself. He's making a fortune by selling government food and goods while the reservation Sioux are starving."

"Why don't you just tell him you know what he's up to?"

"And disappear?"

"What?"

"That's what happened to the BIA agent who was sent out here two years ago. We heard from him once. He said he suspected Hardy of stealing, and then he supposedly became lost during a blizzard."

"Oh, Caleb." Her hand went to her throat. She could feel her pulse throbbing along the vein in her neck.

"Don't worry. I won't make a move until I'm sure I've got him."

"Why doesn't the army do anything?"

"Do you mean the major?"

"No, I mean the army."

He drew up one knee and leaned an elbow on it.

"I can't ask for the army's help until I'm sure that Williamson isn't in collusion with Hardy. They could be splitting the money, or at the very least, the major may be taking a bribe to look the other way."

"I can hardly believe that."

"Because the major has been kind enough to take an interest in you, Mrs. de la Vega?"

"Because," she bit back, "*Professor* de la Vega, I think I know a little about people."

"You have to be very careful, Anja. People are not always what they seem."

He stood, removed the empty glass from her hand, and set it on the table. Pulling her up with both hands he kissed her full upon the mouth. He tasted of brandy.

"Now. Will you please be content to amuse yourself here awhile longer? I can't be worrying about you while I'm trying to juggle my dual roles." He kissed her again and held her hand as he walked over to the lamp on the side table.

"All I ask is that you be here for me, Anja. Welcome me when I come home; brighten the day as you do each time I see you. Wait until this thing is over."

He picked up the lamp and led her toward their room. Once inside he gently closed the door, set the lamp on the bureau, turned back to her, and reached up to remove her hairpins. .

"Will you be here for me, Anja?"

His eyes were blue flames shining in the lamplight, his whispered words caressed her beating heart.

"Always."

Always. She thought of her promise to Caleb again as she helped Kase set the table in the kitchen. She hoped he'd forgive her when he found out that she'd gone to the agency against his wishes. Could she keep Zach from telling him? And what of Kase? She would deal with them after she'd met Buff Hardy. All she was concerned with now was finding a way to obtain information for Caleb. The sooner Hardy was found out, the sooner Caleb could end his dangerous charade. She couldn't rest safely knowing the danger he faced constantly.

Hoping that Zach would feel more comfortable at the simple pine plank table than in the parlor, she added a final touch by straightening the napkins. Whenever Caleb was away, she and Kase took their meals in the kitchen, relishing the warmth of the stove and the intimacy of the tiny room.

Analisa heard Zach ride up and opened the back door. He hitched the two horses to the post near the back wall of the house and swung down from his mount.

"Howdy, ma'am."

She immediately noticed the missing plug of tobacco that usually deformed the side of his cheek.

"Hello, Mr. Elliot. You are right on time." She held the door open for him as he removed his battered hat and beat it against his leg, setting loose a cloud of dust that rose from the faded army trousers.

He shuffled in on heavy feet and stood, awkward and uncertain, in the center of the room. Zach kept glancing skyward as if having a roof over his head posed a threat.

Analisa had never seen a filthier pair of army-issue cavalry pants. The usually bright yellow stripe running the length of each leg was nearly indistinguishable. Perhaps, she thought, she'd made a mistake. Her inclination was to dunk him in a tub of water, clothes and all, and give up the whole wild idea of trekking off to the agency. Her time would be better spent cleaning up Zach Elliot. Another look at the face of the hardened, wiry man wiped the notion from her mind.

"Sit down, Mr. Elliot." She indicated the table, which was flanked by chairs covered with peeling white paint, relatives of the one on the front porch. She had been meaning to paint the table and chairs ever since her arrival. This might be a good day.

Realizing that her nerves were calling up any reason to avoid the trip to the agency, Analisa tried to stay calm. *Remember, you're doing this to help Caleb,* she reminded herself. Since his disclosure the night before, Analisa was determined to help her husband bring Buff Hardy to justice. It was just that she lacked any sort of a plan, and knew that she would not have one until she sized up her opponent. A trip to the reservation seemed to be her only recourse, and Zach Elliot her only means of achieving that end.

"Kase, take your seat. Once a guest is seated, you may sit down."

The boy stared at his new hero, the thrill of having his riding teacher in his own kitchen all too apparent upon his upturned face. Only two places were set at the table, and Analisa explained quickly to Zach that she'd eaten earlier. In reality, she was far too nervous to swallow a mouthful.

"You eat with Zach while I change my shoes, and after dinner we'll all go riding."

"Well, boy, you gonna help me clean out your mama's pantry?"

"You bet!" Kase used the latest expression he'd picked up from Tor.

"If you two will excuse me?"

Analisa turned to leave them, intending to change into an old pair of black shoes. She would travel in the plaid wool dress, for besides providing protection against the cool breeze, the generous old-fashioned skirt would afford her more modesty while she sat astride the horse. After all, she was not setting out to impress the corrupt man she was about to visit.

"Miz de la Vega?" Zach's voice stopped her before she left the kitchen. "You really plan on takin' this boy out there?"

She tried to find a reason for his question and searched his expression. All his face revealed was his usual staring, all-knowing eye and the ever-frowning mustache.

"Of course. Why shouldn't I?"

"Nothin', ma'am. Jest a thought, is all."

"Don't you feel you can take care of us both, Mr. Elliot?"

"Doesn't have nothin' to do with it. As I said, Miz de la Vega, forget it."

Determined to do just that, Analisa left the room with far too many questions on her mind.

Chapter Thirteen

Analisa rode uncomfortably, her jaw set in a stubborn line, Kase riding behind her, clinging to her waist. She sat the horse as if someone had rammed a pole down her spine, and try as she might, she could not seem to stop struggling against the hard leather saddle.

She glanced across at Zach Elliot and watched him spit a stream of brown tobacco juice at the ground, barely missing a flattened round of buffalo dung.

"How far is it?" Analisa managed to ask between bounces.

"Not far. 'Bout two mile."

"Why didn't they just build the agency next to the fort?"

"It don't do anybody good to have a whole passle of yellow legs camped out next to a corral full of Sioux."

"Yellow legs?"

"That's what the Injuns call the cavalry, 'cause of the yellow stripe down their pants."

"Do you know the agent, Mr. Hardy?"

He deliberated a moment too long before he answered. "Some."

After the curt reply, Analisa turned her concentration to the rutted road they were following. The prairie seemed flat, but as they traveled on, she realized the earth was deceptive. It rolled expansively, slowly rising upward from the river valley. Lavender blooms sprinkled the hills in the distance. She longed to get closer to them and see exactly what type of plant they might be, but it was all she could do to hang on to her horse for the last few yards until they reached the agency. She saw the entrance looming ahead and suddenly wondered why she was going against Caleb's wishes, interfering with his job.

She would just meet this man, Hardy, and then leave, she resolved. At least that way she'd know what Caleb was up against. Not that it would matter. He would never give up until Hardy had been dismissed from the post; she knew Caleb well enough to know that much.

Zach slowed up and waited until her horse was alongside his. He rode through the gate beside Analisa and, with a nod, directed her toward a large two-story house on her right. The house seemed sorely out of place, especially as it stood next to a low, ramshackle building made of cottonwood logs and odd-size pieces of lumber. Indian women of every conceivable size and age stood two deep in a serpentine line that disappeared around the corner of the low building. They whispered in small groups or stared blankly ahead while they waited in the sun, beaten by the briskly blowing wind.

"What are they doing? There must be over a hundred of them." Analisa hoped her hushed voice would carry to Zach over the sound of the horses' hooves.

"They're waitin' to be issued their monthly ration. Each of 'em gets thirty pounds of flour and a handful of salt."

She watched Zach's eye squint along the line of women from beneath the lazy brim of his hat. "Is that all?"

"Sometimes they get tobacco or sugar."

It was nearly impossible for Analisa to tear her eyes away from the women standing so patiently, shuffling their moccasin-clad feet forward as the line inched along. She was too far away to study their clothing closely, but saw that it was made of softened hide decorated with colorful trim. Long swaying fringe decorated skirt hems and sleeves. The designs and materials intrigued her, and Analisa wished she could get close enough to see how the clothing was sewn together.

"Miz de la Vega?"

Analisa jumped in response to Zach's voice and turned toward him.

"I'll stay with the horses while you go callin' on Hardy. Want to leave the boy with me?"

Zach dismounted and stood beside her horse, waiting to lift Kase down. Was it her imagination or did his tone hold a warning?

"He'll be fine with me," Zach said.

She waited in the saddle until Kase was lifted down, then stood in the stirrups and tried to unbundle her gathered skirts enough to swing her own leg over the saddle. Zach steadied her, his hands at her waist until she was on the ground.

Analisa felt her legs trembling with fatigue after the unaccustomed ride. The ground swayed beneath her like the deck of a rolling ship.

"It'll be right in a minute," Zach said quietly behind her.

She looked up at the massive flank of the horse and watched the muscles contract beneath the hide as the animal flicked away a pesky fly. The sound of booted footsteps rang out on the wooden porch of the house, alerting them both. Analisa turned toward the sound and found herself staring at the approaching figure.

Analisa was immediately reminded of a fine fat goose when she looked at the man who could only be Buff Hardy. She tried to take in the picture of him all at once, found it too overwhelming, and studied him inch by inch.

His hair was silver white, swept back away from his forehead and slicked down with pomade. A bulbous red-veined nose called attention away from the man's narrow eyes. His thin lips were pursed into a bow, underlined by hanging jowls that sported muttonchop whiskers. An ivory satin vest, embroidered with ivory roses, was stretched to its limit, the buttons clinging desperately to the strained buttonholes. A long gold chain trailed after a pocket watch stuffed into his vest pocket. His legs looked like short, thick sausages encased in white linen pants; the outfit he wore was completed by an oversize white jacket of the same rumpled material. His meaty right fist was wrapped about the handle of a tapered, slim-tipped cane, the glint of its gold handle shining between his fingers. He straightened, as if trying to pull himself up to a greater height, but Analisa could see that he was shorter than she by at least half a foot. His snakelike eyes glittered in her direction, and she felt uncomfortable staring so blatantly.

"Well, well. And to what do I owe this unexpected visit by so charming a guest?" He walked with a noticeable limp to the edge of the porch and waited as if expecting her to approach him. "Come up to the veranda, my dear, and let me see what the fates have sent my way."

The words were spoken in a smooth, drawling accent that forced Analisa to pay strict attention. His words dripped with a honey coating that sent a chill of apprehension along her spine. Chastising herself for cowardice and bolstering her courage with thoughts of Caleb in the renegade camp, Analisa stepped forward, a smile on her lips, her legs somewhat steadier now.

"I would like to introduce myself, sir. I am Analisa de la Vega. I assume you are Mr. Hardy?"

"Why, yes, I am, my dear. I am indeed."

He reached down to assist her as she stepped up on the wide, shady porch. She stretched out her hand and suppressed a shiver when his cold flesh met hers. On level ground with him her estimation proved true: She stood nearly a head taller than he. Hardy seemed not to notice, and was actually preening beneath her stare.

She felt compelled to explain her unexpected descent upon the agency. "My husband is here from the East to study the plant life of the frontier. While we are living at Fort Sully, Major Williamson has suggested that I might enjoy seeing your agency. Perhaps you can think of a way I can be of help."

Buff Hardy stood silent for a moment as if gauging her sincerity. He looked around to where Zach stood watching from beside the horses. Kase was hidden behind the scout.

"Come, come . . . Mrs. de la Vega, is it? Let's go into the house and have a cup of coffee. You must be quite exhausted after your ride."

"Thank you, Mr. Hardy." Hesitantly, she turned in Zach's

direction and tried to avoid his dour expression. "Kase? Come with me."

Kase appeared from behind Zach and ran up the steps of the porch. He looked up at Hardy and tried out one of his new salutes.

"What's this?" the agent said.

Analisa noted the immediate change in Hardy's demeanor. His voice sounded cold and demanding as he stared down at her son.

"Where'd this brat come from? He slip outta here and get as far as the fort? These little devils are almost worse than the big ones. Thank you for bringing him back, ma'am, but I won't pay for the fancy clothes you outfitted him with."

She felt as if the man had slapped her with his thick hand. Analisa reached out and protectively laid her hand on Kase's shoulder, quickly glancing at Zach to see if he'd witnessed the outrageous display of bigotry. Her face was flaming with anger. Zach had obviously heard the crass man's words, for he'd taken a step toward the porch but waited near the horses' heads, fooling with a bit of rawhide.

"This, Mr. Hardy, is my son. His father is Don Ricardo Corona de la Vega."

She was seething. Analisa wondered how she could ever force down the bitter taste of bile in her mouth and still deal with this man. And how dare he speak of a child with such menace in his voice?

The man recovered himself, glancing toward Zach, who stood silent, having turned his back on the scene on the porch. Hardy looked at Kase once again, and Analisa felt he was forcing himself to do so. His lips puckered once more, just as they had when she'd first seen him. It was an unconscious habit, she surmised, one he used whenever he was forced to think.

"Why, yes." He cleared his throat nervously. "I'm sorry, Mrs. de la Vega. I can see now that the boy does have those blue eyes of yours. Please accept my apologies." Hardy shifted uncomfortably and pulled at the pointed tails of his vest straining the buttons even more.

Unable to force herself to speak to him, she merely nodded and then looked down at Kase. Her voice was barely a whisper. "Stay with Zach."

She refused to have her son insulted, even to help Caleb. She would face Hardy alone. What harm could befall her over a cup of coffee? She glanced up at the formidable structure and then stood aside to allow Hardy to lead her to the door. A final glance in his direction told her that Kase was safe; he and Zach were walking toward the well near the trading post.

"You seem hesitant, Mrs. de la Vega." Hardy's tone was as smooth as his satin vest. "Let me assure you that I have two servants who will be in attendance. I'll have one of them stay in the room with us if it will make you feel more comfortable."

Why should he have to assure her that she would be safe? Perhaps he was testing her to see if she was willing to do more than have coffee with him. Analisa mentally scolded herself for having forgotten that propriety dictated she refuse a man's invitation without first inquiring about proper chaperons. Caleb was right. She was naive. And foolish. And afraid. The last admission only served to raise her temper and force her to face Hardy straight on. She could handle this situation, and him, she told herself. Besides, she decided as they entered the spacious entry hall, there was no law against finishing a cup of coffee in a minute or two.

"I was just about to ask if you lived here alone, Mr. Hardy."

"A cook and a maid work for me, Mrs. de la Vega. I'll ask one of them to attend us, if you wish."

"That would be fine. Thank you."

Ushered into a parlor that fronted the right side of the house, Analisa was left alone while Hardy went to find the maid and order coffee from the cook. Wandering about the room, she made note of everything she saw as she threaded her way through the maze of furnishings. Chairs were lined up side by side, most of them upholstered in garish brocade. Four settees were crowded into the room, two at opposite sides of the fireplace and two others sandwiched amid the chairs. Gilt-framed paintings of pastoral scenes hung from picture rails on all four walls, adding to the confusion.

Overwhelmed by the room, Analisa sat down on a brocade settee and thought about Hardy's belongings. The pieces, she realized, were beautiful in themselves, but their elegance was lost amid the color and clutter. She continued to inspect the room, but remained seated so as not to appear to be assessing it too obviously. Three Chinese vases nearly as tall as Kase were displayed on massive, heavy-legged tables. One of the vases contained a bouquet of emerald peacock feathers. A piano stood in one corner draped with an ebony-fringed shawl and topped by a crystal bowl filled with the purple wildflowers she had seen on the distant hills.

Attracted by the colorful flowers, Analisa could not resist the urge to enjoy them at close range. She longed for flowers of her own again, now that winter was past. As she moved across the room, her footsteps were hushed by the thick Oriental carpets that overlapped one another to cover the entire floor. When she stood next to the piano, she reached out tentatively to touch the delicate blooms that appeared to have been thrust into the bowl with no attempt at arrangement. Analisa rubbed a petal gently between her thumb and forefinger, smiling down at the happy, open-faced blooms.

"So, you are attracted to the pasqueflowers?"

Hardy's voice startled her, and she whirled around to face him. He stood just inside the double doors that opened onto the parlor. Behind him waited an Indian woman holding a silver tray laden with a coffee service. Analisa was struck by the servant's beauty as she stood poised behind Hardy, silent and patient, waiting for the man to move his bulky figure so that she could move into the room with the heavy tray. Analisa was so taken by the exotic beauty of the almond-eyed woman in her demure black silk gown that she nearly forgot to answer Hardy's question.

"Why . . . yes. The flowers are quite beautiful. I noticed them on the way here and wondered what they were called. The purple is such a soft, unusual color." She watched as he moved toward the fireplace and the servant followed with the tray. "Pasqueflowers, did you say?"

"Yes." He pointed to one of the settees. "Come, Mrs. de la Vega, sit here and have some coffee. I'm sure you'll find it refreshing after the long ride in the wind. What made you decide to come out here today?"

She thought carefully before she answered. Hardy appeared cordial, but she sensed a reason behind his carefully worded questions. Analisa knew she would have to remain on guard, especially since Caleb had warned her of this man with his story of the missing BIA agent. She thought of Millicent Boynton and tried to affect the woman's attitude.

"Fort Sully is *dreadfully* boring." Analisa wanted to laugh at her imitation of Millicent. "Especially after having lived in Europe and more recently, in Boston."

Buff Hardy handed her a finely shaped cup and saucer. The delicate floral pattern on the china contrasted with his slovenly, overabundant figure. Analisa watched as the Sioux woman poured for Hardy without looking at him. She moved with quiet grace, her shining black hair hanging loose about her shoulders. The elegant cut of her silk dress, its high collar and long sleeves banded by black lace, only served to enhance her dark complexion. Her skin was unlined, flawless. She appeared to be no more than eighteen, but her eyes, when they did meet Analisa's, held the wisdom of one far older.

The coffee served, the maid turned and walked to a chair across the room, near a tall velvet-swathed window. The drapery was swagged to one side, held in place by a length of thick gold braid. From the chair near the window the Indian woman had a view of the agency and the surrounding countryside. She seated herself with a regal air and stared out of the window, ignoring Analisa and Hardy. True to his word, the man must have asked her to act as a chaperon.

"You say you are from Boston?" He leaned over the tray, which sat on a table between them, to select a thick slab of bread from a scalloped plate. His eyes watched her, and Analisa wanted to squirm under his scrutiny.

"We lived in Boston most recently."

"Whereabouts? I have friends in Boston."

She tried not to appear cornered. Boston . . . Boston. Her mind raced for any scrap of information Caleb had related about the city where his stepmother lived.

"Near the water." She quickly took a long sip of the coffee and burned her tongue.

"Beautiful city, Boston. I can see how you are bored here. I can't really think of what Williamson meant by volunteer work, though."

Hardy shifted in his seat, adjusting his vest again. It seemed to be a habit with him, as if by stretching the fabric downward he could somehow disguise his girth. His eyes bored into hers, and then he looked her up and down. She resisted the urge to pull her sweater tight against his blatant stare.

"Perhaps he merely hoped to give me something to do," she

said. "I would, of course, leave it up to you. Perhaps there are some children to teach? Is there a school here, Mr. Hardy?"

The servant woman was quite visible beyond Hardy's shoulder. Analisa found she could study her without seeming distracted from her host. At the mention of a school, the woman looked toward Analisa and met her gaze straight on. Her expression revealed nothing, and Analisa wondered what she was thinking. She wished she could converse with the Indian woman rather than with Hardy.

"There's no school here, and there won't be if I can help it. I'm from the South, originally, Mrs. de la Vega. Being from Europe, you probably don't understand the significance of that statement." He paused as if expecting her to answer.

"You are correct. I don't."

"Well, that means that I believe that some men are created masters over others. It's true of the whites and the niggroes, and it's true of the way the whites ought to handle the Indians. Some people just aren't born to take care of themselves. The problem we have here is that the Indians are even worse than the niggroes. At least the niggroes can work, and work hard. These lazy creatures aren't even good for that. They don't want to work. Even if you beat 'em."

Analisa choked on a mouthful of coffee and was forced to set the cup on the tray until she recovered.

"Are you all right?"

Hardy moved to her side, striking her gently between the shoulderblades to help clear her throat. Analisa waved him away as her coughing spasm died, anxious to have him across the table from her again.

"Thank you." Her voice was a gravelly whisper. She did not think she could look the odious creature in the eye but forced herself. After all, she reminded herself, she was here for Caleb.

"So, Mr. Hardy, how did you come to be here? I'm sure you must find the area as *dimsal* as I do?" *Dimsal?* Was that a word? She hoped it was the word that Millicent used constantly.

Hardy leaned back against the settee, his coffee finished, and folded his hands across his straining vest buttons.

"I foresaw the fall of the South, Mrs. de la Vega. Call it a sixth sense. My parents were gone, the crops failing. I sold our plantation and came west with all of the old family possessions I could move. It wasn't easy ten years ago. Had to come out by wagon train. Everyone who settled here knew that the army would be coming out right behind us. The railroads and settlers were demanding protection from the blasted red men.'' He shrugged. ''I was in the right place at the right time, with connections. When this agency was set up, I was appointed Indian agent. It helps to have friends in high places.''

''You seem to do quite well here. Your house is a palace compared to anything I've seen in the territories.''

''It's not much. I tried to reproduce the old plantation house on a smaller scale. As you can see, none of the things are as elegantly displayed in this small space.''

None of them are as old as you claim, either, Mr. Hardy, Analisa thought to herself. As familiar as she was with materials and fabric, she was well aware that many of the upholstered pieces were of the latest style. They had to have been purchased recently.

''It is still quite beautiful, Mr. Hardy.'' It galled her to have to compliment the man, but he sat waiting, as if he expected it.

Analisa glanced around the room once more. The young woman near the window seemed lost in thought as she studied the view. Analisa noticed that her toes peeked out from beneath the flounced hem of the dress. She was wearing buckskin moccasins, like those of the women outside. Afraid to ignore Hardy for too long, Analisa returned her gaze to him and found that he had been staring at her bodice as she watched the servant. She could not meet his eyes and quickly looked away again.

''More coffee, Mrs. de la Vega?''

He used her name so often that Analisa felt he was attempting to wear her down until she asked him to drop the formality and call her by her given name. She refused to do so. In no way did she wish to become more familiar with this man.

''No, thank you, Mr. Hardy. I'm afraid I must be going. You've been very kind, and I'm so happy to have been able to get away from the fort, even for a short time.'' She stood up, careful to keep her full skirt from brushing against the china service as she moved out from behind the low serving table.

He stood immediately and, limping slightly, ushered her toward the doors.

''You are certain there is no way I can be of help?'' she asked. Hoping she wouldn't push him into any sort of agreement, Analisa attempted to appear sincere in her offer, although she was secretly relieved to think that she would not have to come to the agency again. She didn't relish Hardy's leering company.

"Not at the moment, but I will think about it, believe me. It's not often that a beautiful lady comes out to this godforsaken post to visit, let alone . . . offer her services."

He leaned near her, his hand on the small of her back as she moved into the entry hall. She stepped away quickly, shrugging off his touch. Still, she could not leave without asking about the maid.

"The girl who works for you is very beautiful. Is she a Sioux?"

He turned and looked back into the parlor, his expression contemptuous. The young woman was collecting the coffee, her delicate profile visible to Analisa as she reached for the tray. The well-tailored dress clung to her figure, revealing her high, rounded breasts.

"Mia? Yes. She's one of the renegade women brought in last September. Made a lot of progress, that one. It was a while before I was able to get her tamed down enough to work in the house, let alone dress in a civilized fashion. Animals, the lot of them."

Analisa wanted to argue with him but held her tongue. Millicent Boynton, she reminded herself, would probably agree with the man, and so she remained silent.

As they moved toward the door to the veranda, she asked him about the renegades. He stopped, his hand on the ornate doorknob, and answered her. "If I was givin' the orders out here, I'd have the army hound them until they rode down every last one. Murdering, thieving bunch. They don't aim to be civilized, don't deserve the waste of time and money spent on them either."

"You don't think they'll ever give up and come to the agency?"

"Not that bunch. Most of them have been in here at one time or another, but they run off, break the treaties. They hate it here, won't live under any sort of discipline. Even the Indian police can't handle them."

"Indian police?"

"You'll see them when you ride out. Take some time to look

around before you go. The major can't afford to send men out here, now that they come up with another new law in Washington. The army has to stay out of all agency handling of the Indians. All they get to do is round them up and bring them in. So, to keep the peace, I hired a few of their own kind to work for extra rations, a little whiskey now and then." He shifted his weight, favoring his crippled leg. "Give 'em policemen's coats. Some of these agency men will do anything for a fancy coat or a top hat, even turn against their own." His voice held a condescending sneer.

Mia passed them as she moved toward a door that Analisa assumed led to the kitchen. She gave Analisa one final look before turning her gaze to Hardy. Hate blazed from the black eyes, hatred so fierce that Analisa could feel it. If Hardy noticed the open anger in the young woman's expression, he gave no sign.

Analisa thought he was finished with his explanation, but he continued speaking once Mia departed. "No, Mrs. de la Vega, you can bet that those renegades don't plan on comin' in. Besides, they would have to give up all their white captives if they did, and they don't intend to do that. They set big store in having white slaves."

As his words finally registered, Analisa heard a distant ringing in her ears while a sudden clamminess dampened her palms. The shock of his words forced her to breathe deeply as she tried to stay calm and fight against the light-headedness. Her surroundings slipped away. All she was aware of was Hardy and herself, standing near the double doors of the entry hall.

"White slaves?" Her voice was so weak that he didn't even hear her utterance. "White slaves?" she asked again, forcing the words out as he opened the door. Cool, refreshing air was carried in on the light, steady breeze. It helped to clear her head. She became conscious of the world around them once more.

He stood in the center of the veranda, surveying the surrounding area, reminding her of a king inspecting his realm. Still unable to speak, she looked out at the trading post next door, the Indian dwellings made from hide and adorned with faded paintings of horses, suns, and childlike stick figures. The tentlike structures were scattered over a wide area, the buffalo grass between them beaten into paths that led from one to another and off in the direction of the river. She wanted to be away from the sight of the dismal figures shuffling along between the dwellings or crouched lifelessly before the low doorways, huddled against the sun and relentless chilly wind.

"Sure. They have at least six whites that I know of, just in Red Dog's band. Can you imagine how many whites have been forced to live like animals all over the West? Why, it's a shame. The army ought to be riding them down, if for no other reason than to see that those poor creatures get back to their families."

Shaken, Analisa looked around for Zach and Kase. She needed to get away from Hardy, from this place, and wrestle with her own thoughts. White slaves hidden all over the territories? There was no reason to believe that Meika and Pieter were part of the renegade band living nearby, she told herself. No reason to hope. Still, she did hope. Hope welled in her heart, choking her, threatening to bring tears of joy to her eyes before she could escape this man.

Zach caught her eye from across the small distance that separated the house from the trading post. He was leaning nonchalantly against the hitching post, his hat pulled down low, shading his face, but somehow she knew he was watching them. Her eyes searched out Kase and found him not far from Zach, playing with two children near his own age. A boy and a girl, from the looks of their clothing, their thin, nearly emaciated arms bare against the wind. Dressed in the woolen suit Caleb had given him, Kase appeared abundantly healthy, almost chubby next to them. She watched as Zach alerted the boy and the two of them approached the house. Close to tears already, she swallowed hard when she saw the hardened scout reach down and take her son's hand protectively as they neared the horses tied before the wide veranda.

"Thank you for the visit, Mr. Hardy. You have been a kind host." She refused to extend her hand toward him, and he made no move to touch her again.

"It was my pleasure, Mrs. de la Vega. I hope you'll call on me again, any time." He bowed from the waist, a gesture she thought reserved for royalty. "I'm sorry I could not suggest any way for you to help out here. If I think of something, I'll let you know. Perhaps the next time I'm at Fort Sully, I can pay you a call?"

"Thank you, Mr. Hardy. That would be fine." Her forced

politeness was beginning to nauseate her. Analisa stepped slowly off the porch and moved toward the horses where Zach waited to help her mount. She felt as if she were walking in a dream world. *Hold on a little longer,* she told herself. *You've come this far.* Zach lifted her by the waist as she stepped up into the stirrup and swung her leg over the saddle, then adjusted her skirt modestly.

"I'll put the boy up in front of me, this time, ma'am."

Zach's voice startled her out of her thoughts, and she looked down at his upturned face.

"We'll make better time," he explained.

"Thank you, Mr. Elliot."

"Good day to you, Mrs. de la Vega," Hardy called from the porch.

"Good day, Mr. Hardy." *And good-bye,* she thought as she turned her horse to follow Zach as he headed toward home.

They traveled for at least ten minutes in silence. Zach ignored her while Kase was intent on searching the landscape for any sign of jackrabbits. The wind was increasing, and far off on the western horizon, Analisa saw a storm front gathering as the unpredictable spring weather changed once again.

Her thoughts were jumbled, bouncing back and forth in her mind much the way her insides were being rattled by the movement of the horse beneath her. Her grandiose plan to help Caleb expose Hardy was forgotten, one thought now foremost in her mind: White captives were being held as slaves by the renegades; Pieter and Meika might even now be only a few miles away.

She tried to remember them as she'd last seen them and only recalled the flat, lifeless images in the photograph. Pieter would be thirteen now, and Meika would be a woman full grown, seventeen. Analisa remembered every birthday that had passed, even though her brother and sister were no longer with her. What were they like now? she wondered. Were they still alive? Were they indeed slaves to the Indians who had captured them? Until today she thought she'd finally left the past behind. She held on to her dream of being united with the missing children, but now she knew she would be faced with more than Pieter and Meika as she knew them. What had they been forced to endure? How would she even know them?

"You seem pretty quiet, ma'am. Everything all right?"

She looked across at Zach, surprised to find that she was not alone. "Yes. I am just thinking about all Mr. Hardy told me."

"Such as?"

"What do you know about white slaves?"

Zach looked incredulous. "He told you about *that?*"

"What?"

"The white slaves?"

She wondered why the army scout sounded so shocked, not about the fact of the slaves' existence, but because Hardy had mentioned it to her. News of the white slaves didn't seem a surprise to Zach.

"He told me the renegades will never come in because they hold so many white slaves. He thinks the army should ride them down in order to free the captives."

"He thinks so, huh?"

"Yes. What do you think?"

"I think that's the last thing Hardy wants."

"He did say that it was a waste of money to keep the Indians on the reservation."

"Did he have any solutions?"

"Maybe the same one you have, Mr. Elliot. Kill them off." She wondered if she'd taken leave of her senses, speaking to him this way.

His eye seemed to bore into hers. He spat, and continued to stare at her as they rode on.

"What makes you think I feel that way, ma'am?" His voice was low, angry.

Analisa hesitated. Perhaps she'd let the turmoil of feelings Hardy aroused push her too far. What right did she have to badger Zach?

"Everyone at the fort seems to think you hate Indians as much as Mr. Hardy apparently does."

"People ain't always the way they seem, ma'am."

"So my husband tells me."

"Well, it'd be best to listen to him." He stared ahead, lost in thought for a moment before he spoke. "Havin' the army rescue those whites is the last thing Hardy wants." He spat again.

Suddenly alert to his words, Analisa gave him her full attention. "Why do you say that?"

"Well, he's pretty slick about it, ain't been caught yet, but I happen to know that he makes damn good money *buying* white captives and then reselling them to their families."

"What?"

"Yep. He pays the renegades good money for them, then contacts the families and collects what he calls 'rewards' for sending them back. If they ain't got no family to speak of, well, he can always get a good price for them from the Comanche, who resell them again to the Mexicans. Sometimes he deals direct to Mexico."

She couldn't control the shaking in her voice. "Are you sure?"

"I don't make up fairy tales, ma'am. I ran into Hardy years ago. Nowhere near here, though, and it ain't likely he remembers me. I was a different man then."

"Have you told the major?"

"Nope."

"Why not? Wouldn't he be able to do something?"

"I suspect the major knows something, but he may be one of Hardy's men, or maybe, like me, he's biding his time. A man like Hardy's got connections. That makes him safe. He's got the BIA behind him, too, more than likely."

"But . . ." Analisa started to deny his statement. She knew that the BIA wanted to see Hardy caught as badly as Zach did, but to tell him would reveal Caleb's secret, perhaps put his life in jeopardy.

"Ma'am?"

"Nothing. I don't understand, is all." She shook her head, unable to tell him her true feelings.

"I suspect you won't be makin' any more trips out to visit the agency, will you, Miz de la Vega?"

"No, Mr. Elliot. I don't suppose I will."

"That's too bad. I'll miss the dinners aforehand."

Chapter Fourteen

By the time Analisa, Zach Elliot, and Kase approached the outlying buildings of Fort Sully, gray clouds had gathered and lowered in the sky. The driving wind pushed against them until Analisa's thick wool sweater provided little comfort against the chill. As if he sensed her discomfort, Zach urged his horse into a gallop, and when her own mount followed suit, she was forced to clutch the horse's mane. Analisa was sure the animal knew it was really in control.

They neared the row of officers' houses and passed the doctor's quarters, then the BOQ, which she'd learned meant Bachelor Officers' Quarters, the major's house, and then the Boyntons', beside her own. Analisa suddenly became aware that the porch of her own small house was covered with boxes, barrels, and crates. The front door was blockaded by the goods stacked around it. Analisa was rendered speechless as she stared at her porch. Was Caleb responsible for all of this?

"Looks to me like you got company, ma'am."

Zach chuckled, and she followed his gaze, watching in awe as a rotund, rosy-cheeked woman, with a crown of gray braids wrapped about her head and a pipe clamped between her teeth, stepped around the boxes and lifted a suitcase high above another stack before she made her way back inside the house.

"What in the world . . . ?"

"Do you want me to go in with you, ma'am? You look sorta surprised."

Analisa tried to reason it out but found it made no sense. What was an old woman with a wagonload of parcels doing on her porch, in her house? She suspected it all had something to do with Caleb and realized that her life with him would never be boring.

"No, thank you, Mr. Elliot. I will see to this myself. Thank you, too, for taking me out to the agency." She dismounted alone, her confusion over the woman in the house helping her to ignore the discomfort she felt at the end of the ride.

Zach handed the boy down to her, and Kase bounded toward the house, Analisa hurrying to stop his headlong rush to see what all the boxes meant.

"*Dank U wel,* Mr. Elliot." She called out her thanks as she hurried after Kase, who was almost to the door, his head barely visible over the boxes and barrels.

"Kase! Wait," she commanded, and the boy stopped, although he continued to bounce with excitement.

"Hurry up, Mama. Somebody's in the house."

Before Analisa could reach for the doorknob, the portal swung open to reveal the woman she had seen moving about on the porch moments ago. They stood exchanging startled glances until the hearty woman put her hands on her ample hips, shifted the clay pipe from the right to the left side of her mouth, and looked Analisa up and down.

"You must be Caleb's wife. Leave it to that boy to find a beauty." She called to someone over her shoulder. "Mrs. Storm! She's a picture, just like you thought, but you're in for a surprise."

Glancing over her own shoulder to see if anyone was passing

by, Analisa quickly ushered Kase inside, her hand on his shoulder as she brushed past the stranger. If this woman continued to shout, the entire fort would soon know who Caleb really was.

It seemed the older woman was not the only shock she was to receive, for crossing the parlor to greet her was a dark-haired woman with a glowing expression of affection in her eyes. The woman's enthusiasm forced Analisa to smile in response. Someone so genuinely happy to see her could not mean any harm.

"You look as if this is all quite a surprise, my dear, and I'm sure it must be. Analisa, isn't it? I'm Caleb's stepmother, Ruth Storm. We didn't mean to intrude on you like this, but we all decided it would be best to come straight to the house and act as if we were expected rather than question the major. I'm not quite sure what Caleb is up to this time, but I know that it's important to keep silent as to his identity."

The woman finally paused for a breath, leaving Analisa to stare as she tried to sort out all she'd heard.

"You are Ruth?"

"The same. Caleb has told you about me, hasn't he?"

Analisa nodded. "Yes. But I imagined that you would be much older."

"I am much younger than his father was, but I'm still old enough to be Caleb's mother."

"Barely," the gray-haired woman added as a cloud of smoke issued from the pipe and floated on the air about her head.

"Oh, Analisa, I'm sorry. In my excitement I forgot to introduce you to Abigail Oats. Abbie is my cook. She refused to stay behind when I told her my plan to visit you and Caleb. This must be Kase!" Ruth bent down and looked the boy square in the eye. "*You* are certainly more grown up than I imagined. What a *wonderful* boy you are!"

The boy smiled up at Ruth, well pleased with her praise.

"What's in all those boxes?" he asked, staring at Abbie. "And why does that lady smoke a pipe?" The child looked up in awe at the old cook, who stared right back.

"Kase!" Analisa tried to cover the embarrassing situation but didn't know how to answer the boy.

Abigail Oats spoke up for herself. "Always smoked a pipe,

boy, since I was your age, most likely. If you're real good, I'll let you try it."

"Oh, for heaven's sake, Abbie, don't tease the child. Just look at his mother's expression. She's not used to your teasing." Ruth turned to Analisa. "About the boxes, I'm afraid I may have overstepped my bounds." She continued apologetically, "I thought I'd bring out just a *few* things that might help you set up housekeeping. But, as usual, I became carried away. I think I packed up half the house."

"*I* packed up half the house. *You* gave directions," Abbie said, and Analisa realized the cook was more of a friend to Ruth than a servant.

"Yes, I gave the directions, and I'm about to give more. Get Analisa a cup of tea, please, Abigail. She looks ready to collapse. Kase, would you like some pie? I'll bet Abbie has one of Caleb's favorites wrapped up inside that hat box she's been guarding all the way from Boston." Ruth sent the two off to the kitchen.

"Come, my dear." Ruth led Analisa to the dining table. "We need to talk. Abbie will have the tea here in no time. Would you rather sit in the kitchen near the stove? We haven't had a chance to light the fire here in the parlor yet, and you look quite chilled."

Feeling like a guest in her own home, Analisa let Ruth pull out a chair for her before the woman seated herself at the table. Overwhelmed, Analisa couldn't help admiring the woman's calm self-assurance and poise. She seemed to have everything well under control without being intrusive. Analisa watched Ruth as she smoothed out her forest-green skirt and straightened the prim white blouse. Caleb's stepmother perched on the edge of her chair, expecting Analisa to begin the conversation. She could feel Ruth's calm hazel eyes studying her, assessing her. How much had Caleb told this woman about her and Kase? He'd last seen Ruth in December, before his return from Washington. At that time, Analisa wasn't even certain that he would be coming back to her. Had he told Ruth the story of their hurried wedding? At a loss, Analisa sat quietly, unsure exactly where to begin.

She finally decided on the most important issue: Caleb's hidden identity. Ruth must be made aware of the danger her stepson was in. Had she spoken to anyone out of turn and placed Caleb in danger already? Taking a hint from Ruth's own straightforward manner, Analisa asked the woman directly. "How much do you know of Caleb's reason for being here?"

Ruth kept her voice low, following Analisa's example. "Before he left Boston, he received his orders from General Parker. He told me I could reach him here until I heard differently, and that he would be using the name Don Ricardo Corona de la Vega."

"You haven't mentioned his real name to anyone?"

"No, of course not. My dear, I have known Caleb since he was eighteen. I'm quite used to his escapades."

"Escapades?"

"I'm sorry." Ruth searched for another word. "His . . . adventures."

"This is hardly an adventure, Mrs. Storm." Analisa felt herself becoming protective of Caleb's position. "Caleb's life is in danger."

She watched as Ruth smiled at her with understanding. "Caleb's life is always in danger, Analisa. It's the nature of his business, but even if it weren't, he'd be doing something equally dangerous. He thrives on it."

Analisa remembered the urgency and excitement she'd experienced as she rode toward the agency to seek out Hardy. The danger of what she was doing was thrilling in a way she'd never imagined it could be. Did Caleb feel the same excitement each time he rode into the renegade camp, every time he confronted anyone as Don Ricardo? A different energy had surged through her when she faced the danger of intrigue. She understood Ruth's comment, because she'd experienced the feelings that Caleb apparently thrived on.

"I can tell by your expression that you are worried about him. Perhaps I've come at a good time after all." Ruth leaned toward Analisa, diminishing the space between them. "I was married to his father, Analisa. They were very much alike. Caleb, like Clinton, must be free to seek the challenge he needs. Never hem him in. Do you understand what I'm saying?"

Analisa nodded. It was a relief just to sit and talk quietly with Ruth. It had been so long since she'd had her mother to comfort her, guide her. Sophie had been her friend, but her equal. With

Ruth she hoped she might find the joy that came from having a gentle adviser.

"I think I am beginning to understand Caleb, and so I do understand what you have said."

Abigail bustled into the room with a steaming pot of tea and a large wedge of apple pie for Analisa.

"Don't mind me. I'll be gone in a minute." Abbie paused to look at Analisa, her blue eyes snapping, the pipe missing from the corner of her mouth. Although the ring of silver-gray braids about her head was neatly arranged, wisps escaped here and there. Her forehead was beaded with sweat from her recent flurry of activity. Abbie leaned toward Analisa, assuming the role of conspirator. "You don't have to worry about me, honey. I may seem like a loudmouth, but I'm closed as a clam when I have to be. And," she added in a stage whisper, "I was only teasin' about letting the boy smoke. It'll be a year or two before he's ready for it."

Rearing back with a hearty chuckle, the woman turned away. Analisa watched the starched bow riding above the cook's wide derriere as Abbie bounced into the kitchen.

Before she continued, Analisa relished a sip of the steaming tea. The tart aroma of orange peel floated above the liquid. Abbie was beginning to bang pans about in the kitchen, and Analisa listened to Kase as he asked the woman a string of questions in between telling her where household items were kept. Ruth seemed to want to relax and chat, but Analisa found it hard to do so with a strange woman working in her own kitchen. Shouldn't she be preparing dinner for her guests?

"You just relax." Ruth's voice intruded upon her thoughts. "Your worry is as plain as the nose on your face. Abbie doesn't need or want any help. I guess now is the time to apologize for coming out here on a whim to visit you two without any notice, but you see, I just couldn't wait any longer to meet you and Kase. Abbie refused to be left behind, and once she's made up her mind there's no arguing with her. She's become part of the family. We gave up trying to act like employer and employee years ago." Ruth stopped long enough to refill her own cup and then continued.

"We told the soldier who met the steamboat that we were guests of Don Ricardo, and believe me, I breathed a sigh of relief when he brought us directly here. I wasn't even sure you'd still be at Fort Sully." She looked at Analisa with eyes that begged for understanding and forgiveness. "I realize that our accommodations will be cramped, but I don't intend to put you to this trouble for too long. We'll be going back on the next steamboat. I hope you'll forgive me, though. I just had to meet you."

Abandoning a forkful of pie, Analisa reached across the table and took one of Ruth's hands in her own.

"You can't leave without seeing Caleb, and he may not be back for weeks. We'll be crowded, but please stay for as long as you like." Analisa looked around for a moment before she had second thoughts. "Perhaps the house is too small for your taste. I . . . I know that it is simple, but it is clean. Maybe the major can find housing for you elsewhere, but you must stay."

"I can manage anywhere, but I'm concerned about you and your privacy."

Analisa felt her face flush as she realized that Ruth must be thinking of sleeping arrangements when Caleb returned. It was a moment before she could meet the woman's eyes again. Ruth's were sparkling.

"Kase will sleep with me," Analisa began, mentally arranging everyone in her mind. "You can sleep in his bed, and Abigail can have a cot in there, too. The room is large enough. We'll worry about moving Kase later."

Analisa's voice was drowned out by what sounded like the shriek of a very angry cat. While the shrill screech still hung in the air, a black and white streak hurled itself from the kitchen, followed close behind by Kase. The boy ran through the doorway, heedless of the commotion, and tripped headlong over the edge of the carpet. The fall threw him to his knees, and he remained stunned for a moment before both Ruth and Analisa jumped to his aid. Analisa looked him over, saw that he was unhurt, then brushed off the knees of his trousers and adjusted his suspenders.

"You are all right," she assured him, noting his darkening expression. "Don't run in the house, Kase. You know that. Did you put your jacket away?"

He nodded. "But, Mama, they brought a cat. He was asleep under the stove and I saw his tail, but I couldn't get him out."

"Did you pull on it?" Ruth asked.

"*Ja*. I pulled on the tail, but then he jumped up and screamed and scared me and ran in here." The boy looked around for the missing animal.

"Come with me, Kase," Ruth said, extending her hand to the boy. "We'll find Galileo, and I'll help you apologize to him. I'm sure you'll want to be friends. It may take him a while to get used to you, though. He doesn't know any children, and he gets a bit upset when he travels in a box for very long."

"Is he yours?"

"Yes. I've had him many years now."

Analisa listened as they walked about the room, searching under the furniture and behind the drapes. Ruth calmly instructed the boy as to how to treat a cat gently and quietly if he wished to make friends.

"Here he is," Ruth whispered. She knelt down in front of the sideboard. "Come out, Galileo. Come and meet Kase."

Muddy water lapped in and out of the shallows along the riverbank, surging and swirling around the tree stumps and other natural debris carried along by the steady current of the Missouri. Caleb urged Scorpio forward, letting the big stallion find his own footing through the shallows. He glanced over his shoulder anxious to leave no trace of his passage. There was no sign of anyone following him. He reined to the right in the direction of the bank and began to make his way through the dense undergrowth that lined the shore beneath the bluffs that had been carved away by the water's force.

Once he reached the wide plateau at the top of the riverbank, Caleb could see for miles in every direction. The sky was clear, the sun shining down over the rain-freshened landscape. Scorpio shook his head, impatient to be off. Caleb made the horse wait while he tightened the rawhide band he had tied around his forehead to hold his hair away from his face. He pressed his knees against Scorpio's ribs, gently controlling the horse without the aid of saddle or stirrups, for he'd left his tack and his white man's clothing in a small cave a few miles from Fort Sully. He knew that anyone who came upon him now would mistake him for an Indian. His clothing consisted of buckskin leggings, cut-beaded moccasins, and a buckskin pullover. His rifle was thrust into a fringed scabbard decorated with beads and porcupine quills. He reached down to straighten the knife that hung ready in a smaller sheath at his waist. In an hour or two Caleb would arrive at the cave where his "Don Ricardo" suit and saddle were hidden. As he rode toward the fort, he mentally tallied the hours it would take him to get home.

Impatience assailed him. It was a feeling he didn't welcome, for he knew that an impatient man often made mistakes. He squinted into the distance and tried to make out the dark shapes circling in the sky not far away as he sorted through his thoughts. His own plans seemed at an impasse, for he was no nearer to curtailing Hardy's duties at the agency than he had been when he first arrived. Everything was moving far too slowly, and Caleb was aware that most of the problem stemmed from his living in two places at once. Caleb knew that he would remain under suspicion as long as he kept disappearing to visit Analisa. One of these days Red Dog would send someone to trail him, someone whom Caleb would be unable to shake. He didn't relish the thought of having to face Red Dog and the others if they learned of his identity before he'd put Hardy away for good.

Things had seemed easier when he had only himself to worry about. He let his mind drift to Analisa, and his body began to respond the way it always did when he thought of her. Damn. The woman had gotten into his blood in a way no one ever had before, and she'd done it effortlessly. He smiled, thinking of his last night at home and the magic she'd worked on him. He'd been gone only two weeks this time, hardly long enough to settle into the routine in the renegade camp, before he felt the nagging need to return to Analisa. "Trust your intuition." That was always Ruth's advice. So, when the feeling wouldn't leave him, he'd decided to go back to the fort. Caleb had left the camp before dawn with a hurried word to the scout who was guarding the Indians' horses. He told the man he was going hunting and would return in three, maybe four days. The guard hadn't questioned him, for there was always too great a need for food among the renegade band to deny anyone permission to go off hunting.

Looking to the east once again, Caleb was certain now that a flock of carrion crows had gathered above the open plain. They

had probably found a dead antelope, he told himself as he tried
to shake off the nagging feeling that he should go find out for
sure. His impulsive trek to see Analisa was already costing him
valuable time. He didn't need to waste any more by taking a
detour.

Glancing once again at the circling crows, he muttered a
curse under his breath and then turned his horse toward the
ominous black figures in the sky. What difference would a few
more minutes make?

Scorpio sensed his mood and broke into a gallop as soon as
he felt the touch of Caleb's knees. As they approached the
crows, Caleb saw that a dark form lay huddled on the ground in
the distance, and although he could not make out what sort of
creature it was, he thought he saw it move. Within minutes,
horse and rider drew close enough to the huddled figure for
Caleb to see clearly that it was a person clothed in black. With a
practiced move he was off of the horse as soon as it reached the
limp body lying huddled against the onslaught of the crows.
Caleb swung his arms in the air, shouting to drive the more
brazen ones away from the broken figure of a woman. He knelt
beside her and turned her gently onto her back. Long, thick
strands of ebony hair lay tangled over her face. He brushed it
away.

It was a girl of about eighteen, and Caleb could see that she
was a Sioux, although she was dressed in a black silk gown that
had once been exquisitely tailored. The dress was torn and
ragged now, the sleeves pulled away from the shoulders,
brambles and tears covering the skirt. He cradled her in his
arms, and she pressed her face against his chest until he tilted it
up gently with his thumb and forefinger to get a closer look. Her
left eye was swollen shut, her lips caked with dried blood. Caleb
put her down gently and strode back to Scorpio to retrieve his
water bag.

Raising her head once again, he forced the mouth of the bag
between her lips and whispered in Sioux, ordering her to drink.

The girl opened her eyes at the sound of the Sioux words and
did as he commanded, slowly sipping the water he offered.

As understanding filled her eyes, Caleb withdrew the bag and
set her away from him, allowing her to lean against his bent
knee.

"Who are you?" He spoke to her only in the Sioux language, knowing she understood.

"Mia." She looked him over, studying his clothes, then his eyes. "Who are you?"

"Raven's Shadow, of Red Dog's band."

Caleb watched as she relaxed at his words, her wary look replaced by one of hope.

"I was going back to him. I am Red Dog's woman."

He frowned, his eyes taking in the dress, the condition of her face. She answered his questions before he could ask them.

"I was forced to live in the agent Hardy's house. I worked as his servant. Last night he wanted more. He beat me. When he was asleep, I ran away."

"How did you escape?"

"I knew the guard. I told him if Red Dog came to get me he would kill all of the ones who call themselves *police*." She spat out the white man's word. "Will you take me to Red Dog?"

Caleb nodded. His journey to Anja would have to wait. Finding this woman might be the break he needed to gain Red Dog's trust. Perhaps she was the reason he had felt the need to leave the camp this morning. Fate had demanded that he rescue Red Dog's woman. "Can you ride?"

At her nod of assurance, Caleb lifted Mia and carried her to Scorpio. Once they were both mounted, he held her securely before him, one arm looped around her waist. She relaxed against him, her head on his shoulder, and fell immediately asleep as he turned the giant horse back toward the renegade camp.

It was late afternoon before Caleb rode into the camp, which lay hidden in a wide ravine near the river. From the open plain above it could not be seen, nor could it be sighted from the Missouri, lying as it did along one bank of a narrow tributary of the river. Dogs barked as children ran through the settlement of buffalo-hide tepees. Women worked over open fires while the men sat in small groups around the camp, some busy repairing or replacing valuable weapons. Tender shoots of spring grass were beginning to sprout in the less traveled pathways as well as along the high banks of the ravine. The scent of simmering food hung in the air, reminding Caleb of his hunger. A youth of about twelve summers spotted him first and, with one glance at the woman in Caleb's arms, began to run for Red Dog's shelter. Within moments, people had begun to cluster around Caleb's horse.

A sudden movement in the crowd caught his eye, and Caleb glanced over the bobbing heads. There, between two Sioux women, stood a girl who looked enough like Analisa to make him want to call out to her. Caleb stared wide-eyed before he quickly tried to cover his amazement by looking away. Concealing his curiosity, he let his eyes scan the crowd as he guided Scorpio toward Red Dog's tepee in the center of the encampment. Slowly he passed his gaze over the place where he'd last seen the girl and noted with some relief that she was still there between the two women. Her hair was parted in the center and braided in the Indian fashion, and a beaded headband encircled her brow. Her clothing told Caleb that she lived with a family of some stature in the camp. Why had he never seen her before? Without openly staring, Caleb let himself take note of every feature of the blond girl who was now almost hidden among the crowd. He wanted to tell himself that it could not be Anja's sister, Meika, and yet the likeness between them was too great to be a coincidence. Could the brother be here as well? His next thought hit him as suddenly as a prairie thundershower: If Meika was among these people, was Analisa's attacker also one of them? He wondered if he knew the man who had fathered Kase. Forced to pay attention as he maneuvered Scorpio through the pressing crowd, Caleb made his way toward Red Dog's shelter.

Caleb felt Mia stir as she straightened, forcing herself to sit unaided. Red Dog, alerted by the young runner, pushed through the throng and stopped when he reached them. He looked up at Mia's face for a moment, then reached up to take her from the horse. She leaned down and surrendered herself to the leader's strong arms.

"Come with me." Red Dog tossed the order over his shoulder to Caleb, who gave Scorpio up to the runner's care. He knew the horse would be watered, fed, and rubbed down immediately. As he followed the man into the tepee, Caleb knew that Red Dog's mind held many questions.

Caleb sat cross-legged on a buffalo robe and listened while the young leader issued orders for Mia's care to the older women of his family. Red Dog watched in silence for a time before he turned his back on the hovering women and joined Caleb on the mat.

Dispensing with the usual ceremony that preceded conversation, Red Dog confronted Caleb directly. "Where did you find her?"

"Half a day's ride away, between here and the agency land." Caleb met the man's questioning stare, but did not admit what he was doing so near the fort.

"She was alone?"

"Yes. And exhausted. She could travel no farther when I found her."

Silence grew heavy between them as Red Dog watched Caleb. The women's voices behind them in the shadowed interior of the hide dwelling were indistinguishable from one another. A low cook fire burned in the center of the room while a wisp of smoke rose through the smoke hole at the apex of the willow shafts that supported the buffalo hides. The air was scented by a bowl of rabbit stew simmering near the flames and by the heat of so many bodies. Caleb watched Red Dog draw himself up and fill his lungs with air. His obsidian eyes did not waver as they met Caleb's blue ones.

"I owe you a life. You have returned one who is very precious to me."

"I will remember." Caleb knew it would be an insult to ignore the man's words or pass them off with a show of humility.

The renegade leader allowed himself a glance toward Mia, who was now sleeping on a pile of mats. His mother sat at the girl's side in attendance.

"How was she injured?"

Caleb paused before answering. If he raised Red Dog's ire with the truth, by telling him of Hardy's guilt, the young chief might take matters into his own hands and attack the agency himself, ending Caleb's chance to arrest Hardy. Caleb's job would be over, yet an attack on the Sioux agency would lead to more bloodshed. The troops from Fort Sully as well as others from the surrounding area would then be called out, and Red Dog's band would be ridden down to the last man. Caution was required, even though Red Dog demanded an explanation.

"She said she was beaten," he told the renegade.

Anger welled up behind Red Dog's eyes. "By the white chief, Hardy?"

Caleb nodded. "You know of him?"

"Yes. He deals in women. The next time he comes to deal with me, I will kill him."

"You have sold him women?" Caleb hoped to gain answers before Red Dog took offense at his question.

Anger was apparent even in the man's hushed tones. "We were making plans to trade for Mia and for other women of our band who were taken in by the soldiers before the winter came."

"What does Hardy ask in return?"

"Furs sometimes, if we are trying to reclaim our captives. In the case of our own women, he would have asked for others to replace them—Crow or Blackfeet, perhaps, but he prefers whites."

Trying to cover his astonishment, Caleb gently prodded the man with more questions. "What else does he give you in such exchanges?"

Red Dog smirked, contempt for Hardy etched on his face. "He gives us guns in return for some of the women we take him, or gold so that we can buy guns to kill his kind. This time he has gone too far. He will walk right into my trap. The guns will be used on him. All I need to do is send word that I have a white woman to trade."

Red Dog was giving him all the information he needed in order to trap Hardy, but unlike the younger man, Caleb did not wish to see the agent dead. Justice would be served to the letter of the law, for Caleb intended to see that Hardy stood trial and that his atrocities became public knowledge. There were too many agents like him scattered over the frontier. If the BIA was to improve its services, men like Hardy would have to be paraded before the highest powers in the land. That was Ely Parker's secret dream, and Caleb hoped to help to make that dream a reality.

"I saw a white girl among the people when I rode in. Will you use her to tempt him here?"

Red Dog's expression became guarded at the mention of the white girl. "She is not for trade. She is the wife of Swift Otter."

"I had not seen her before."

Contempt was heavy in Red Dog's tone when he replied. "Does the white blood mixed in your veins tempt you to have her?"

Ignoring the statement, Caleb met Red Dog's stare. "I am curious. I thought I had seen all the people of the camp."

"Swift Otter and his band arrived this morning. We camp apart for the winter. Now that the snows are gone, many more will join us."

Standing, Red Dog turned his back on Caleb, ending the discussion. Any other guest would not have been treated in such a rude manner, but Caleb knew that his white blood as well as Red Dog's lack of trust in him had prompted the abrupt dismissal.

Rising from the mat, Caleb ducked low and stepped out of the tepee. Dusk shrouded the camp while the people inside their dwellings shared the evening meal. Now more than ever, Caleb missed Analisa and Kase. He had no one here. He knew he wasn't likely to get another glimpse of the white girl before morning, even if he prowled the camp. Perhaps it would be just as well if he set out toward the fort, as he'd done earlier. It would not be that late when he arrived. He had to send a message to Parker, with details and documentation of the incidents proving the agent's guilt. Caleb knew that someone could be killed before this drama was played out. It was imperative that he send word to Washington before that happened.

Chapter Fifteen

"Mama? Mama!" The boy tugged at her shoulder.

"Mama, everyone is awake and Abbie has breakfast ready. This is the dance day, Mama. Don't you want to get up?"

Analisa pulled herself up on one elbow and leaned toward her son, touching his cheek with her lips. The sun was already high, the bedroom flooded with light. She stretched, raising her arms high over her head, and remembered that tonight the long awaited dance would be held in honor of the Boyntons' sister, as well as her own guests.

"Yes, I'd better get up, hadn't I, Kase? We have to prepare the food, and Tor is coming in with some of the men to take the organ over to the commissary." She flipped back the sheet and quilt and moved to the edge of the bed. "You run along, and I'll be there in a moment. Tell Abbie I'm sorry I overslept."

As Kase opened the door, Ruth peered into the room. She

was already dressed in a crisp white blouse and green skirt, her hair pulled into a tidy roll. Her glasses rode atop her head, crowning the wavy mass.

"I'm sorry he woke you, Analisa. I intended for you to sleep a while longer. You've been working so late that I thought you could use a little extra rest."

Ruth crossed the room to inspect two beautiful dresses hanging along the wall. As Analisa slipped her stockings on and then her *klompen*, Ruth fingered the material of the gowns, straightening ruffles and fluffing the skirts.

"You've done a marvelous job on these, Analisa. What a task, and what a talent you have!"

Analisa flushed at the compliment and thanked Ruth before she quickly pulled off her nightgown and drew on her old yellow calico dress. She walked to the dresser and, while she continued her conversation with Caleb's stepmother, parted her hair, separated it into two sections, and began to braid it.

"It was a job I enjoyed," she told Ruth. "I could not have done it without the aid of your gift, Ruth." Ruth had brought a new sewing machine from Boston for Analisa. The overwhelming gesture was such a surprise and delight that she had insisted on making dresses for Ruth and Abbie as well as one for herself. Even though Abbie declined the offer and there was one less to make, the task had forced Analisa to work long hours in order to complete the gowns before the dance.

"For a time I thought you were ready to send that sewing machine back home with me." Ruth laughed, turning once more to face Analisa.

Deftly, Analisa plaited the second braid, wound it about the crown of her head, and pinned it securely, forming a golden coronet.

"The little booklet with the drawings and instructions didn't help much."

Ruth laughed as she recalled Analisa's attempts. "I'll never forget the look on your face once you got it threaded and were able to make the treadle pump the needle. It was priceless. You looked as if you'd just invented the thing yourself." Ruth thought for a moment before she added, "You know, you could make a fortune in the East if you were to open your own salon. You have quite a talent for design."

A soft smile turned up the corners of Analisa's lips as she

remembered Pella and the discoveries she'd made as she learned from one experimental dress and then another. All the nights she'd spent poring over pictures and making patterns in the dim lamplight of the soddie had helped her develop a talent that was second nature to her now.

"What a difference the machine makes, Ruth. I am so lucky to have it." Analisa stood in the doorway, waiting for Ruth to join her. She smoothed the waistline of her dress before she looked at the woman once again. "And I'm lucky to have you, too."

Ruth took her by the shoulders and studied Analisa's eyes before she spoke.

"I'm so pleased to have you in my family, Analisa. Caleb made a wonderful choice when he married you. For a time I thought that he would never marry. He's always been such a loner. You are a very special lady." She gave Analisa a quick hug and then added, "I'm going to skin him alive, though, next time I see him. He should be checking on you more often."

It was Analisa's turn to laugh. "I'm trying not to 'hem him in.' Didn't you warn me about that yourself, Ruth?"

"I guess I did, but this is ridiculous. Besides, I'm anxious to see him myself. Come, dear. Abbie has breakfast waiting for you."

The day passed quickly, with everyone in the household engaged in preparations for the party. Abbie and Ruth worked in the kitchen, determined to bake pies that, as Abbie declared, "would cause a man's heart to stop beating." Analisa hemmed and pressed the new gowns and was well pleased with her handiwork. For Ruth, she'd worked with a raspberry watered silk. The material had been packed inside a box of fabric intended as a gift for Analisa, but she insisted on using it for Ruth. The shade was too overpowering for her own fair coloring, but perfectly enhanced Ruth's dark hair and hazel eyes. Since Abbie had refused a new gown, Analisa had stitched a full length ruffled white apron for the cook to wear over one of her own dresses.

For herself, Analisa had chosen a material unlike any other fabric she'd ever worked with. It was a pale pink muslin striped with ribbons of white that were embroidered with tiny blue flowers. From it she had fashioned a gown with a narrow skirt and a lower neckline than any she'd ever worn—but only due to a miscalculation on her part. The pattern she'd drawn had seemed perfect, but when Analisa tried on the finished dress, she found the neckline far lower than she anticipated. The material was too precious to discard, however, and Ruth thought the gown stunning, insisting that the bodice was flattering and Analisa's figure well suited for it, so Analisa was finally convinced she should wear it, with a shawl for modesty's sake.

By the time evening arrived, the members of Analisa's new family stood assembled in the parlor awaiting Private Jensen, who was to escort them across the parade ground.

"Is it time to go, Mama?" Kase asked impatiently.

"As soon as Tor gets here. Why don't you go out on the porch and watch for him?"

The boy ran quickly to the door, his dark hair bobbing as he moved. He looked quite the young gentleman in his wool suit and suspenders, his shoes shined to a high gleam.

"I hope nobody cuts that pie before we get there," Abbie spoke up as she walked impatiently to the window and drew the curtain aside. The woman seemed as anxious as Kase for the party to begin.

"He's here!" Kase shouted as he popped in the doorway and then out again.

Analisa drew a lightweight shawl over her shoulders, knotted it across her breasts, then ran her hand up the back of her neck to catch any stray wisps of hair that might have slipped from the coil on her head.

"You look lovely, dear," Ruth whispered behind her as they moved toward the doorway. "I only wish Caleb was here to see you. He would be so proud."

Unexpectedly Analisa felt her eyes mist over with tears. She, too, wished Caleb were here. Suddenly she knew she was anxious to see him, not because of the information she wanted, but because she truly missed having him beside her. Ruth's presence only made that fact more apparent to Analisa. Her excitement over attending her first social gathering was lessened by Caleb's not being here to share it with her. Apprehension assailed her at the thought of moving among so many people as an equal. Indeed, in their eyes she was supposed to be something more than an equal, as the wife of Professor Don Ricardo Corona de la Vega. All week she'd been so involved in her sewing efforts that the thought of what this night would mean had escaped her. Overwhelmed, she stopped before she reached the threshold. Kase and Abbie were already moving toward the pathway as Tor stood looking back toward the house.

"Analisa?" Ruth's voice sounded far away, but it served to call her back to the present.

"I can't go." Analisa was surprised at the sound of her own voice, a croaking whisper. Fear constricted her throat.

"Are you ill, dear? You look so pale."

She blinked twice as she studied the worried look in Ruth's eyes. Unable to speak, Analisa merely shook her head.

"What is it?"

"I can't do this, Ruth," she said at last. "I don't know how. I have never been among such a large group of people . . . since . . . I . . . I don't belong there. It is not right."

Ruth was silent for a moment before she spoke. Analisa watched as the smaller woman drew herself up and reached out to place a hand on each of her shoulders.

"Listen to me. You have every right to be there tonight. If Caleb were here, you know he'd tell you the same thing. Make him proud of you, Analisa. Hold your head high and walk into that place as if you own it. Do you understand?"

Analisa took one deep breath and then another to calm her racing heart. The palms of her hands were sweating. She knew that there was no sense in looking back, there never had been. Through the open door she could see the lights shining in the commissary windows, and she watched as silhouetted figures moved across them. When would it become easy? Would she ever be able to leave the past behind? One thing was certain, she would never forgive herself if she did not face her own fears. Analisa toyed with the ends of her shawl. Finally she nodded at Ruth and whispered her answer.

"Yes. I'm ready."

"Good, then, let's go. The others are waiting."

Caleb dismounted slowly and held his spine straight in order to conceal his usual fluid movements. Bowler hat poised atop his head, he stood beside Scorpio and surveyed the darkened stable yard. The sounds of horses shuffling around in the corrals and stalls that lined the long wooden building filled the night air. He could hear music in the distance and wondered for a moment if it came from the enlisted men's quarters, for often in the evenings the soldiers amused themselves with song. Light from a single lamp inside the tack room slipped through a slight opening where the door stood ajar. Listening intently, Caleb heard the sound of bootshod feet moving about in the small room. He guessed it was Zach Elliot.

Several burlap bags full of plant samples and cuttings hung from Caleb's saddle, many with root balls intact. He'd give a month's pay just to see the expression on Ely Parker's face when he opened the first crate of plants shipped to an address established for their exchange of information. None of the plants were of value or the least bit extraordinary. Caleb collected the samples at random on each return trip to the fort in order to provide some cover for his absence. Now that he'd discovered proof that Hardy was guilty of illegal dealings with the Indians, he hoped that the charade would end soon.

Releasing the bags from his saddle, he lowered them to the ground and gave Scorpio an affectionate scratch beneath his jaw.

"Your friend doesn't look as happy to be here as you are, boy." He whispered softly to his own mount as he unwound the lead rope from the pommel of his saddle. At the end of the line skittered a nervous pinto, its soft eyes round with fear. The pony was one of six that Caleb now owned and let run with the renegade herd. Horses stolen from other bands comprised the lot. A Sioux's wealth was judged by the string of horseflesh he owned, and so Caleb had begun to amass his own small herd as soon as he joined the band.

He hoped the spirited pinto would eventually make a fine mount for Kase. For now he would warn Elliot to keep the boy off the pony and secure it, for the animal would most likely attempt to return to the herd if given its head. The trick would be to convince Zach Elliot that, as Don Ricardo, he had no knowledge of the worth of the pinto.

He took a deep breath, straightened his glasses, and wrapped the lead rope around his hand before he set off toward the tack room to face Elliot.

"Señor Elliot," Caleb called out as he stood near the slightly open door. He listened as the man inside set something down on the wooden workbench that lined one wall.

Zach opened the door wide, and light spilled out, staining the crooked back step with its yellow light.

The man in the doorway nodded a silent greeting.

"Señor Elliot," Caleb began again, heavily lacing his words with the lisping Castilian accent, "I have returned with a new horse for my son. Perhaps you will be so kind as to look the animal over for me?"

Stepping aside as Zach moved wordlessly out of the tack room and into the path of light cast by the oil lamp suspended from the ceiling of the tiny closetlike room, Caleb fumbled with the rope wrapped about his hand. Finally allowing the line to pull free, he passed it to Zach and stepped back to allow the other man to lead the pony into the arch of lamplight beyond the doorway.

Caleb cleared his throat and met Zach's stare before the scout turned his attention to the pinto. Running his hands over the horse's chest and down each leg, Zach chose to remain silent as he assessed the worth of the animal in the darkness, his hands telling him more about the horse than his eye could see. The man finally straightened and moved to stand near the pony's head, holding fast to the rope bridle.

He spat into the dust. "Where'dja get this horse?"

Caleb noted the suspicion that tainted the man's tone. "My friend, it is a long story. I was on my way back from gathering plant specimens when I came upon an Indian and his family camped near the river."

Zach stared out from beneath the floppy brim of his hat and spat again.

Don Ricardo cleared his throat nervously and continued. "They were in need of food, and I had supplies left. Knowing I would be here within a few hours, I offered them food. The man insisted I take the horse in return. I gave them a gold piece in trade as well, but I have no idea of the animal's worth."

Elliot expressed himself in what Caleb could only describe as a doubtful grunt and spat one more stream of tobacco juice before he spoke. He pushed the brim of his hat back with a gnarled thumb and indicated the pony with a quick nod.

"It'll do."

"Will it run off, do you think?" Caleb asked, knowing full well the horse would bolt if given half a chance.

"Yep. I'll keep him corraled till he gets used to bein' here. Wouldn't do for the boy to be hurt."

Caleb's eyes widened in alarm at the man's words. "If you think there is a chance of my son's becoming harmed by the worthless animal, I'll turn it loose immediately."

"I'll watch 'em both." Zach stroked the pony's nose.

"*Gracias*, Señor Elliot. *Gracias*." Caleb bowed slightly, formally, before he turned to lead Scorpio into the corral.

"Mr. de la Vega?"

Zach's voice cut the air, demanding Caleb's attention.

"*¿Sí?*"

"How'd you understand that Indian fella you ran into?"

"*¿Perdón?*"

"How'd you know he wanted to trade the horse for food?"

Zach's face was blank. Caleb could detect no suspicion there and yet he knew the man must have a reason for asking such a question.

"*Señor*, a man learns through traveling that one can be understood in any language if he desires to be. The hands tell many things, as do the eyes." Caleb returned the man's stare unflinchingly.

"I guess they do at that, Mr. de la Vega. They do at that."

Bowing slightly again, Caleb reached for Scorpio's reins.

"I'll see to your horse, de la Vega."

The man's kind words surprised him, but Caleb covered his response by handing the reins to Zach and reaching into his pocket for a coin.

"Forget it," Zach said. "I thought you might like to hurry so's you can join your wife at the fancy fandango they're throwin' in the mess hall."

"How kind of you, *señor*."

"*De nada*." Elliot answered in Spanish.

Caleb wondered if it was an attempt on the man's part to let him know he was familiar with the language. Perhaps not. He rejected the idea, for many men who traveled the frontier knew a few words of many languages. Zach Elliot was probably one of them. Handing the reins over to the scout, Caleb stopped long enough to remove his bags and baggage from the saddle and, shouldering them, moved off into the night. He could sense Zach's stare through the darkness and so made a great show of tripping on the uneven ground, regaining his balance just before he dropped the bags of cuttings. Shifting the weight of the bags, he turned toward the row of houses across the open square.

The commissary had been transformed into a most unusual ballroom. Analisa stared around the room again as she stood behind the serving table with Abbie Oats. Her cheeks hurt from smiling, but she found it not too unpleasant a sensation. Ruth had been right. Analisa discovered she was not only accepted at the gathering but welcomed. Soon, she hoped, the wounds of her past would heal.

The room was festooned with swags of red cotton, the fabric having been generously loaned to the ladies of the decorating committee by the trader, Wilber Gentry. Bouquets of wildflowers stood at either end of the long serving table and formed a ring around the punch bowl as well. The table was laden with pies, cakes, cookies, and breads, some nearly entirely eaten by men long starved for home-cooked meals. The long tables used by the soldiers during mealtime had been pushed back away from the center of the room; they were lined up three deep in places, but no one seemed to notice the inconvenience. Analisa watched as couples danced past the refreshment table, whirling and bouncing to a lively tune played on banjo, fiddle, and harmonica. Her eyes scanned the crowd as she sought out Kase and found him standing on a bench with two other boys. Both were slightly older than he, and from the similarity of their looks, Analisa guessed they were brothers. The trio giggled and pointed at the dancers, caught up in the high spirits of the adults.

She ladled a cup of punch made from lemon extract for one of the enlisted men who stood gazing at her appreciatively. Analisa was forced to look away, embarrassed by the open admiration in his eyes. She had chosen to help Abbie tend to the table in order to rest her throbbing feet after nearly an hour of continuous dancing. No sooner had they entered the room than she'd been asked to dance by first one and then another of the men. Frank Williamson had no chance to claim her and immediately asked for an introduction to Ruth. Analisa obliged him and noted that Ruth had danced with him more than a few times since and even now stood beside the tall officer, laughing gaily up into his eyes as he inclined his head in her direction.

The contrast of colors, Ruth's raspberry silk beside the midnight blue of Major Williamson's uniform, presented a stunning picture that Analisa could not help but admire.

"Have you ever seen such a show?" Abbie's voice rode high above the music as she drew Analisa's attention back to the dancers. The colorful gathering moved in a jumbled mass about the room with no attempt at organization. Lively dance steps degenerated into out-and-out stomping. The dancers were allowed no time to rest, although none seemed to require such, for the musicians merely exchanged instruments with others and took up dancing once their repertoire had been exhausted. Occasionally, someone would join in and play Analisa's organ, which stood against the wall, pounding joyously on the keys as he pumped the pedals mercilessly.

As her thoughts turned to Caleb, Analisa wondered what he would think when she told him she had traveled to the Sioux agency against his wishes. She knew instinctively that he would be angry, but just how angry and for how long she could not guess.

"A penny for your thoughts, Mrs. de la Vega."

"Major!" Analisa looked up quickly in response to the words spoken so close to her side. "You startled me."

"Allow me to apologize, then, by asking for a dance."

Analisa suddenly remembered Caleb's assertion that the major was attracted to her. If she accepted, would she encourage him without intending to? She was determined not to cause a rift between this man and her husband.

"Has Ruth lost your attention so suddenly, Major?" Analisa glanced around, hoping that he would be distracted by Caleb's attractive stepmother, but was unable to find her in the maze of dancers.

"Not at all. She stepped outside for a breath of fresh air. Actually, I want to talk to you for a moment about your guest, but first, how about a dance to put a smile back on your face and a blush in your cheeks?" He laughed down at her, his green eyes sparkling, his usual riot of flaming auburn hair tamed with pomade. Analisa wanted to trust her own intuition about the man; she truly felt he acted only out of friendship.

"I think I've rested long enough. Abbie?" Analisa turned to the other woman, who was cutting a thick wedge of mock apple pie. "I am going to dance with the major. Would you mind to keep an eye on Kase?"

"Not at all. You just go on, now." The woman drew herself up importantly and nodded in Kase's direction. "I've got him well within my sights."

Analisa allowed Frank Williamson to lead her into the melee. She soon found that he was a graceful dancer and willing to teach her the steps, unlike the others who had merely grabbed her about the waist and propelled her like a sack of potatoes about the room. They moved in time to the lively tune until the music stopped abruptly while the musicians exchanged instruments and loudly argued over the next tune.

Analisa caught her breath for a moment while the major surveyed the crowd. She stared at the shining brass buttons that adorned his jacket, suddenly awkward at his nearness in the pressing crowd. Analisa had earlier forsaken her shawl for the sake of comfort in the stifling heat of the crowded dance floor. Now, as she stood with Frank Williamson only a breath away, she was all too aware of the low neckline of her pale pink dress, which revealed far too much of the deep cleavage between her full breasts. Unsure exactly where to look, she began to search out Ruth in the crowd. Then suddenly the music started again as abruptly as it had stopped. This time it was a slower tune, and the major did not hesitate to place his right hand at the small of her back while his left lightly held her fingertips. He dipped slightly in the direction he wished to lead her, and Analisa followed, unsure at first of her own ability to master the flowing steps. For the first few bars of the song she watched her feet, hoping to keep them from hampering the major's own smooth movement.

"Relax," he whispered softly. "You're doing just fine."

His words drew her eyes to his face, and she found him smiling down at her, his lips suddenly too near her own. What was she doing? Abruptly she began to speak, trying to fill the silence between them with words that barely carried above the sound of the music.

"You wanted to ask about Mrs. Storm, my guest?" She reminded him once more of Ruth.

"I did indeed." He chuckled and pulled back in order to see her better. "Am I making you uncomfortable, Mrs. de la Vega?

You suddenly seem ill-at-ease. Your cheeks are a delightful shade of pink.''

"Somewhat uncomfortable, yes.'' She answered without hesitation.

"It's nice to run across an honest woman for a change.''

"I don't understand, Major.''

She felt him loosen his grasp on her waist, opening the space between them.

"It's nothing, Mrs. de la Vega.'' They moved along to the music, Analisa careful to count the steps in her mind while she listened to his words. "What is your relationship to Mrs. Storm? She's quite charming, and a widow, I understand.''

"We are friends, Major. We met in the East.'' Analisa looked up and found him smiling down at her, a mischievous glint in his green eyes. "Are you finding something funny about me, Major?''

"Not at all. It's just that it's quite easy to make you blush, and I'm afraid I like nothing better than to tease beautiful women. But you needn't worry, for I'm sadly convinced that you are content with your professor. Actually, it's your friend, Ruth Storm, that I'm interested in. Would she mind if I called on her?''

"You must ask her, Major.''

"I intend to.''

They continued to glide around the room, Analisa becoming more confident now that she could relax and enjoy the man's expert guidance without fear of his intentions. She nodded politely to Millicent, who stared with open admiration at Frank Williamson as she waltzed by in her husband's arms. Analisa avoided Captain Boynton's narrow gaze. She supposed the man was annoyed by the fact that she seemed able to enjoy herself while her husband was away. If only he knew how much she wished it was Caleb teaching her to waltz instead of the major. She'd never had the pleasure of dancing with her husband, yet she knew in her heart it would truly be just that, a pleasure.

The music lulled her with its haunting sound, the fiddle singing out the waltz as the dancers moved around them. Analisa soon forgot she was in the major's arms, as her mind filled with thoughts of Caleb. Her feet began to move with little effort as they circled the room. When the tune ended, Analisa leaned back and smiled up into the major's eyes, almost surprised to find it was not Caleb who held her, for she had been so lost in her daydream.

"Thank you, Major."

"Thank *you*, Mrs. de la Vega."

Before Analisa could say another word, the fiddler began again, another tune filled the air, and the major, after a glance around the room, began to dance once more.

Chapter Sixteen

No one noticed Caleb when he stepped into the crowded commissary and stopped just inside the doorway. He clutched his bowler hat between his hands, pressing it against his vest front. His hair was still damp from a hurried washing, his usual white shirt replaced by a new one he'd found hanging among his others. He had known immediately it was a gift from Analisa and had donned it with a deep sense of pride, not at all surprised by the expert workmanship. The shirt was a brilliant blue cotton. He looked at the cuff that extended slightly beyond the edge of his coatsleeve and realized that he'd never owned a shirt of such a vibrant color before. He shifted his round-lensed glasses, slid them up the bridge of his nose with one finger, and quickly resumed clutching his hat against his shirt front. He hoped he gave the appearance of a man holding on to it for protection.

He'd seen Analisa the minute he entered the noisy gathering, his eyes drawn by his wife's shining white-blond hair as she moved across the far side of the room in the arms of Major Frank Williamson, a dreamy faraway look in her eyes. Caleb noted the tall officer's gaze continually scanned the room, yet the green-eyed stare had not connected with his own. A slow, roiling boil was beginning to build inside Caleb, stoked by the necessity to stand by and play the part of the polite, bumbling professor while his instincts told him to lash out and claim what was his alone. He fought the urge to assume his more casual demeanor, to lean back against the door frame and watch the unsuspecting couple. He knew that inaction on his part would tell him more than an abrupt appearance on the scene. He tried, but soon failed to force himself to take in the rest of his surroundings. Caleb nodded politely whenever someone caught his eye, but he hoped his rigid stance would put off anyone who wished to engage him in idle conversation.

The waltz continued, the moving melody haunting him as much as the sight of the elegant figure of his wife as she swayed in another man's arms. It was not until the dancing couples parted and the music stopped, not until Analisa pulled away from the major for a moment, that Caleb noticed every detail of the dress she wore. Elegant in its simplicity, the gown was made of some dusk pink fabric that appeared entwined with ribbons. The bodice was cut low across her breasts, a style Caleb never dreamed Analisa would be bold enough to wear, although her appearance sent his blood singing through his veins.

Couples moved away from the center of the room toward the tables lining the walls. Analisa stood beside the major, and as Caleb watched, the two of them chatted amiably. Caleb stepped forward, feeling as if his stomach was lodged somewhere near the region of his throat, his nerves taut, unable to watch the couple a moment longer. He moved with quiet determination across the room.

"Don Ricardo."

The voice was familiar and yet out of context in the surroundings, and so Caleb failed to recognize it was Ruth's until he turned and saw his stepmother standing beside him. He became aware of her hand on his arm, halting his forward progress.

Caleb stood speechless. Ruth had called him by his assumed

name, but he was not quite sure how to address her. His silence alerted her to his dilemma, and she immediately began to explain. Thankful, he blessed his stepmother for her keen intuition.

"I'm sure you're surprised to find me here, Ricardo, but, as I told Analisa when we arrived two weeks ago, you did extend an invitation and I always enjoy traveling. Welcome home. We've all missed you, especially Analisa."

"No doubt."

He let his gaze cut back to the place where he'd last seen his wife talking to the major. The music started up once again, and the couple had resumed dancing. Caught just inside the edge of the dance floor, there was nothing for Caleb to do but dance with Ruth or step back toward the doorway, a move that would take him away from Analisa. Without bothering to ask, Caleb reached for Ruth's hand and began to dance.

"May I ask the reason for the dark scowl?" Ruth kept her voice low. "Your lack of response at finding your beloved stepmother here is very touching, Caleb."

Caleb answered in a tightly controlled whisper, devoid of the thick Castilian accent, "Welcome to Fort Sully, Ruth."

"I know that look of yours. Someone is likely to get hurt before the night is over if you don't calm down. What is wrong, Caleb?"

"What's wrong? Nothing's wrong. Nothing except that every time I come home I find the illustrious Major Williamson entertaining *my wife*."

"Ah." She looked at him with a mischievous twinkle in her eye. "Would it help if I told you that a few moments ago the major was very seriously entertaining me?"

"It might." He looked down at her, hoping to find the truth in her expression. They were nearer the major and Analisa now, but the other couple remained unaware of Caleb's presence.

"He was indeed," Ruth assured him. "Come, now, Caleb, you don't look as if you believe me . . ."

Caleb turned away from Ruth, abruptly leaving her alone as he turned to face Analisa and Frank Williamson. He stepped forward and watched his wife's reaction as she recognized him. Her eyes widened as her lips parted in surprise. Caleb knew a desperate urge to crush her to him then and there, seal her lips with his own, and loose the pins from her hair. Instead he was forced to stand and watch as the major released her hand and Analisa remained standing, caught between the two men.

He saw her lips silently form his name before she caught herself and merely whispered, "You're home."

"Quite a surprise, is it not, my dear? And just in time for the *fiesta*." He waved his arm wide in a gesture that took in the entire room.

"Welcome home once again, Don Ricardo." Williamson bowed slightly in greeting, his mustache-framed smile wider than Caleb remembered. When the man turned toward Ruth, Caleb was surprised to find her still at his side.

"Would you do me the honor, Mrs. Storm?" Frank Williamson asked formally, and Ruth readily accepted.

Finding himself in the center of the dance floor, his wife standing before him, lovelier than ever and stunned by his sudden appearance, Caleb felt his anger slowly ebb. He lifted his hand and before he could formally ask his wife to dance, she moved into his embrace. Hastily he cleared his throat and stepped back the proper distance, widening the space between them. He slipped his forefinger between his shirt collar and his throat, hoping to relieve the sudden constriction that choked him. Her nearness after so long an absence nearly unhinged his reserve.

"I am supposed to be Don Ricardo, remember?" he whispered near her ear as he began to move in time to the music.

"And I am Analisa, your wife," she teased. "I am pleased to make your acquaintance, Mr. Don Ricardo."

He could not help but pull her near again in a brief, warm hug of greeting before he resumed dancing at a polite distance. "You look beautiful tonight, Anja."

"*Dank U wel.*" She smiled as she thanked him, caught up in the charade his role of stiff propriety forced upon them both. "I see you found your shirt. Do you like it, Don Ricardo?"

"*Gracias, mi esposa. Es muy hermosa.*" Caleb hoped his eyes expressed the warmth he felt for her at that moment.

He deftly squired her through the waltzing figures, pausing long enough to allow an overenthusiastic enlisted man to lead his partner past them on the way to the punch bowl.

"That's a lovely dress, Anja. Was it a gift from Ruth?" He watched a rosy blush stain her cheeks in reaction to his appreciative glance at her revealing décolleté.

"In a way," she managed to stammer, regaining her composure. She went on to explain about the sewing machine and the fabrics Ruth had transported from Boston along with a set of china that had graced the Storms' table for generations.

"How long has she been here?"

"Since the day you left . . . nearly three weeks. Mrs. Oats is here also."

"Both of them in *our* house?"

The waltz halted abruptly as did their chance for private conversation. The musicians halted long enough to choose the next selection, and Caleb quickly surveyed the room. He located Abbie behind the serving table and, placing his hand at his wife's waist, urged her in that direction. "I'd better give my regards to Abigail or suffer the consequences."

As they approached the serving table, Caleb quickly noted that his stepmother stood near the punch bowl flanked by Frank Williamson and a man he had never seen before. The stranger's portly bulk was emphasized by a poorly fitted white suit. The planter's outfit, complete with panama hat, looked incongruous in those military surroundings. Caleb felt a sense of foreboding as he assessed the stranger. Even before he asked, he was certain he knew what his wife's answer would reveal. "Anja, who is that man?"

Caleb's words sent a chill through her. She raised her eyes to follow his gaze. Her heart dropped to the pit of her stomach and immediately climbed to lodge in her throat, for there, standing beside Ruth, was Buff Hardy. The stifling room felt cold as Analisa's skin went from warm to clammy. There was no escape, no time to explain to Caleb why she had acted against his wishes and visited the Sioux agency. No time to tell him that Hardy was indeed guilty of dealing incorrectly with the Indians, as the bureau suspected. Caleb would learn without explanation that she had let her stubbornness rule her actions.

"Anja?"

She'd stiffened involuntarily at his first question. Now she feared it would be obvious why she chose to avoid his query. Before she could collect her thoughts, Caleb had led her to the trio standing near the refreshment table. Ruth was holding court between both men, but Analisa noticed she had moved nearer to Williamson, as if unwilling to share a closer proximity with Hardy.

"Don Ricardo," Williamson began as Analisa and Caleb joined them. "I'd like to introduce you to the Sioux agent, Buff Hardy."

While Analisa stood mute beside Caleb, the major completed the introductions and explained why Caleb and his family were living at Fort Sully. Analisa felt Hardy's eyes on her, prayed that he would not mention her visit to the agency, and knew without a doubt that he would. Her fears were soon realized as Hardy raised his ever present gilt-handled cane and twirled it between his fingers.

"Don Ricardo." The agent acknowledged Caleb with a nod, his cool-eyed stare assessing her husband carefully before he turned a telling smile upon Analisa. "And Mrs. de la Vega. It's a real pleasure to see you again, ma'am." The words were coated with syrup.

Buff Hardy rocked forward onto his toes and then back to his heels as he spoke, giving her the impression of a man standing on the deck of a rolling ship. It seemed his crippled leg was not hampered by the movement.

"It's a shame you weren't able to visit the agency with your wife, de la Vega. She explained a little about your work."

"My wife is good with explanations, *señor*. She has many things to explain to me."

Analisa was all too aware of the hidden meaning behind Caleb's compliment.

The pressure of his fingers against her waist tightened before she felt them drop away. He stood rigid at her side, anger emanating from him in waves like heat off of a rock. She was aware of little else, her smile frozen into place.

"Shall we go outside, Analisa?" Caleb asked abruptly.

She nodded. Words caught in her throat. Quickly her mind raced ahead as she tried to reason out exactly how she would explain her actions to him. She realized there was not much she could say. Yes, she had gone against his wishes. Yes, she had visited the agency. No, she was not sorry in the least. With that realization came her strength. Determined not to be cowed by Caleb's silent anger, she moved through the door and out into the April night. Too late she realized she'd forgotten her shawl.

They walked away from the commissary and were halfway across the parade ground before Caleb spoke. The air was crisp, the night sky filled with countless stars that seemed to hang just above them from horizon to horizon. Analisa took a deep breath and held it for a moment. The effect was calming. As she looked skyward, studying the pinpoints of light, she realized how small her problem seemed in the face of the great universe. It gave Analisa a sense of strength as she turned to face Caleb.

He stood very near, ramrod straight and unyielding. She could not see his expression in the darkness. Only his features stood out, the smooth forehead, high cheekbones, and straight, finely shaped nose. Even in the shadowed night she could see his full lips set in a grim, taut line.

"Well?"

She watched his lips move briefly as he demanded an explanation.

"Yes. I went to the agency." It was best to get it over with, she thought. "I went with Zach. And Kase."

His tone remained flat, stilted. "You took Kase with you?"

"I could not leave him home alone."

He turned away and looked across the square. Caleb's profile was a darker shadow against the night sky. She thought she heard him sigh.

"Why?" he asked.

"Why what?"

"Why did you do it, Anja? Why did you go there after I expressly asked you not to? I explained everything to you the night before I left. Hardy is a dangerous man. A killer. I know for a fact he'll stop at nothing." He shifted his weight and continued while Analisa listened intently.

"All it would take is one mistake and our cover would be blown to pieces. Did Kase say anything while you were there? Did you stop to think that he might have slipped up and referred to me as Caleb or talked about Iowa? The boy's only five, Anja. Hardy could pick up on any slip he made and start snooping around." She saw him drag his hand through his hair and thought he was through.

"I—"

"And what of you?" he interrupted. "What excuse did you give for just dropping in to see Hardy? I'd like to know just what in the hell you thought you were doing."

His terse statement hung heavily between them. No longer was his anger under tight control, although Caleb had not raised his voice as he ground out the words.

Analisa remained silent for a moment while a guard drifted like a specter past the whitewashed wall of the quartermaster's storehouse. The man was out of hearing range, but his appearance drew their attention for a moment. The pause gave her time to steel her nerves and answer Caleb.

"I thought I might be able to help you find out something you were unable to learn while you were living with those . . . those . . ."

"Say it, Anja: those savages."

"No." She shook her head adamantly. "That is not what I was going to say. Never. I suddenly lost the name for them."

"Sioux?"

"Yes. You spend all of your time with them when the answer has been with Hardy all along. Well, not really with Hardy, but right here at the fort."

"What are you talking about?" He grasped her upper arms and pulled her closer, his voice a harsh whisper.

She looked over her shoulder, suddenly aware that they were standing in the open square protected only by the shadows of the night.

"Please, Caleb." She waved in the direction of the house. "I have so much to tell you. Let's go home and sit down and talk about this like civilized people. Please."

"Now I'm not even civilized?"

"Caleb . . ." Her patience with him was wearing as thin as she knew his was with her.

"Come on."

None too gently he led her across the parade ground, past the tall, naked flag pole, along the gravel walk to their porch. Without hesitation he threw open the door and stepped inside, drawing Analisa in with him.

"Sit down, Caleb, and I will tell you what I have discovered." Analisa drew away, refusing to let him intimidate her.

She thought she saw a hint of a smile pulling at the corner of his mouth.

"You are certainly getting used to giving orders around here," he said. "Are you sure you didn't enlist in the army while I was away?"

Her eyes met his as she tried to read his mood. Sensing capitulation, she chanced a smile.

"You told me once," she began, "that I could boss around

an old man and a little boy, but not you. But I think that once in a while I have to try."

He slouched against the back of the settee and locked his hands behind his head. "You might be right." He crossed his ankles and gave her his full attention. "But don't think that I'm not angry. You had better do some fairly fast talking, Anja."

She took a deep breath. Where to begin? She worried that she might not recount the tale correctly and thus confuse him.

"Well? I'm waiting."

"I asked Zach to take me to the agency," she began slowly, building confidence as she explained. "When we got there, I told Hardy that I was bored here and wanted to offer my help at the agency . . . to help with the Indians, perhaps teach the children. We had coffee. Caleb, he took me into his house, and I am sure that you are right. He has so many expensive things . . ." As she spoke, her excitement took over. "And he has a big house, too. He said that they were old things, family pieces, but I could tell that most of the furniture was new. Costly, too." She nodded for emphasis and watched him as he could not help but smile.

"What else?"

"Well, just before I left, he told me that the renegades would never come into the agency. He said they had white captives that they sell and keep as slaves." Analisa stopped for a moment, her train of thought broken by a vision of Meika. *Wait*, she told herself. *Ask him later. Stay with the story.* "I was upset about that, but I left without asking any questions. On the way home I asked Zach about the captives." She leaned forward to emphasize her next words. "Zach knew about them, Caleb. He said he was surprised that Hardy had told me about the whites. Zach told me Hardy *sells* them back to their families."

Disappointment washed over her when she realized Caleb was not at all excited or surprised by her revelation. Perhaps he required proof. Perhaps, she thought, he didn't even believe her. She watched him stand up and cross the room to the sideboard. He poured a hearty swallow of brandy, drank it down, and poured another. This one he carried back to the settee with him. He did not sit, but stood in the center of the room, staring down at her contemplatively. He seemed to be weighing his next words.

"Hardy not only sells them to their families," he said finally.

"He sells them to other tribes or to people in Mexico, too. He doesn't only deal in whites, either. The man buys and sells Indian women, too."

"You already knew?" She watched him, her eyes wide, her voice tinged with disappointment.

"I didn't find out until this morning. Hardy roughed up Red Dog's woman, a girl named Mia, but she managed to get off the agency land before he found her."

"Mia!"

"You know her?" His expression told her he was amazed that she seemed to recognize the name.

"She was Hardy's maid."

"He tried to use her for more than that."

Analisa was silent as a cold chill passed through her. She remembered Hardy's leering stare all too well and the hatred in the eyes of the young beauty who served him. Caleb tossed off the brandy and returned to pour another.

"Did Zach tell you how he learned all about Hardy?" he asked.

"He said he ran into him years ago and that Hardy does not remember him."

"What if they are in this together? That puts you in as much danger as I am."

She thought for a moment and tried to put her feelings into words. "If Zach is part of Hardy's crimes, why would he tell me about them?" She worried her bottom lip with her teeth and then remembered. "I know! Zach said that he is . . . is biting his time."

"Biting his time?"

"Yes." She nodded with assurance.

"Who?"

"*He* is. Zach . . . Zach is biting his time until he can catch Hardy. Zach is not certain if the major knows about Hardy or not." With a short laugh she added, "I know a man like the major could not possibly be a part of anything so . . . so . . . terrible."

"You seem to know more than I do already." He set his glass on the patterned *tafelkleed* on the dining table and began to slowly pace the small room. "So, Zach is *biting* his time until he can catch Hardy, Red Dog is planning to set his own trap for the man, and I'm one step behind my wife in my investiga-

tions.'' He looked up at the ceiling and spoke to himself.
''You're doing one hell of a job, Storm. Wait until Parker hears
about this one.''

She watched in amazement as he turned on his heel and
walked with purposeful strides toward their room.

''Caleb?''

He ignored her.

Analisa trailed after him and stood just inside the doorway as
he quickly lit the lamp on the dresser and moved to close the
curtains. Without a word he began to strip off his coat and
unbutton his shirt. Hastily he pulled the material from the
waistband of his trousers. Analisa watched in amazement. Was
he never going to speak to her again?

''Caleb, what are you doing?''

He paused long enough to look across the room at her before
he tossed the shirt on the bed. His hands went to his waist and
he unbuttoned the waistband of his trousers and began to shuck
them from his long form. At the sight of him standing so
blatantly nude in the lamplight, Analisa turned her back, only to
find she was standing before the mirror, where his lean,
well-defined form was clearly reflected. She moved toward the
bed, her eyes averted, her attention riveted on his clothes. She
lifted the crumpled garments and began to shake them out. Still
refusing to look in his direction, she carried his clothing to the
row of hooks that bordered one wall.

''I have decided, dear wife, that it is high time I set aside all
of these trappings and got to work. It seems that you are capable
of flushing out the quail before I am. I want to get back to Red
Dog's camp before he sends word to Hardy that he has a woman
to trade. The last thing I want''—his voice was calm and
determined as he strode to the dresser and yanked open the top
drawer—''is to have anyone kill Hardy before I can arrest
him.''

''You have the power to arrest Hardy? Oh, Caleb, why don't
you go to the dance and get him now? The major can put him in
the guardhouse, and we can forget all about this.''

''I do have the power to arrest him, Anja, but first I need
proof that he is guilty. I have to set my own trap for Hardy
before Red Dog or Zach can get hold of him. I want that man
tried for his crimes. Then we can begin to round up all the
others like him.''

Caleb pulled on his black shirt, the one he'd been wearing the day he rode into her life. He stood buttoning the shirt, his back toward her, the movement of his well-defined, powerful muscles visible even beneath the dark material, and spoke to her over his shoulder.

"Get me my black pants, would you, Anja?"

She moved to do his bidding and held the trousers out at arm's length. As he shoved one leg and then the other into his pants, he looked up at her with a smile.

"Did I tell you how beautiful you look tonight?"

"*Ja*. You are not angry with me now?"

"No. I must admit, I was disappointed in you, and I know now that you can't be trusted not to interfere with my work."

"Oh, Caleb, please . . ." His words hurt her, although she knew he spoke the truth.

"It's all right. I figure this experience just served to show me that sometimes I move a little too slowly. Not you, though; you just take the bull by the horns and jump right on his back."

"What?"

"Nothing. Forget I said that." He reached for his worn leather jacket and mumbled loud enough for her to barely catch his words, "Next thing I know, she'll be out looking for a bull."

She followed close on his heels as he went to his trunk and opened it. Beneath a stack of folded shirts rested his gun and holster. Fear clutched at Analisa's heart as she watched Caleb buckle the gun belt about his waist and tie the rawhide thong around his thigh. Absently he lifted the gun and felt its weight, as if he needed to reacquaint himself with the feel of it.

"Caleb, please . . . tell me where you are going. What are you going to do? Shouldn't you let me know before you walk out of here? What if something should happen to you?"

Frantic now with worry, trying to swallow her fear, Analisa stepped nearer and took his hands in her own. She forced him to slow down, to stop his movements and meet her gaze. "Tell me."

"I have to go, Anja. It may already be too late."

She thought back over his words. "You said Red Dog had a woman for Hardy, a woman to trade . . ."

"It's just a trap. Red Dog means to trick him."

"Are there any white women in the renegade camp?" She paused to be sure he was paying attention to her words. "Caleb, is my sister one of the captives?"

He seemed all too still for a moment. Although he did not look away, Analisa could see that he was somehow able to hide his thoughts, as if his mind were suddenly shuttered. The pause between her question and his words was too long, and too heavily silent. He knew something about Meika. She was sure of it.

As he looked down into her pleading, upturned face, Caleb knew he could not tell her he'd seen Meika, not until he was positive the girl really was Analisa's sister, and certainly not until he could be sure of obtaining her release from the Sioux. He would risk telling her a lie and losing her trust in him in order to avoid leading her down a trail of false hope. Caleb's fingers tightened around hers as he spoke.

"No."

She barely heard the reply and yet knew that it was a lie, the first lie he'd ever told her. Analisa dropped his hands and turned away. She fought back tears, blinking rapidly. Perhaps she'd earned this, she thought. She'd betrayed his trust by going to visit Hardy. Now, to repay her, he would keep the truth from her. Could he do something so cruel, knowing how she longed to find her missing sister and brother?

"Anja, I'm ready . . . I'm going."

Did he expect her to turn and kiss him good-bye?

"Aren't you even going to say good-bye?"

"*Ja. Ja*, Caleb." Whirling, she faced him, her fear for him heightening her anger. "Good-bye. Ride away to be killed. Ride away, knowing that my sister is out there with the Indians. Why not tell me the truth? You can't. You are still angry and wish to punish me." She had to turn away from him now; she could not face his closed look. "*Ja*. Go. Good-bye."

There was nothing left for her to do but listen for the sound of his footsteps as he left the room. The sound did not come. Analisa could feel him behind her, standing, waiting, perhaps weighing the meaning behind her outburst. Suddenly she felt his hands on her shoulders. Caleb forced her to face him once again. Before she could speak, he lowered his head and pressed a searing kiss on her lips. He held her so close she could feel the wide buckle of his gun belt cutting into her waist. He pulled her closer, his hands playing along her spine, and pressed his hips to hers.

His arms encircled her as his lips ground against hers, forcing her to open her mouth and welcome his insistent tongue. Without relinquishing his hold, Caleb stepped forward, pressing her backward, maneuvering her toward the bed. Analisa felt the mattress dip beneath her thighs as Caleb bent over her, forcing her down on the coverlet. She was helpless to stop him, nor did she want to. His touch set her senses reeling just as they had when he first held her in his arms. She could not hold on to her anger while his body worked its magic on hers. Analisa began to return his kiss full measure. Her tongue toyed with his, exploring, darting, exchanging the maddening sensations that caused her to feel the sudden delicious warmth that radiated from deep inside her. She moaned, pulled her lips away from his, and buried her face against his shoulder.

"Oh, Anja." His voice sounded far away, unsure. "Nothing ever comes easy for you, does it?" He sighed, his breath teasing the column of her throat. "I would tell you everything if I thought it would help. But it won't. For now, you will have to trust me."

When she failed to respond, he gave her a squeeze. Analisa kept her eyes closed against his shoulder. She refused to believe he would not come back. Caleb would be fine. He could do anything.

"Are you listening?"

"*Ja.*"

"When this thing is all over, when Hardy's on his way back to Washington, I'll ask Ely for all the men he can spare. We'll be in contact with posts all over the West. If your brother and sister can be found, I'll find them . . . but not now, Anja. Not now. One problem at a time is all I can handle."

Her heart went out to him. She knew she was pushing Caleb too hard, asking for far too much, but she could not seem to stop.

"Are you sure, Caleb? Tell me you have not seen any white children who might be Meika and Pieter."

Again he paused. "They are no longer children, Anja."

"I know that, but—"

He began to pull away, to straighten his clothes. She watched him with regret, her eyes misting over with tears.

"They may not want to be found," he said finally.

"I must try."

"We will try together," he assured her, and then added, "when this is all over."

He pulled her to her feet. Unable to resist, she linked her arms about his neck.

"You must go now?" she whispered.

"*Ja.*" He gave her a crooked smile and disengaged himself. He crossed the room. Caleb reached for his dark, wide-brimmed hat and put it on. His hair, still in a queue at the nape of his neck, was hidden by the lowered brim. "I'll be back."

Chapter Seventeen

God go with you, she thought, as she watched him walk out the door. Suddenly, Caleb was gone. A helpless feeling settled over her like a sodden cloak, her worry compounded by the knowledge that he had lied to her.

Analisa tried to shake off her tension as she crossed the darkened parade ground, this time alone. It was time she collected Kase and took him home to bed.

She entered the commissary and searched the crowd for Ruth. The deep raspberry gown caught her eye, and Analisa hurried across the room to join her friend.

"It seems you've lost Don Ricardo," Frank Williamson commented. Analisa noticed the familiar way the man's hand now rested on Ruth's waist. He was fairly beaming, his smile spread from ear to ear, his ruddy complexion flushed redder from the heat of the room as well, it seemed, as Ruth's nearness.

Analisa smiled up at him. "He has retired for the evening. He must leave before dawn."

"He is certainly devoted to his work. I'm afraid I'd find it hard to leave my wife—if I had one, that is—to go off digging up a lot of weeds." The man shook his head as he smiled down at Ruth.

Caleb's stepmother returned his smile and then added, "Well, I have only known Don Ricardo a short while, but I know he is committed to his cause. Is everything all right, dear?" Her eyes searched Analisa's face.

"Of course. I have returned to collect Kase, as well as Ricardo's hat and my shawl. It's time Kase was in bed."

"I'll be happy to take him home," Ruth volunteered easily, "if you care to stay."

Analisa looked around the room. The crowd was thinning now, many of the couples content to chat while seated on the short wooden stools scattered about the room. She noticed Zach Elliot leaning near the side entrance, his hat in his hand, his usually unruly white hair somewhat tamed into place.

"No, I don't want to stay." She shook her head, pausing to remember the feel of Caleb's arms about her as they waltzed together. Wanting nothing to detract from the memory, she chose not to dance with anyone else. "I think I'll go home now. You come along whenever you are ready, Ruth." Although she wanted desperately to talk to Ruth, Analisa did not intend to keep her friend from enjoying the major's attentions.

Excusing herself, Analisa sought out Abbie at the refreshment table. The buxom woman no longer bustled to and fro, but was seated on a stool behind the table. The crumbly remains of cakes and pies gave testimony to the party's culinary success.

"Abbie, is Kase with the other boys?" In her perturbed state Analisa had failed to notice him when she entered the room. Now she looked around apprehensively.

Abbie hefted her bulk off of the squat stool and pointed to a spot under the table. Analisa peered beneath the long table-cloth. The sight that met her eyes warmed her heart, and for a moment her problems were forgotten. Kase lay curled up beneath the table, his cheek resting on her folded shawl, his head covered by Caleb's bowler hat. Typical of an exhausted child, he was oblivious to the noise around him and slept blissfully. Analisa bent down and gently pulled him toward her. She lifted him carefully and tried to disturb him as little as possible while Abbie retrieved the hat and covered the boy with the shawl.

"I'll bring the hat with me," Abbie decided, seeing that Analisa's hands were full. Kase slept undisturbed against his mother's shoulder.

"Thank you, Abbie. I'll see you at home."

Analisa turned to cross the room, choosing to exit through the side door rather than make her way among the dancers. As she reached the open door, she smiled at Zach. He seemed content to stand in the doorway rather than ask anyone to dance.

"You haven't danced tonight, Zach?" she asked lightly.

"Naw. Ain't no one going to want to get that close to this ugly mug, Miz de la Vega." She noticed his mouth was free of the usual plug of tobacco. He looked as if he wanted to spit anyway, out of sheer habit.

"I would have, if I had known you would be here."

He seemed to sense her sincerity, and a half-smile broke his usual stern countenance and played tricks with his scarred cheek.

"Well, if I'd a known that, I'd a sure been here earlier." He turned to look out into the darkness behind him and then glanced at the sleeping boy before he spoke again. "I told Don Ricardo I'd take care of that pinto he brought the boy, but I been thinkin' that mebbe we'd better not say anything to the kid about it. It'll be a while before I can trust that pony not to hightail it back to wherever it came from. If Kase knows about it, he'll be badgerin' the hell outta me to ride it."

"Pinto?" She didn't understand the term. Her confusion was apparent to Zach.

"He didn't tell you yet?"

"No, we have barely spoken. Don Ricardo was exhausted and went to bed early."

"Well, he brought the boy an Indian pony. Traded his vittles for it. Got himself a fine deal, too. Only thing is, the animal's half wild and sure to run back to his herd first chance he gets. It's not even shod." Zach looked fondly at the boy in her arms. "He's sure gonna be excited when he does find out."

"Can I carry the boy home for you, Miz de la Vega?"

Gratefully she nodded at Zach. "That would be very kind of you, Mr. Elliot. Thank you."

She transferred her son to the scout's waiting arms, and although he opened his eyes and looked about, Kase was soon asleep once more, this time with his head on Zach's shoulder.

When they reached the front door, Analisa refrained from inviting Zach to enter and took Kase back into her arms. Bidding Zach good night and thanking him once again, she carried her son indoors. Soon he was tucked between the sheets of her own bed, and within moments, Galileo was kneading the quilt near Kase's feet, preparing to sleep beside the boy, as usual. *It should be Caleb sleeping next to me tonight,* she thought as she stared down at the boy's midnight-black hair.

She smoothed the coverlet drawn up beneath Kase's chin, and suddenly she was reminded of Zach's words. Caleb had brought Kase a horse, an Indian pony of some sort. She tried but failed to remember the word Zach used to describe the pony. If the scout felt it best not to tell Kase about the horse, she would defer to his wishes.

Analisa undressed and slipped into her nightgown. It had become her habit recently to pull on Caleb's flannel robe over her nightdress. As she cinched the belt tight about her waist to close the wrapper, Analisa recalled something else Zach had said. "It'll be a while before I can trust that pony not to hightail it back to wherever it came from . . ." She sank to the side of the bed and sat lost in thought. Slowly an idea began to take shape in her mind, and with every passing second Analisa became more certain about what she intended to do.

The front door opened and closed. Stepping into the parlor, she found Ruth and Abbie just returning from the dance.

"Analisa! I hope we didn't wake you." Ruth looked concerned as she watched Analisa close the bedroom door behind her. "Is Caleb asleep?"

"Caleb is not here, Ruth. I need to talk with you for a moment." Analisa saw the curiosity in Abbie's eyes as the cook left the two women alone.

Ruth's face was shadowed with worry. She crossed the room and draped her ivory shawl over the back of a chair.

Analisa admired Ruth's calm. She never pushed or expressed

impatience. The woman was content to wait until Analisa was ready to talk.

"I am going to leave here tonight, Ruth, and I want you to give me your word that you will not tell anyone that I have gone. Please watch over Kase for me."

"What! Where are you going?" Ruth's eyes were wide and searching. "You aren't going after Caleb, are you?"

"Yes, in a way, but I am not going to let him know I am following him."

"How in the world are you going to track him in the dark? Even if you knew where you were going, you would be insane to travel alone."

Analisa shook her head. "I can't tell you, Ruth. The more you know, the more you could tell the major if he asks. Caleb's safety depends on secrecy."

Ruth stood and walked across the room only to sit down again, this time on one of the straight-back oak chairs beside the dining table. She leaned an elbow on the *tafelkleed* and turned her worried expression on Analisa.

"What about your own safety?" Suddenly Ruth's face took on an expression of anger that Analisa had never thought to see there. "Did Caleb ask you to do this? If he did—"

"No, Ruth," Analisa tried to explain. "He knows nothing about it."

"What do you hope to accomplish, dear? Have you thought this through?"

"Yes." Analisa nodded. "I have to go, Ruth. It may be my only chance to find out if my brother or sister is nearby."

"What?"

"There is much to explain and very little time. I am asking for your trust and your help. I cannot tell you more."

"But surely Caleb knows what this means to you and would help you."

"Not this time, Ruth. He has asked me to wait until he has finished his work here. This may be the last chance I have; his job here is nearly over."

Ruth sighed, and Analisa knew that the woman must have sensed the depth of her determination, for she did not attempt to sway her. "I want to look into something before you go. It won't take very long."

Analisa started to protest.

"Please?" Ruth asked.

"I will change. That will give you a few moments, Ruth, but I am leaving soon."

Ruth Storm moved toward the door to the room she shared with Abbie. Her hand on the knob, she turned to face Analisa and asked, "When is your birthday, Analisa?"

"My birthday?"

"Yes." Ruth nodded. "When were you born?"

Although she was puzzled by the question, Analisa told Ruth the date of her birth.

Without another word, Ruth entered the smaller room.

It took Analisa little time to change once again. This time she donned her plaid wool dress. Glad that she had not discarded the old-fashioned gown, she smoothed the wide skirt and then changed her shoes. The worn black high-tops would do. All the while, she tried not to think of the darkness outside or of the miles of open country she would have to cross alone. If she allowed herself to dwell on the dangers ahead, she knew her courage would fail her. Hastily, she took down her dark wool winter shawl and crossed it over her breasts, tying it at her waist. It would protect her from the cool spring night.

Opa's gun rested on a high shelf that bordered the room. She could not see it from where she was, nor could she reach all the way to the back of it, so she pulled her trunk away from the wall and stood on it. She groped among the folded clothes until she felt the cold metal of the shotgun. Carefully, she lifted it down and then replaced her trunk against the wall. Opening the lid, she dug out the tin of bullets and, clutching them, stood up.

The soft light from the lamps in the parlor crept through the open door of the bedroom. Glancing around the shadowed room, Analisa checked one last time to be certain that she was ready. As a final precaution she repinned the crown of braids upon her head. She was ready. Moving to the side of the bed, she bent and kissed her son's brow, careful not to disturb him. Nothing would happen to her, she vowed. Nothing would keep her from coming back to Kase.

Quietly she withdrew from the room and closed the door behind her. Ruth was seated at the dining table, her head bent as she studied a sheet of paper. A worn leather-bound book rested

beside the page. When she noted Analisa's entrance, she lifted
the volume and thumbed through the pages. Ruth's glasses were
once again in place, perched on the end of her nose.

"I'm ready, Ruth."

"Give me a few minutes more, my dear. I've made a pot of
tea, and I suggest you have a cup before you leave. Did you
think about packing yourself some food?"

Analisa felt the blood rush to her cheeks. Embarrassed at
having almost forgotten such an important item, she walked into
the kitchen to pack food and water. When that was done, she
poured a cup of tea and joined Ruth at the table.

"It's not much, but enough to help, I believe. At least I am
reassured." Looking up from her work, Ruth peered at Analisa
over the rims of her glasses.

Wary, afraid that Ruth would try to talk her out of leaving,
Analisa was hesitant to ask her to explain and so sat in silence.

"This," Ruth said, indicating the page before her, "is your
horoscope. It is a chart that maps out the twists and turns your
life will take, according to the position of the stars on the day
you were born."

"Stars?" Analisa stared down at the paper. Strange squiggles
and lines that resembled worms and arrows surrounded a circle
in the center of the page. The sphere was divided into
pie-shaped wedges, the whole drawing making as little sense to
Analisa as Ruth's words did. She sipped her tea and tried not to
lose her patience. Eventually, everything Ruth did made sense,
although the reason was not always apparent at first.

"It would take too long for me to explain all of this to you
now," Ruth said, "but it is something I find very helpful when I
have a major decision to make. You see, you were born under a
certain sign that was determined by where the stars were on the
day that you were born. You are a Pisces, your symbol is the
fish." She pointed to a small mark on the page that looked like
a floating water beetle.

Analisa sighed and stared at Ruth.

"Oh, dear." The woman appeared frustrated by her lack of
time as well as Analisa's failure to find her words comprehensi-
ble. "Although I am not at all delighted about this scheme of
yours, Analisa, I don't think you could have chosen a better
time. Your stars are all favorable right now, and anything that
you attempt, should succeed."

"Good." Slapping her palms against the decorative tablecloth, Analisa stood and looked down at Ruth. She had delayed long enough. "I do not know what you just said, but I will hope that you are right about my chances for success. I am going now."

Chapter Eighteen

The sun seemed intent upon exerting the strength it had gained with the arrival of May. Although the heat of midday had abated, the sun still blazed hot enough to rouse Analisa from a fitful sleep. Stretched out beneath the shade of a budding maple, she awoke with a start, to discover that exhaustion had forced her to abandon her vigil. She sat up and with an open palm pushed back the wild tangle of sun-bleached hair from her eyes. Opa's gun lay on the ground beside her. Rubbing her hand against her hip, Analisa tried to ease the ache in her side as she searched the ground for the cause of her discomfort. A sharp rock was embedded in the soil, one she had overlooked earlier. Her intent had been to close her eyes for a moment or two, but she could tell by the sun's position that she had slept for hours. Drawing her knees toward her chest, she rested her elbows on them and propped her chin in her cupped hands.

The pony grazed lazily nearby. Analisa noted thankfully that the knot she'd tied in its rope halter still held. The pinto seemed content to graze and drink from the small spring she'd discovered trickling out of the rocks not far from the maple. She scratched at the irritating wool of her plaid gown and wished for the hundredth time that day that she'd worn one of her old calicos; she'd never expected such warm weather. Wide awake at last, she stood and stretched, her hands at the small of her back, her gaze ever alert to the surrounding area.

She'd come upon the small stand of trees in the dark and after a cursory walk around its perimeter, decided it was as safe a vantage point as she would find so near the renegade camp. Virtually surrounded by rocks and trees, the small grassy area stood high up on a bluff above the river valley that harbored what she assumed to be Red Dog's camp. True to Zach's prediction, the pony had returned home, bringing Analisa with him. She started toward the animal and, with her first step, became all too aware of the quivering fatigue of her overworked muscles. There was not a bone in her body that didn't ache from the long ride. As she stroked the pony's velvety soft nose, she glanced skyward, tried to judge the time of day by the position of the sun, and guessed it was nearly three in the afternoon.

Kneeling near the small puddle formed by the underground spring, she cupped her hand and lifted a mouthful of crystal water toward her lips. The liquid trickled from between her fingers and soaked the front of her wool dress. She sighed; she had always disliked the thick smell of damp wool. Another handful of the cold water quenched her thirst, and she used a third to splash her face, smoothing it over her eyes before she pushed back her hair once again.

Last night, shortly after the pony ambled into the clearing, Analisa had discovered the Sioux camp in the valley below the bluff. In the clear, chilled darkness that surrounded her, she had walked as near to the edge of the bluff as she dared and then knelt down. Carefully using her hands to explore the ground ahead of her, she'd crawled to the very edge of the bluff that jutted out over the valley below, and peered down into the darkened chasm. Campfires burned low before many of the Indian dwellings. The flames danced and flickered, illuminating the sides of the conical structures with sinister, wavering shadows. Except for the occasional yelp of a dog or whinny from the shuffling herd of horses near the river mouth, the village remained cloaked in silence.

Analisa had watched the firelight in the valley below and wondered if Meika and Pieter were indeed in one of the crude shelters. And what of Caleb? Did he ride in and out of the camp at will? Was he disguised? She had no intention of entering the camp, and certainly not in the dark, nor did she have an inkling as to what her next move should be. Exhausted, she had decided to rest while darkness provided a cover. She'd felt her way back along the ground and, once she was certain she was out of sight of the village below, prepared to rest.

Sleep had evaded her. Every sound drew her spine as straight as if she were a soldier at attention. While the long hours of darkness crept on toward dawn, her mind had played over and over the events of the previous evening. The dance, Caleb's return and subsequent departure, and her decision to find the camp—all these events plagued her thoughts and kept sleep at bay. She had cradled Opa's gun to her breast, clutching it tighter with every sound, every sigh of the wind in the new leaves above her, every slight disturbance the pony made during the night.

Sometime after dawn, the sun's heat had heightened her exhaustion, and Analisa had finally slept. Now she was awake at last and determined to enter the village and seek out her siblings. She gave the pony one last pat on the nose and tugged playfully at the shock of mane that fell forward between its ears before she turned it loose to find its own way down into the ravine below.

Her heart beating rapidly, Analisa tasted the dry metallic flavor of fear in her mouth as she edged toward the rim of the bluff on her hands and knees, dragging the gun along beside her. She stayed close to the ground and when she reached the edge of the cliff, raised her head just enough to see out over the ledge.

Analisa caught her breath. The quiet village she'd last seen in the darkness now rivaled an ant colony for activity. Paths worn in the grass between the hide dwellings were filled with busy figures of men and women passing to and fro. Packs of children ran about, darting and hiding between the trees that grew along the riverbank. If she listened intently, Analisa discovered she could hear their laughter above the rushing water. She found she was much closer than she had anticipated. The darkness had been deceiving. Dropping her head, she rested her cheek against her forearm and swallowed nervously. She could smell the fresh grass, the pungent scent released by the blades bent beneath her weight. She took a deep breath, fought to still her hammering heart, and raised her head for another look.

Nowhere did she see anyone who resembled Caleb. For that matter, she did not see anyone who might have been white. It dawned on her that Hardy and Zach might have lied to her about the white captives . . . but for what reason?

Analisa began to damn her own impulsiveness, wondering if perhaps she had the wrong camp, assailed with the fear that she would never find her way back to Fort Sully. Then her eyes were drawn to a pair of figures that emerged from one of the dwellings near the river. She pulled herself forward with her elbows in order to get a better view, sliding her stomach along the new grass. Only a deep-seated appreciation of the danger she was in kept her from calling out to the girl she saw below. Could it be? she wondered as her heart rattled inside her breast. Strolling along with carefree strides was a young blond woman who stood at least a head taller than the Indian girl beside her. Even across the distance that separated her from the women, Analisa could see the fine white line of the blond girl's scalp where her hair had been parted into two even braids. They hung down her back, swinging gracefully with every step.

The girl faced the river, her back to Analisa. She found herself wishing the blonde would turn around and look her way, but then Analisa realized the distance was too great. She would never be able to make out the other woman's features.

Analisa scanned the sides of the bluff in every direction until she found exactly the formation she sought. A crevice was eroded into the walls of the bluff. Further inspection proved it was negotiable. Before she could hesitate and perhaps change her mind, she sat down and slid forward toward the opening. Stretching the toes of her dusty high-top shoes as far forward as she was able, Analisa finally connected with the closest boulder and then lowered herself with her arms until she stood securely on the first step down toward the valley floor.

Rock by rock she worked her way down, alternately crawling and sliding, always remembering to drag the old hickory-stock gun along with her. Her shaking limbs forced her to make frequent stops, and she realized with dismay how quickly she had grown weak from lack of strenuous work. Silently she berated herself for her lack of strength and made a promise that once she was out of this predicament and safely home she would plant herself a garden behind the house even over the objections of Caleb and the entire U.S. Army.

When she reached the valley, Analisa paused to catch her breath and look around. The crevice yawned wide in the face of the hill behind her. For a moment she wondered how she had managed to get down, shaking aside the dismal thought that she might not succeed in climbing back up should she be forced to escape that way with Meika. If the girl she saw *was* Meika. *Go forward,* Analisa warned herself; *never look back.* What was it Ruth had said? She would succeed at whatever she tried today. Analisa held to her friend's encouraging words and prayed the stars told the truth.

She found herself near the eastern end of the valley, on the village side of the wide, gently flowing stream that fed into the Missouri. Not far away was a well-worn path that led to the water's edge. Analisa crouched down among the brush that lined the bank of the stream and waited, hoping that she would be able to move toward the camp once evening cast shadows across the land. Long moments passed before the sound of voices drew her attention to the nearby pathway. She took a deep breath and held it, scrunching herself farther back into the bushes, waiting. She felt the blood pulsing along the veins in her neck, urged on by the pounding tattoo of her heart. Wide-eyed, she watched as two, then three Sioux women chatted amiably together and dipped their water containers into the stream.

Although she was close enough to hear some of their words, she was unable to understand any of the lilting language. Their laughter and gentle gestures were universal though, and in seconds Analisa felt herself relax as she watched them, her perilous position all but forgotten. It seemed to be the time of day when all the women gathered water from the stream. Would the white girl be allowed to do so? Would she be alone?

Nearly twenty women had come and gone. From her vantage point Analisa noted every detail of their dress and habits. The women all wore simple dresses fashioned of hides. Curious

about the beautiful materials, she wondered how they had cured
and tanned the hides to achieve so soft a texture. The basic
pattern of the clothing was a straight-seamed sheath, cut wider
at the shoulders to provide for the sleeves. None of the women
wore cloth dresses, although many had adornments, which
surprised Analisa. Scraps of velvet had been sewn into pouches.
Calico strips bound their braids. While there were a few items
that hinted at contact with the whites, the women adorned
themselves with natural fibers and animal skins.

She'd relaxed her position, slipping out of her wary crouch to
sit amid the brush. Analisa rested her head on her arms for a
moment and longed to stretch, hoping it would not be long
before she could stand and make her way closer to the
dwellings. The women were fewer in number now, most having
collected their water, exchanged greetings, and departed.

More voices called out along the trail, and Analisa looked up.
She swallowed, choking back a cry, and felt her eyes flood with
tears, which blinded her so that her vision wavered. Pressing her
hands against her lips, she let the heavy tears scald her cheeks as
she watched the tall, long-limbed blonde approach the stream
beside her Sioux companion. There was no doubt: The girl was
Meika.

Meika. No longer a child of twelve, but a beautiful young
woman of seventeen. No longer the little sister Analisa remembered, but Meika nonetheless. Her hair was white-blond, fairer
even than Analisa's. The girl's complexion glowed a deep
honey gold, attesting to her outdoor life. Her eyebrows were
stark white arches above her nearly translucent blue eyes. She
was dressed identically to the others except that she wore a
decorative beaded headband.

So stunned was Analisa that it was a while before she realized
her sister was speaking amiably with the others, smiling and
laughing with some of the women, nodding politely to others.
In no way was she treated as a slave. It was as if Meika belonged
with them, as if they were her friends.

Analisa slowly, carefully returned to a crouch, never taking
her eyes off of Meika. She gauged the time it would take her
sister to dip the soft skin bag into the stream. There might never
be another opportunity to locate her among the crowded
dwellings that resembled one another so closely. She seemed to
be accepted by the others, so perhaps there was no need for

fear. Determined to step forward and call out to her, Analisa reached out and touched the pliant limbs of a low shrub. Surely, with so few women near the stream now, she was in little danger of attack.

Go. Go now. Analisa tried to summon the courage to step out from her hiding place and reveal herself to her sister. Two of the women walked away, one of them so stout that she was forced to walk alone along the pathway behind her companion. Only Meika and her friend were left beside the stream. The sun had slipped behind the ridge high above them, throwing the valley into cool shadows. The stream bubbled past, rippling over the rocks, swirling in and out of the tufts of grass growing along the bank. All was quiet. In the village, the sounds of life and smells of cooking filled the air and wafted toward the stream. It was an idyllic setting, one that lured Analisa, urging her to act.

"Forgive me, Caleb." She whispered the thought aloud and then straightened. Pushing aside the surrounding brush with her forearm, Analisa stepped out from her hiding place and moved toward the two girls beside the stream.

Analisa hoped the two women would not look up until she was near enough for Meika to recognize her. Slowly, quietly, she edged toward them, careful not to lose her footing on the damp grass near the water's edge. Stepping forward, intent on the women by the stream, Analisa did not feel the loose gravel beneath her heel until it was too late. The sole of her shoe slid across the smooth, wet pebbles, and her left leg shot out from under her. Quickly she regained her balance just short of a fall, but not swiftly enough, for the sound of her shoe scraping across the pebbles alerted the two young women, and they turned in unison toward Analisa. For a moment all three stood frozen, staring across the short distance that separated them.

Analisa stared in disbelief at her sister. Meika's skin fairly glowed, unlined and healthy despite her deep tan. Her cheeks were tinged pink, her eyes clear and bright. At close range Analisa could see the intricate pattern worked in beads on her headband. As Analisa looked on, neither of the others moved, but stood silent, ready for flight, as they assessed her.

"Meika, it's me. It's Anja," she said in Dutch.

Analisa extended her hand toward her sister and felt her heart rushing in her ears. She watched as Meika shook her head in confusion and then, without looking at the girl beside her, issued orders to the startled Sioux. The water skin slipped from the Indian girl's hand to lie forgotten on the ground, its contents soaking the trampled grass at Meika's feet while her companion backed away from the scene. With a last, uncertain look in Meika's direction, the Indian girl turned and bolted toward the settlement.

"I'm so sorry. I've frightened your friend." Analisa continued to speak to her sister, all the while reaching down to place the gun on the ground. She then moved forward unarmed, her palms open, arms wide and pleading. "Meika, don't you know me? What have they done to you?" The Dutch words seemed to have no effect on the girl.

Analisa's vision blurred, and her sister's image wavered as her own eyes filled with tears. The warm droplets soon spilled over her lower lashes to course down her cheeks. She had waited so long, held such hope of finding Meika and Pieter. What had these people done to her sister to cause her to forget her past? Analisa stepped forward, her tears forgotten as they continued to pour down her cheeks. She brushed her hair back and continued to move toward Meika, never taking her eyes off of her sister's face. The girl stood as if turned to stone as she stared back at Analisa.

"I have no gun." Analisa's words were a hurried whisper in Dutch. She could only hope she was making sense. Her heart continued to pound, and her tongue no longer seemed to fit inside her dry mouth. "Come with me, Meika. Quickly. I have come to take you home."

The younger girl placed her right hand protectively above her heart and began to back away from Analisa who had slowly closed the distance between them. Meika shook her head, as if to deny Analisa's presence, or the reality of what she was seeing.

"*Komop,* Meika. Come."

"*Nee.*"

As the girl shook her head to emphasize her answer, Analisa felt her heart soar. *Nee.* The simple denial spoken in Dutch erased every trace of doubt from her mind. She'd found her. She'd found Meika.

Close enough now to reach out and touch her sister, Analisa made an attempt to grab the girl's hand but felt her own arms suddenly grasped from behind. Her wrists were forcefully brought together and bound so tightly that the leather thongs cut into her skin. She tried to writhe away from her captors, but only succeeded in causing her captor to grip her upper arms even tighter. Fingers cut into her flesh like steel bands.

"Meika . . . why? *Why?*"

Twisting and kicking out at her captors, Analisa craned her neck to look over her shoulder. Two half-naked Sioux men held her firmly, their eyes hooded, their faces immobile masks. Before she was able to speak to her sister again, Analisa found herself carried along between the two tall men, her feet barely touching the ground as they hurried her toward the encampment. She turned in a frantic attempt to call out to Meika and was rewarded by a resounding slap that snapped her head back around.

Stay calm. Caleb is here somewhere. You are safe. Her mind chanted the litany over and over as the two silent men pushed her along the narrow path toward the center of the village. All around her people gathered. Most stood silent, content to stare, while others shouted at her. She recognized the angry tone and somewhere in the back of her mind realized that insults must be universal. A sea of brown seemed to ebb and flow around her as she was jostled through the growing crowd. Hides adorned the Sioux's bodies. Their dark eyes, some almost coal black, bored into her. Shining black hair hung long about their shoulders. Analisa felt the darkness closing in on her. How had Meika survived it for so long? Nothing was familiar. Nothing was safe. The old panic returned, and Analisa fought against the iron grip of her captors. One man now stood on either side of her, holding on to her upper arms, forcing her to stand at attention between them.

Analisa stared at the crowd, searching frantically for Caleb. Surely he would step forward and explain. Wouldn't he? Somehow, as her mind raced ahead and her pulse pounded along her veins, she realized he might be waiting in order to conceal his own identity a while longer. She must trust in his judgment. If she had only listened to him in the first place, she would not be here now.

The luxury of such speculation was no longer hers, for her captors now jerked her forward without ceremony, signaling for her to wait before the closed flap of one of the dwellings. Standing only a few feet away from the structure, Analisa could see that its sides were decorated with faded paintings of horses, riders, and walking figures.

A thick, cloying odor emanated from the men beside her. It tickled her memory, touching off waves of fear, and caused her skin to crawl. She risked a glance at the man to her left. He was as tall as she, his nose long and bent to the side, as if once broken. He stared straight ahead, ignoring her. The man on her right was at least a head shorter than she, but sturdily built, his skin stretched tight over wadded muscle. His face was round, unlined, yet showed no kindness. He leered up at her, and if his expression was meant to intimidate, he had succeeded.

The sound from the crowd around her swelled to an angry crescendo, then suddenly gave way to silence as the tent flap was pushed aside. As if unfolding from a cocoon, the stooped figure that emerged stood to tower over Analisa. The hush of the crowd warned her this man was someone to be reckoned with, and so it surprised her to find him so young. She guessed him to be not much older than herself, and younger than Caleb. In a way, the young leader reminded her of her husband, not in appearance so much as in stature and bearing. In a glance he took in the angry crowd around him before he let his eyes drop to meet hers. As the fathomless ebony eyes met hers, Analisa felt her blood run cold. This man would show her no mercy, for his eyes mirrored the depths of his soul. Hate radiated from him, hatred for her kind and the life he was forced to lead.

The man's lips were pressed together in a rigid line, one corner lifted in disdain. His hair was swept back from a high, smooth forehead, worn long in the Sioux fashion and hanging nearly to his elbows. Unlike her captors, he was completely clothed, his fringed and beaded buckskin shirt serving as a backdrop for the array of jewelry adorning him. Thick strands of white beads hung in graduated lengths around his neck. Beneath the longest strands he wore a breastplate of tubular shells and beads edged with dancing feathers. Loops of metal holding round flat shells hung from his earlobes.

The leader's deep-set hooded eyes were further recessed by his high cheekbones. She was aware of his nostrils, flared in anger, beneath his long, straight nose. Analisa was drawn to his stare, unable to look away while fear radiated through her. Before she had time to react, his hand shot out and grasped her chin, forcing her to meet his eyes. He studied her features as carefully as if reading a hidden trail. Where his fingers touched her sensitive skin, she burned, and felt her face redden with anger and embarrassment. Analisa tried to pull away, to force him to release his grip, but failed. Finally, his perusal of her over, he pushed her chin aside in dismissal. He spoke, not to the waiting crowd, but spat out words to the men at her side. His voice was low, guttural, and curt.

At once the two men pulled her away from the leader and dragged her unceremoniously across the camp.

"Stop! Where are you taking me?" Attempting to dig her heels in the ground and force them to halt, she was soon overpowered by her silent guards.

The crowd closed around her again. Analisa noticed the men of the village no longer seemed interested in her, but the surge of angry women grew. Their sharp, screeching catcalls reverberated in her ears, and as they pressed closer, Analisa expected the men beside her to bark orders at them to back away, yet nothing was said to the maddened crowd. Where was Meika? Analisa frantically tried to see her sister among the women who were now pushing against her and jeering. An old woman, her hair more gray than black, reached out with a wizened, claw-shaped hand and rent the sleeve of Analisa's gown from the shoulder. The plaid wool slid down her arm to gather at her bound wrists. Another hand reached out to pluck a button from the front of her dress, and at the woman's success, others followed suit. Soon the bodice of the dress was hanging open, Analisa's camisole exposed to their view.

As she sought to escape their clutching, grasping fingers, Analisa twisted toward her guards and succeeded in trodding upon the shorter man's foot with the heel of her shoe. His muffled grunt sounded in her ear and was followed by a resounding slap to the side of her head that nearly knocked her senseless. Analisa fought to stay conscious, knowing full well that, should she falter, the angry women would most likely tear her apart.

"Stop it!" she screamed as a hand wound itself in her hair. "No!" Unable to fight back in any other way, Analisa turned her head toward this new attacker and sank her teeth into the woman's wrist. A sense of satisfaction overwhelmed her when she heard the woman's startled cry and the hand entangled in her hair was released.

The mob parted. Analisa was thrust into a hide-covered dwelling. Momentum impelled her forward, and she fell head-long onto the hard-packed ground inside the dark hut. Her hands still bound behind her, she was unable to break her fall and cried out as her cheek slammed into the ground. For a moment she lay stunned, her face pressed against the cool dirt floor as she listened to the sounds of the angry crowd slowly diminish. The place was damp and musty, the air close and still. Slowly she rolled to her back, her gaze drawn upward along the slanted walls of the shelter, up the slender poles that formed its skeletal framework. The apex was open to the sky, and she stared at the clear, bright blue above her, surprised to discover so familiar a piece of her world in the midst of the hellish scene.

The moment of peace was shattered when a crouched woman stepped through the opening and stood to her full height. She was soon followed by a second. Analisa quickly rolled to her side and pushed herself up on her right elbow. Dizziness attacked her in waves; her vision blurred and then cleared.

"Don't you touch me. Keep away!" She pushed herself to a sitting position and tried to scoot backward across the floor, away from the women.

They moved toward her, undaunted by her shouted com-mand, and set to work. One held her thrashing legs until Analisa was forced to sit still. The other worked to unlace and remove her shoes. Her thick *sokken* followed. The two then examined the wool dress and spoke quietly between themselves as if deciding how best to remove it.

"Oh, no, you don't!"

Analisa shimmied farther away from them while they con-curred, but found herself wedged against the wall of the shelter. She was forced to wait until they approached her again.

The heavier of the two then drew a knife from a sheath at her waist, and Analisa screamed. The woman reached out, not with the weapon, but with her open palm, and silenced Analisa with a firm slap that rattled her teeth.

Her voice reduced to a whimper, Analisa hated the fact that she was cowering now, but exhaustion and pain were fast eroding her courage. "No. Please." She shook her head, hoping to dissuade them, but the heavy woman proceeded to cut away the sleeves of her dress, first the left and then the already ripped one. Swiftly the woman parted the rent bodice and cut it away from the gathered waist. Her companion pulled the skirt down over Analisa's hips and thighs until it was free. Clad only in her thin cotton chemise and the bodice of the dress, which now hung open like a tattered vest, Analisa was released. The women turned and left the dwelling as suddenly as they had entered, abandoning Analisa once more to the semidarkness.

Nerves stretched to the breaking point, Analisa lay tense and alert, staring at the sky, trying to hold on to the patch of light high above her, trying to ground herself in reality. No one else came in to disturb her. As time slowly passed, she felt herself slowly relax as knotted muscles loosened up. Pain shot upward along her arms from her bound wrists. She could tell by the burning sensation around the leather cords that her skin was raw, perhaps even bleeding. She tried to reason with herself in order to fight down her fear. Caleb would come. He would find her and talk to these people. She would wait.

What if this was not Red Dog's camp? The doubt nagged at her, for she had no real proof that the Indian pony had indeed carried her to his settlement. *This has to be the one*, she reassured herself. Hadn't she found Meika here? She would not give up hope. Perhaps her sister might help her escape. She clung to her dream, to the image of Caleb walking through the door, her sister beside him. It would all work out. Analisa was convinced she had come too far to have it end this way.

Analisa was certain of only one thing as she stared up through the darkness and watched the sky transform itself from blue to radiant rose to pale twilight lavender. She knew that if and when all hope vanished, she would never allow herself to be taken by another man the way it had happened years ago. No man would touch her in lust, no one would force himself on her again, even if she had to fight to the death. No one.

Chapter Nineteen

Dampness seeped into the hide dwelling, chilling the figure lying curled up on the dirt floor. Analisa roused herself and stared up toward the smoke hole to gauge the passing of time. It was early evening. The rising moon's light reflected off the clouds that shrouded the stars. Tonight was cooler than last. As she lay trussed up like a Christmas goose and forgotten in the deserted shelter, Analisa wished for the warmth and security of home. The cotton chemise and torn wool bodice did little to protect her from the chill that rose from the ground beneath her.

She realized she must have slept, and wondered how. Her wrists were still bound tight despite her struggles, her lips parched and dry. Analisa prayed that someone would come to ease her discomfort and in the same breath prayed that the Sioux would leave her alone. What of Meika? Surely the girl

knew Analisa was a prisoner. Perhaps her sister would rescue
her. And what of Caleb? Was he here at all?

Her right shoulder was numb from lying on it, her fingers
devoid of feeling. Analisa rolled to her left side and faced the
doorway again. The flap was closed, and, she assumed, secured
on the outside. Her eyes had become accustomed to the
shadowy light inside the dwelling, but all she could see was a
circle of charred stones that marred the open expanse of the
floor. Ashes remained in the center of the fire pit, ashes and the
lingering scent of wood smoke, the only reminders that the
place had ever been inhabited.

The numb sensation in her right hand gave way to sharp
tingling. She tried to wiggle her fingers, but the pain that shot
through her wrist forced her to stop. She closed her eyes against
the reality of her situation. *Kase. Think of Kase.* She pictured
him safe, tucked into his bed between clean white sheets. Ruth
would see to that. Ruth and Abbie. They would care for her son
until she returned. She would not even allow herself to think of
the alternative. *Ja,* she would return from this, she knew she
would . . .

At the sound of footsteps Analisa's eyes flew open and she
watched, tense, as the door flap was thrown aside. For a
moment a dark shadow filled the opening, then moved inside.
Uncurling to its full height, the figure proved to be that of a
man, tall and finely honed, from what she could see in the
darkness. She forced herself to rise up, first on her knees and
then to a sitting position. Without a sound, the man began to
cross the shelter toward her. As he moved closer, she pressed
herself back against the hide wall. He did not speak. Uncertain,
Analisa guessed from the height and build of the man, it could
be none other than Red Dog. As he passed beneath the circle of
light that shimmered down from the smoke hole, she caught a
glimpse of shining shoulder-length hair and a naked upper
torso. His face was cast in shadows. He carried a bundle of
some sort, perhaps a crude pouch, she could not tell, but she
became aware of the heavy scent of hair grease that often clung
to Caleb when he returned home from the camp.

He had not spoken. She found she could not. Her lips were
sealed with a terror so stark that Analisa feared her heart would
burst. It was all too real this time and yet exactly like the dream
that had haunted her over the years. The man who attacked her

was but a shadow in her memory. Now she lay at the mercy of another shadow, one that was alive and real and edging slowly toward her. Analisa shook her head from side to side in silent protest. She did not want to remember it at all, but the old dream began to mix with this new, dark menace. Her lips parted, and she summoned every ounce of strength in order to cry out, but all that escaped was a hoarse, shuddering sob.

"Anja?"

Caleb stopped when he heard the pitiful, heart-wrenching cry. Could it have come from his wife? His proud, stubborn Analisa?

Early in the evening Caleb had listened intently as he sat crouched before the old woman's tepee, careful to keep his eyes downcast while he cleaned his rifle. He heard the women speak of the tall blond one who'd tried to speak to Swift Otter's young wife. He let his fingers lightly ply the soft leather cloth over the highly polished hickory stock of his rifle and hoped that he appeared lost in thought.

He had returned to the camp bearing a brace of pheasants, a welcome surprise for the ancient one, the childless widow older than time, who cooked for Caleb when he chose to eat in the camp. With no one to provide for her, the nearly toothless hag was forced to rely on the generosity of others. Caleb's offerings were always welcome. While she cleaned the fowl and prepared the evening meal, Caleb sat before her tepee and worked on his rifle, cursing the fact that it had taken him longer than he had anticipated to return to the camp.

A rock had slipped between Scorpio's hoof and shoe, forcing Caleb to slow his pace. Stopping at his hiding place to change into his Sioux clothing had caused another delay as well as the time it took to kill the pheasants in order not to return empty-handed. Caleb finally arrived, only to hear the women softly talking about the white captive, speculating as to how she had come upon their camp. His heart seemed wedged in a steel trap of his own making when Caleb heard them describe Analisa. He had no idea how she'd located the camp alone and unseen in broad daylight, or how she'd found her sister so easily, but now that the damage was done, he was forced to think of a way to rescue her and take her out of the settlement.

All that led up to the moment at hand was quickly forgotten when he heard the gasping sobs that pierced the stillness in the darkened interior of the tepee. He knelt, at the same time setting his bundle down beside him. Reaching out, his hand connected with Analisa's shoulder, and he leaned forward to wrap her in his embrace. The soft sound of her anguish became muffled against his shoulder as he knelt with her in his arms. Caleb stroked her bare arms and felt the chill on her skin. The faint scent of her talcum was so familiar that he found himself forced to choke down the knot that lodged in his throat. His hands quickly found the rawhide ties that bound her wrists, and he swiftly drew his knife from the sheath at his waist and sliced the bindings. Setting her away from him, he pulled her arms forward and rubbed the circulation back into her hands. She had not spoken a word, nor had she acknowledged him by name. Caleb waited to speak until she had calmed.

"Anja . . ." He again cradled her with one arm while he continued to stroke her with his hand. "Are you all right? Come on, say something." He whispered near her ear.

"Oh, Caleb . . ." Her voice was ragged between sobs. "I was so . . . scared. I did not know it was you. I saw . . . Meika . . . and she didn't . . . she didn't even . . . know me." Her last words were nearly inaudible.

Caleb felt her arms encircle his neck and could tell by her weak attempt to draw him close that she was near collapse.

"Shh. Let me light a fire to warm you. I have some food and water." She did not respond to his words, nor did she lessen her hold. "Anja? Come on, now. Let go."

He reached up to unlock her arms from his shoulders and draw her hands down to her sides. With quick efficiency he unrolled a length of buckskin and removed from it a few pieces of firewood, a water bag, and a packet of cold cooked pheasant. From a small pouch at his waist he drew a shard of flint, and soon a low fire crackled in the stone-ringed pit. The dim, shimmering light cast its glow upon Analisa, and he glanced across the small distance between them to find her staring at him, her knees drawn up to her breasts, her matted hair hanging about her shoulders.

The firelight played upon the swell of her breasts beneath the thin camisole. The tattered bodice of her plaid dress hung open, providing little protection from the chill of the night air. Her short pantalets revealed the curves of her long, shapely legs all too clearly. His anger at her impulsive act and his fear of losing her dissolved at the sound of her broken sobs. He added another small piece of wood to the low-burning fire and watched the smoke curl up toward the apex of the tepee. Drawing the water bag toward him, Caleb returned to Analisa's side and crouched beside her, offering her the container.

She took a sip and then another, all the while avoiding his steady gaze. Finally, her thirst slaked, she poured a small amount of water into the cupped palm of her hand and bathed her face with it. Reaching down, she drew up the corner of the torn bodice and wiped at her eyes. Still she avoided looking at him. Caleb watched her silently for a moment, the sight playing havoc with his insides. One part of him wanted to rail at her. Was she pleased with the mess she'd gotten herself into? The rest of him wanted to hold her close until the frightened, wary look was banished from her eyes. The overwhelming sense of relief that flooded him only stoked the fire that burned in his loins. Now that he'd found her safe and relatively unharmed, he longed to press her down on the earthen floor and move within her as he'd done so often, reveling in the feel of her, always pleased and awed by her immediate response. But Caleb knew he had to wait. What she needed now was his love, not his lust.

"Are you hungry?" He leaned close, brushing her hair off her cheek and tipping her chin up so that he could see into the blue depths of her eyes. They sparkled with unshed tears.

"No." The word came out a whisper, and she cleared her throat. Her eyes did not leave his face, but clung to his as if she feared he might disappear.

"How did you get here, Anja?" he asked, trying to keep his voice light and understanding. He rested an open palm on her shoulder. Her skin had warmed.

She took a deep, shuddering breath. "I took the pony you brought home to Kase. Zach said it would return to its home if it was turned loose."

"Why?"

"I guess ponies do that." She shrugged.

"No, Anja. I mean, why did you come here?"

He watched her blink twice as if unsure of his question, or perhaps, unsure of her answer.

"You already know why I came here: I came to find Meika."

"How did you know she was here?"

"I knew because of what I saw in your eyes, what you did not tell me. I knew that you had seen her, but trapping Hardy was more important to you than freeing my sister. So I came to get her myself."

He sat beside her, drawing her into the circle of his arm.

"Why do you always rely only upon yourself, Anja, never anyone else?"

"I am used to having only myself to rely on."

"When will you realize that has changed?"

"You told me Meika must wait, Caleb."

"And I would not have forgotten my promise. Now I must get you out of here before Red Dog changes his mind."

She sat up straight and looked into his eyes again. "He said I could go?"

Caleb felt her shiver and rubbed her arm. She leaned against him and curled her legs beneath her.

"Not in so many words, but he didn't say I *couldn't* take you out of here."

"You told him I was your wife? Did you have to tell him what you are really doing here?"

He looked down into her eyes. There was so much to explain. "No. I didn't tell him you were my wife and I didn't tell him why I'm here. I bargained for you; I reminded him that he owed me a life."

Analisa was silent for a moment, gauging his words. "So . . . he gave me to you?"

Caleb nodded.

"For . . ." she asked.

"For whatever I wanted to do with you."

She turned to him then, her breasts brushing against his naked chest. Caleb caught his breath as he looked down into his wife's eyes.

"You would probably like to beat me." A tear slipped over her lower lashes and ran down her cheek. "Caleb, I'm so sorry."

He reached out and held her chin in the palm of his hand. With his thumb he gently brushed away the tear and then used both hands to lift her hair away from her face. His fingers caught in the tangles, and he gently pulled them free.

"Your face is bruised." He stroked her purpled cheek with his fingertips and wished he knew who had inflicted the pain.

"I fell."

Her eyes met his briefly before they moved to his lips. Analisa mirrored his movements and reached out to hold his face in her hands. Tears continued to slip down her cheeks.

"I knew you would come," she whispered.

Caleb's full lips met hers in a soft, tender kiss that built in intensity as the tip of his tongue touched hers. He felt her hands creep up to link behind his neck, and she pulled herself against him. He drew her closer, pulling her onto his lap, and sat with her cradled in his arms, tasting of her honeyed sweetness, exchanging a kiss that said what his words had not. His relief at finding her alive, his need for her, his anger, too, at her defiance, all were communicated through the delicate exchange of that one heated kiss. Above all else, he hoped his love was apparent to her. Finally, she was forced to pull away first and take a deep breath, all the while staring up into his eyes.

Pulling her back to him he whispered against her lips, "I want you, Anja."

"I am afraid."

He stroked her hair. "Of me?"

She shook her head. "I am afraid in this place. What if they come back?"

"No one will enter without asking."

"No?"

"No one."

He kissed her once more and, as he did, began to press her back upon the earthen floor.

She glanced toward the doorway. "Shouldn't we leave?"

"Not yet. Not until the camp is quiet. Until then, you need not worry." His hands stroked her hip and moved down along her thigh. "Relax."

"Caleb?" She linked her arms about his neck, and he stretched out above her.

"Hmm?"

"Is it strange that I want to . . . that I need you here in this place?"

"No. Not strange. I feel the same way. We came close to losing each other. To share our love now will be an act of celebration."

Her breath fanned warm against his cheek as she spoke. "A celebration."

A log in the fire ring popped and broke in two, shattering into ash and embers. Caleb slipped his arms beneath her shoulders and cradled the back of her head in his hands. His fingers buried themselves in the wild tangle of thick silken tresses. He let his lips play upon her languorously, prodding hers into response. Soon, as he knew it would, her kiss intensified and she clung to him, unconscious of time and place, lost in a world of sensation and pleasure.

Analisa was trapped in his arms as surely as he was trapped in her heart. He released her hair, feeling the need to explore her with his hands. She relished the feel of his callused, gentle palms as they rode over the plains and valleys of her skin, and waited in rapt anticipation for him to unerringly find and fondle all the secret, sensitive places that he knew gave her so much pleasure.

She burrowed her face into the hollow above his collarbone and let her tongue slither across his heated flesh. Partly because she feared intrusion from outside, but mainly because of her mounting need, she began to tear at his clothing with sudden urgency. Caleb needed no further invitation, but pulled away from her in order to slip out of his buckskin leggings.

A blush heightened her coloring in the vibrant glow of the firelight. She lay pliant and waiting, lips parted, her breathing uneven and shallow. He peeled off her remaining garments and knew a throbbing urgency as she readily opened her thighs in welcome. Blood thundered through his veins as he gazed down at her, so open and willing, lying there on the earth.

They did not speak. Words were unnecessary. The act of love was older than time, alive long before the need for language. Words could not express what Caleb felt for Analisa. His heart stretched with a fullness that caused him to ache with want of her in every fiber of his being.

Their shadows entwined on the wall of the dwelling. Analisa was mystified by the giant, wavering images that swayed with every movement of the flames. She stared up at Caleb, shuddering with her need of him, trying to slide nearer that part of him that only teased and probed the beckoning entrance to her velvet womanhood.

His well-honed muscles rippled in the firelight as he reached down and held her still, his hands on her shoulders. She mirrored his movements, reaching up to meet him as he lowered himself toward her to fuse them together. Their shadows merged and beat against each other, larger than life, capturing Analisa's attention with their erotic movements. Her body was alive and pulsing with the primitive beat that echoed between them, charged with frantic energy as they engaged in the ritual of celebration and exchange in the confines of the buffalo-skin tepee.

Caleb burrowed deeper, delving into the farthest recesses of her body until she was forced to lock her limbs about his waist to still the frenzied staccato movements of his hips. She clung to him, enfolding him with her arms, thighs, and inner core until he gasped out her name and shuddered convulsively in her arms.

The velvet warmth that spewed from him at the peak of his ecstasy sent Analisa vaulting into an abyss of pleasure. Caught in a storm of quicksilver sensations, she hung suspended, pulsing with supreme satisfaction, savoring the echoes until they died away.

"I don't think, at this point in time, you have any reason to lie there looking so smug, Mrs. de la Vega."

"Smug?"

"Self-satisfied."

"Ah." She shook her head in understanding. "But I do. I have discovered that when my husband becomes unbearably angry, all I have to do is take his mind off of his anger."

He smiled tenderly in response. "I had every right to be angry. You placed yourself in great jeopardy."

"Speak English."

He slowly enunciated each word for her: "Thanks to you we are not safe at home in our own parlor."

She answered him in kind: "Thanks to you we are not even safe when we *are* at home in our own parlor."

"What?"

Analisa ticked the names off on her fingers. "Ruth, Abbie, Kase, the cat . . ."

"Kase we already had."

Her eyes took on a faraway look, and he watched them fill with tears. She whispered, "*Ja*. Kase I already had." She turned her head away.

"Anja," he asked softly, "what is it?"

He sensed her change of mood and knew the reality of their situation had once more come crashing down around her.

"When they brought me here, all I could think of was Kase. I knew I had to get out of this for him." She turned to him. "Caleb, if anything ever happened to me, you would care for him always, wouldn't you?"

He realized that he was seeing her through his own film of tears. He rapidly blinked them away.

"Of course." He nodded to emphasize his words. "You know I think of Kase as my son." He pulled her close, anxious to still the erratic beating of his heart at the thoughts her words had conjured up.

They were silent for a time. The dry wood popped and spit in the fire pit as the flames burned low. Caleb rocked her gently as she lay quiet in his arms, and smoothed her long hair against her back.

Analisa's hushed voice broke the stillness. "When you came in through the door, I thought you were him . . . I thought you were the leader, Red Dog." A shudder ran through her as she recalled the experience for Caleb. "It was like that other time, just like before. I almost remembered it all, I almost saw the man who attacked me, but when you spoke, and I knew it was you, Caleb, all of the memories vanished."

He fought to keep his breathing even, his movements slow and steady as he gently rocked her back and forth. What if someday she did remember the face of the man who raped her and fathered Kase? Caleb realized then with sudden clarity that the sooner his job was over and he moved his family away from the Sioux, the better for all concerned.

His only comment was silence. He hoped it would be enough. Moments passed and soon he felt her relax against him. In an hour or two he would make his move. Red Dog had not forbidden him to take Analisa out of the village. Caleb fully intended to try. Somehow he had to get her away and intercept Hardy before the man reached the settlement. Red Dog's messengers had carried word to the agent that the renegade chief was ready to trade him a white woman. Red Dog felt that Hardy's cruelty to Mia would only be avenged by the man's death, and all of Caleb's work would have been for naught if he could not stop Hardy before the Sioux killed him. For now he would let Anja sleep and let Red Dog think that he was having his way with this white woman whom he'd all but begged to possess.

He laid his wife gently on the ground near the fire and placed a deer-hide robe over her. He then lay down beside her and sheltered her within his embrace. Sleep would not come to him. Instead, he remembered his exchange with the volatile young chief. When Caleb had asked for the white captive in exchange for Mia's life, Red Dog was adamant. No, he'd said; he would use her to bait Hardy and then give her to the highest bidder.

Caleb had been hard pressed to control his anger, forced as he was to barter with Red Dog. The memory of his own words still rang in his ears.

"I want her. Is Red Dog such a poor man that he must sell the captive? I delivered your own woman to you. A life for a life."

"Why do you want this white scarecrow?" The younger man had scoffed at Caleb, deep loathing burning in his eyes along with the mistrust that he no longer hid. "Is your father's white blood so thick in your veins that you lust for her white skin next to yours?"

"Is my choice of women a concern to so great a leader?"

Red Dog turned away, part of his hair braided alongside his face, the rest left to sway free behind him. "She will be offered to Hardy."

"That's a lie. You don't really need a woman to draw him here. Word alone will bring him running to you."

"I wish to toy with him. To watch the puffed-up toad gloat and strut before he dies. He will strike a bargain, pay us in rifles, and then I will turn the rifles on him. But slowly . . . he will die slowly."

Frustrated, Caleb tried again, inwardly seeking calm to match his outward control. He would succeed. He had to, for Anja. "I say again, you owe me this woman. You don't need her. Is your word of so little consequence? Or do you want her for yourself? I hear she is beautiful."

Red Dog turned on him, anger dark and brooding in his eyes. "She is a white scarecrow. Her eyes are colorless, her skin pale as ground corn. She is filthy. Maybe she *is* the fitting woman for you, Raven's Shadow." Red Dog looked Caleb up and down before he offered a cunning smile. "Take her."

Caleb pulled Analisa close and tried to forget the heated exchange. There was little chance Red Dog would deal with him now as a government representative. Why should the man trust any white or even half-white official after the treatment his people had received from Hardy? Now Caleb had personally angered him, as well. Reminding himself that he must awaken within an hour, Caleb shut his eyes and tried to sleep. First things first, he thought, his father's words echoing in his mind. Always handle first things first.

A gentle hand was shaking Analisa awake.

"Anja? Get up."

"Ga weg."

"No, Anja, I won't go away. Wake up. We have to get out of here."

She forced her eyes open, recognizing the urgency in Caleb's voice, and stared up at him in the dim light cast by the glowing embers in the fire ring. Fearful, she glanced around the circular expanse. They were alone. Every bone in her body ached, every muscle cried out in distress, but she forced her arms up and wrapped them around his neck as he leaned over her. What was he saying? They had to get out of here. But it was so warm, so quiet. And she was so tired. She tugged on his neck and knew he would be unable to resist the invitation to kiss her. He did kiss her, but quickly, then raised his head and looked toward the door.

"Come on." He swatted her rump and she groaned. "Up."

"Ik houd van jou."

"I love you, too. But I'll love you more when we are safely back at Sully. Let's go."

He rose to his feet and reached down to pull her up. Standing beside him, Analisa experienced a wave of dizziness and reached out to him for support. She watched as he unwrapped the cold pheasant meat and held it out to her.

"Eat. Then drink some water."

While she did as he asked he moved about the room, grabbing the deer hide and the water bag, rolling them up in preparation to leave.

"Do you have anything I can wear?"

"Here." He tossed the hide in her direction.

She threw it across her shoulders like a shawl and wrapped the ends about her. It covered her from shoulder to ankle. "Caleb?"

"What?" He'd moved to the doorway and flung the flap back to peer outside, then signaled for her to join him.

She whispered in his ear. "How are we going to get Meika out of here?"

"We aren't. Step through here and I'll follow. There are no guards."

"No."

He stared at her. "Anja . . . what in the hell do you think you are doing? What do you mean, no? This isn't the time or the place to—"

"I will not leave here without my sister. If I do, all of this will have been for nothing."

He took a deep breath and held it as his eyes bored into hers. Analisa took a step backward.

"All of this *has* been for nothing. Try to understand, Anja, that your sister would not go with you even if we tried to force her. Her place is here, Analisa. This is her home now. She accepts that; now you must."

His words hurt her so that she could only shake her head in denial.

"It's true. She's married now, Anja. Just as married as you are. I saw her tonight, walking through the camp with her husband at her side. Do you think she'd just ride off and leave him?"

He was lying to her. He had to be. "She has been forced to live with them. She is afraid of what might happen if she tried to leave. We must find her. I know if I could talk to her that she would go with me."

"Where? Back to what? Do you remember the treatment you had to learn to live with? Do you remember what people thought of you for living through something that was over with in minutes? Anja, she's been here since she was twelve. Do you know how long it takes for a child of that age to become assimilated into a new culture? Sometimes a year or two at the least." He grabbed her forearms, pulling her down to kneel with him before the doorway. "She's seventeen now, Anja. Married. And pregnant, or didn't you notice? Even if she wanted to leave, which she doesn't, do you think the whites would ever accept her?"

Analisa felt hot tears course down her cheeks and suddenly realized she was crying. Again. She wondered when it would end. Caleb's words stung her, but she could not deny the truth that she heard in them. Before Caleb, her life had been hell.

Although she could not fathom her little sister choosing to live among the Sioux of her own free will, she could believe that Meika had learned to adapt to the Indians' way of life. But Analisa needed to hear it for herself. Let Meika tell her she wanted to stay with the Sioux. Wouldn't Caleb grant her that? It seemed little enough to ask.

"Caleb, please . . . let me talk to her."

"No. We haven't time to waste. I'm telling you the truth, Anja. Let it be."

"I won't, Caleb. I cannot. She is still my sister, and I must know for certain that she wants this for herself."

He pulled her close, his fingers rough on her arms as they bit into her flesh.

"I'm leaving *now,* and you, wife, are coming with me."

She tried to pull away, the tears flowing faster as she defied him.

"Let go, Caleb. I'm not leaving until I speak to her. You cannot make me." Analisa knew her voice was getting louder as it broke the stillness of the night. She felt as if for the first time in a long while she was losing control.

When he released one of her arms, Analisa was nearly convinced that Caleb would acquiesce. His eyes, deep blue now, as dark as the midnight sky, caressed her face. For a moment she thought she saw the glitter of tears reflected in them.

"I'm sorry, Anja," she heard him whisper.

As his words died away, blackness engulfed her.

Chapter Twenty

Pausing to shift the burden he held in his arms, Caleb took in the surrounding landscape. The walls of the narrow canyon were bathed in milk-white moonlight. The deep shadows cast by jagged outcroppings of rock were fathomless against the ravine's silver walls. A breeze blew across the land, rustled the leaves of the trees lining the riverbank behind him, and gently lifted his hair as it brushed his shoulders. He looked down at Analisa, wrapped in deer hide and cradled in his arms, then glanced at the sky and offered a silent prayer to the moon and the stars that she would forgive him.

As he worked his way upward, leading Scorpio behind him, Caleb was ever wary of his footing on the rocky path, which was all but nonexistent. He climbed slowly along the gentle rise toward the plain above. Forgive him? He knew he would be lucky if Anja didn't put him under with a frying pan once she was safely back at Sully. *You had to do it,* he told himself. Ever since his fist connected with her jaw, Caleb had been trying to convince himself that knocking her out had been necessary. It was no consolation knowing he hadn't hit her half as hard as he would have a man. He touched his lips to her forehead without breaking stride.

As he walked on, his mind wandered. Caleb envisioned Analisa, regal in her crown of braids, presiding over the dining table, an older more mature Kase seated between them, himself dressed in a three-piece suit, looking every bit the successful Boston lawyer.

"Remember the time I knocked you out, dear?" he would ask.

The Analisa of his fantasy would smile and nod. "Of course, darling. What a night! But you had to do it. I realized that the moment I came to."

The scene faded, and Caleb groaned inwardly. What if Analisa did not understand? He hoped she would not go so far as to leave him. He'd never struck a woman before and hoped he would never have to again.

Caleb stopped to listen to the night sounds carried on the breeze. Analisa moaned and shifted slightly in his arms. He glanced back toward the river, illuminated now by the moonlight. He had nearly reached the plateau that stretched eastward, away from the river, a flat rolling expanse. No one had followed him.

The hint of a sound alerted Caleb. His attention was drawn to the river valley far below. Two men rode along the narrow, winding trail along the riverbank. They moved slowly toward the Sioux encampment from the direction of Fort Sully. Quickly veering to the right, he continued to follow the Missouri southward, all the while remaining just below the rim of the plateau. Scorpio followed behind, surefooted on the narrow pebble-strewn trail. The cave was just ahead. Caleb knew that he could safely leave Analisa there while he intercepted Hardy and convinced him not to ride into Red Dog's camp. Caleb formulated a plan as he carried Analisa out of harm's way. If luck was with him, or, as Ruth said, if it was written in the stars, everything would soon fall into place.

Moving carefully, he quickly arrived at the well-hidden opening in the wall of the bluff. Tall cuttings masked the mouth

of the low-ceilinged cave from view. Pushing them aside, he left
Scorpio at the entrance and carried Analisa inside. Swiftly, he
knelt on one knee and carefully laid her on the cool, sandy floor
of the cave. He drew aside the deer hide that covered her face
and smoothed back the golden hair that fell across her forehead.
She was still unconscious, but he knew she would not remain so
for much longer. Locating his saddle and saddlebags, which
he'd hidden near the back wall, Caleb pulled aside the worn
wool blanket that he had covered with sand to hide his
belongings. He picked up a coil of rope and then searched
through the clothing folded beneath the saddle. From the pocket
of his dark trousers he withdrew a cotton bandanna. Pulling two
of the corners taut, he quickly flip-rolled the bandanna and
carried it to where Analisa lay.

Caleb gently worked the twisted cotton between Analisa's
teeth and then tied the ends behind her head.

Gingerly he pulled the deerhide about her and bound her
securely with the length of rope. If his plan succeeded, he
would lure Hardy back to the cave and the man would mistake
Analisa for a captive.

Caleb stared down at her, knowing full well that Analisa
would be furious when she awoke and found herself encased as
tight as a sausage. He shook his head and loosened the rope
around the deer hide. That way, if anything were to happen to
him, Analisa would be able to work free with little effort. He
laid his knife on the ground beside her. She would have the
weapon at her disposal if she needed it for protection. Covering
his saddle once more, he reached for the fringed and beaded
scabbard that held his rifle and slung it over his shoulder.
Moving outdoors once again, he replaced the screen of cuttings
and picked up Scorpio's reins. As he began to lead the horse
away from the mouth of the cave, he paused to look back and
hesitated for a moment, his mind on the woman bound inside.
With a slight shake of his head, he began to make his way down
the trail once more.

Not again. Analisa tried to cry out into the darkness as she
realized that her arms were pressed to her sides. She felt the soft
warmth of the hide wrapped about her and realized immediately
that she was no longer in the Sioux tepee. There was no sign of
light where the smoke hole should have gaped open above her.

Afraid to squirm and roll herself too far in the darkness, she chose instead to peer around, searching for any sign that might tell her where she was.

Where was Caleb? Tears formed in her eyes as she remembered his last words: "I'm sorry, Anja."

Furiously she blinked the tears away and remembered how she had thought he was referring to his refusal to help Meika. Now it was all too clear that he had rendered her unconscious before he brought her to this place. *If* he had brought her here. Perhaps Caleb himself was a prisoner somewhere nearby. If not, if he had deliberately tied her up and carried her out of the camp, he would have to face her wrath.

She tried to speak, to call out, but the gag caused her to retch. Fearful of choking, Analisa fell silent and waited. The place smelled of dampness and must. Pain pounded at her temples and the rag in her mouth was maddening. Lifting her head, she felt the throbbing pain increase, but before she lowered her head to the ground once more, she glimpsed dim light filtering through a curtain of leaves.

Eyes closed, her brow creased as Analisa tried to sort out her jumbled thoughts. She could do nothing bundled in the hide that held her arms against her sides. As she began to strain to free herself, a sound from beyond the curtain of leaves alerted Analisa. She stopped. Her breath caught in her throat. She waited, listening to the approaching footsteps.

There was a brief silence. Then she heard the crackling of leaves and branches. Raising her head, Analisa peered over the edge of the hide. The curtain of foliage had been removed. Stars dotted the night sky beyond the opening. Her eyelids lowered as in sleep, Analisa watched the thin silhouette of a man approach. She shut her eyes tight and heard him stop, his feet only inches from her face. He was still for only a moment before she heard him strike a flint to light a fire.

Analisa fought the urge to open her eyes and see the intruder. When she became aware of a bright light, she could not feign unconsciousness any longer. She opened her eyes.

The summer-sky blue of Caleb's eyes did not stare back at her as she'd half expected. She looked into eyes as dark and fathomless as the night sky. The man was thin and old; at least his dark, deeply creased skin made him look old. Unlike the other Indian men she'd seen, he wore no headband. His body was wiry, his arms and legs as stringy and brown as jerked beef. His clothing appeared to be a mixture of Indian and military. The coat he wore looked like a U.S. Army jacket, but Analisa did not recognize the insignia. Memory nagged at her. She'd seen the same type of jacket before, but could not remember where.

He did not move to touch her, but studied her intently for a moment before he turned abruptly on his heel and walked away, snuffing the torch in the sand before he walked through the opening. His footsteps faded away.

Afraid that she had been left alone to die in this unknown place, Analisa struggled to break free of the hide tied about her. Twisting and rolling back and forth in the loose, sandy gravel, she grew frustrated to the point of tears. Giving one final thrust forward as she tried to sit up, she felt the rope fall away. Her arms were no longer pinned beside her. Analisa shrugged out of the hide and tried to stand. Shaking from exhaustion, she knelt for a moment to catch her breath. The opening to the shelter remained exposed, the brush no longer filtering out the moonlight. She could see nothing beyond the opening but the night sky.

Analisa reached down to brace a palm against the earth. Her head was reeling, her heart pounding, her stomach a twisted knot. She took a deep breath and drew herself up. Standing in the center of the small earthen shelter, she kept her eyes on the entrance and with soundless steps, moved slowly toward it.

She looked out at the sky and then down. In the valley below, the waters of the Missouri flashed in the moonlight. A narrow ledge fronting the cave continued on, forming a path just beneath the ridge that led down to the river. By judging the direction of the current, she knew that Red Dog's camp was somewhere to the north.

The sky was beginning to brighten to a pale blue-gray in the east. Her wrists ached from the bonds she had endured in the renegade camp, and she rubbed them as she watched the dawn. She looked to the right and saw a lone rider negotiating the narrow path. Analisa wondered how the mount could find his footing in the weak light. She stepped back into the shadows of the cave and waited. Unafraid, she recognized the rider as Caleb. It was impossible for her to mistake the outline of his strong shoulders or the proud way he sat the horse. She wondered if he could see her standing just inside the mouth of the cave. Although she'd stepped back into the interior, the rising sun was casting a wider glow every moment. Her white undergarments would not be hard to see.

Analisa fought down the biting anger that stirred within her as she watched him draw near. Her body began to betray her as she warred with her emotions. She watched him dismount a few steps from the cave, and although she longed to run to him and feel the warmth of his protective embrace, she knew she could not do so without hating herself. He had much to explain.

Caleb approached her, his footsteps nearly silent in the shifting gravel. He led Scorpio into the shelter without a word, although his eyes never left her face. She did not move or speak, but chose to wait. Uncomfortable in the silence, she crossed her arms beneath her breasts. Caleb was toying with the horse's bridle as if avoiding her. She glanced down and found that by crossing her arms she'd succeeded only in pressing her breasts upward. They looked as if they might flow over the top of the camisole at any moment. Analisa quickly dropped her arms to her sides. It would not serve to arouse him now. Her anger was too great; her pride ran too deep to allow him to touch her.

He dropped the bridle. She watched him turn and walk toward her. Caleb stopped an arm's length away. The new morning sun bathed the walls of the cave and the bluffs around them with rose-tinted hues. Analisa stared at Caleb, trying to read his thoughts.

"How could you?"

She knew her tone was flat, expressionless. She could not seem to say it any other way.

"I had to."

"But . . . to hit me . . ." Analisa still could not quite believe it herself, and her disbelief echoed in her voice. The expression in his eyes changed; if she had not known him so well, the difference would have been imperceptible. Was it remorse she saw in them now? Sorrow?

Caleb reached out to gently touch her chin. She flinched, unable to control the movement. Caleb closed his eyes for the briefest moment, then looked into hers again.

"Anja, if I could take it back I would."

She shook her head. "You would do the same again."

"You're probably right, given the same circumstances." He

sighed and dropped his hand. His eyes searched her face before he turned to look down into the valley below. "I didn't have time to argue."

"Nor time to let me see my sister."

He turned and faced her once again. "No, Anja. No time to find her tepee. No time to ask if she could spare a minute to chat with a sister she didn't care enough about to even acknowledge before that sister was taken prisoner. No time to sit and wait to see if Red Dog wanted to change his mind and keep you prisoner." Angry now, Caleb turned his back on her and walked to the farthest wall of the cave. She watched him dig in the soft earth until he uncovered a blanket. Beneath it lay his saddle.

He continued talking while he hefted the saddle out of the depression in the floor of the cave and then pulled out his shirt, pants, and saddlebags.

"This isn't exactly a tea party you know."

She ignored the remark.

"Here." He tossed his black shirt at her and then the trousers.

Analisa held them in her arms and stared at him. Anger forced her to end her silence. She marched toward him, a piece of clothing in each hand.

"*Ja*. I know this is no tea party. Even though I go to *so* many."

"Calm down. You aren't making any sense." He threw the saddle over Scorpio's broad back and reached for the strap.

"You know what I mean." She shook the shirt at him as she spoke. "I have longed to find what is left of my family for five years. I have prayed. Do you know what it is like to just ride off and leave her? No."

"Yes." He stopped his packing long enough to stand and face her again. His eyes were dark with pain. "Yes. I know what it's like to ride away from your family. I had to leave one world and enter another. Nothing was the same. Even when I returned to the Sioux as an adult, I found that my life with them could never be the same as it was before my father took me east."

He reached out and grabbed her shoulders. She tried to step away and shake off his hands, but his hold was too tight. Analisa stopped moving when she saw the pleading look in his eyes. It was something she had never thought to see there.

"Listen, Anja. We haven't time for this. We—"

"There is never time," she interrupted. "Always you have to go off to something else. You are never here, never there." She let her hands drop, the clothes trailing from her fingers as she looked at the ground. It was like talking to the bluffs outside the cave. He was stone.

"Don't . . ." He stepped close. She stepped back.

"Don't what?"

"Don't look so dejected." His words were sad.

She stared at him. "Do not try to comfort me, Caleb. I cannot stand it just now."

"Anja, listen. I promise you that we will come back and talk to Meika. I don't know how we'll work it just yet, because after tonight Red Dog won't greet me with open arms." Scorpio moved restlessly and drew his attention. He stroked the big animal's nose.

Analisa pulled Caleb's shirt over herself. The sleeves hung past her fingertips, and she worked at rolling them up to her elbows. She pulled the front panel across her breasts and began to button the side buttons. The squared-off hem fell past her hips to midthigh. While Caleb continued to strap his saddlebags behind his saddle, she pulled the trousers. He stopped to watch, and when she straightened to face him, a half-smile played upon his lips.

"Let me roll up your pantlegs."

She stood quietly as he knelt in the sand and rolled the pants up until they hung about her ankles. He squeezed her calves before he stood. She could see that he was ready to leave.

When Caleb rolled up the deerhide, he found the bandanna gag. Without looking at her, he quickly tied it about his throat.

"You probably wish I still had that on."

"It crossed my mind when I first came in."

She watched him pick up his knife from the floor.

"Where did that come from?" She stepped forward in order to see it more clearly.

"It's mine. I left it here for you to find, but you must have rolled right over it. It was under the hide, which, by the way, was tied so loosely a child could have worked it free."

He would not be stared down but met her eyes.

"Who was that man?" she asked.

As if sensing the angry moment had passed, he returned to

his horse and tied the rolled hide on the rest of the pack. He spoke over his shoulder. "One of Hardy's Indian police. He sent the man up to see if I was telling the truth." Pulling on the reins, Caleb led Scorpio to the cave entrance. "I managed to stop Hardy before he got to Red Dog's camp. I told him that he was sure to lose his life if he rode in there, that Red Dog was furious over his mistreatment of Mia and planned to kill him."

"He believed you."

"He was afraid not to. I made his trip out here worthwhile, though. I told him I had stolen a white woman from the camp and that if he let me keep her two more days I would sell her to him, along with one other."

"So his man had to see me?"

"Yes. There was no way Hardy would try to negotiate that ridge in the dark. He sent his man while I waited with him."

"Hardy didn't recognize you?"

"Not in these clothes and in the dark. He didn't spare poor de la Vega a glance the night we met anyway. Come on. I'm taking you back."

She continued to question him as she walked toward the horse. "He agreed to your plan to buy two women?"

"Of course. As soon as his man told him I had one young blond woman in the cave, he decided to wait to get hold of one more."

"When does he expect to make the trade?"

"Day after tomorrow. Let me help you up." He moved to grab her about the waist.

"Wait. You said you had *two* women. What other woman did you mean?"

"None." He shook his head and she felt his fingers tighten about her waist. "I hope to get two of Williamson's men to disguise themselves as women."

She put her hands on his shoulders to stop him. "That will not work. Ruth will go with me."

"Anja . . ."

"Hardy will not come near if he thinks you have set a trap. You must have real women he can see from a distance. Ruth and I will do it."

"We'll worry about it later."

She could tell by his tone he hoped to put her off. "Nothing to worry about, Caleb."

He rolled his eyes toward the ceiling. "Does this mean I am forgiven?" He pulled her closer.

Analisa knew her anger had ebbed. Caleb had promised her he would take her back to Meika. She would believe him. As she looked up into his eyes she read uncertainty. More than anything else, she wanted him never to feel uncertain of her love.

"Does it mean so much to you?" She wanted to know.

"Yes."

Analisa paused for a moment as her eyes fell to his lips. "You are forgiven. But do not think I will forget your promise."

"I wouldn't even try to forget. I know you better than that. You'll see your sister." He pulled her into the circle of his embrace.

"I believe you."

His heated gaze made her blush. She looked over his shoulder and saw that the morning was full blown now, clean and brilliant. It was a new day. She was ready to go home.

He turned her in his arms and, as she stepped into the stirrup, hoisted her up from behind before he spoke. "Too bad we can't stay here a bit longer."

"I thought you were in a hurry." She looked down and watched him glance once more around the shady interior of the cave.

"I was just thinking . . . We've made love outdoors, in the cow shed, and in a tepee." His eyebrows shot up as he smiled devilishly at her. "But not in a cave. Yet."

Chapter Twenty-One

The solid white-washed pine door of the house at Fort Sully had never looked so welcoming to Analisa as it did when she crossed the plank porch with Caleb, his hand riding gently at her waist. Pausing before the door, she glanced up at her husband and smiled. He stood tall and proud beside her, his blue eyes alive with excitement and determination. Without appearing grim, his lips were set in a firm line. Although he had not slept for two nights, his face showed no sign of fatigue.

There was still much to be done, but Analisa knew that Caleb would push himself to the limit to bring Hardy to justice. Determined to share the load, Analisa drew herself up and stood proudly beside him. Reassured by his promise to return to the camp for Meika, she knew she could wait until he captured Hardy.

They met little resistance when they returned to the fort.
Caleb rode behind her, one arm firmly wrapped about her waist
as he held the reins. Two enlisted men on guard duty halted
them as they reached the west perimeter formed by the crude
buildings.

Recognizing Analisa, the guards allowed them to pass,
although one of them immediately rode off in the direction of
company headquarters. She knew that in a matter of moments
the entire fort would learn that Analisa de la Vega had just
ridden into Sully in the arms of a Sioux brave. She could tell by
the wary expression in the soldiers' eyes that they had no idea
the formidable figure who held her firmly against him was none
other than the soft-spoken Don Ricardo. Somehow the thought
of becoming the subject of idle gossip meant little to her this
time, and she knew that it was because of Caleb.

It was impossible to recognize him as Don Ricardo now. She
smiled up into his stormy blue eyes. Caleb's long hair hung free
about his shoulders. Buckskin leggings clung to his thighs. A
finely sewn shirt of the same material hung open and exposed
his smooth bronze chest, the fringe adorning the sleeves
swaying with his every movement, and hide moccasins protected his feet. The red bandanna was tied jauntily about his
throat, a startling contrast to the natural buff-colored clothing
fashioned from hides.

Now as they stood together, ready to enter the house, she
turned to face him and placed her open palm against his heart as
he reached around her for the doorknob. Caleb stopped and
stared down at her.

"I love you, Caleb," she whispered. "Thank you for loving
such a hard-headed woman."

Eyes wide, she watched his lips until they met her own in a
swift, firm kiss.

"I love you, too. Don't ever forget it." He kissed her quickly
once again. "Besides, I knew you needed a keeper the first time
I laid eyes on you." He touched his fingertip to her lower lip.
"You were wearing pants then, too."

She looked down at her hand, which held the bunched
waistband of his trousers against her. She looked back up and
laughed as Caleb patted her behind before he opened the door.

Once inside the house, Analisa tried to take in the scene
before her. The ever-present breeze billowed the curtain out and

away from an open window. Ruth Storm was crawling on hands and knees, her skirt hiked up to allow her to move. Gathering up papers that covered the carpet, she stacked them under various books scattered about the floor to weigh them down, all the while unaware of Caleb and Analisa's entrance.

Across the room, Galileo howled piteously, voicing disgust at being tied with Analisa's apron strings to one of the ladderback chairs near the dining table. Kase knelt on the floor beside the cat's chair, his back to the front door. Unaware of his mother's entrance, he continued to wield a small paintbrush as he attempted to paint the animal's front paw with green watercolor. Pages covered with the boy's earlier artistic endeavors littered the tabletop along with a thin, open tin containing a child's watercoloring set.

While Analisa and Caleb stood unnoticed drinking in the confusion, Abbie Oats appeared in the kitchen doorway, puffed furiously at her clay pipe, and feigned a swat at Kase with her dish towel.

"Untie that creature this minute, lad, or you'll get no dinner from me."

"Aw, Abbie! Ruth said I could paint him." He pointed at the struggling black and white cat.

"Now!" the cook bellowed as she sent him a threatening look. "She meant paint a *picture,* not the cat. You know very well what she meant."

Kase shrugged and began to comply as he fought with the knots in the apron strings. He grumbled to himself as he worked.

"She should have *said* what she meant."

"Kase Van Meeteren Storm!"

Analisa stepped forward, embarrassed by her son's apparent lack of respect for the cook. What had happened to the orderly home she'd left only two days before? At the sound of her voice, pandemonium broke loose as Ruth, Kase, and Abbie all spoke at once.

"Mama!"

"It's about time!" Abbie barked.

"Oh, Caleb!" Ruth rose, papers forgotten, and moved across the room to greet them.

Galileo gave one last howl before he wriggled free of his bonds, and Kase ran to his mother, grabbed her around the knees, and held on. She lifted him up and hugged him to her, pressing her cheek against his. He pulled away and planted a kiss on her lips before he turned to greet Caleb.

"Kase!" Startled, Analisa stared at the boy's face. "What happened?"

A blue-green shadow darkened the hollow beneath his left eye.

"Nothing," Kase said. "What happened to you?" He traced the bruise on the side of her face.

"I fell down. Now tell me what happened."

Caleb broke away from Ruth's welcoming embrace and caught the boy's chin in his hand. Analisa felt her stomach knot as she inspected her son's black eye, fearing he'd been forced to face prejudice so soon.

"What happened, Kase?" The seriousness of Caleb's tone warned the women not to interfere.

"I ran into a gate at the stables." The boy met his stepfather's stare straight on. "I did not cry, though. Zach said I could if I felt like it, but I didn't."

Both Caleb and Analisa looked to Ruth for confirmation.

She nodded. "That's really all that happened." She tousled the boy's midnight-black hair, which was cropped in an even line just above his eyebrows. "He's going to watch where he's going from now on, aren't you, dear?"

"*Ja.*" With a final hug, Kase looked at his mother. "Put me down, Mama." When she complied, he stared up at Caleb, studied the man intently for a moment, then in a piping voice asked, "Why do you look like a dirty Red Indian, Papa?"

With the important business at hand, Analisa knew full well that Caleb could ill afford to spare even a moment and so was touched when he knelt down and spoke to Kase with quiet patience.

"Where did you learn those words, Kase? Dirty Red Indian?"

The boy looked at Caleb with uncertainty, puzzled by his concerned expression. "From the other boys."

"What do they mean? Do you know?" Caleb laid his hand gently on the youngster's shoulder.

Kase shrugged, glanced at his mother, and continued, "The Red Indians are those people that live out there." He pointed in the direction of the agency, which lay a few miles away. "They dress like you are now. They kill people and cut off their hair and roast 'em.''

Eyes smarting with tears, Analisa pivoted and moved to the table where she began stacking up her son's paintings. Abbie moved to her side immediately and began to help while Ruth remained beside Caleb and listened while he spoke quietly to Kase.

"You went to the agency once with Zach and your mama. Did you see the Indians there?''

"*Ja.*''

"What were they like?''

"Huh?''

"What were they like?'' Caleb pressed him.

The boy shrugged. "People.''

"What else?''

"I played with them.''

"Did they hurt you?''

"No.''

"Did you see them hurt anyone?''

Kase shook his head.

"They are just like you and me and Mama. There are good and bad Indians, just as there are good and bad people in every land.'' Caleb sighed and stood up, looking down at the boy's open, upturned face. He cupped Kase's cheek in his long brown hand, his thumb gently tracing the bruise beneath the boy's eyes. "I don't want you to call them dirty Red Indians ever again. Never call anyone names, Kase.''

"No, Papa.'' He dropped his gaze to the floor. "I'm sorry.''

Caleb placed his forefinger beneath the boy's chin and tilted his face upward. Their eyes met again. Analisa watched silently from across the room and felt her heart trip at the sight.

"And always look people in the eye when you say you are sorry, so they know you mean it.'' Caleb smiled down at Kase to lighten the mood before he went on to explain his appearance. "I am dressed like this because I have been living with the Sioux Indians. It is part of my job.''

"Mama, too?''

Caleb glanced in Analisa's direction and sent her a wry smile. "She thinks it is her job, too.'' He laughed, and the seriousness of the moment passed. He then issued instructions to the child. "Go clean up that mess while I talk to Ruth.''

Hurrying to do as he was told, Kase ran to the table. Caleb strode across the room to lower the window, and Ruth sat on the settee and watched the fluttering pages of her work settle to the carpet.

"Why didn't I think of that?" she asked of no one in particular. Patting the top of her head, she swiftly located her glasses and, satisfied that they were securely anchored in her hair, left them there. She looked first at Caleb and then at Analisa, her snapping hazel eyes taking in every detail of their disheveled appearance as well as Analisa's bruises. "What happened to you two?"

Abbie crossed the room to stand, hands on hips, and listen to the exchange. A ring of smoke hovered over her head as she puffed nervously on her pipe. Analisa glanced up, too exhausted to remind the woman she was to smoke only in the kitchen or outdoors. Abbie remained standing while Analisa lowered herself to sit beside Ruth on the settee.

"I'm done!" Kase announced before Caleb could begin.

"Good," Caleb said. "Now go outside and sit with Scorpio. I had to leave him out in front of the house. Be sure he doesn't eat your mama's flowers."

Kase folded his arms across his chest, stood his ground, and stared pointedly at Caleb. He crooked an eyebrow and studied the man before he asked, "How come every time the grown-ups talk, you tell me to go outside and see Scorpio?"

Caleb turned to Analisa and indicated the boy with a nod of his head. "He's yours all right." Then to Kase: "Go."

With a deeply exaggerated sigh, the boy scuffed out of the room and the door closed soundlessly behind him.

After briefly relating their experiences, Caleb quickly outlined his mission at Sully for Ruth and Abbie. After giving them the essential facts in the case, he turned to Ruth for help. He continued to stand beside the settee.

"What do you think of Williamson, Ruth? Do you trust him? Could he be involved with Hardy?"

Ruth did not hesitate before she answered. "No. I've gotten to know him quite well since I've been here, and I truly believe he is too honest to become involved in illegal dealings. After all, he's only here to relieve General Stanley while he is in the east. Besides, he's a Libra." When they both stared blankly, she explained, "He's a romantic; he's sensitive and, very judicious. I don't think he would support or even condone the agent's actions.''

Caleb reached down and began to rub Analisa's neck and shoulders as he spoke. She felt the tenseness in her muscles dissipate with the strong kneading of his fingers.

''Why do you ask, Caleb?'' Ruth wanted to know.

''I'll need his help. Either that, or I'll have to use the power given me to commandeer a company of his men.'' He glanced down at Analisa. ''You look exhausted.''

With this declaration, she realized how tired she was. The warmth of his hand against her skin and the steady movement of his fingers as they worked her stiff muscles quickly suffused her with lethargy. His fingers gently crept up and lightly brushed the dark bruise along the side of her cheek and then the one he had inflicted on her jaw. His touch made her forget the presence of others, and she turned her head, raising her shoulder, to bring his fingers to her lips. The kiss was quick, a gentle, reassuring movement, intended to show her forgiveness. Analisa looked up to see Ruth smiling warmly.

''I'm sure the major would be more than willing to help,'' Ruth said, her eyes on her stepson once again.

An insistent pounding on the back door commanded their attention, and Abbie hurried to answer the summons.

Almost immediately following the silence that ensued, someone began knocking on the front door. It was Ruth's turn to rise. As she opened the door to admit Frank Williamson, Abbie returned to the room with Zach Elliot, who trailed behind her, hat in hand.

Caleb turned toward the front door, while Analisa acknowledged Zach with a smile and a nod and was surprised to see his sun-roughened face smile back at her.

''Welcome home.'' Zach spoke so softly that she was forced to read the words as they were shaped by his lips. His eye seemed to question her as he took in her appearance, and she felt the need to cross the room to explain it to him. Although until now they had only shared a silent respect for each other, Analisa knew by the look on the scout's face that she had somehow earned his friendship. Frank Williamson demanded attention, though, and so her chance to speak directly with Zach was lost as she listened to the major's inquiry.

''I think it's about time someone let me in on what's going

on here." He stood tall and commanding in the center of the room, his hands on his hips, legs spread wide.

Caleb stepped forward, undaunted by Williamson's stature, for he was of an equal height. He sought to put the major at ease, for he knew his own appearance was the cause of Williamson's militaristic attitude.

"You have every right to demand answers, Major. Please come in and sit down."

"I'll stand, thanks." For the first time he acknowledged the women. "Miss Ruth, Mrs. . . . de la Vega." He hesitated using the name as he looked first at Analisa and then at Caleb.

"The name is Storm, Major. Caleb Storm. Analisa is indeed my wife; Ruth is my stepmother."

"And I'm still the cook," Abbie quipped. It was clear that she'd worried and waited for two days and wasn't about to miss this scene. Zach snorted, observing them as he leaned against the kitchen doorway.

Caleb remained standing and began to explain. "I'm an undercover agent for the Bureau of Indian Affairs, Major, sent out here expressly for the purpose of investigating Buff Hardy. We suspected him of withholding government funds and supplies meant for the Sioux in his care, and we believe he was responsible for the disappearance of one of our agents."

"Can you prove it?"

"I believe I can, once he's under arrest. I do know he is guilty of extortion, buying white captives as well as Indians, and selling them back to their families or into slavery in Mexico. Analisa and I have just returned from the camp of the renegade leader, Red Dog. Hardy has dealt with him on more than one occasion, and tomorrow morning he plans to meet me to buy what he assumes are white female prisoners."

Williamson stood speechless. He turned to Ruth as if to silently seek her affirmation of the facts.

"I'm afraid he's right, Major." Ruth spoke softly as she stood beside the commander. "Caleb works for Ely Parker, head of the BIA. I'm sorry we had to keep you in the dark, but Caleb didn't know whom he could trust."

"You have the proper papers, of course?" Williamson's hard stare returned to Caleb.

"Of course." He turned to Analisa. "Anja, the lining in the

lid of my trunk contains a packet of government documents. Will you bring it to me, please?''

Hitching up the bagging trousers, Analisa crossed the room, squeezing Caleb's hand as she passed by. She could hear their voices and searched the trunk with silent motions so as not to miss the exchange of words.

"Were you aware of Hardy's dealings, Major?" Caleb's tone was firm but not accusing.

"Of course not." The major's green eyes flashed above his thick auburn mustache. He brushed his hat against his thigh as he spoke, the brim curled into his palm. "I'll admit there was something I didn't like about the man. He's always whining about a lack of supplies and monies." He turned to Ruth, and his voice was apologetic as he explained. "I know there's no excuse for my ignorance of Hardy's crimes, but I've only been stationed here a few months myself. There's so much to attend to that I'm afraid Hardy was low on my list of priorities."

Ruth looked up at him in understanding. The man's gaze returned to Caleb.

"You realize I have the power to commandeer a detail of men if need be," Caleb was saying. "But I trust that, if what you say about your innocence is true, you'll be more than willing to cooperate?"

Offended by the slur on his character, Williamson blushed nearly as dark as his hair. "*If* what I say is true?" He took a step toward Caleb. "Listen, Storm, or whatever your name is, no one calls me a liar. Especially someone who's been parading around as something he's not for months now." He made a grab for the open front of Caleb's buckskin. Zach stood away from the doorway, ready to move if need be. Analisa watched from just inside the bedroom, afraid of Caleb's temper, tired enough to drop, and wishing this was all over. She never thought she'd see violence in her own home. Before she could utter a protest, she heard Caleb speak. His voice was barely above a whisper, but deadly as he stared Williamson down.

"Take your hand off me."

For a moment Analisa was afraid that neither of them would back down as they stood like a pair of fighting cocks, staring eye to eye. Ruth was dwarfed beside them, but she reached up to touch Frank Williamson's sleeve.

Suddenly the commander of Fort Sully smiled, then winked at Ruth.

"You don't think I'm crazy, do you?" The tension eased and he laughed. "Anybody who had me as fooled thoroughly as you did would know more than his share of fighting tricks." He slapped Caleb on the shoulder and then asked, "Do you know what a bumbling idiot I thought you were? I couldn't figure out how a man like de la Vega ever won such a beautiful wife." He smiled at Analisa as she returned to the room, the large packet in her hand. "Now I know."

"Here are the papers, Major." She handed them over and moved to stand beside Caleb.

After a cursory glance at the material, Williamson spoke. "Everything seems to be in order. Let me know how many men you need, when you need them, and all the details. I plan on riding with you."

"So do I." Zach's gruff voice carried across the room. For the first time Caleb and Williamson acknowledged the scout's presence.

Caleb turned to question him. "Do you know Hardy personally, Zach? Did you have any knowledge of his dealings?" Caleb glanced at him sharply, awaiting an answer.

"Let's just say I have a score to settle with him," Zach said, crossing his arms over his chest.

Caleb stared, waiting for Zach to elaborate.

Finally the scout spoke again. "I've seen Hardy's slave trade dealin's. I rode with the Comanch' down in Texas years ago, even married one." Zach shrugged, trying unsuccessfully to hide his hurt. "Hardy was responsible for the death of two of the people closest to me."

He glanced in Analisa's direction for a brief second before his eyes met Caleb's evenly. "Let's just say I got a stake in Hardy's future. Or lack of it."

"I want Hardy alive. He's going back to Washington to stand trial." Caleb looked at each of the men in turn.

"Agreed," Williamson quickly assented.

Caleb turned to Zach. The man was silent as if Caleb's statement weighed heavily on his mind. Finally he spoke. "He'll get what's coming to him?"

Caleb went to stand directly across the table from Zach Elliot.

"He'll get what's coming to him. I'll see to that. So will the others like him."

"We'll take him alive, then."

"Well, now," Ruth spoke up as the tension visibly eased from Caleb's shoulders, "I'm sure you men have plans to make, but they'll be best made after you've all had some supper."

Analisa watched Ruth move among the tall men like a small brown squirrel, her eyes sharp and bright, and marveled at the way she could pull everyone together in a crisis. She briskly took command of all of them and began issuing orders in much the same way she had the day Analisa met her.

"Analisa, you look ready to drop. I'll start heating water for your bath, and I want you to go in and take those things off and lie down until it's hot. Abbie, add to the supper, enough for an army." Smiling at her own joke, Ruth turned to the major, and Analisa knew by their expressions that they were fast becoming more than acquaintances. "Caleb, sit down before you fall down, and—Mr. Elliot, is it?—please go spit that wad of tobacco out before you sit down to dinner."

Analisa watched in admiration as the men obeyed Ruth's imperious commands. Suddenly she was certain that if she did not lie down soon she, too, would fall down. Every muscle in her body cried out in pain and exhaustion. Barely able to clutch the sagging waistband any longer, she entered her bedroom on slow, shuffling feet and turned to close the door. Caleb stood framed in the doorway behind her. She had not heard him follow her.

Silently he stepped inside and closed the door. He leaned forward and pried her hands from the waistband and drew the trousers down over her hips until they fell into a puddle at her feet.

"Step."

She stepped out of them.

"Raise your arms."

She raised them, and he drew the shirt up over her head and tossed it aside. She felt herself sway and fought to keep her eyes open.

He folded back the quilted coverlet, and the bright splash of tulips disappeared from sight.

"Get in."

Analisa looked at the pillow with longing. She stretched her arms forward as if diving into a shallow pool and slid between the cool, crisp sheets. The delicate scent of violet talcum clung to the pillow that cradled her head. The feeling was far better than she'd imagined.

"I've never gone to bed dirty before," she mumbled into the pillow.

"Forget the bath, Anja." Caleb's lips touched her face with a soft caress. His tongue traced the outline of her ear, and then he kissed the soft, vulnerable spot just below it. "Get some sleep. *Ik houd van jou.*"

Her husband's voice whispering the Dutch words, I love you, floated with her into her dreams.

"Aren't you finished yet?"

Caleb called out to her from the bed where he lay propped up against the headboard, his hair washed and brushed to a fine silken sheen, his upper torso dark copper against the pillow at his back. He was covered with the bedclothes from the waist down, his hands locked behind his head as he waited for Analisa to finish her bath.

"I'll never be clean again." She spoke to him from behind the folding screen, the sounds of her splashing loud in the stillness of the night. The other occupants of the tiny house were all in bed. They would rise long before dawn.

"Clean by whose standards? Did anyone ever tell you that too much washing could be unhealthy?"

"*Ja?* You were in here for nearly half of an hour."

"And how would you know? You were still asleep."

"I woke up off and on and you were splooshing and sploshing away."

He heard water sloshing over the side of the tub and then the padding of her feet on the floorboards. Caleb could see his wife's nude silhouette outlined on the chintz screen as she toweled herself dry, and he felt his blood warm to the sight.

Her hand reached up to grab the nightgown that hung over the top of the screen. Seconds passed before she emerged and walked to the dresser, all the while roughly towel-drying her hair.

"What did I miss while I slept?" she asked, bending forward from the waist to fling her hair down toward the floor. Without looking, she felt around on the surface of the dresser, closed her fingers over the hairbrush, and began to work through the tangles in her hair.

"Why do you comb your hair upside down?"

Her answer was a short, lilting laugh. Ignoring his question, she repeated hers. "What did I miss, Caleb?"

"I told Zach exactly where I plan to meet Hardy. He knew where I meant and left tonight with Williamson and eight of his men. They'll be there well before Hardy arrives."

"There is no way Hardy will find out?"

"That could only happen if the major or Zach sends word to him, but they seem sincere. The other men will not be told of their destination or the assignment. They'll find out when they get there. Tor Jensen is going along with them as one of the eight."

"When will *we* leave?"

He shifted his gaze to stare up at the ceiling. He'd been adamant during the dinner discussion, arguing all the while against the women going along. Analisa had slept through dinner and the planning, but Ruth had insisted that the two of them should pose as captives. Outnumbered, Caleb argued that soldiers disguised as women would work just as well, but even the major and Zach Elliot had insisted that Hardy might sense a trap if the women he was to buy were bundled and covered and appeared at all suspicious. Even the fact that Hardy had briefly met Ruth at the dance and knew Analisa on sight could not dissuade the group around the table.

Ruth decided that Abbie would stay home and take care of Kase. Caleb, Analisa, and Ruth would leave before dawn in order to arrive at the rendezvous site ahead of Hardy. If all went well, Zach and the soldiers would by then be hidden among the rocks along the rise.

"Caleb?" Analisa was still standing before the mirror awaiting his answer.

Caleb hesitated. God, he didn't want her to go tomorrow. An ominous feeling nagged at him, pulled at his guts, and warned him not to take the women, but he'd been urged by the others to use reason and go against his instinct. When had this whole affair gotten away from him? he wondered. It had been hard for him to acquiesce to the group decision at dinner, but although he knew full well he had the final say, Caleb knew, too, that the others were probably right. The women were needed. He just hated to admit it. Hated to think that he was willfully putting Analisa and Ruth in danger.

A sigh escaped him before he realized it. He watched her as she began to braid her hair into the long honey-gold rope she sometimes wore down her back.

"Leave it loose." *I'm beginning to bark orders like a general,* he thought, and added, "Please."

She did as he asked and picked up the brush to loosen the beginnings of the braid. He had not moved, his hands still locked behind his head as he lay reviewing every detail of tomorrow's rendezvous.

"We *are* going with you, aren't we?"

He lowered his arms, stretched, and then pulled her close to him. "Yes. But I have to tell you that I'm against it, Anja." He looked down at her. "At the first sign of trouble, I want you to head out of there. You'll be on the lead pack horse, so you'll have to ride like hell and be sure Ruth is behind you."

Her breath was warm against his shoulder as she spoke. "Nothing will happen to us, Caleb. You worry too much."

"Ha!"

"Your hair is very soft without that grease on it."

"You're changing the subject again."

"I think maybe I hear an argument coming, that's why." She ran her fingers through his hair, pulled it back into a queue, then spread it out against the pillow. "Will you cut it off when this is over?"

He nodded.

She sighed. "I think I will miss it."

Caleb felt her left hand move across his chest before it slipped down to rest on his stomach. When he looked at her again, she was staring up into his eyes; her own were twin pools of aquamarine aglow in the light from a single lamp. Her lips were slightly parted, waiting, and he knew he could not resist her invitation. He dipped his head to taste the nectar of her kiss, his tongue slowly tracing the outline of her lips. He watched her lashes flutter as her eyes closed and she lost herself in his kiss. He rolled to his side and pressed himself against her length, capturing her face between his hands. Her arms slipped up around his neck, her fingers threading through his hair. Caleb took his time, savoring every sensation that rocked through him. Nose to nose, heart to heart, thigh pressed to thigh, they clung to each other, making no demands, just sharing the moment. As the kiss ended, Caleb pulled away to rest his cheek against hers and stare into the shadows.

"What did I do before I had you?" he whispered.

She hugged him close. "Rode around and caught the measles," she whispered back.

"Anja, do you know how much I love you?" He reached up to tuck a stray lock behind her ear. "Sometimes I'm overwhelmed when I realize how dear you are to me. I never expected to love anyone this much. I didn't even know I could."

"Just as I love you, Caleb. I never thought anyone could love me, not after all that had happened, and yet you came to me and brought this amazing love of yours . . . and you share it with Kase. For that I love you even more."

He put aside thoughts of the morrow as his fingers began to tangle in the satin bow at the neck of her nightgown.

"I thought you were tired," she whispered, her hands replacing his to free the knot he'd made.

"Not anymore, sweetheart."

"Sweetheart? I never heard you say that word before."

"A man in love says many things." He pulled aside her gown and lowered his head to her breast.

"I like it better when you stop talking."

And so he did.

Chapter Twenty-Two

Caleb rode ahead of the women as he led them over the flat terrain clotted with thick tufts of buffalo grass. Analisa followed directly behind, clinging to the rope halter of the pack horse, fighting to keep her balance. She rode bareback and astride, her skirts hiked up and bunched about her knees. A good inch of her calves showed white between the hem of her dress and the tops of the socks that extended above a pair of Abbie's black shoes. Analisa had refused to wear her best gray kid shoes after the Sioux women had taken her old black high-tops. Abigail had stuffed a pair of her own with straw and handed them to Analisa, insisting she wear them. Over her worn yellow calico, she wore a dark shirt of Caleb's that nearly covered her dress entirely.

Her hair was tangled by the incessant wind that gathered the steely gray clouds above them. She glanced down at a fall of

hair that hung over her shoulder. Her gaze returned to it
countless times that morning, yet she never failed to be startled
by its brassy orange-red shade. Her honey-gold tresses had been
rinsed with henna at Ruth and Abbie's insistence; it had taken
no little persuasion to convince Analisa that the color would
rinse out easily and that she needed it to keep Hardy from
recognizing her. She'd been adamant, stubbornly refusing to
pour the henna concoction over her hair until Caleb threatened
to leave them behind unless they hurried. Closeted in Ruth's
room long before dawn, the two women had collaborated on
each other's disguises, Ruth's flair for the dramatic tempered by
Analisa's subtle restraint.

Careful not to lose her balance, Analisa turned to glance over
her shoulder at Ruth, who was riding a mule. The mule's lead
rope was tied securely to Analisa's lead, which Caleb held
loosely in one hand. Analisa had sworn to Caleb that at the first
sign of trouble she would lead Ruth to safety. She could not help
smiling through her nervousness as she looked back at Ruth.
Caleb's stepmother reminded Analisa of a painting she'd once
seen of a Gypsy caravan. Ruth's curling, silver-streaked mahogany hair was unbound and hung in wild disarray about her
shoulders. A silk scarf of midnight blue was wound about the
crown of her head and tied behind her right ear, the ends left to
trail behind. She'd refused to wear her glasses.

Caleb led them toward a hilly area that had appeared on the
horizon. They'd been traveling southward since dawn. The
river, always to their right, was well hidden by cottonwoods and
thick growth along the banks.

Analisa let her gaze roam over the tall, broad-shouldered man
riding before her, his senses attuned to every sight and sound
around them. She knew Caleb was not afraid. He would never
fear such a confrontation. The entire mission was well plotted,
the product of much thought and planning. She sensed a
hesitation in him, though, and a reluctance brought on by the
fact that the others had forced him to agree that the women were
a necessary part of the plan.

Although she realized the burden her presence placed on
him, Analisa knew, too, that she could not have waited at home
for Caleb to return. She had no doubt that this venture would
succeed, for she never questioned his ability to bring Hardy to
justice. But she did know that in this, as in all things, there were

factors over which they had no control. Whatever the outcome, she was convinced that the meeting with the agent was necessary. She wanted Hardy caught and convicted as much as or more than anyone else involved. The fear and anxiety she had suffered over the years since her brother and sister were taken captive only stoked her anger at Hardy's crimes. That he had preyed upon the hapless victims of similar tragedies made him less than human in her eyes.

Caleb slowed his horse and waved Analisa up beside him.

"We are nearly there." His eyes searched her face as he spoke. "Stay behind me and try to keep your eyes down. I don't think Hardy will be there yet, but let's not take any chances. He might recognize you."

"I understand."

His eyes took in her face and the brassy color of her hair. "God that's awful," he announced and shook his head in disbelief. "Thank God it's not permanent."

"I know."

"Are you scared, Anja?"

"No." She answered honestly and knew he believed her.

"Good. You need to keep your wits about you." He bobbed his head toward his stepmother. "You are supposed to be captives, remember. Be sure to tell Ruth not to look as if she's enjoying this so much."

Analisa nodded and smiled back at him.

"From here on out, no more smiles," he warned, "and no more talking."

"How much farther is it?"

"A couple of miles." He pointed up ahead. "Do you see that low ridge of hills? Zach should have the men scattered just behind the rocks and trees at their base. We're going to meet Hardy in the open, and we're going to stay in sight of the men. Once Hardy pays me off, I'll let him lead you a few feet away before I signal Williamson." He reached out to caress Analisa's cheek. His touch was warm and gentle and matched the blue fire blazing in his eyes.

"All set?" Caleb asked.

"*Ja*. It will be the first time I see you arrest a criminal."

"And the last."

"Maybe."

He signaled Scorpio with a slight movement of his knees, and the horse lunged forward, pulling Analisa's and Ruth's mounts along behind. They covered the two miles of open ground in no time at all, and before Analisa could even think of becoming frightened they had arrived at the meeting site. As they neared the low hills that rose from the open plain like lazy giant buffalo, Analisa could see Hardy's squat, rotund figure seated on his mount in the center of a small grove of trees. Two of his men were beside him. Beyond him, large boulders and rocks lined the sides of the low hills. Smaller, gnarled trees clung to the rocky ground, their roots like twisted fingers clutching for a hold in the soil. She glanced up quickly, searching for some sign of the men hidden there. She saw nothing that even hinted at their presence.

While they approached Hardy she kept her eyes downcast and tossed her head forward, letting the hideous orange hair partly cover her face. She was unable to watch Hardy as he rode forward to meet them, but tried instead to steal glances at his two companions. They were his Indian police, dressed in dark blue coats adorned with an array of shining brass buttons and epaulets. Their legs were bare beneath the hems of the coats, and they wore long white loincloths and ankle-high beaded moccasins. One cradled a rifle in the crook of his arm while the other rested his upright, the stock against his knee.

The men reined in their mounts as the parties met and remained on horseback. Analisa turned around to see how Ruth had survived the ride. Ruth's face was now streaked with dirt and sweat, which enhanced her disguise. At the sound of Hardy's voice Analisa turned around again, keeping her head bowed. She told herself that in a very few minutes it would all be over.

"I brought two women. Did you bring the gold, Agent?" As Caleb spoke, he held his own rifle ready, the barrel aimed casually at Hardy.

The man chose not to answer Caleb, but instead drew a bag of coins up by its rawhide drawstrings from where it hung over the pommel of his saddle. He tossed it at Caleb, who caught it deftly with his free hand. He weighed it in his palm and then loosened the ties with his teeth.

He addressed Hardy in broken English.

"Plenty gold in here, Agent. I'll make trade."

"Where'd you pick 'em up?" Hardy nodded toward the silent women.

Analisa listened to the exchange and wondered if they should be sitting like cattle awaiting their fate or arguing with the men. After all, she thought, if she were truly being sold to the agent she would indeed protest rather than sit idly by and watch the exchange.

Ruth must have had the same notion, for Analisa heard her cry out to Hardy in a tight voice, "My family will pay whatever you ask if you'll only write to them!" Theatrical sobbing rode on the air behind Analisa.

Hardy spared her barely a glance filled with disdain and prodded Caleb again. "I said, where'd you pick 'em up, boy?"

Analisa watched her husband's fingers tighten around the lead rope.

"Near Fort Randall."

"How long ago?"

"Three, maybe four days."

"Funny," Hardy mused, "I haven't had word of any raids around there. Place would be buzzin' with news by now if anyone was missin' these women."

"One don't speak English. The old one talks too much." Caleb spoke loud enough for the women to hear his words.

A sudden gust of wind swirled the dust around the horses' hooves. Analisa pulled the shirt tight around her and noted the darkness that crept over the hills. Giant, splashing droplets began to fall around them. They slapped against the backs of her hands as she held the horse's reins.

"If you're satisfied with the gold," Hardy said, "I'll take the women now. I don't relish getting soaked."

He signaled one of his men with a wave of his hand, and the man rode forward to take the lead rope from Caleb. Without even inspecting the merchandise he'd purchased, Hardy rode past the women. The Indian tugged on the lead rope as he passed by, and the women's mounts wheeled around to follow. Hardy's second companion followed behind Ruth.

They hadn't gone ten yards before Caleb called out, "Hardy!"

At the new, commanding tone in Caleb's voice, Hardy drew his horse to a halt and half turned in his saddle. Sensing danger, he signed to his men, who swiftly turned their rifles on Caleb. Analisa's heart stopped as she sat frozen and watched the exchange.

"I wouldn't try it, Hardy." Caleb's clear, concise English rang out above the gathering storm. "I've got the barrel of this rifle aimed at your gut. Even if your men get off a shot you'll be dead before I am. I'm placing you under arrest in the name of the United States government." Caleb rode toward them, his eyes locked with Hardy's. The man made no move to comply.

"Tell them to drop the guns, Hardy."

Buff Hardy stared at Caleb, his face flushed with color, his rat's eyes skimming from Caleb to the women and back again.

"If my word's not good enough for you, maybe you'd better take a look over there." Caleb nodded toward the hills, but never took his eyes off the agent.

A few yards away, men in army uniforms dotted the hillside, advancing with rifles at the ready. Analisa recognized Tor and Frank Williamson at once, for they were much taller than the others. Zach was riding forward, leading a string of horses, as the men ran down the hill dodging boulders and trees.

"You can't prove anything," Hardy blustered.

"I have a bag of gold that says I can. Tell them to drop the guns." Then, without waiting for Hardy's command, Caleb spoke rapidly to Hardy's policemen in Sioux. They lowered their rifles, and the elder of the two answered. His words seemed to reassure Caleb. When she saw that Caleb no longer pressed the men to drop their guns, Analisa knew they had agreed to cooperate with him. They cradled the rifles and moved away from Hardy. The man holding the lead rope to Analisa's and Ruth's mounts dropped it as he maneuvered his horse away from the agent's.

Rain pelted them now, falling in steady streams. Analisa wiped the hair away from her eyes and then stared at the palm of her hand. The henna ran rust red, staining her fingers and dripping on her bodice and skirt. She tugged on the lead rope connected to her own bridle and pulled Ruth's mule up beside her.

"Dismount, Hardy!" Caleb shouted over the increasing sound of the wind and rain before he sprang to the ground.

Zach arrived and shouldered his horse between Analisa's and Scorpio, keeping a wary eye on Hardy. Analisa was thankful for his presence and let herself relax somewhat, the first time since they had left the fort.

"We did it!" Ruth called out to her.

Hardy stood on the ground now, his lips clamped in a tight line, refusing to speak to anyone. Caleb was tying the agent's hands behind him, all the while grimly listing the man's offenses.

". . . and if that's not enough, Hardy, we're going to prosecute you for the murder of a BIA agent, one Chuck Reynolds, missing for nearly two years."

"Try it." The man fairly spat the words at Caleb.

"We intend to."

"Looks like we've got trouble comin'," Zach called to Caleb and pointed toward the north.

A mounted band of Sioux was fast approaching the group. Five riders were bearing down upon them. Analisa motioned to Ruth, who watched with wide-eyed fascination as the group thundered closer. All of them were armed with rifles or long lances decorated with feathers. A woman rode at the front of the riders beside the leader, her long hair plaited into two braids, her legs exposed to the thigh as she sat astride her horse. They seemed oblivious to the pouring rain that turned the ground to mud beneath their horses' hooves.

The soldiers, still on foot, surrounded Caleb, Buff Hardy, and the two women, and raised their rifles in readiness. Analisa had nowhere to run, trapped as she was by the troops around them. She looked to the right and saw Frank Williamson. Their eyes met, and he motioned to her as he stepped away from the man beside him. The opening he left for her was just wide enough for the horses to pass through. She glanced back at the approaching Sioux, then at Caleb who had yet to react at all.

"Hold your fire," Caleb called out in a low voice, and Frank Williamson repeated the command to his men as he shouldered his way toward Caleb.

"Red Dog?" the major asked when he reached Caleb's side.

"Yes. Have your men stay calm. We don't want an all-out war on our hands."

As Caleb spoke, Analisa looked up and recognized the young Sioux chief riding beside the woman. The picture was a striking one. The woman sat her horse as regally as the man, her dark eyes burning with undisguised hatred. Even the impulsive young leader, Red Dog, appeared less hostile than his female companion. Recognizing her suddenly as Mia, Hardy's maid, Analisa remembered all that Caleb had told her concerning his own part in the woman's rescue. Mia looked far different riding beside Red Dog than she had in the ostentatious surroundings of Hardy's house. She radiated such power that Analisa could not take her eyes off the girl.

Ruth leaned close to Analisa and asked in a voice barely above a whisper, "Who is she?"

"Red Dog's woman. She was Hardy's . . . slave." There was no other way Analisa could explain the girl's relationship to the agent. Ruth understood immediately.

"She's magnificent," Ruth commented.

Analisa nodded, wiped the streaming rainwater from her eyes, and watched as the gap between the two parties lessened.

The Sioux showed no signs of hostility. Their rifles remained lowered, their lances pointed toward the sky as they reined in to face the men.

Red Dog called out to Caleb in Sioux. Zach translated rapidly for the others.

"Raven's Shadow. You have the man Hardy. I claim him."

Caleb did not move away from Hardy but spoke to the young renegade from where he stood. His voice was strong enough to carry above the wind and rain without shouting.

"I have come from Washington. Even there we have heard of this man's crimes. I was sent here to make peace with you and your people, to be sure that the Sioux were given the goods promised by Washington. Hardy must be taken back to the East to face the high chiefs of the government. They will deal with him. All of the people must be made aware of his crimes."

Red Dog stared down at Caleb, his expression scornful. "The white man's justice is not good enough. We, the Sioux, are entitled to this man."

Analisa looked at Caleb. He had not moved, had not looked away from Red Dog's stare. His hands remained at his sides. As far as she could see, he was determined not to relinquish Hardy to the Sioux leader.

"You will have to take him from me, Red Dog."

As Zach's translation died on the wind, Analisa gasped, her eyes riveted on the tall warrior whose fury was so evident in his flashing eyes. Still he did not move as Caleb continued.

"Know that if you try, more will die here today, men of both sides, fighting over a man who is not worth the loss of even one life. I swear to you on my own life, on my honor, that he will be brought to justice. I ask you to trust me."

All was silent until thunder crashed in the distance. Red Dog stared at Caleb, who stood unwavering. Rain streamed from his hair. His clothing was soaked and plastered to his skin. The soldiers in blue were frozen in poses of readiness, their fingers poised on the slippery triggers of their rifles. Ruth's mule skittered nervously, nudging the side of Analisa's mount. To Analisa the entire scene seemed to have been captured in time; it was real and yet unreal, like the images in a photograph.

Caleb spoke again, his words echoed in English as Zach translated.

"Hardy will be replaced here by an agent who will deal fairly with all Sioux who sign a new treaty and agree to come into the agency."

"Another like him will come," Red Dog said.

"I give my word, the new agent will be an honest man."

"The word of a half-breed. The word of one who sought to deceive us. I was never fooled by you, Raven's Shadow. I knew you were not what you claimed."

"I had to find proof the white judges would believe. Now I have Hardy, and he will stand trial in Washington. It is time the fighting and running stopped, Red Dog. Your people need food. They want peace. At least try it."

Red Dog sat deep in thought. Analisa sensed that the young man wanted to believe Caleb, and she could guess what a weight he had to bear, with the responsibility of so many on his shoulders. She glanced at Mia and saw the dark hatred that burned in the woman's eyes as she looked at Hardy. The Sioux woman sat rigid, her eyes feverish with revenge. The men's attention was riveted on Caleb and Red Dog. Hardy stood all but ignored while his fate hung in the balance.

As Analisa stared at Mia she sensed a change in the woman's expression; the slightest, almost imperceptible hint of a smile teased the girl's lips. A cruel smile, a smile of death. Mia's hand moved stealthily toward her waist. No one else moved, or noticed. Analisa watched in disbelief as the girl drew a small revolver from her beaded belt.

"Caleb!"

Analisa's scream rang out a heartbeat before the gunshot rent the air around them. The Indian ponies pawed the earth, and Analisa's own horse jerked its head up with a start. She clung to the reins as she fought to maintain control. When she looked up again, chaos reigned around her. A stray shot echoed on the air, and Major Williamson called out, "Hold your fire!" Ruth shouted something Analisa could not understand above the uproar.

Red Dog held Mia against him, her wrist in his grasp as he forced her to let go of the gun. Analisa turned away from them, fully expecting to see Hardy lying in the mud. Instead, Caleb lay near the hooves of Zach's horse. Hardy stood rooted to the spot, having narrowly escaped death when Caleb stepped into the bullet's path.

Analisa tried to dismount but only succeeded in catching the toe of one oversize shoe in the hem of her skirt. She tripped forward and over, half jumping, half sliding into the mud. Wiping her muddied hands on her skirt, she pushed her way past the crowd gathering around her husband. Her mind was blank, no sound issuing from her lips as she hurried to Caleb. Frank Williamson rose from where he bent over Caleb's silent form, his emerald eyes haunted and searching as they met hers.

"My God, Analisa. He's dead."

Chapter Twenty-Three

Moving like a sleepwalker, Analisa brushed past Frank
Williamson's outstretched hands toward her fallen husband.
Kneeling at his side, her senses numbed by the shock of the
major's pronouncement, Analisa was oblivious of the mud and
the steadily falling rain. She barely heard the voices shouting
around her. All she saw was Caleb. Her heart pounded out the
echo of Williamson's words. *He's dead. He's dead. He's dead.*

"Elliot, make certain none of those people leave!" the major
demanded. In rapid-fire Sioux, Zach began to speak to Red
Dog's men who sat in stony silence.

"Hays. Riley. Get the prisoner mounted and ready to ride. I
want no less than four of you around him at all times."

Analisa became aware of a presence beside her and looked
over to find Ruth kneeling nearby, staring down at Caleb, one
hand pressed against her throat. When her eyes met Analisa's,

Ruth shook her head in disbelief and then covered her face with her hands.

Still refusing to believe what was happening around her, Analisa looked at Caleb once again. Blood covered almost the entire right side of his buckskin shirt. The steady rain did little to wash it away, and only served to spread the oozing red stain and carry it dripping into the mud. Caleb's usual high color was now ghostly, his vibrant eyes closed.

As Analisa stared at him, she noticed that his every feature seemed to stand out, one against the other. The thick black lashes were spiked by raindrops and looked like detailed crescents where they rested on his cheeks. His finely tapered nose and full, even lips gave him the appearance of a stone statue. She reached out with shaking fingers to touch him, fully expecting his skin to feel as cold and lifeless as he appeared. The fingertips of her right hand touched his cheek, and she slid them up to caress his face with her palm. His skin felt warm, a sharp contrast to her own cold, wet fingertips.

She watched his eyelids flutter open, and shock waves echoed through her as his deep blue eyes unerringly connected with her own. He did not speak or try to move.

"Oh, Caleb!"

At her joyous whisper, Ruth glanced up, startled, in time to see Caleb's eyes close once again.

"My God, Analisa! He's alive." She pressed her hands to Caleb's throat and found his pulse before she continued in a strained voice, "But he won't be for long if we don't hurry."

Analisa stood and, without even a hesitant glance at the men around her, lifted up the skirt of the worn yellow calico and pulled off her petticoat. Avoiding as much of the muddied front as possible, she folded the white material in a great wad and leaned over Caleb once again. As she did, she called out to Zach who immediately dismounted and joined her.

"Cut his shirt open," she demanded and watched as the scout quickly obliged.

Analisa saw the full extent of Caleb's wound for the first time. A small hole pierced his right side between shoulder and chest. She promptly but gently pressed the wadded cotton petticoat against his wound and then drew the stained buckskin shirt across it.

"Hold this," she instructed Ruth. She rose from her knees to stand tall against the gray sky, her hair plastered down by the rain, her dress muddied from knee to ankle, hands clenched at her sides. Analisa called out to Frank Williamson who stood holding the reins of Hardy's horse as the main body of the detail mounted. Red Dog and his band watched in silence, the Indian leader's face set, an unreadable mask. Six soldiers began the journey to Sully, Hardy sheltered between them.

"Major!" Analisa called out in a tone that demanded his attention. Williamson was at her side immediately. "My husband is alive," she said, ignoring his expression of disbelief, barely able to look at him after his too hasty declaration. "I want him moved out of here. Now."

Without another word she was back at Caleb's side. Her own hand ceased shaking as it replaced Ruth's on the makeshift bandage.

"You will not die, Caleb Storm," she whispered fiercely as she leaned near. "You would not dare!" As she brushed his rain-slicked hair off of his forehead, Analisa thought she saw a flicker of a smile on his lips.

Around her all was chaos again. Zach bade the agency Indians to hastily construct a litter out of saplings and army blankets. Analisa insisted Caleb be moved out of the mud, and so Frank Williamson and Tor Jensen gently lifted and wrapped him in a blanket from Tor's bedroll. Within moments, the litter was prepared and another blanket securely lashed to saplings and slung between the agency Indians' mounts. Analisa remained at his side as they carried him to the litter, struggling through the hoof-torn earth in Abbie's oversized shoes, pressing her hand against Caleb's wound as if she could hold life within him by sheer force of will. She knew that Ruth followed closely behind, as unwilling as she to leave Caleb's side.

The men laid Caleb on the litter as tenderly as if they carried a newborn babe. Zach instructed the Sioux agency police with words and signs while Analisa adjusted the sodden blanket that covered her husband. The touch of a hand on her arm made her look up and discover Mia standing beside her. The Sioux woman's expression was suffused with remorse, her dark eyes deeply tinged with sorrow.

"I did not mean—" Mia choked on her words and shook her head as if to deny everything that had happened.

Analisa stared at the woman who had wounded her husband and was silent for a moment while she gathered her shattered nerves. She took a deep breath and adjusted her hand on Caleb's bandage before she spoke.

"The innocent are often harmed by hatred. This is one of those times. Caleb wanted only the best for your people, for his people, too, in both worlds."

Mia's eyes brimmed with tears that quickly spilled over to mingle with the rain on her cheeks. She did not brush them aside before she spoke.

"Red Dog has let the soldiers take Hardy. I have shamed him. He says he will talk of peace to Raven's Shadow, if the man lives."

"He will live," Analisa assured her.

Without another word or gesture, Mia conveyed her sorrow to Analisa, her dark eyes begging forgiveness. A tense, silent moment passed between them before Analisa nodded once to Mia and then turned away, knowing she could not bear to look upon the Sioux woman any longer. Analisa was determined not to allow herself to hate Mia for what she had done. Hate would only poison her own heart as it had Mia's. Besides, she knew Caleb would not want her to carry such hatred, and so she let it go. He needed Analisa's care now as well as love uncluttered by hatred for the woman who'd done him harm.

She watched Zach Elliot approach and sensed by his grim demeanor that he was none too happy with his task.

"Miz Storm, you're gonna have to let the men take him back now. It'd be better if we got movin'."

"Come, Analisa," Ruth added, touching her shoulder in a gesture of comfort. "We must move quickly."

The thought of relinquishing her position beside Caleb's litter tore at her heart, yet she knew she could not walk all the way back to the fort. With a heavy sigh she tested Zach with a look.

"Come on, now, ma'am," he insisted. "They'll make better time without you holdin' them back every step o' the way."

"You'll tell them to take care?"

"I told 'em once and I'll tell 'em again and again if they need remindin'."

Analisa felt her shoulders droop with exhaustion as she looked at her husband's face again and felt as if it were her own life's blood that ebbed away. She asked for Ruth's scarf, carefully eased it beneath and then around Caleb's body, and knotted it to hold the bandage in place.

"You can ride up behind me, ma'am."

Gratefully she acknowledged Zach. "I'd like that, Mr. Elliot. I don't think I could manage alone right now."

Ruth walked beside Analisa to Zach's pony and waited until she was mounted behind the scout. Frank Williamson joined Ruth, and Analisa watched them share a whispered exchange. Soon the remainder of the group was mounted and fell in behind the litter bearers. Frank Williamson offered Ruth his saddled mount and rode bareback on Analisa's pack horse. The one remaining trooper led the pack mules.

Red Dog and his band of warriors followed close behind the small procession of women, soldiers, and agency Indians, all traveling through the rain that had slowed to an irritating drizzle.

"Why do they stay with us?" Analisa asked, nodding toward the renegade band.

Zach answered over his shoulder. "They'll escort us until we get closer to Sully. You don't need to worry. Red Dog's been humiliated enough by the girl's act. He won't tarnish his honor any further by attacking us when we're down. He only wanted Hardy, not a full-out war, but now he's given the agent up to the government to make up for the girl's shootin' your husband."

She did not speak again during the rest of the journey. The uncomfortable ride in clinging, sodden clothing was nearly unbearable, the discomfort only adding to her misery. Although Analisa tried to relax against Zach, knowing full well she would need all of her strength in order to nurse Caleb, she found herself unable to glance away from the litter that carried her husband's prostrate form.

The events of the morning repeated themselves in unbidden fashion in Analisa's mind. How could Caleb be hovering near death? She had feared for his safety since she'd first learned of his mission, but despite her fear she'd never faced the reality of his being critically wounded. Fear and reality were two far different things, she realized. Caleb was the strong one, self-assured and independent despite his status as a man of mixed blood. Why had this happened now? she wondered, as the horses jolted along at the fastest pace Zach felt Caleb could endure. Why now when the promise of a life together stretched before them? It seemed so unfair to think he might be taken from her just when his assignment had come to a close and their lives were no longer overshadowed by his work.

She shook her head to rid herself of such dismal thoughts and felt a shudder run through her. Caleb would not die. She was determined that he should live, for her, for Kase, for the future that stretched before them.

Somehow the next few hours passed and the weary party finally arrived at Fort Sully. Red Dog and his men departed, the young leader giving his word to Zach Elliot and Williamson that he would deal with Raven's Shadow and only Raven's Shadow. The message was clear enough. Should Caleb die, Red Dog would feel no obligation to surrender. Mia was allowed to accompany Red Dog only after Analisa insisted she be released to her people.

"She's responsible for wounding your husband," the major had reminded her unnecessarily. "I'll have her arrested if you want to press charges. Red Dog left the decision up to you."

Analisa answered without hesitation. "She shot Caleb by mistake, Major. I cannot find it in my heart to blame her. Hardy is a cruel man. Heartless. In her place I might have done the same."

She had felt Red Dog's stare across the distance between them when she gave the commander her decision. She met his eyes as she watched the small group of warriors and the woman ride away as proudly as they had thundered across the plain that morning. Analisa wondered what chance she would have had of seeing Meika or Pieter again if she had insisted that Mia be arrested. She wondered, too, how her sister had survived all these years among a people so vastly different from her own, leading a life far removed from the one they had known in Holland.

The small party of bedraggled travelers was greeted at the house by Abbie who could now be fully in her element, the only woman fit to command. Ruth was far too exhausted to exhibit her usual cool authority, and Analisa refused to leave Caleb's side.

The company doctor was there to meet them, alerted by the troopers who had returned earlier with Hardy. The young medic was hardly older than Analisa. His white-blond hair was close cropped and curly, his skin clear and only slightly tanned. She could tell immediately he spent less time out-of-doors than the other soldiers. An evenly trimmed mustache covered his upper lip.

Analisa had met Dr. Matthew Benton soon after she'd arrived at Fort Sully and knew him to be polite as well as friendly toward everyone, civilian and military personnel alike. Shivering, she stood beside him as he ministered to Caleb, amazed at the young man's confidence. His hands were steady as he probed for the bullet buried deep in Caleb's chest. Analisa winced with every move of the long forceps. Finally, Dr. Benton dropped the offending metal on a piece of gauze, swabbed the wound once more, and stitched it closed. Caleb had not regained consciousness. "A blessing," Benton said as he turned bleak eyes on Analisa.

"That's about all I can do, ma'am." He dipped his arms in a pan of sudsy water up to his elbows and then toweled them dry. His gaze held steady as he spoke to her; and for that Analisa was grateful. He dealt with her frankly, and she thanked him for his honesty.

"The bullet may have pierced his lung. I haven't seen anyone recover from this type of wound before, but he's a strong man and miracles have been known to happen."

"*Dank U wel,* Doctor." Analisa extended her hand as he collected his black bag and moved toward the door. "I never believed in miracles, but Caleb has taught me they can happen. He will live."

That the young doctor did not agree with her failed to discourage Analisa. Wearily she turned away from the bedroom door and drifted back to Caleb's bedside. She could hear the others speaking to the doctor in hushed tones beyond the door. The scent of bacon wafted through the house, and Analisa was immediately assailed with nausea. Although she had not eaten since before dawn, the thought of food made her weak.

There was no chair in the room and so she stood staring down at Caleb. His breathing was shallow, his muscular chest bandaged and covered by the sheets, barely rising and falling. She traced his arm, which lay beneath the covers, with her fingertip and then hugged her arms about her. Taking a deep breath, she looked up toward the ceiling and fought the tears that threatened to overwhelm her. Never before had she felt so

alone, so shut out. Even with the house full of people, Caleb's
inability to respond to her was almost more than she could bear.
Analisa knew she would welcome his silence, even his temper,
if only he were conscious and aware that she was beside him.

Outside the gray skies had yet to clear. Their gloomy pall
shrouded the room in shadows. It was nearly dusk, but Analisa
chose not to light the lamp on the dresser. Too tired to go for a
chair, she rubbed her arms again, trying to generate heat in her
frozen limbs. Exhaustion forced her to lean against the wall at
the head of the bed. Her eyes closed wearily and her chin
slumped to her chest. The bedroom door creaked as it opened
slowly; a shaft of light and a current of warm air from the wood
stove in the parlor were ushered in on a draft. Abbie poked her
head into the room, took one look at Analisa standing against
the wall for support, and opened the door wide.

"Come on out of here now, ducks," the old cook encouraged Analisa in a whisper that was overloud in the silent room.
"It's as cold as a well in this room. You need some vittles and
then a bath, and I'll not take no for an answer."

Analisa shook her head but lacked the strength to shake off
the determined cook, who had her by the arm and was leading
her toward the parlor.

"Caleb" was the only word she could utter.

". . . will be asleep anyway and won't know if you're here
nor there." Abbie grabbed Caleb's robe from the wall hook as
she passed by and led Analisa straight through the parlor, where
Ruth was lying on the settee with her eyes closed, and into the
bedroom that Ruth and Abbie shared. A hot washtub of water
stood in the center of the room, a stack of warm towels folded
nearby.

"Get out of that wet dress and get yourself washed and
wrapped up; then come out and I'll give you some supper."
Abbie held up her hand as Analisa started to protest. "You're
not gettin' out of this room until you do."

"Please . . ." Analisa implored and watched the old woman's face soften. ". . . Ask Ruth to sit with Caleb until I can go
back in."

Tears filled Abbie's round blue eyes before she could turn
away and hide them. She looked suddenly old, as her crusty
demeanor crumbled. "You just get in the bath and I'll go sit
with Caleb myself."

As soon as Analisa began stripping the muddied dress from her shoulders, Abigail Oats turned and left the room, hastily wiping her eyes with a corner of her apron.

Four long days passed, days in which Caleb continued to hang on a precipice above the valley of death. The doctor came and went, offering Analisa solace, changing the bandage, and sprinkling medicinal powders on the infected wound. He told Analisa to force water into Caleb and to try to keep his fevered body cool. He could do little else. The old Van Meeteren rocker was moved into the room for Analisa to use, as well as a cot commandeered by the major. Abbie brought her meals in to her. She had to force herself to eat the delicacies. After the first day she allowed Ruth to sit with Caleb while she left the room for fresh air and to stretch muscles cramped from sitting. Kase was her companion, walking at her side whenever she went outdoors to sit on the porch and watch the rain or, if the sky was clear, to wander a few yards along the gravel path that fronted the houses.

During her brief periods outside, Analisa became aware of a change in the attitude of some Fort Sully inhabitants. The most obvious was Millicent Boynton, who no longer spoke to or even acknowledged Analisa. One sunny morning Analisa and Kase were walking slowly along the lane when Millicent returned home, and they crossed paths.

"Good day, Mrs. Boynton," Analisa greeted the pert blonde as she usually did, only to be met with an icy stare of disgust. As Millicent Boynton swept past, she held her skirts aside as if unwilling to let even the hem of her garment brush against Analisa's.

"Why is she mad, Mama?" Kase asked innocently.

Staring at the back of the retreating figure, Analisa spoke softly to her son. "She's in a bad mood today, I guess, Kase. Do not worry."

Analisa knew immediately what had caused the change in Millicent and some of the others, women and soldiers alike. The word was out that her husband was not the Spanish professor he'd claimed to be but a half-breed Sioux. It mattered little that he worked for the Bureau of Indian Affairs, that he was better educated than most of them, or that his background was one of wealth and society. What mattered was that Indian blood ran in his veins. They would never condone her marriage to him, nor would they forgive her for having chosen to marry an Indian.

She no longer cared what the bigoted residents of Fort Sully thought. She took her brief outings with her head held high. Unlike the shame she had felt while living outside Pella, this new emotion was one of pride, for she knew that Caleb was far superior to those who held such prejudice against him. He had fought for their safety as much as for the lives of the Sioux who needed protection. She knew in her heart that if Caleb possessed two heads and one of them were green, she would love him all the same.

No, she thought, as she sat in the rocker at his bedside late one evening, bundled in his robe and sipping hot tea, *it is I who feel sorry for these people. They have so little love and so much hatred in their hearts*. She knew then that never again would she allow others to cause her to feel shame.

The world was hot and dark, so dark that Caleb almost feared he was blind. He knew he'd been in this place before and tried to force his fevered mind to remember where or when. He tried to call out to Analisa. He knew she would come if only she knew where to find him. Or would she be afraid to enter this darkness? Caleb hoped she would not, and trusted his love to guide her.

A cool, fleeting touch entered into the strange, close heat that seemed to engulf him. Feather light, the touch moved against his brow and down along his cheek and neck. He tried to speak and thank the bearer of the soothing relief, but could not. His throat was parched and dry, his lips unwilling to move. He thought he heard a voice calling him from afar and forced himself to look through the black, endless night that imprisoned him. Caleb fought to lift his weighted eyelids and saw a wavering light somewhere nearby.

A figure bent toward him, a face he'd seen before in a vision, an apparition with wisps of silver hair that framed her face like a halo. He could see her eyes but not their color, yet he knew instinctively that they shone like blue crystals. Again the specter was dressed in white and he called upon his mind to recognize her. It was the princess he'd seen once before, the fairy princess of his father's people's legend, the princess who lived in the house of dancing, bobbing sunflowers.

Happiness suffused him when he recognized her. Where had she been? Perhaps in this land of darkness she had waited for him. Caleb tried to speak to her, to implore her not to leave him alone here, at least not until Analisa could find him.

"Are you the princess?"

Had he spoken, he wondered, or just imagined the words in his mind?

"Or are you *wanagi,* the ghost in my mother's tales?"

"Sleep," the spirit commanded. He felt the soft touch of her hand on his cheek. "Your fever is gone, Caleb. You will be well soon."

"Wait." He tried to call out to her, but already the vision was fading and he felt his eyes closing against the weak light around her.

"Analisa!"

He called out his wife's name in hope that the spirit would lead her to him, but he knew it was too late. He felt himself drifting back into the darkness. It was cooler now, but just as deeply black.

"I am here, Caleb."

He heard a voice at the edge of the darkness and his fears vanished. It was Anja. She'd found him at last. He smiled then, and allowed himself to drift into a peaceful sleep.

"Mama?"

Kase kept his voice down to a whisper as he tiptoed into the room, Galileo dangling from his arms. The cat was wild eyed, sensing sure strangulation if he wasn't freed soon.

"Do you think Papa will feel better if I let him see the cat?" he asked.

"He's still asleep, Kase." Analisa reached out to rescue the black and white animal, and Kase released it into her arms. She scratched the haughty creature on the top of his head, and he settled down on her lap, purring loudly. The boy scrambled up beside her, squeezing himself into the small space she made for him on the wide seat of the rocker.

The past few days had been as hard on Kase as they had been

on Analisa and the rest of the household. He had haunted the bedroom doorway, a small, silent shadow, sometimes waking late at night to crawl from his makeshift bed on the settee and stand beside Analisa as she sat awake in the rocker. Often he would startle her as she dozed, forcing her to catch her breath, startled at the sight of a small figure draped in a long white nightshirt who'd appeared without warning beside her. The experience of losing his *opa* was still fresh in his mind, and he would often voice his fears, asking if Caleb was going to die like his great-grandfather and leave him. She had reassured him over and over that Caleb would live, only to find herself praying fervently that it would come to pass.

She pushed her feet against the floor to set the rocker in motion and welcomed the calm she experienced as she watched Caleb sleep peacefully for the first time in nearly a week. Sometime during the night the fever had left him, and now she waited impatiently for him to awaken.

"Mama?"

"Hmm?"

They spoke in silent whispers as they sat side by side staring at the figure stretched out under the tulip-patterned quilt.

"When will he wake up?"

"Soon, I think."

"*Ja?* What if I put the cat on his stomach? You think then he'll wake up?"

"You put that cat on my stomach and I'll tan your hide."

For a moment they were both too stunned to move, and then Analisa jumped to her feet. Galileo hissed as he tumbled unceremoniously to the floor. She reached out to touch Caleb's forehead and then took his hand between her own. His face was stubbled with a light growth of beard, his hair matted and much in need of a wash, and his eyes were rimmed with deep purple shadows. But he was alive, lucid, and smiling at her beguilingly.

"Miss me?" His voice sounded hoarse, a dry, rasping whisper, but the light in his eyes shone for her alone.

She nodded and smiled, blinking away tears as she reached for a glass of water and gave him a drink.

"*Ja,* I missed you."

"Want to show me how much?" He tugged on her hand and

drew Analisa down toward him. She perched gingerly on the side of the bed, afraid that the least motion would cause him pain.

Kase immediately scrambled up beside Caleb and leaned close enough to plant a kiss on his cheek. "I'm glad you're awake, Caleb," Kase said.

"You don't want to call me Papa anymore?" Caleb raised an eyebrow as he teased the boy.

"*Ja*. I forgot."

"I'm glad I'm better, too, because I missed you . . . and your mama."

Caleb laced his fingers between Analisa's as he continued to stare into her eyes, telling her without words the things he longed to say but could not because of the boy.

"Kase, go over to Ruth's and tell her that Caleb is awake. Tell her to come over later to see him."

"Do I have to?"

"*Ja*. You are the only one who can go right now."

Kase clung to Caleb's neck a moment longer, burrowing against him until Analisa was forced to remind him of the wound.

"It's all right," Caleb reassured her, his voice husky with emotion as he soothingly stroked the little boy's shoulders and then gave him a firm hug before he set him away from him.

"Do as your mama said, Kase. You can come right back, you know."

After a quick kiss to Caleb's cheek, Kase crawled off the bed and flashed a winning smile at them before he ran out of the room.

"Your turn." Caleb tugged on her hand. "Or am I too much of a mess?"

"You look *wonderful*." She leaned forward and pressed a light, quick kiss on his lips, a kiss that Caleb sought to deepen before she pulled away.

"I feel as if I'd been dragged behind a horse. How long have I been out?"

"Six days. It is not noon yet, the twenty-sixth of May."

He studied her face, his expression intent, searching.

Analisa felt her heart begin to gallop.

He patted the empty space beside him. "Sit with me."

She complied. Easing into the space beside him, she leaned

against the headboard and nervously smoothed her apron over the skirt of her gray batiste gown. Analisa could not fathom why she felt so awkward with Caleb, as nervous and unsure as if they'd just met. Perhaps, she thought, because the circumstances were so similar to those of their first meeting. Then, too, he'd been in her care. She'd blushed and shied away from his every look, every word. Now that he was well, she felt awkward, and so she lay beside him and stared at the toes of her stocking feet.

"Are you all right, Anja? Everything okay here?" he asked as if he sensed her skittishness.

"*Ja*. Everything is okay now."

"You look bad."

Just as he knew it would, his comment drew an immediate reaction and she turned to question him. "Bad?"

"Tired," he amended.

"You kept me from sleeping for five nights. Last night you were talking and tossing. Something about a princess." She waited for an explanation while Caleb silently mused over her comment.

"Well," she prodded. "Do you know some . . . some princess?"

He did not hesitate to carry her hand, fingers still entwined with his, to his lips to kiss the back of it.

"Yes. I know a princess. I married her."

Although Caleb seemed content to talk, Analisa was all too aware of the strain in his voice. He needed sleep, sleep unburdened by fever, and he needed sustenance.

"Let go, Caleb, and I'll have Abbie fix something for you."

"Where's Ruth?" He continued to toy with her fingers and gave her arm a slight tug that caused her to slide down the headboard in his direction.

Analisa knew it would do no good to protest and so shifted her weight and made herself comfortable as she leaned against his good shoulder. Just feeling the familiar warmth that emanated from him helped her relax.

"Ruth moved over to the major's house."

"What?"

"*Ja*. He moved to the bachelor officer's house and offered his home to Ruth because he knew it was so crowded here. Ruth plans to stay until you are well again."

"And that old pipe-smoking tyrant, Abbie? Is she still here?"

Analisa giggled at his description, for Abbie had indeed become a tyrant while Caleb lay ill. "She's been more than good to me, Caleb. To you, too."

"I know. I'm only teasing."

His eyes closed and Analisa rested contentedly beside him, waiting for him to drift off to sleep. It surprised her when the sound of his voice broke the peaceful lull.

"I'm sorry, Anja."

"Sorry?"

"Yes. For putting you through all of this. You and Kase. I'll make it up to you both. I promise." He opened his eyes and tried to roll onto his side but found he lacked the strength to accomplish even this small task. "I'm quitting as soon as the BIA sends out another agent. No more of this intrigue for me. You and Kase deserve a decent, normal life, and I intend to see that you get one."

For some reason Analisa felt suddenly saddened by the words she'd so longed to hear. She wondered if her feelings stemmed from the tone of resignation in his voice or from her own uncertainty about how she would react to what Caleb called a decent, normal life.

"Wait until you are well before you decide, Caleb. Right now you are too exhausted to worry about it."

"I won't change my mind." He thought for a moment longer before he spoke again. "What happened to Hardy?"

"Red Dog did not try to take him from the major after . . . after what happened. He is in the guardhouse until you can give them instructions. Messengers have come each day from Red Dog. He said he will talk peace with you and *only* you."

"Sounds as if I don't have time to waste lying in bed."

"If you try to get up, General Abigail and I will hit you over the head with cooking pots."

He laughed and shook his head. "I wouldn't doubt that you'd do just that."

"Caleb." She laid her palm alongside his cheek and leaned forward to kiss him. The kiss was chaste and brief, yet held a promise of more. "Please. I must get up now. You need to eat, at least some good, rich broth. The doctor said you must not get dedryhated."

"De-*what*?"

"Are you teasing me?" She tried hard to appear stern and forbidding.

He shook his head, but she did not miss the twinkle in his eye.

"De-dry-hated." She pronounced each incorrect syllable distinctly.

"That's exactly what I thought you said." He dared not smile, but let go of her hand and quickly closed his eyes again.

Analisa slipped from the bed to go in search of Abbie. She paused in the doorway long enough to reassure herself that Caleb was resting comfortably, then let herself out. As she closed the bedroom door, Analisa heard him chuckle contentedly and then smiled to herself and whispered, *"Dehydrated,"* in perfect, unaccented English.

Chapter Twenty-Four

The *Deer Lodge*, a Missouri paddle wheeler, steamed against the current as it fought its way upriver, looking like a two-story cabin plopped on a raft. The upper deck consisted of a large, airy salon whose walls were composed of a long row of glass doors. Relief from the summer heat was carried through the open doors on a gentle breeze, cooled by the waters of the Missouri.

Analisa sat just inside the salon of the riverboat, with Caleb and Kase beside her. She dabbed at her brow with a handkerchief, then folded the dainty square of cloth and tucked it into her beaded reticule. She thought of Sophie and the day her friend had given her the little purse. It all seemed so long ago.

"Kase," she admonished as she watched her son sneaking toward one of the open doorways, "please try to stay clean."

She shifted nervously in her chair and tried to concentrate on her needlework.

Caleb watched her intently from where he sat across the passengers' dining table. He sipped at a tall glass of iced tea, a pleasant afternoon refreshment.

"Anja?"

At the sound of her name she immediately looked up at him, concern etched around her deep blue eyes.

"Are you all right, Caleb?"

He shook his head, resigned to the fact that she would never cease to inquire about his health.

"I'm fine," he answered gently, then leaned forward and whispered for her ears alone. "I thought last night was proof enough?"

It pleased him to watch her cheeks deepen to a ripe peach shade as she hid the easily rekindled fire in her eyes with a sweep of her lashes. He relished the fact that she glowed with love and life, and he was sincerely grateful to have played a part in helping her blossom into full-blown womanhood.

The picture she presented was one of elegance and refinement as she sat trying, he knew, to ignore his teasing. Her gown was a new one, periwinkle blue the trader called it, and store-bought for the occasion. She'd even agreed to wear her best kid shoes, the gray ones, after Caleb promised to buy her another pair should they be ruined. She did him great honor, this headstrong wife of his, and he was more than proud to have her travel at his side on his final journey in the employ of the Bureau of Indian Affairs.

Besides, it would have been impossible to leave her behind, he thought, and smiled to himself as he finished his tea. Both Analisa and Kase accompanied him, dressed in their finest. For this trip to the renegade camp, even he wore his finest suit. The utmost honor and sincerity would be shown to Red Dog and his band of Sioux. Caleb was determined to do his best for the people he had persuaded to come in peace to the agency.

The decision to take the steamboat proved to be a wise one. The miles between the fort and the renegade camp were long, arduous if attempted on horseback. Caleb knew them well, for he'd made the trip many times in the previous months. Now, on this final journey upriver, he was able to relax as well as spare

Analisa and Kase the hard ride. The boat ride also saved further aggravation of the bullet wound, which still pained him on occasion.

He pushed his chair away from the table and offered his arm to Analisa. "Would you care to stroll around the deck, Mrs. Storm?"

She folded her embroidery into a small square, pinned on the needle and thread, and deposited them inside her reticule. With the purse once again dangling from her wrist, she stood and tucked her hand into the bend at his elbow.

They stood by the rail and watched the sandy, willow-lined banks of the Missouri sweep past. Caleb stared down at the swirling, mud-yellowed water and was thankful that they had not been delayed by hidden sandbars or engine fires, so often impediments to river travel.

"Mr. Storm?" A young deckhand interrupted Caleb's thoughts with a hesitant inquiry. "You said to tell you when we'd made eighty miles, sir. Captain says we're about there."

"Thank you. Tell the captain he can put in anywhere he sees fit and we'll take a skiff to shore."

They watched the boy walk away with a jaunty bounce in his step, his hands swinging freely at his sides.

"Will anyone pick us up here in the middle of nowhere when we are ready to return?" Analisa wanted to know.

"Williamson is going to alert the next boat to watch for us when they leave Sully."

She looked above the tree-lined riverbank to the sandy bluffs beyond. Endless miles of rolling grasslands stretched toward the horizon. Although her stomach fluttered as nervously as if it were filled with tiny flitting moths, she realized that she loved this land in all its austerity. Each and every day was different from the one before, and yet the open prairie was the same, ever constant. The colors changed with the seasons and with the passing hours of the day. The land itself, as well as the river that shaped the land it carved, was as alive as the wildlife and humankind that took nourishment from it. She leaned against the rail and filled her lungs with the warm summer breeze.

Caleb stood beside her at the rail, his mind registering little of the natural scene that held Analisa spellbound. His own thoughts lingered over the coming exchange with Red Dog, for what he felt in his heart and what he was to tell the young Sioux warrior were worlds apart. He leaned forward, his elbows propped up on the rail, and stared out at the passing scenery, seeing nothing. If he followed his heart, he would tell Red Dog to take his people and flee to the wooded wilds of Canada to buy themselves a few years before they were forced onto a reservation.

He knew far too well, though, that that solution would last only a short time. Sooner or later all of the Indian nations would be forced to surrender themselves to the care of the overlord government of the United States. The alternative was extinction. The sad but inevitable fact was that the two civilizations could never live together in the same land and retain their own ways of life. One must indeed give way to the other, and Caleb knew only too well that it was the people of his mother's blood who must lose.

The sooner men like Red Dog brought their people to safety, the greater chance there remained to save the lives of the children and help them and future generations to coexist. Still, the task was a mighty one, bitter and poignant, and Caleb dreaded the eventual outcome. He hoped with all his heart that the peace he made with Red Dog would prove to be lasting.

"Your thoughts are miles away." Analisa touched his shoulder and drew him back to the present.

"It looks as if the captain has found a safe landing." The roar of the boilers ceased as the riverboat neared the shore. Caleb whistled for Kase, using the secret signal they had devised during Caleb's recuperation, and Analisa laughed as the boy's dark head and then his shoulders appeared hanging over the rail directly above them.

The topmost deck of the steamboat was surrounded by an observation rail, but most passengers were discouraged from using it, because of the fierce sunlight that beat down on it and the flying sparks of wood and ash that spewed from the tall chimneys and fell upon the unwary, singeing hair and clothes alike.

"*Komop, wij gaa nu,*" Analisa called to her son as she leaned back and shaded her eyes with her hand. "We go now.

"Will there be anyone here to meet us?" she asked as she followed Caleb through the salon to a stairway leading to the deck below. She lifted her skirt and held it out of the way in order not to trip as they made their way downstairs.

"I'm sure one of Red Dog's messengers will be there as soon as the boat has pulled away. We won't see anyone before then. You can be sure they are watching, though."

They reached the lower landing, and Kase soon clattered down the steps behind them. While Analisa brushed off his clothing and straightened his jacket and collar, Caleb watched several crewmen load their suitcases into the skiff. Analisa and Kase were soon handed aboard the rowboat, which bumped continually against the side of the steamboat, and sat waiting for Caleb, who shook the captain's hand as the man said farewell.

"I don't feel right letting civilized folks off in the middle of Indian country," the captain called down while a nervous deckhand waited to row them the short distance to shore. "Are you sure someone's gonna be here to meet you?"

"I have Red Dog's word on it, Captain," Caleb assured him.

The captain looked skeptical as he scanned the shoreline for any sign of a greeting party. He pushed his cap back off his forehead with a thumb and looked at the departing passengers.

"Still," he began again, "you can't trust the word of a savage . . ." His last words died to a whisper that was carried away on the breeze.

At least, Analisa thought, the man had the grace to blush with embarrassment. Word had spread along the river like a prairie fire, traveling from one fort to the next, of the undercover BIA man who had lived in their midst masquerading as a Spanish professor. In a few short weeks Caleb had been elevated through such gossip to a position that rivaled that of President Grant. Still, Analisa noticed that even though most people treated him with courtesy, the warmth of sincerity failed to spark a light in many eyes. He was still an Indian. A red man. A Sioux. A savage. Still, she never thought of him as anything but Caleb until a bigoted remark like the captain's reminded her of how he was so unjustly regarded.

There was an awkward silence as the deckhand awaited the command to depart and the captain stood in silent embarrassment.

"Thank you for your hospitality, Captain," Analisa volunteered and smiled up at him to fill the void. Caleb pulled Kase onto his lap, nodding his thanks to his wife for combating the remark with kindness rather than with a vicious retort. He'd

learned to live with such unconscious cruelty, but was sorry that
Analisa and Kase would always be subjected to them as well.

The small skiff moved away from the *Deer Lodge*, thrusting
forward with each pull of the oars. Kase, oblivious of the
captain's remark, waved gaily to the passengers who lined the
rail to watch their departure. Caleb was once again reassured,
happy with his decision to bring Analisa and Kase along for the
peace talks. He hoped the meeting would see the matter of her
sister settled as well.

During the weeks of his recovery, messengers from the
renegade camp had frequently arrived carrying information
concerning Red Dog's demands, and had returned with Caleb's
replies. The main points of the treaty were refined in this
manner until all that remained was the official signing ceremony. Both men had agreed not to include army officials, for Caleb
was entrusted with the government agency's power to sign the
agreement. Major Williamson had questioned the arrangements, but the matter was ultimately left to Caleb's discretion.

Caleb had sent word to Red Dog that, as a sign of his great
faith, he would bring his wife and son along to the festivities
and accept Red Dog's offer of hospitality. Caleb chose to make
no mention of Meika, although he knew that Red Dog was
probably aware of his reason for bringing his wife along.

Dealing with the Sioux was a game of cat and mouse that
Caleb understood well, far better than any white man ever
could. He knew that the Sioux looked upon certain questions as
rude, and that some subjects could never be mentioned at all.
He knew that Red Dog, after seeing Analisa with him on the
day of Hardy's arrest, was well aware that the white woman who
had crawled into the camp to speak to Swift Otter's wife was
Caleb's woman. Caleb wondered if Meika would make any
effort at all to speak to her sister while she was in the settlement,
and knew that only time would answer his questions.

"I hope I can remember everything you told me." Analisa
fretted with the ties of her shoes as she made final preparations
to leave the tepee.

"Just watch me, and if you are in doubt, don't do anything
until I give you a signal." He pulled her close and planted a
sure, swift kiss on her lips.

The shadowed interior of the tepee was warm even though it was not yet midday. Analisa smoothed her skirt and then reached up to be sure her hair was still neatly combed and bound in a knot upon her head. She fought the few stray wisps that had escaped the pins and worried her lower lip with her teeth.

"Relax as much as you can, Anja. It will all be over soon."

"But what will be the outcome, Caleb?" Her eyes were haunted as she looked up at him, and he tried to smile in return.

"The outcome," he began, "will be for the best."

"She is not *your* sister."

"No, but she is my wife's sister, and so I do care what happens today. Try not to get yourself worked up into a fighting state; it will do no good."

She sighed and moved toward the opening of the tepee. It was finally time for her to meet with Meika and try to persuade the girl to return to Fort Sully with them.

Three days she'd waited for this moment, and now that it had finally come, Analisa was not certain her legs would carry her to Red Dog's tepee for the meeting. Her heart pounded and her mouth was dry. She hesitated, waiting for Caleb to step outside and then followed a few steps behind him as was the custom of the people here.

The peace council between Red Dog and Caleb had gone successfully; the treaty was signed and ready to be delivered to Washington. Feasting for all had followed the day-long discussions attended only by the men. Before their arrival at the camp, Caleb taught Analisa many Sioux customs of propriety and good manners, but she realized it would take many weeks of living among the people before the customs became habit.

Finally the time had come for her to see her sister, a meeting agreed on by Red Dog and Meika's husband, Swift Otter, after Caleb had first asked permission for Analisa to speak to her sister alone. Instead, Red Dog had chosen to officiate and had offered his own tepee for the meeting. The entire village was alive with the news, and although Analisa could not understand the words of the people who watched them pass by on their way to Red Dog's tepee, she could feel the excitement in the air.

Kase tripped along beside them, having joined his mother and stepfather as they wound their way through the village that bordered the stream. He had been free to run and play at will, following the custom of the Sioux, who raised their children with freedom and loving words rather than with harsh punishment and admonitions. The boy had abandoned his clothes in exchange for a loincloth presented to him by one of his numerous new acquaintances. He joined readily in the rough-and-tumble games with the other boys, and although younger than most of them, seemed to enjoy himself thoroughly.

As they neared their destination, the old widow who'd cooked for Caleb separated herself from the crowd and approached them. Caleb greeted her kindly and stooped to hear her rasping words. She reached out a gnarled finger and pointed toward Kase, shaking her head and staring at the little boy who was oblivious of her actions. ''Red Dog's Shadow,'' she whispered over and over, staring first at the boy and then at Caleb. He listened uneasily to the quiet whispers of the people who lined the route, all speculating on the old crone's words, and was thankful Analisa could not understand them. The women were chattering among themselves, and more than a few times he heard them refer to Kase as Red Dog's Shadow. It tore at Caleb's soul to think that Kase so resembled Red Dog as a child.

Caleb was thankful that he had not been aware of the likeness before the peace council began, for he doubted that he could have shared a mat with the young warrior and carried out his mission, knowing as he knew now with only a shadow of a doubt, that Red Dog had fathered Kase.

How was he to sit placidly across from the man and translate the coming proceedings to Analisa, knowing full well the man who had once brutally violated her and nearly ended her life sat across from them? Caleb's mind was in bitter turmoil, his heart heavy as they reached the tepee of Red Dog.

The flap was open, a sign that they were free to enter without first seeking admittance.

''Oh, Caleb.'' Analisa stopped him with a hand on his sleeve. ''I'm so nervous.''

He stared at her silently, wanting for all the world to tell her to turn around and give up this whole scheme, to leave the camp with Kase in tow, before he lost control of his senses and harmed the very man he had come to befriend. Instead, he choked down his hatred and hid it behind the unreadable, closed expression he'd learned to affect so well.

"You will do just fine. Remember not to beg your sister to
return. It will only shame her if she refuses you."

"I will remember." She nodded and then looked down to
check her appearance one last time. She wished her dress were
freshly pressed and clean as it had been when they arrived. The
past three days had taken a toll on her clothing, but this was the
best of the lot, and she'd been determined to put on her finery to
honor the Sioux. Now, in her nervousness, nothing seemed
fitting.

Taking a deep breath, she followed her husband into the tepee
and immediately moved to the left of the door to sit with the
other women on the south side of the room. Caleb entered and
walked to the right, as custom demanded. The men were seated
opposite the women. It was a moment or two before Analisa
recognized her sister in the muted light; she was tempted to
speak to her but remembered her manners and remained silent,
awaiting Caleb's signal. Unlike Meika, though, Analisa was
unable to sit with her eyes downcast and could not bring herself
to look away from her sister.

Meika was dressed in a beautiful garment made of white
skins and covered with beads and quillwork the likes of which
Analisa had never seen. Before her lay a pile of goods on a fine,
thick pelt. Behind and beside Meika sat her husband's relations,
many openly staring at Analisa. Had it not been for her sister's
shining blue eyes and white hair, Analisa would not have
recognized her as being any different from the others. Mia was
also seated among the other women, but she was as close to Red
Dog as custom would permit.

Red Dog began to speak, and Analisa's attention was drawn
in his direction. It was then that she noticed Caleb's dark
expression. Something was very wrong. She listened to the
incomprehensible exchange with trepidation. The men spoke
together for a time, ignoring the women and the reason for the
meeting. Swift Otter, Meika's husband, remained silent, his
eyes slowly moving from his wife to her sister. Analisa caught
his stare once and was forced to drop her eyes under the burning
intensity of his gaze.

"Analisa, if you wish to speak to your sister, now is the
time."

At the sound of her husband's hushed voice addressing her in

English, she was so startled that she sat bolt upright and blinked twice before she realized what he'd said.

"*Ja.*" She cleared her throat. "Yes."

Analisa turned to Meika and asked in Dutch if she was happy here with her new family. It tore at her heart to say the words, but it hurt worse to realize that her sister seemed to understand little, if anything, of what she said. Caleb had warned her that since Meika had come to accept her place among the Sioux, that the girl would most likely refuse to speak Dutch, preferring to use her adopted language out of loyalty to her new family. Meika turned to Caleb, her eyes wide and questioning. He repeated the words in Sioux.

"She says she is more than happy here and that she has a good family, a family of wealth who treat her as a daughter of their hearts." Caleb stopped translating long enough to listen to Meika's soft, halting speech. "She says that her husband, Swift Otter, is most kind and generous." Then he gently reminded Analisa to speak first to him in English.

"Is she so happy that she will not consider returning to her old life." Despite what Caleb had instructed her to do, Analisa asked Meika in Dutch and twisted her hands together in her lap to stop their shaking. She then told Caleb what she'd asked, and he translated. Before her sister answered, Analisa knew in her heart what the answer would be.

"I have no other life. These are my people. This is my home."

Meika stared down at the pile of goods before her as Caleb translated her words to Analisa.

Can she not face me? Analisa wondered. *Is she being forced into this?*

Meika did not ask about their mother, father, Jan, or Opa. She asked Analisa nothing at all.

Analisa stopped speaking directly to her sister in Dutch and tried to see Caleb through the tears in her eyes.

"Ask her if she knows where Pieter is."

At the sound of their brother's name, Meika looked up and waited for Caleb to ask the question.

"He is with a band of Sans Arc Sioux. He is becoming a skilled hunter and warrior. She says he has forgotten all of the old ways."

Analisa sat in silence. Dizziness assailed her in the close, crowded space inside the huge tepee. The scent of sage filled the air, burning slowly as an offering to Wakan Tanka, the Great Mystery. The smoke served to purify the air and carry their thoughts heavenward. She knew now that what Caleb had warned her of was true: Her sister was lost to her, the shining, golden-haired girl who had been her closest companion in her youth. A stranger now, Meika would never again be a part of Analisa's life. Pieter was lost to her as well. All that Analisa retained of the old life was a fading photograph and the memories locked in her heart.

"Anja? Do you want to ask her any more questions?" Caleb's voice was gentle now. He knew her pain.

She straightened her shoulders before she faced her sister once again. "Does she need anything? Is there anything I can do for her, or her . . . family?"

Caleb hesitated before he repeated the younger girl's reply to Analisa.

"What did she say?" Analisa pressed him to repeat the words.

"She needs nothing from you. She said to take the whites away with you. Go back across the wide sea to the land you came from and leave the Sioux to live in peace once more."

Analisa bowed her head and stared at her hands clenched tightly against her skirt. She blinked back tears and then searched the faces in the room. Surprisingly, many looked upon her with compassion. Even Meika seemed to regret having caused her such pain. She straightened again and then searched the room for Kase. He sat with three other children near the door, all silent as they watched the exchange. Analisa signaled for him to come to her. Custom could be damned, she decided. She wanted Meika to see her nephew.

When Kase crawled into his mother's lap, she stroked his hair and then pointed to the blond girl across the room. "That is my own sister, Kase," she whispered in his ear. "She is your *tante*, aunt." Then she directed Caleb to explain to Meika. "Say that this is my son, her nephew. His name is Kase. Tell her I hope that her sons will be as strong and as brave as mine. Tell her that I will never go back across the sea, but that I hope we will be able to live in peace."

Caleb did as she asked, his heart heavy with his wife's

sadness. He felt his own anger toward Red Dog ebb as the minutes passed. As he stared at the younger man, his mind churning with unwanted visions of Analisa's defilement, he realized suddenly that Red Dog could not have been much older than Analisa at the time of the rape. The warrior would have been a youth of no more than seventeen summers when he participated in the attack on the Van Meeteren family. Even now, as a man, Red Dog was hard-pressed to subdue his temper. What must he have been like in his youth? Caleb would never forgive the man his act, but he sought to understand the circumstances.

For the first time Caleb realized what it must have cost Analisa to forgive Mia after she shot him. He wrestled with his emotions, trying to find as much compassion and understanding in order to forgive Red Dog's violation of Analisa. It was time the past was laid to rest once and for all. He was reminded of Ruth's simple philosophy: Everything happens for a reason. Surely he would have never met and married Analisa had she been living a placid life in the Dutch settlement. Surely Wakan Tanka, the Great Mystery, was behind this web that formed the pattern of their lives.

Meika's relatives shifted uncomfortably in the tense atmosphere, and Caleb realized it was time to draw the discussion to a close. In the Sioux custom, no sign was needed from their host. When it was time for guests to leave, they merely stood and announced, "I am going." Caleb was prepared to leave. He glanced at Red Dog. The sight of the young chief staring pointedly at Kase with obvious speculation forced Caleb to watch as icy cold fingers of fear closed around his heart. Never once by word or deed had Red Dog so much as hinted that he recognized Analisa. Indeed, he might not have known who she was, or remembered his part in the massacre. Thankfully, Analisa still had no recollection of the man who had raped her. But now, as Red Dog stared at the boy, Caleb felt his own scalp prickle. He acted quickly to remove his wife and son from the tepee.

"Go now, Analisa. Take Kase with you."

She stood to do his bidding, and Caleb was forced to endure another wait while Meika spoke to him in Sioux. She had gifts to present to this sister of her old life; she indicated the beaded household items on the rug before her. Caleb nodded and informed Analisa, who took her place once again on the mat while the younger girl carefully tied up the gifts in the beautiful wolf-skin pelt.

"Thank her for me, Caleb."

"I will. You go now. Take Kase."

Analisa stooped to leave the tepee, clutching her sister's gifts in her arms. Kase ran out behind her, but not before bestowing a sparkling smile upon Caleb that chilled him to the bone. He knew that Red Dog watched the exchange and held his breath. He stood to leave behind his wife and the boy.

"Wait," Red Dog commanded and waved the others away. Swift Otter and his family then filed out, leaving Caleb alone with the other man.

Caleb sat, determined to say only enough to be polite. He counted each breath as he sought to ease the tension within him. Red Dog stared at Caleb and neither man looked away from the other.

"The boy is your son?" Red Dog spoke first.

Caleb alone knew why Red Dog dared ask such a personal, offensive question.

"Yes." Caleb's voice never wavered with the lie.

The silence between them was as charged as summer lightning. Finally, Red Dog commented, forced to speak, as the exchange was held at his demand. "He is well cared for. A fine strong boy."

Caleb did not hesitate to respond to the compliment. "I am pleased with him."

For a moment a flicker of doubt flashed behind Red Dog's eyes. To call Caleb a liar, to claim the boy as his own would have serious, far-reaching repercussions. Without proof, Red Dog was forced to back down. In that moment, Caleb knew he had won.

Red Dog remained silent, giving up any claim to the boy.

"I am going," Caleb announced. Without ceremony he stood and left the tepee.

With sure and steady strides he moved through the village to Analisa and Kase. He did not look back.

Chapter Twenty-Five

The sound of someone scratching on the tepee flap startled Analisa, for Caleb had no need to seek permission to enter. She wiped her teary eyes and crossed the interior of the tepee, pulled aside the flap, and was shocked to find herself face to face with Meika.

"*Kom,*" Analisa invited, wondering what the unexpected visit meant, and realized Meika must have followed her directly from the formal meeting in Red Dog's tepee. Before she stooped to enter, Meika spoke in hushed tones to someone near the entrance. Analisa noticed Swift Otter waiting outside the door.

"He is welcome," Analisa said, using the Dutch words as she gestured toward Swift Otter, but he chose to wait outside.

Meika refused to sit on the mat Analisa offered, visibly

uneasy in her sister's presence. Her eyes took in every detail of Analisa's appearance.

"Are *you* happy?" Meika asked, her attempt at communication a combination of halting Dutch and hand gestures. Yet Analisa understood what her sister struggled to ask.

"*Ja*. I am happy." Analisa tried to smile. It was a beginning.

"The others are all dead?" Meika asked.

"*Ja*." Analisa found no gentle way to acknowledge the harsh facts. "All dead. Only you and Pieter and I remain."

Meika was silent as she seemed to digest the words. She then spoke again. "Do you understand?" she asked, her eyes wide and pleading. "I cannot go with you, but I do not hate you. The old Meika is no more."

Staring hard at the girl dressed in her Sioux finery, Analisa took in the white braids bound with beaded ties, the soft fringe at the hem of a skirt that swayed gently with every movement, and became aware that the old Meika was indeed no more. Not because she had assumed the clothing and mannerisms of a Sioux wife, but because what she had once been inside had changed as well. *Just as I have changed,* Analisa realized. Yes, she thought as she watched the beautiful girl stand uncomfortably before her, I do understand. Meika had clearly expressed what Analisa was only beginning to realize. Their old lives were gone forever. Each had found a new way, a new life, and new loves. It was time to let the old life go.

On impulse, Analisa reached out, not to try to bind Meika to her, but to assure her sister that she loved her still, loved her enough to let her go. At Analisa's touch Meika stood rigid, but as she heard Analisa whisper, she relaxed and returned the embrace.

"I understand," Analisa said softly and pulled back to bestow a smile upon her sister. "I understand. The old Anja is gone, too." She hugged Meika close one last time and then told her, "Be happy, little one. *Ik houd van jou.* I love you."

The sisters smiled, mirroring each other in feeling as well as appearance. Meika glanced toward the door and then murmured, "I am going now."

She moved away. Soon the buffalo-hide flap closed behind her, and she was gone.

Alone in the silence of the empty tepee, Analisa sat down and removed her shoes and stockings. She hiked her skirts up to her thighs, exposing her long legs to what little draft filtered down through the smoke hole. Rolling up her sleeves, she leaned against the back rest Caleb had hung for her against the ridge pole and sighed. She unbuttoned the bodice of her dress in an effort to seek release from the heat and closed her eyes, feeling the need to think over all that had transpired.

She'd found her sister only to lose her again, yet this time she could put the past behind her, knowing that Meika and Pieter were living the life they chose, not one that had been forced on them.

Shifting to a more comfortable position, she let her mind wander over the past few years. She knew in her heart that she, like Meika, was an entirely new person, one forced to grow from the hardships life had shown her.

This time, as she thought about the past, she dwelled not upon the massacre but upon the changes that it had wrought, changes that forged this new self. The innocence of youth had been stolen from her along with her family, and during the months that followed she had battled her own shame as well as that heaped upon her by the community. Still, mingled with the hurt and degradation were the few happy memories the years had given her. She remembered vividly the day Kase was born. Never would she forget the moment, when Opa had laid the tiny brown boy-child with rosebud lips in her arms. The love she had felt for him was so great that it had overshadowed her shame and lightened her heart.

She recalled, too, those first freezing Iowa winters in the soddie, winters so cold she'd been forced to tie Kase in his bed, lest he crawl out from beneath his covers at night and freeze to death. She'd learned to pack her *klompen* with straw to protect her feet from frostbite whenever she went outdoors.

Then she had put aside her shyness and insecurity for independence. To provide for her son and Opa, she'd spent long evening hours learning to design patterns and piece together fashions. No longer forced to face the townsfolk and accept their handouts, she had gained their business, if not their respect.

Now, as Analisa mused upon the past, she was suffused with pride in her own accomplishments, certain the women of Pella would not have hired her to sew their finery out of mere kindness, for their dollars were far too dear, but because her skills were superior to anyone else's.

A typical day in the soddie had consisted of cooking three full meals for Opa and Kase, tending the animals and the garden, weekly baking, the endless laundry and cleaning —accomplishments any woman could be proud of, and she'd taken them on when she was but sixteen years old.

Then there was Caleb. Her lips curved into a dreamy smile as she remembered the first time he had made love to her beneath the cottonwoods. Was he surprised, she wondered, to find her so eager to lie with him, a man she barely knew, simply because the minister had pronounced them wed? He must have understood her need to give something in return, for had he not come back to her? And what a homecoming! Recalling that passionate lovemaking in the cow shed caused her blood to surge. A pulsing warmth invaded her senses.

It was too hot to think of things that only raised her temperature, so she tried to picture Sophie and Jon as she'd last seen them, tearfully waving good-bye at the station. Analisa said a silent prayer that they would someday meet again. She thought of the new family she had in Ruth and Abbie. Although they were none of them related by blood, they'd grown as close as family over the past few weeks.

Yes, Analisa decided. Her life had indeed changed, and would continue to do so, for that was the way of life. For the first time, she was eager to see what the future held in store for them, and wondered if Caleb intended to keep his word and quit his job with the Bureau of Indian Affairs.

Where *was* Caleb? Impatient, she lifted her skirts and fanned them up and down. It was at that moment that he chose to appear.

"Is that a new sort of signal?" He beamed appreciatively at the sight of his wife's silken thighs. "Are you in distress?"

Caleb ducked inside and circled around to the right to join her. She noted how the customs of the Sioux were second nature to him.

"*Ja*, I am in distress. I am boiling like a potato." She started to push her petticoat and skirt down to cover her legs.

"Don't do that on my account." Caleb joined her, assuming a cross-legged position directly opposite. He smiled wickedly, his strong white teeth enhancing the deep bronze of his complexion.

"Where have you been?"

"Checking on Kase. He is off with his band of friends. Taking his knocks, I'd say, from the looks of him."

"Knocks?" She was suddenly concerned.

"He's fine. I told him to be back here before supper." He took one of her feet in his hands and began to massage the sensitive arch. Lethargic from the heat, she fought to keep her eyes open as Caleb's ministrations lulled her into deep relaxation.

"I thought you might want to be alone for a while." His voice sounded far away, and she forced her eyes open to gaze at him with a dreamy faraway expression.

"It was good to think for a while alone."

"I'm sorry about your sister; I know how much taking her home meant to you."

"She came here."

"She did?" As he voiced his surprise, his fingers stopped momentarily, then began the slow deep kneading once more.

"*Ja,* because she wanted me to understand."

"Do you?"

"I do now. We are not the same anymore."

She nodded in agreement and added, "To live is to change, I think."

What we have is very good, she thought, as she watched him through lowered lashes. This moment is good. It felt so right to sit and talk with him, to share her thoughts and feelings, that Analisa wished the moment could go on and on, for it was a beautiful, peaceful exchange that seemed as natural as their lovemaking. She added the moment to the collection of memories in her mind, her photographs of life, ones to be taken out and studied in times of reflection.

She closed her eyes as he began to work on her other foot.

"Caleb?"

"Hmm?"

"You look very silly sitting there in those clothes."

"They're the best Duffy and Peak had to offer. New trousers, white linen shirt, suspenders, clean socks . . ."

"Not good for a tepee . . ."

"Would you rather I took them off?"

The rustle of clothing reached her ears, and her eyes flew open immediately.

"I'd rather we were at home," Analisa admitted and began fanning her skirt again.

"What you need is a swim. *Komop.*" He stood and pulled her up without hesitation. *"Wij gaa nou."*

"Oh, no!" she moaned as she let him lead her toward the door. "I think you must be turning Dutch!"

The stream was wide and slow moving, far deeper than the creek behind the soddie, and Analisa hesitated when she saw Caleb dive in and then stand in shoulder-deep water near the shore. The sparkling surface rippled above the green depths, and the cool relief the clear water offered soon overshadowed her fear as a nonswimmer.

"No one will see?" She stared suspiciously at the open landscape. The bluffs above provided a lookout over the entire stream bed.

"Do you see anyone around?"

"Not right now, but maybe someone will come along . . ."

"This time of day everyone is resting. You stay there and watch my clothes, and I'll swim alone." He disappeared, his dark head a blur, his skin flashing like the coat of a sleek brown beaver beneath the water. With sure, steady strokes he moved upstream, turned over on his back, and then floated lazily past. The sight was far too tempting for Analisa to resist any longer.

She unbuttoned the bodice of her dress and untied the waistband, then loosened her petticoat, and shucked the garments as quickly as she could before she changed her mind, all the while keeping a wary eye on their surroundings. She left her camisole and pantalets on and struggled down the slippery bank. The water lapped cool and inviting around her ankles, and she waded contentedly until she lost her footing and found herself sliding down the muddy bank farther into the water than she had intended.

Thrusting her hands down to her sides to stop her descent, she only succeeded in plunging them up to the wrists in mud. Caleb's strong fingers closed around her ankle and Analisa tried in vain to pull away as he forced her to slide downward until she was sitting waist deep in the water.

"Oh, Caleb!" she wailed. "Look at me."

"I am."

She followed his heated gaze and saw that her wet camisole was as revealing as if she wore nothing at all. If anything, the sight of her peaked nipples pressing against the wet, transparent material was more seductive than nudity.

He bobbed before her, floating upon his back, his arms extended and supporting him in the water, just inches from her. "You have to come all the way in to wash that mud off."

"No."

"Come on. I'll hold you."

Tempted more by his smile than by the thought of being clean, Analisa complied and rubbed the mud off her hands before she reached out to him. He drew her into the current, and she was forced to cling to him for support. Soon they were in shoulder-high water, and Analisa found herself molded against Caleb by the slow steady current flowing around them. He turned onto his side and drifted lazily along, guiding them with easy, scissoring motions while she held on to his shoulders and reveled in the feel of his well-honed muscles as they bunched and relaxed beneath the palms of her hands. Caleb half swam, half floated until he reached a quiet pool midstream. The water eddied and flowed about the edges, but the surface of the pool was nearly still. A large rock at the far end provided a perfect resting place, and Caleb stopped before it, using the boulder as a backrest to keep from floating farther down stream.

"Feeling cooler now?" His hands moved lazily along her back, and she found it quite natural to loop her arms loosely about his shoulders. His hair was short again, in the style he'd worn when she first met him. It waved about the nape of his neck in thick, luxuriant curls and glistened blue-black in the afternoon sunlight.

She nodded in answer to his question, yet felt anything but cool in the intimate embrace.

His lips were silky smooth as they brushed against hers, tempting, teasing. She glanced at him coyly from beneath lowered lashes.

"I think I'm getting warmer," she teased.

He lowered his lips to hers once more, and her senses were filled with him. The coolness of the water was a sharp contrast to the warmth inside his mouth as he opened his lips and teased her tongue with his own. In the open air the scent that was

Caleb was all the more apparent. Strong and masculine, it was his and his alone. His skin was silk and honey beneath her fingertips, the cinnamon sheen of it standing out in sharp contrast to her own.

The sensations running up and down her thighs were far from cool as she realized that it was his arousal that pressed so eagerly against her. She strained against him in return, excited by the feel of his urgency. When his hands reached up to tangle in her hair and pull it down around her shoulders, she moaned in need and anticipation. Clinging to him, she let herself return his kiss with the first truly wild abandon she'd ever dared. Caleb reacted to her excitement and delved deeper as he ground his lips into hers, pressing his hand against the back of her head as if he wished to draw her into himself.

Throbbing with urgency, she rubbed against him, entangling her limbs with his, thankful that he was able to maintain his balance against the smooth boulder. She felt his hands at the waistband of her pantalet and wondered why she had left them on. The water caused the knot to stick, and as he fought with the twisted ties, she buried her face against his neck, peppered it with feather-light brushes of her lips, and then moved down to cover his throat and smooth, hairless chest with kisses.

She heard the underclothes come loose with a rending tear as Caleb's patience came to an abrupt halt. Before she could stop him, the offending garments were cast aside, caught in the current to disappear down stream. His hands then cupped her derriere and he pressed her naked hips to his own. She opened her legs invitingly and felt the rush of water between her thighs, its chill offering a sharp, tantalizing contrast to the warmth that flowed within her.

Aching with need, wanting desperately to feel him inside her, Analisa was consumed with desire such as she had never known. Her hands moved up to trap his face between them, and she kissed him as he usually kissed her, demandingly, possessively, expertly, and she thrilled to hear Caleb groan, low and uncontrollably.

He lifted her then, swiftly and easily, the water aiding him in his delightful task, and murmured soft words of encouragement. His fingers slipped into the warm passageway that opened for him, his other hand tight on her waist, holding her above him. Waves of excitement pulsated through Analisa when he touched her, excitement that built as his hand caressed and teased the hidden entry between her thighs. As he held his body away from her, she yielded all to his scalding touch, moving in rhythm with his strokes while his lips continued to tease hers, his tongue darting between her teeth. Fires consumed her from the inside out, and finally she gave herself entirely to the feeling and cried out softly as intense, spiraling reverberations shook her.

Caleb let her down slowly until she rested against him. She trembled in his arms, her head against his neck, her eyes closed as she floated, detached and dreaming. He kissed her lips, softly, gently, and invitingly, waiting for her to garner her strength after the intense onslaught of sensation, but he was not to be denied his own pleasure. When she raised her lips in anticipation of a deeper kiss, he complied and, as he kissed her, raised her once more until he could slide into the welcoming, heated confines of her womanhood.

Never dreaming that she would find herself aroused again so suddenly, Analisa looked up into the intense blue depths of Caleb's eyes, only to see them close in ecstasy. She clung to him then, her hands raking through his hair as she tried to move against him. The water created a buoyant, liquid atmosphere that surrounded them, lapping against their backs and shoulders as they bobbed beneath the surface, aiding them in their frenzied movement. Analisa felt the tension building rapidly inside her once again and welcomed it, reveling in the fact that she was discovering more and more how to control and direct her ever mounting need and ultimate release.

She wanted to give him the same pleasure he had given her and followed her instincts. She clutched at his shoulders and drew herself along his heated, pulsing shaft for nearly its entire length before she lunged forward, drawing him into her very core once again. Moving back and forth again and again, she threw her head back in wild abandon, forgetful of time and place, and called out his name. He grasped her hips and held her immobile as he stifled his own cry and spilled his seed into her; then, shuddering violently, he folded her protectively against his wildly beating heart.

Epilogue

Boston, July 1873

"Anja."

She awoke to the sound of her name on his lips, felt Caleb's warm breath tease her ear, and tried to ignore his summons, nearly an impossible feat, since she was lying with her head on his shoulder. The shrill complaint from the nursery continued, as did Caleb's insistent nudges. Analisa groaned and lifted her head, only to move away from him and seek her own pillow. Its surface was crisp and cool, and she nestled down into it with a sigh. She soon felt the mattress rise as Caleb left it, and heard him pad across the carpet toward the nursery door. She smiled to herself and relished the few moments' reprieve. Her actions were not entirely fair, for she knew that Caleb would eventually give in to his daughter's demands for attention. He spoiled Annika Storm outrageously.

Dragging herself to a sitting position, she pulled the sheet over her breasts and tried to finger-comb her wild hair into some semblance of order. She tossed it back over her shoulder, so that it would be out of the way of the baby's grasping fingers.

Naked, his daughter riding high against his shoulder, Caleb strode across the room. The baby squealed with delight when she saw her mother and smiled wide enough to show off all four of her teeth. Analisa reached up to take the kicking, laughing child from Caleb before he slipped back into bed beside them.

Annika Marieke Storm, or Annemeke, as they all called her, was now ten months old and possessed her parents' deep blue eyes, her mother's honey-colored curls, a lighter shade of her father's warm-toned skin, and her step-brother's ready smile. Above all, she possessed all of their hearts.

Conceived in the Dakotas, Annika had been born in Boston here in the Storm mansion. At Caleb's insistence, Analisa was attended by the best doctor money could provide. The baby was born on October 7, 1872, exactly nine months to the day of her conception. Her "Granny Ruth," as Ruth Storm insisted she be called from that day forward, announced that Annika was a Libra, and told Analisa that her daughter had been born with the ruling planet of Venus, to which Analisa shrugged, knowing it was useless to try and understand.

Now Annika bounced happily from Caleb to Analisa as he contorted his mouth into various comic expressions with the aid of his index fingers. Soon Analisa was laughing as well, more at her daughter's shrieking cries than at Caleb's antics.

Finally the teasing ended, and Annika found a soft spot between them and settled down quietly again, to sleep for another hour or so. Analisa played with the baby's fine-textured curls and watched as they looped about her fingers.

"Anja?" Caleb hesitated as if he sought a way to put his thoughts into words, "are you happy here?"

She looked around the massive room they had shared for a year now and wondered how anyone could ever admit to not being happy here. Theirs was the master suite, consisting of not one, but four rooms—a bedroom, sitting room, dressing room, and nursery—all of them appointed with furnishings fit for a palace. When they moved into the mansion, Caleb had told Analisa to decorate the rooms in any way she saw fit, but she doubted that she could improve on the tasteful royal blues and greens that Ruth had chosen before her.

Beyond their suite was a wide hallway. Kase was ensconced in Caleb's old room, which was still filled with the collection of Sioux implements and beadwork items. Ruth's sitting room and bedroom were at the opposite end of the hall; three guest rooms completed the second floor.

The night they had arrived in Boston, Analisa had wandered from room to room, unable to believe the size, elegance, and grandeur of her new home.

"I told you it was big . . ." Caleb had shrugged and reminded her.

"You did not say it was a castle, Caleb!"

For weeks she had roamed about, lost in the various twists and turns of the hallways and stairways, searching for something to occupy her time.

Abbie's domain was the huge kitchen on the first floor with its massive brick fireplace. The room was larger than the entire soddie had been, but here Analisa found a ready companion in Abbie and so spent as much time in the kitchen as any place else while Caleb was at work. When Abbie finally agreed to allow Analisa to bake, she showed the old woman her gratitude by teaching her all her Dutch favorites. Abbie reciprocated by showing Analisa how to make Caleb's favorite pies and Cornish pasties.

The library had offered her solace, especially during the last weeks before Analisa delivered Annika. Often she would curl up in Clinton Storm's huge leather armchair and read for hours while Ruth sat across the room and muttered over her own work. Analisa had neither the talent nor the desire to learn the complicated method by which Ruth plotted the astrology charts.

"Anja? You haven't answered my question." Caleb prodded her back to the issue at hand.

Was she happy? She wasn't unhappy, she thought with a heavy sigh, but if she were to tell him the absolute truth, she would have to admit that, for her, life here was almost too placid, too orderly, too—boring.

He heard the sigh and smiled to himself, crossing his arms over his chest as he stared up at the ceiling.

"I've been offered a job," he began and felt her staring at him with rapt attention, "but I told them that it would be up to my wife."

"What kind of a job?"

With that he rolled to his side to face her and pulled the sheet up to cover the sleeping child between them.

"If you're against it, Anja, just say the word and I'll tell them no."

"What kind of a job?" she repeated.

"Francis Walker is the new head of the BIA. Naturally I thought he wouldn't want any of Parker's men around once he took over, but he called me in to see if I'd agree to go back out to the Indian territories again—this time out near the Black Hills." She heard his excitement mount as he explained, "Settlers are encroaching on the lands that have always been sacred to the Sioux. He wants someone out there who can work with both sides, maybe help ease the pressure. After Hardy was prosecuted so swiftly, thanks to *our* evidence, and after the successful negotiations with Red Dog's band, well . . ." He shrugged, modestly proud of his accomplishments. "Who else would they ask?"

She could not keep her eyes from straying to the jagged scar that marred the otherwise flawless skin on his chest. He would carry it forever, a memento of his assignment for Ely Parker. She looked up into his eyes and saw what she knew she would find. They were alight with excitement as he spoke of the challenge he would face working for the Bureau of Indian Affairs again.

"Fine. When do we go?" What else could she say?

Caleb went on as if he hadn't heard. "He thought that maybe if . . . What did you say?"

"I said fine. When do we go?"

He propped his head on his hand and rested on his elbow. "Are you sure? I know I'm asking you to give up a lot."

"I'm sure." She reached out to smooth his hair away from his forehead and trace the outline of his jaw with her fingertips. "I think you already knew what I would say, Caleb."

He nodded and turned his head in order to kiss the palm of her hand.

"I've seen that look in your eyes, Anja. You miss it, too, don't you?"

"*Ja*. I miss it." Her eyes took on a faraway look, and she glanced toward the open window. Fresh July sunlight poured in and splashed across the shining border of hardwood floor then crept along the carpet. Traffic noise drifted up from the street below along with the early morning cries of the vendors who peddled their wares to the housekeepers in the big homes along the avenue.

"I miss the open sky and the peace of the prairie, Caleb. I didn't know how much I loved it until we left. It is too crowded here, so many people and carriages, trains and buildings. I long for the earth and sky that stretch out far and away, so far until they come together."

As she put her thoughts into words she could almost feel the never-ending breeze and smell the tall waving grasses after a summer storm. She looked forward to seeing Sophie and Jon once more and caring for her own home again. She wanted to till the soil, to struggle and work and fall into bed exhausted and pleased with her accomplishments.

Analisa knew that Ruth would not be opposed to moving west with them. Not only was she attached to the children, but over the past year, she had continued to receive numerous letters from Frank Williamson.

"What about your business?" she asked Caleb after a time.

"I'll transfer my clients to another firm." He shrugged and voiced the truth. "There aren't that many to lose. Let's face it, there isn't much demand around Boston for a lawyer who's half Indian, even if his last name is Storm."

"Caleb"—she suddenly straightened—"why can't you practice law out West? Isn't there a need for someone like you? You can be an Indian lawyer."

"I *am* an Indian lawyer."

She sighed with exasperation. "I mean a lawyer for the Indians."

"I've thought about it," he assured her.

"Tell them yes." Analisa was up and moving. Her pale backside flashed in the shaft of sunlight as she hurried toward the dressing room.

Caleb was having a hard time keeping up with her train of thought.

"Tell who yes?" he called out in a hushed tone, trying not to awaken Annika, who slept on oblivious to their discussion.

Analisa's head appeared around the open doorway as she shrugged on her dressing gown and belted it tight around her trim waist.

"Tell the BIA yes."

She moved around the end of the massive cherrywood bed and sat on the edge nearest him and soon found herself trapped in the circle of his arms.

"I didn't realize you hated all of this luxury so much," he teased as he nibbled on her earlobe.

"I do not hate it. It is just very . . . orderly . . . and boring."

She found it hard to talk while his tongue did delicious things to her ear. His lips soon found their way down the slender column of her throat and then played at the edge of her gaping robe.

"Next time you're bored, ma'am, please let me know." His hand strayed before it slid lower.

"*Ja.*" Analisa untied the sash and let her gown slip off her shoulders. "I will do that." Before he could stop her, she twisted out of his grasp and, in a graceful movement, seductively reclined on the thick Persian carpet beside the bed. She lifted her arms in a tempting invitation for him to join her there.

"Don't be boring, Mr. Storm. Or is it Señor de la Vega? Or Raven's Shadow? Come down here so that you will not awaken the baby."

"I always aim to please, ma'am." He smiled and moved to join her.